Reini

POLLY L. HUGHES

HORSESHOE PUBLICATIONS, WARRINGTON, CHESHIRE

COPYRIGHT © P. L. HUGHES 1995

ALL RIGHTS RESERVED

No part of this book may be reproduced in any form by photocopying, or by any electronic or mechanical means including information storage or retrieval systems without permission in writing from both the copyright owner and the publisher of this book.

ISBN 1 899310 25 8

First published 1995 by
HORSESHOE PUBLICATIONS
Box 37, Kingsley, Warrington,
Cheshire WA6 8DR

Book cover designed by Cheshire Artist
TRACY WALKDEN

Printed and bound in Great Britain by
ANTONY ROWE LTD
Chippenham, Wiltshire

FOR A FATHER'S LOVE

&

THE NUMBER 145

~ ~ ~ ~ ~ ~ ~

Acknowledgments to :-

My husband for his patience and support.

My Dad for his love.

My Mum for her guidance.

Moira Anderson for the world of Shakespeare.

Barbara Papademetriou for her encouragement.

Grace Corne - Flora, Facts and Fable Magazine, for the positive thinking.

Graham Fisher and the Chester Library.

Barbara Tudor and the Damariscotta Region Chamber of Commerce.

&

John Hibbert for his faith in my work.

INTRODUCTION

SARAH - 1828

Inflamed by the excellent white wine from Joseph's own cellar, they went to bed. In the firelight Sarah slipped on Jenny's gift. An alluring nightdress, of blue-grey silk and lace, with tiny shoulder straps and a revealing low neckline. She stood by the flickering flames, filled with desire at the sight of his strong naked body, the nightdress tantalisingly showing off her breasts, and the gold crucifix shining against her fair skin. He fell on his knees before her, and lifting the beautiful silk, kissed the hot wet place, the centre of her yearning, as she gasped with pleasure at this new experience. He carried her to the bed, tasting her desire for the first time and she moaned in ecstasy as he put his mouth to her.

> "Open afresh your round of starry folds,
> For great Apollo bids,
> And when again your dewiness he kisses,
> Tell him, I have you in my world of blisses."

With the poetry, wine and new found pleasure, she wept as he skilfully brought her to climax. This was a different kind of pleasure, and after, as he held her, she found herself longing for the deep satisfaction of his full erection. He seemed to know all her feelings, leaving her wondering, if indeed he did have that All Hallows Eve, double sight, but again he did the unexpected. Kissing her breasts, he took the crucifix from her neck, and threaded the chain between her legs, before lowering himself gently inside her. She sighed with delight at his fullness. He did not move, but once again brought her to thrilling rapture, this time by rubbing the gold chain against her with his hand.

Then with his ache for her almost unbearable, they began mutual love making. Relishing the joy of kissing her, gently nibbling her neck and breasts, feeling her writhe beneath him, and hearing her strange little cries as they reached the height of passion together. Swathed in happiness, never would they have believed that anything could wreck their perfect love, as they slept in that delightful bedroom, without moving until morning.

Chapter One

Part One - The Beginning

SARAH - 1809

Icy wind howled around the house, and Mary woke again. The pain in her back was becoming unbearable, she bit her lip and waited hopefully for it to subside. James her husband slept soundly beside her. "How can he sleep?" she thought irritably, "all this wind, and my fidgeting, he wouldn't wake if the house fell down." The pain lessened to a dull ache, and she felt cold and clammy, her hair and nightdress damp with perspiration. James was warm and she cuddled up to him for comfort, as much as was possible as she was expecting a child in about six weeks.

This pregnancy had not been like her first. That was two years ago. She had been fit and strong, and hardly shown at all until the seventh month. James's mother had voiced her concern, but Mary dismissed the older woman's knowledge because she felt so well, and because Jane rather frightened her. Jane was experienced in all herbal remedies and had taken over as local midwife. She did not agree with doctors and their methods of bleeding patients. In fact she never seemed to agree with anyone, yet she was well respected for her skills. Mary had felt that her mother-in-law was something of a witch, and refused even the raspberry leaf tea which Jane had begged her to take in the last few months, to help towards an easy labour. The pregnancy had ended tragically.

Mary endured a horribly long and painful labour, in fact she felt sure that if Jane had not been with her, she would have given up and died, rather than face any more of the intolerable pain. The baby was born dead. A tiny, but beautiful little boy, with James's pale skin and dark hair, everything they wanted, but with no life.

Mary had clung to James, and they cried for what seemed to be days. Her mother-in-law, herself with a broken heart, was a tower of strength, taking charge of the running of the farm, and keeping an eye on the corn mill, until the grief had ebbed a little, and life slowly began to return to normal. By then Jane had become a mother to Mary, and the old animosity had gone. "I still think she is a witch though," Mary smiled to herself, thinking how Jane seemed to be able to read her thoughts, and would often wag her finger saying, "I can read you like a book, Mary my girl. I know exactly what you are thinking."

Although they longed for another child, nothing happened for a long time after the first. Mary was beginning to worry that she would never conceive again, but her mother-in-law's advice of, "give it time", had paid off and here was another baby nearly ready to be born. Mary patted her huge stomach fondly, the child was so active, surely nothing could go wrong now. This time she had begun to develop 'the bump' at three months, and had gone on to be an enormous size. James teased her that she was getting to be a big as Rosie, their house cow. This had become their own private joke, with Mary's smiles and giggles resulting in confused looks from Jenny, a simple girl who came up from the village to help in the house. "Well Rosie," thought Mary, "you have got your baby now, and I will soon have mine."

By now the dull ache was almost gone, and the room was slightly lighter. "Winter solstice today, the year's shortest day, Christmas in four days," she thought as she drifted off to sleep.

In her cottage, by the mill, Jane her mother-in-law slept fitfully. She was worried about Mary. Although she had obediently followed all her advice through this pregnancy, Jane was sure that something was wrong. The previous afternoon, she had called at the house, only to find her daughter-in-law scrubbing the kitchen table, and looking dreadfully pale and tired. "What on earth are you doing?" Jane had scolded, "let Jenny do that." Mary looked quite weepy, "I just felt I needed to do something, I don't know why," she sighed. She resisted going to bed, so Jane ordered her to a chair by the cooking range and made her as comfortable as possible, with her feet on a stool. Then, while Mary sulked, she took over the kitchen. Jenny snivelled as she was ordered about, and the meal prepared. By the time James returned, the kitchen was glowing, table laid and a delicious meal ready. Jenny looked more bedraggled than ever, but Mary was cheerful and the colour was back in her cheeks. "Ankles badly swollen," Jane noted mentally and worried.

James wanted his mother to stay for the meal, but Jane had a rich savoury stew cooking at home, and was determined to go before the weather worsened. "I can smell snow," she said, in such an authoritative voice, making Mary smile, but Jenny cower. "Keep warm", she added, for James had ushered his mother to the door, she knew he did not want her to start upsetting that silly superstitious mousy Jenny. Why they bothered with her she could not understand, but at least she was staying now at night to keep the range fire going while it was so cold. "If she lets it go out, I will do more than make her sniff," Jane thought as she left for home. She would return first thing in the morning, with an infusion of fennel and nettle for Mary's swollen ankles, and would make sure there would be no more scrubbing of tables!

As always, James woke at daylight. He turned in bed to his wife. "Good morning my love," he whispered and gently touched her soft fair hair. She felt too warm, and her cheeks were flushed. He sat up in alarm, waking her far more suddenly than he had intended. She struggled to sit up, but was defeated once more by a wave of relentless back pain. "What is wrong?" he tried to ask calmly, but anxiety betraying his voice. "Just backache, I did too much yesterday," she whispered through the pain. "I will go for mother," he said calmly, but with panic churning his stomach. "No, no," she pleaded, "it will soon pass, I have just got myself overtired". James told her to rest, and quickly pulled on his clothes, he would go for his mother, whether she liked it or not, but he said nothing, trying to stay as outwardly calm as possible. "I will send Jenny up with a drink of that special tea, and then we will see how you are."

Down at the mill cottage, Jane woke with a start. something was definitely wrong. Mary's baby was not due for more than a month, but Jane had an intuition for disaster, as well as for snow. It was almost as if she really did smell it. She quickly dressed, and pushed a bottle of camomile oil, and some little packets of herbs into her pocket. Soon she was into her heavy coat and woollen shawl. She had been right about the weather, as she opened the door, the snow reached almost to her knees and swirled from the sky as if it would never stop. She pushed her way through, everything was obliterated by the dense blanket of whiteness, so she set off following the stream, now full of ice, which flowed past the farm to the mill. The two pigs, still shut in the sty by the house from the previous night, squealed when they heard her, anticipating food, but were ignored as she plodded forward against the snow filled wind, only determination kept her going, against the breathtaking cold.

James made the raspberry leaf tea. He was well used to Jane's teas and potions and to his relief, during this pregnancy, Mary relied completely on his mother's advice. With Jenny dispatched upstairs, carrying the tray, James pulled on his coat and opened the door onto the snow. Before he could kick the entrance clear, there was a crash upstairs and a startled scream from Jenny as she dropped the tray and came thundering down the wooden stairs, as if chased by hounds, and almost as white as the snow itself. "The, oh, the baby," she wailed in a hoarse, frightened voice.

James was in the bedroom in what seemed to Jenny a single leap, leaving her to wrestle with the door against the wind and snow. Mary was in the grip of a violent contraction, not just backache this time, but the real thing, and her waters had broken. The look of pain and fear on her face tore at James' heart as she reached her hand out to him. "It's too soon," she sobbed through the pain, tears rolling down her face. When the contraction subsided, James turned to see Jenny standing by the door like a fox-scared rabbit. "Get your coat, and go for my mother," he ordered. The girl stood and blinked, "But it's snowing," she whimpered. "You had better get going, or I will take the brush to you," scowled James, who had never, and would never actually do such a thing.

Mary groaned as another violent contraction took hold, followed by a horrible tearing sensation, as she gave birth. James and the terrified Jenny ran to her side at once. The baby was born, but to their horror it was not properly formed. A poor, partly developed foetus, which had obviously been dead for some time, "Is it all right, is it a boy?" poor Mary gasped. Jenny retreated from the bedside, and ran downstairs, falling headlong into Jane, just as she came through the door, with a flurry of snow blowing into the kitchen behind her. Jane did not wait to listen to the girl's garbled cries, "See to that fire, and get some water on," she snapped as she ran up to the bedroom.

Mary was hysterical when the next contraction hit, she did not even seem to know her mother-in-law who was now taking charge. Jane took in the situation at once. The sorry mess on the bed, which had been the promise of a much loved child, was now not of her concern. It was obvious that this was a twin birth, and another baby was trying to come into the world, by a mother almost mad with pain and grief. She held Mary's thrashing head gently between her strong hands, and looking closely into her face, firmly and convincingly explained. "Hush, hush, it was just a dream, your baby is not yet born, you must help it, be calm. Look James will stay. You must do as

I say and all will be well." The wildness began to fade from Mary's eyes, and she looked from her mother-in-law to James, who nodded in encouragement. "Just like with Rosie's baby," he smiled and winked, provoking a look of rebuke from his mother, who had not shared their private joke during the pregnancy.

Bewildered, but with faith in her husband and mother-in-law, Mary calmed down and worked with the contractions. This time the birth was much less painful, and there in Jane's arms was a perfect baby girl. Mary stared almost in disbelief, "A little girl, oh, I am so happy," she sighed.

This baby, though perfectly formed, was indeed a few weeks too early, and although not tiny, was going to need a great deal of care. Jane skilfully wrapped her in a piece of clean linen and turned to her son. "Undo your shirt," she commanded. James, already stunned by the recent trauma, stood looking as uncomprehending as the simple Jenny. "James!" his mother barked. She took the baby and tucked her into her son's shirt, against his bare chest and arranged his arms to support her. Then she gently touched his cheek, "She has come into the world a little too soon," she explained softly, "cold is her biggest danger now, and it's too cold up here. Go down and sit in the kitchen with her while I see to your wife." He obeyed, like a man in a dream, hearing, as if somewhere in the distance, his mother shouting at Jenny to bring hot water.

He sat in the large chair by the fire, and did not move, trying to come to terms with the horror of that morning. Then he became aware of the baby stirring, and came to his senses. He peeped at his daughter, seeing her really for the first time. She was small, but not as small as their first child two years ago. "So beautiful," he breathed, almost scared to look. Her hair was stuck to her head in little curls and her long eyelashes were of the same dark brown colour. He looked at her tiny hands, she curled her hand around his finger and for a fleeting moment, opened her sleepy little eyes, seeming to look straight at him. James was filled with an all consuming, overwhelming surge of love for his child. He knew at once that here was a person who he would willingly sell his soul for. "Such a small living being, but oh so precious," he sighed, not even noticing when Jenny came down on Jane's orders to brew a cup of camomile tea for Mary.

Jane quickly and efficiently wrapped the dead child and afterbirth in the soiled linen, and kept it away from Mary's sight. She bathed her with the hot water and applied a dilution of camomile oil to her abdomen, to soothe the strained muscles, all the time keeping a blanket around her to keep off the chilly air. "Under the circumstances, there is very little damage done," she thought, "but I must watch for infection."

Mary in clean warm nightgown, and heavy woollen shawl, sipped gratefully at the camomile tea, though anxious to hold her baby. "James will bring her up as soon as you have finished your drink," Jane assured her, "but we are going to have to move you downstairs as soon as possible."

James took the baby up to Mary, never had he trodden with such care, he felt her move against him, and wanted to hold her for ever. A bond had formed between father and daughter, a bond of love never to die, that was one day to reach through time itself.

What a change there was in his wife from just an hour ago. She lay, propped up on pillows and seemed to glow. Her soft fair hair was brushed, hanging loosely around her shoulders, and even her eyes seemed to be smiling. She put out her arms and he handed their daughter, to be held by her mother at last. The baby took to Mary's breast with no fuss and began to suckle well, to Jane's relief, early babies were often slow to feed. James kissed the top of Mary's head. "How do you feel my love?" he whispered, "I am so proud of you both." "I am a little weak, but so happy," she smiled, "I am so glad you were with me, Jane says I had some sort of fever. Did you know I had terrible dreams?" "Yes, you were very ill, and you gave me quite a fright, but it is all over now, and here is our beautiful daughter," he reassured her.

Jane felt relieved and amused that both the new parents had forgotten the fact that they had longed for a son, and were so delighted with this little girl. Secretly she had longed for a granddaughter, now she would have someone to pass on all her medical skills to, just as her own mother and grandmother passed them on to her.

Putting thoughts of the enjoyable future aside, Jane set to work. "Now," she ordered in her bossiest tone, "We must get these two young ladies downstairs, where it is warm." James carried his wife and child down to the kitchen, and arranged them in the most comfortable chair, with footstool and blankets. "We will bring the bed down, and you will have to keep her next to your skin for the next few weeks, until she begins to thrive," Jane instructed. Concern filled James' eyes., "Is she going to be alright?"

Jane gently took her son's hand. "She is here a little too early, but she is strong, and girls will hold on to life, when boys will let go. We will love her, and keep the cold winter away from her, she will be just fine."

With her son and daughter-in-law reassured, Jane went with Jenny to bring down the bedding, asking James to follow soon, to help with the bed. It looked as if the winter was going to be long and hard, and there was no way her baby granddaughter was going to sleep in a room without a fire.

James and Mary kissed, with a passion that surprised themselves. The proud father smiled at his wife, there seemed to be some squabbling upstairs, so he thought it best to sort out the bed problem as soon as possible. He kissed his baby daughter's curls and headed up towards the angry mutterings. "Why does my mother always try to upset the girl," he thought, "She should know better, with Jenny's simple mind."

He was right, Jenny was upset, but that was nothing to the look on his mother's face. He had seen her look like this only once before, her pale skin a deathly grey, and her dark eyes blazing with anger. That had been the time when a typhoid epidemic took Mary's entire family, and then his own dear father, just before he and Mary were to be married.

"What in Christ's name is going on?" he demanded. Jane pointed at Jenny, who just cowered and trembled even more. "Jenny, SPEAK!" he said as quietly as his rising anger would allow. The girl opened her mouth, but it seemed an eternity before she spoke, then she stammered. "The baby, stillbirth, twins, winter solstice, dead, deformed, witchcraft, evil . . ."

"Stop," yelled James, grabbing the girl roughly by the shoulders. "My daughter will be as good a Christian as any. She is beautiful and perfect, and I will, with my bare hands, tear apart anyone who says, or does anything to hurt her, understand!" "It is she who is evil," Jane began to exclaim, pointing at Jenny, only to be silenced by a furious look from her son. Neither women had ever seen him like this. He had been a sweet, even tempered child, and that temperament continued into manhood. The room fell silent.

Mary down below, unaware of the reason for the affray, smiled and whispered to her daughter. "Your father has sorted them out, don't worry, you are going to love your grandmother, it just takes time to get used to her."

In the bedroom James's fury had not abated. "We will hold an emergency Christening, right now," he said in a strange, fierce, low whisper. "The Church allows it in such circumstances of early birth, and you will stand as Godmother," he growled, pressing his fist into Jenny's shoulder. "You will never repeat such wicked things again, and you will forget the stillbirth, it did not happen, understand?" he demanded. The girl nodded dumbly, and his mother opened her mouth as if to speak, but changed her mind and nodded also. "Right, let us get this bed down," he said brightly.

The moving of the bed did prove to be a problem, as it was a heavy wooden base structure. The head and legs were carved with flowers and leaves, very ornate and unusual. It had been made by James' father, originally a carpenter by trade, he had gone on to be a musical instrument maker and repairer.

As James removed the bolts and gently hammered apart the dove tail joints of the bed, his mother sighed and thought of the past, when they first came to the little village outside Eastham. John, her husband had been a bright intelligent man, with a thirst for all things new. He heard of the new farming methods, and saw the potential of the four crop rotation practised in Norfolk, growing turnips, barley, clover and wheat in alternate fields, with none left fallow. This provided food for animals in winter, and therefore fresh meat all year round. Even King George himself set up a farm at Windsor, following the new trends, and John was determined to be part of this lifestyle.

James was twenty at this time, and had been established, working with his father, with a great flair for musical instruments. Jane was very surprised when he so readily agreed to move from Manchester, to work on the land. As for herself, she longed to live in the country, as her parents and grandparents had always done, so the move had met with all round family enthusiasm. They bought the sturdy little house, and a good sized parcel of land, which led down as far as the corn mill.

The mill, owned by Alan Williamson, was powered by the same stream which flowed alongside John's new farm land. Alan was a big, friendly man with a kind petite wife, a son who was his mirror image, and a slender daughter with grey blue eyes and fair hair which glinted in the sunlight. Her name was Mary, and James had immediately fallen in love wiyh her.

The farming project had been hard work for James and his father, but thanks to enthusiasm and fair treatment of their farm labourers, they soon began to reap the benefits. "Oh John, my beloved husband,"

Jane sighed to herself, "Never to see our son's first child." She shook herself back to the present, there was much to do, and no time for such memories at the moment.

After a great deal of effort, the bed was reassembled in the kitchen, with Mary and the baby settled in it. Mary thought that Jenny and her mother-in-law still seemed a little sullen, but they had all laughed when both of them stumbled down the stairs with the huge feather mattress. James fluffed up Mary's pillows and explained that although the snow had stopped, it was so deep, and the air so cold, that it would be some time before she could go out with the baby. "We should have an emergency Christening for her now, especially as she is so early," he told his wife calmly and as persuasively as possible, trying not cause alarm. To his relief, Mary voiced no objection, she would have agreed to anything, feeling so happy and comfortable now. She had hoped to have influential Godparents for their child, but now, looking at the baby and soothed by the camomile tea, that no longer seemed to matter.

James filled the large glass bowl with warm water and took the heavy old bible down from the dresser. He opened the holy book at the first blank page, then took from his neck, the gold chain and crucifix, which had been passed down through his father's family for many generations. They stood around the bed. James dipped the cross into the water, and then gently touched it to the baby's head.

"We name this child, Sarah Jane,

in the name of the Father,

Son and Holy Ghost,

Amen".

He then wrote in the bible, in his beautiful neat script, which was just like his father's.

> *Sarah Jane Brand*
> *born and Christened*
> *this day*
> *21st December 1809*

He and Jane signed it and Jenny made her mark. Jane gave Jenny a very strange look, but Mary said nothing, just smiled at her husband. "As soon as she is old enough, she shall have this," James whispered to his wife, as he slipped the crucifix back over his head.

Chapter Two

It was soon mid-day and by then, Jane had organized a light meal. James milked the cow, fed the hens and gathered the eggs. The animals were fretful, being cooped up was not usual for them. "Not many eggs," he thought, "Perhaps we should have roast chicken, but as the hours of daylight increase, they will all start laying again. After all, this is the shortest day of the year, everything gets better from now on. It will soon be winter's end, and I have a little girl now, to see all the spring flowers, and my growing corn!"

Outside he could see that the stream had frozen to a solid silver ribbon of ice, and knew that the corn mill would not be able to function in such conditions. A warm glow spread through the new father as he realised that he would be able to stay all day with his wife and new baby, until the ice thawed. The snow was now a dry icy powder, in places, blown into high drifts, altering the landscape. "How on earth did my mother get up to us from the mill in that storm?" he wondered, "and what made her come at such an early hour." He would ask her later, but knew that she would be evasive, saying that she had a feeling for such things. "Actually, I really think she has," James smiled to himself as he headed back to the house.

Mother and baby were now asleep. Mary had been surprised at her own appetite, and pleased that Sarah had fed well again. Jane fussed about letting the cold in, as he came through the door but handed the eggs and milk to Jenny in a fairly good natured way. "I am going back to my cottage for an hour or so," his mother announced, pulling on her coat. Before he could protest, she insisted. "No James, I must go by myself, if you like, follow down in an hour and walk back with me, I will have things to carry." Although James had over the years, become a skilful businessman and negotiator, he was not going to argue with his mother when she was in such a frame of mind, so he helped her on with her coat and shawl and watched as she set off for the cottage.

It was not easy walking through the snow, but Jane pushed on with determination. The sky was now a clear blue, but there was no sign of a thaw, in the icy wind. There was something that only she could do. Inside her coat was the soiled linen, wrapped around the malformed foetus and afterbirth. It could not be buried in this weather, but disposal was of the utmost importance. Mary believed that the stillbirth had been a dream, caused by a fever, and Jane was determined that she would never know the truth.

She reached the little cottage next to the mill, feeling numb with cold. Before entering, she went to the pigsty, to be greeted by the two excited, un-fed and extremely hungry pigs. She closed her eyes at the sight of their frothing, anticipating mouths. It had to be done, she fought her rising nausea and tossed the bloody remains from under her coat to the slavering animals. Turning, she fled to the cottage, forcing herself to think only of Sarah Jane, that precious baby girl, named after Mary's mother and herself.

The cottage gave shelter from the bitter wind, but with no fire it was cold and unwelcoming. With shaking hands she began to light the fire with tinder wood, always kept alongside the range. George from the mill appeared at the door, his face full of concern. "Saw you'd gone early this morning, no smoke from your fire you see. Me and Emily looked in, most concerned we were in this weather and all." He held his cap in his hands humbly, feeling guilty for looking into the cottage earlier.

Jane explained about Sarah's birth being at least a month early, and was rewarded by sympathetic oh's and grunts from George's wife Emily who had now arrived on the scene. The couple had a reputation for being rather too inquisitive, but she knew they meant well, and that they both thought the world of James. If it had not been for his intervention, George and his family might have been starving or working in the mines by now.

Even little children went down the coal mines in those days, Jane had heard terrible stories of their misery, deaths and injuries. It was wicked, children needed fresh air, sunshine and good food. People were trying to protect such children, by laws, but action was slow, and the mine owners did not seem to care. She heard once, of a terrible fire damp explosion. It had been caused by some sort of underground gas in the mines, ignited by the miners' lights. Those men who survived the explosion, were then suffocated by something left behind after the ignition, before they could be rescued. Miners said that this was a silent killer, they could not smell, see or taste it. Whatever it was, it turned a man blue, and his blood bright red as it killed him. "What great fear those miners must live with," she thought.

James had given George the job at the mill, and the other little cottage next to Jane's to live in, after the terrible typhoid fever swept through the district.

Mary's family, the original mill owners were wiped out by it, along with James' own dear father. Jane fought to save him, using all the skills passed down through her family. To no avail, she lost the only person who had ever understood her, husband, friend and lover, and through the loss, she also lost her faith in the Church. "Part of me died with John," she sighed to herself.

Jane had insisted that James and Mary should not delay their marriage. "Life must go forward," she maintained, "We cannot keep dwelling on our sadness." The wedding was a simple ceremony, but Mary's plain cream silk dress, sewn deliberately with modesty and restraint, made her look even more beautiful than anything frivolous. Jane herself had worn black, since the death of her husband, and was not ever going to wear anything coloured again, so Mary made her a beautiful black silk outfit, embroidering the top with tiny intricate flowers in matching black silk thread. Jane was touched by the beautiful work, and said so, with almost the first kind words to her daughter-in-law to be, she was a talented seamstress, that had to be admitted.

The corn mill and two tiny cottages, were then left standing empty and desolate, with Mary's family gone, so James set to work with his wife to start up the business again. At this time Jane decided to move to the smaller of the two cottages, the one with the garden and pigsty, and to leave the young couple to themselves in the farmhouse. It was full of reminders of her husband, which tore at her heart and sapped her strength, she felt that she needed some solitude.

Mary, of course, knew about the running of the mill, but it was all too obvious that they would need to employ someone, and quickly. During that same week, George and his family arrived at the village. He was a very tall, muscular man, but his face was pale and drawn. His wife looked even worse, she was thin and stooped, with a babe in arms, while George led a child of about two, and carried their few possessions.

George's family had retained a small piece of land and a tiny house in a village many miles away. It had been passed on from father to son for generations. They owned a couple of hens, grew most of their own food and kept a goat which they tethered on the common, every day.

The new farming style of crop rotation and enclosure was proving a success, and the government started to make laws to enclose land and create bigger farms. Wealthier land owners bought up small pieces of land, and unless ownership of property was available in writing, it could be confiscated. None of George's family could read, and as there were no documents, he was forced to sell for a pittance, his family turned out onto the road. Even the common land was taken over, leaving nothing for the poor. There were many such families all over the country. Most drifted into the towns to work in the new factories, or went to the mines. George and Emily saw the filth and disease in the overcrowded conditions of the factory workers, and knew all about the mines, so decided to take their chances as farm labourers. In the countryside, at least they might catch a rabbit, and pick wild berries and mushrooms to stave off the hunger. They were tired and hungry now, and the hopelessness which they felt in their hearts, was showing on their faces. There seemed to be so many labourers looking for work on the farms, and those who were employed were paid so little.

Someone in the village sent them up to see James, but did not give them any words of encouragement. Mary opened the door, and almost straight away looked past George to Emily, so dusty and bedraggled, seeming to sag under the weight of such a small baby. Mary earned a stern glance from James when she asked them in, before giving him a chance to access the situation, but when he saw Emily's haunted eyes and the little bundle of a baby, he understood his wife's swift and sympathetic action, this poor woman was on the verge of collapse. They sat her down with the children, but the tall man remained at the door respectfully. "I have come looking for work, Sir," he said with surprising dignity, "I am strong and willing, and I am well used to farm work." "Have you ever worked in a corn mill?" James enquired. George swallowed the temptation to lie. "No Sir, I am afraid I have not," he admitted, with his already heavy heart sinking even further. James was touched and slightly amused by the stark honesty of this man. "Would you be willing to learn? We have a mill here which we must get working, perhaps between us we could do it." A flicker of life glowed in the big man's eyes. "Yes indeed, I am a quick learner, and will work all the hours God sends if need be." So it was settled George would start work the next day.

He was persuaded to sit with his wife and children at the table. Mary gave them all a bowl of warm bread and milk, with some honey for the little boy, and a little red wine to revive his parents. James explained the sad situation of Mary's family, the reason for the empty corn mill, and tried not to notice the tears in George's eyes when he realised that he was being offered not only a well paid position, but a house for his family as well. "We'll not let you down Sir, you can be sure of that," he said with a quiver in his strong voice as he looked at his wife.

The family's introduction to Jane at the cottage was predictable, but James had warned that his mother's bark was worse than her bite, and that she always meant well. In fact Jane's frostiness thawed at the sight of the poor little children. Emily was grateful for any advice, and made no protest at all at Jane's bossiness. Emily in fact proved to be an excellent cook, and despite her first appearance, very clean in her ways, and although the two women became friends, she always treated Jane with the greatest respect.

George, a man of his word, worked as hard as two men, and soon learned the workings of the mill. It was not long before the business was running smoothly again and James was able to leave the mill in George's care with confidence, freeing himself once more to get on with the farm.

All this had been three years ago, and now here were George and Emily, shining with health and strength, full of anxiety for Mary and the baby. Jane, of course, would be up at the farm for most of the time during the next few weeks, but asked Emily to feed the pigs in the mornings with the turnips and grain from the store, and also to light the fire in her cottage. "There will be washing to be done," she explained, "and I don't want the baby exposed to damp, so I will do it here." Emily was glad to be able to help, and promised to give a hand with the wash, looking forward to hearing all the news and progress of the baby at the same time.

Her own two boys were now five and three, sturdy healthy little people, seriously interested in everything their father did, but full of mischief, especially the youngest. Much as she loved them, she longed for a daughter. It would be wonderful to have a little girl, but after losing everything they owned, once before, George cherished the position they now had at the mill, and wanted the best for his family. He knew about the poverty caused by having too many children, and so continued to limit their family, by practising withdrawal when they made love. It did not spoil their sexual pleasure, but to be pregnant now, with a little girl, when life was so good, was Emily's burning desire.

James arrived, and was greeted by hearty congratulations from George and Emily, the joy on his face warmed their hearts. He hurried Jane along as she fussed about the cottage, collecting her nightclothes, packets of herbs and a bottle of strong red wine. He almost asked if all these were necessary, but knew for the sake of peace that it was better not to. With covered basket in one hand, he took his mother's arm with the other and headed back to the farm.

Chapter Three

In those first few weeks, Sarah settled into an easy routine. She was a contented baby, and received every attention. She slept and fed well, and when carried about, was always kept in her father's shirt or Mother's shawl, against their skin. Every night Jane made a posset for Mary. She warmed some milk, and added her special strong red wine. This made a thick, slightly curdled drink, to which she then added a pinch of powdered borage seed. The posset insured a good night's sleep for mother and baby, and the borage helped to keep up Mary's milk supply. Jenny now went home at night, and James made sure the fire stayed lit, as they slept in the kitchen.

James and his mother went down to the mill, the morning before Christmas, to help George kill and prepare one of the pigs. Jane was reluctant to leave Jenny in charge, but Mary insisted, in fact she felt that she could have managed by herself.

The pigs now sickened Jane, but she could say nothing about the reason why, and got on with the gruesome task. The pig, once jointed, was to be shared. Some for James at the farm, part for George and Emily, and a joint each for James' farm labourers.

There was no work now, at this time of year for the labourers, who lived in rather miserable huts, with their families. Most farmers left these people to their own devices, and abandoned them to parish charity, often they would be starving at such times. James was unusual in his attitude towards them. They did an honest day's work for him when they could and treated him with respect. James was not going to forsake them during the hard winter months. He instructed Emily to give a loaf of bread for each family every day, from his own flour, together with a jug of milk or whey. This was given, as an extra, whether they were working or not. Emily baked wonderful bread, even Jane had to admit, and now baked it also for James's family every day. She said that her secret was that she was so happy making it!

In the afternoon, with the pork jointed, Emily and Jane set to work to make some pies. Stock, which would set to a jelly, was made by boiling bones. Small pieces of meat simmered in the stock, with herbs and seasonings until tender. With some of the hot rendered fat and water, they made a delicious pastry, and packed the meat into the deep pies. Jane had preserved some cranberries that summer, and these were placed on top the of meat, a little stock added, and a top of lattice cut pastry, brushed with egg, showing the cranberries through, finished off the pies. These took an hour to cook, so the women cleaned up Emily's kitchen while they baked. George and James went off to deliver the gifts of pork, a mission much delayed by handshaking, enquiries and congratulations on Sarah's birth. Jenny's family, in the village was the last call. Her parents were old, her birth had been a great surprise to them both, an unexpected sixth child. The couple accepted the meat graciously, and James assured them that Jenny would be home soon, although he and George noticed that they showed very little interest in news of the girl.

It was late by the time they trudged back to the mill and both men, although strong and warmly wrapped, felt frozen to the bone. The delicious smell and sight of the freshly baked pies was almost too much to bear, but Jane and Emily were too good housewives not to expect this, and had also baked two small pies, just for this reason.

Feeling contentedly full, with the hot savoury pastry, and a glass of spicy mulled wine, James bade farewell to his good friends at the mill, and set off with his mother back to the farm. It had been a long day, and he had missed being with Sarah and Mary.

What a pleasure it was to be home. The kitchen was warm, and was filled with that unique smell of clean baby. Mary looked lovely, and Jenny looked very pleased with herself. She had, with Mary's patient guidance, prepared a stew, which of course would not come up to Jane's standards, but promised to be very good all the same. The table was laid and everything was in good order, so much so that the girl earned a, "well done," from Jane.

With Jane out of the way for the day, Jenny for the first time really got to know Sarah. It started that morning, with a visit from the village parson, who laboured through the snow to the farm, to confirm James' presence in the orchestra on Christmas day. He blessed the baby for Mary, but had looked with great disdain at Jenny when he realised that she was Godmother, he most certainly did not approve. He seemed a virtuous man, with good intentions, but he had no understanding of the poor. He taught them to be humble and know their place beneath the landowners of the area. The misguided man thought this was part of good Christianity. His attitude was abhorrent to Mary and James, who in fact earned more respect with their own ways, and Mary was tempted to tell this pompous parson so. Instead she graciously took Jenny's part.

"Jenny was with me when Sarah as born, she is also my friend, and I am pleased to have her as Godmother," she firmly persisted. Having once before experienced the wrath of a mother with a new baby, the parson let the matter drop. "If they are content with a simple serving girl, from a poor family, so be it," he thought, and left.

Mary, angry at the parson's attitude and sorry for Jenny's hurt feelings, began to involve her with the baby. As for Jenny, she felt so honoured by Mary's speech in her defence, no one had ever spoken of her in such a way, and she became determined to take her new elevated position seriously. The baby fascinated her, such little hands and long eyelashes, she would always do her best for Mary and baby Sarah. Mary could see all these thoughts written on Jenny's face, and was amused and pleased to see such a reaction, where before there had been so little.

From that day, Jenny tried to listen and concentrate, she would watch Mary and her mother-in-law, and try to copy them to improve herself, Sarah must never be ashamed of her. She was pleased at Jane's praise of the meal, and was filled with a strange joy as she set off home, to be with her parents for Christmas.

Christmas came and went quietly. James attended church, mainly because he played the violin in the orchestra, and they relied upon him for organisation.

Some visitors braved the snow, to see Mary and the baby, but the relentless east wind continued to blow, and there was no sign of a thaw, so most people kept to their houses. James' new little family were content to stay in the warmth of the farm, and count their blessings.

Jenny's Christmas was disturbing, and she found herself longing to go back to work. Mary had said that she need not return until the 28th, in her kindly way, giving the girl time to spend with her parents.

For the first time in her life, of nineteen years, Jenny looked at her home life and saw that it was strange. There were no affectionate greetings at her home, not like that at the farm. Her parents mostly ignored her, unless giving her orders for cooking or other chores. She was their daughter, just like Sarah was Mary's, surely her parents must have felt the same joy at her birth as had Mary and James. Something was wrong. She also realised that she never offered them any love either, "Why?" she asked herself, but there was no answer. She tried to be kind to her parents, but was rebuffed with cruel thoughtless words. "They think I am stupid," she thought to herself. "They are always saying so, and I have never thought about it before, I must prove that they are wrong."

That night she looked at herself in the small kitchen mirror. The image looking back at her was a dishevelled creature, with lank untidy hair, and bad looking skin. She looked down at her clothes. "These are as bad as me," she critically thought, "Why am I like this?"

Over the next few days she washed her hair and clothes, and scrubbed her face. Lye soap was all they had, and her face became sore, so she bathed it with milk, which was surprisingly soothing. "See," she said to herself, "I am discovering new things, I will watch and copy Mary and Mrs. Brand."

She experimented with her hair, and managed to catch it up at the back, but it looked nothing like Mary's or Jane's. Her parents did not seem to notice any of this. The only reaction was that her mother slapped her for using so much soap. "Do you think we are made of money, girl, what have you done with the soap?" her mother grumbled, without waiting for, or expecting an answer. "Get some more, and if it happens again, your father will take his belt to you."

On the morning Jenny returned to work, she set off looking different. Her clothes, although still shabby, were as clean as she could get them, and tears had been stitched, if somewhat clumsily. She made a point of saying goodbye to her mother, but was rewarded only by a disinterested grunt.

Jane noticed the difference in the girl, straight away, and full of curiosity mentioned it to Mary. When she heard of the parson's cruel comments, she too was angry. "I think she is trying to better herself because she is Sarah's Godmother," Mary had whispered. "We will see," commented Jane, in her usual sceptical tone, "If you are right, we should help the girl. I have heard that her mother rejected the child from birth. She was born after her five brothers had left home, and the father is almost senile. Children absorb what we teach them, perhaps she is not as simple as everyone thinks, perhaps it is just parental neglect." Tears sprang to Mary's eyes, "How could anyone reject their own child?" she thought, feeling Sarah stirring beneath her shawl, "You are right, we will keep watch and help her if we can."

Jenny continued to be obedient, but with a new and increasing curiosity. She asked, timidly, how things were done, how food was cooked, could she watch as Mary sewed, to see the tiny stitches forming, while hers had always been so big and clumsy. Mary was very patient, and began to teach Jenny to sew, with quite reasonable results, in no time. Even Jane, who thought that no one could do anything as well as herself, was tolerant, and made a real effort not to upset the girl.

As time went by, Jenny decided to ask Jane a question. She had never asked her anything out of turn before, and it took much courage, as Jane was to her so venerable. Jane's skin was always pale and clear, while her own was becoming more red and sore with the strong soap. Jenny explained this to Jane, and was astonished at the concerned and kindly reaction. "Oh dear, your poor skin," Jane sympathised, "Come down to the mill to help with the washing, and we will see what we can do, James will be here if Mary needs anything."

Emily had the fire ready at Jane's cottage, with water boiling for the wash, and was surprised to see Jenny arrive as well. Jenny helped, but was quiet as the other two women chatted away. Jane's system was working well. The washing was left to dry on the large airer, over the fire, while Jane went back to the farm. Emily came in and lit the fire every morning, folding and ironing the clothes when they were dry, ready to take back next time, in order to keep any damp away from the delicate baby. When all was done, Jane brewed some birch tea. It was made with very young birch leaves, which she had dried the previous spring. A refreshing wood flavoured drink, which was pleasant after the hard work. Emily brought over the bread for the family, and also three pieces of caraway seed cake, which was her speciality. Even though naturally curious, she did not ask about Jenny's presence, knowing that Jane would explain in good time. After the welcome break of cake and tea, Emily went back to her family, promising to keep an eye on the fire later, and left Jane with Jenny to carry home the bread and clean clothes.

Jane explained that the birch tea was good to clear the complexion in winter. "You must only use the youngest leaves," she said as she tipped some into a small jar, and gave them to Jenny. "Have a cup, three times a day. You must not use that soap any more as your skin is so sensitive, and we will make some soapwort, to wash your hair, the soap is only making it dull."

The soapwort plant grew by the mill stream, and Jane gathered and re-planted some every year. The little pink flowers produced seeds for re-planting, and only the root was used. Into an earthenware jar of water, Jane put two handfuls of crushed root, to this she added three drops of undiluted camomile oil, and two drops of lavender. "I use borage seed oil, but camomile will be better for you as your hair is fair," Jane instructed, "and you must use it twice a week, until the condition improves." The mixture was to stand for at least two hours, so Jane explained that they would strain it through some muslin and put it into smaller jars when they were back at the farm.

"For your face, we must make something soothing," she carried on to Jenny's delight, rummaging through her supplies. She took a large spoon each of rosewater, and distilled witch hazel. Together with three large spoons of honey she stirred the mixture in a bowl then poured it into a small jar. "Rub this all over your face, night and morning, rinse off and then splash on some elderflower water," she said as she handed over a bottle of the liquid.

"How is this made?" questioned Jenny, who was by now fascinated by it all. Jane was pleased and amused by all her enthusiasm, the girl seemed to be coming to life before her eyes. Elderflower water took a whole day to make, but Jane promised that in June, Jenny should help her pick the flowers and they would make some together.

"Now come, come, the morning has almost gone, let us get back with these linens for the baby," Jane commanded, but the bossy tone in her voice had lost it's edge, and the two women trudged happily back through the snow.

It took five weeks before there was a complete thaw, now they were into February. Sarah changed with the melting of the snow. From a hungry but sleepy baby, she now lay awake, watching her family. Her first smile was for James, who could hardly believe it. He took her over to his wife, with such pleasure on his face. He put the baby into Mary's arms, and gently stroked her little cheek. She opened her eyes wider smiling and gurgling.

From then, she came on in leaps and bounds. Strong and full of interest, Sarah was pulling herself up, and then with help, sitting straight by April, when James was able to take her out to see his growing corn, and the spring flowers.

Chapter Four

Sarah was a happy contented child, the darling of everyone. Emily and George loved her, as she made up slightly for the daughter they did not have themselves. Their boys, Jonathan and Roger, liked to pretend that she was their sister. Jonathan, now a strapping boy of five, loved to carry Sarah about, showing her all his secret places round the mill, and she always rewarded him and his little brother, with gurgles and giggles. Emily watched and sighed, "Doesn't it make you want a daughter of our own?" she would so often say to George, but he would just kiss her and be evasive. His two growing boys would be an asset to him in the mill, but as for another child, Emily would not be satisfied until they produced a girl, and who could say how many children they might have by then. No, George was determined that large families only caused poverty.

Jenny blossomed along with Sarah. Mary gave her pieces of material, and helped her to make new clothes. She also made, all by herself, three white aprons, which she kept spotlessly clean, and wore to work in the house. Thanks to Jane's preparations, her skin was now smooth and clear, and her shiny light brown hair, which before had been dull and mousy, was caught back in a becoming loose plait. She worked very hard at improving herself, trying desperately to remember Jane's recipes, and copying Mary's gracious ways. She became as part of the family, but always treated them with great respect, and did everything she could for them. The only sad part of her life was her home. Nothing had improved, or even changed, but Jenny was now painfully aware of the lack of love. The only spark of interest was when she took her mother to one side, explaining that she would be keeping a small amount of her earnings from the farm, for herself. Never had she seen such anger. Spiteful words roared from her mother's mouth, and she raised her hand to hit her daughter, but Jenny caught her by the arm. "Don't you think I deserve a little for myself?" she questioned calmly, copying James' tactful way. "Deserve," her mother snarled, "You deserve nothing. You have never been any use to me. You came into the world just as your father and I had got rid of your idle brothers, do you imagine that we wanted another child to feed? You have always been stupid and selfish. What about your father's medicine? I still have to buy that, and now you want money for yourself." Although the outburst hurt Jenny, she showed no emotion, but stood her ground and kept some money for herself. She looked at her father's medicine bottle. She could not read, but that night she carefully copied the letters on the front of the bottle onto a scrap of paper. Next day she showed it to Jane, and asked her what it was for.

Jane read the shaky letters on Jenny's piece of paper. "Heavens child, why do you want this?" Jane declared. Jenny explained that her father had always taken it, but did not know why. The letters on the piece of paper spelled laudanum. It was made from opium and was something Jane would never touch, having seen people driven mad by it's degenerating power. Whether the girl's father had a medical reason for taking this, Jane did not know, but it would explain his apparent senility and occasional outbursts of temper. Jenny, to her credit, never said anything against her parents. Jane's knowledge of them had only been gained from Emily's gossip, so she gently explained about the addictive characteristics of the drug and said that it would be best for Jenny not to mention it at home.

That summer was unusually wet, and crops all over the country were failing. James fared better than most. His late father John, had studied the new farming methods with tireless zeal, and insisted on good drainage of all the fields. As James expanded the farm, he kept to his father's principals, and the initial hard work was now paying off.

At this time he was also approached by other local landowners, to form a 'Turnpike Trust'. This was a group of people, who together financed the repair of roads, which were mainly rough, muddy tracks, full of holes. Every year for six days, villagers were required by law, to do road repairs in their district. Of course the government did not pay for this, with the result that everyone only repaired the part by their own home, and the main routes to the towns fell into even worse disrepair.

The country's best road was the old Roman, Great North Road, which still had some of it's original paving intact. It reached from Chester to London, and the 'Turnpike Trust', wanted to connect with others to join Eastham to this. James could see the wisdom in such a proposal, and so made his investment. Each section of the toll road was to have a gate at the beginning. Spikes, or pikes were fitted along the top of the gates to stop anyone from climbing over. They became known as toll pikes. Different rates were to be charged, more for coach and horses, and less for a man on foot.

As well as his toll road investment, James also bought more land, two cows, and six sheep in lamb. The two cows joined the house cow at the mill, on some of the new adjoining land, and the sheep occupied the rest. The sheep were a short term investment, to be sold off for meat along with their offspring at the end of the year. Thanks to his efficiency, James held a good stock of turnips and clover hay, which would keep his animals fed when grazing was scarce.

On the other hand the two extra cows were to be a permanent investment. From his own house cow, and those at the mill, the family was producing Cheshire cheese. A delicious mild crumbly cheese, which was in great demand. On Jane's recommendation, they fed hazelnut leaves to the cows every day, increasing the butterfat content of the milk, and improving the flavour of the cheese. It was now being sent off to London, via boat from the ferry at Eastham and was fetching a very good price. Jane and Emily made the cheese, sometimes with Jenny's help, and Mary told Jenny she could go more often if she liked, with an increase in wages.

James employed another labourer, who had been travelling the roads, looking for work. He was to look after, and milk the cows, and to keep an eye on the sheep. An unusual young man, even after weeks on the road, he was reasonably tidy with an insatiable sense of humour, and a sparkle of laughter in his eyes. His story though, was sad. He had always worked with his father in the coal mines, his mother and sister, having died of a terrible fever which closed their throats, and choked them to death in a horrible unrelenting way. He and his father could do nothing to help them. Jane recognised the description of the symptoms right away. Martin had watched his mother and sister die from diptheria. She said nothing, but wondered why these diseases took some, but left others untouched.

With the invention of the new steam machines, all over the country, the demand for coal to power them increased. The mines were dug deeper and longer in the quest for coal. Miners were paid only for the amount of coal produced by each man at the end of the day. The deeper mines needed more roof supports and props, but the miners were expected to erect these themselves as they went along. This took too long, so they became careless about safety. Martin was working with his father when the roof of the mine collapsed. It seemed to happen at heart stopping slow speed, a loud crack, black dust, and his father crushed under a wooden beam and rocks. Most of their fellow workmates lay dead around them as work parties above, dug in a frantic rescue bid.

Somehow he managed to light his lamp, illuminating the horror and showing the agony on his father's face. He was afraid to put it out, but his father reminded him of the danger of explosion, so Martin sat holding his hand in the dark until rescue came. "Always keep your sense of humour son," his father gasped. "Your smile will be your fortune, you will see."

When they broke through, everyone but Martin was dead. He washed off the coal dust, and with nothing left, but memories of his father, he took to the road, and made himself smile.

He settled down happily to work for James, always delighted to spare time to see baby Sarah. Her smiles were such a delight, with her little dimples and tiny teeth. If she was around at milking time he would with Mary's permission, lift her to sit on the back of one of the placid cows. Other days he would carry her off, to see the lambs, and help her to pick a flower on the way back for her mother.

Sarah, now eight months old, although placid in other ways, refused to sleep anywhere but in her parent's bed, but after the first months of her life, this was hardly surprising. Mary felt sad that the beautiful crib, in which James had slept for his first two years, was standing unused, and was not amused by James' joke that she would be in their bed until she was married, and would probably expect them to make room for her husband too!

Sarah also discovered that she could crawl, and then there was no stopping her. James solved the dangerously mobile child problem, by building a pen in the corner of the kitchen. He carefully made wooden bars, and left spaces between them of a size that she could not get her head through. Then he rubbed all the wood down to a smooth surface, so that there would be no splinters for her little hands. Mary and Jenny pegged a blanket to the sides on the floor, put in a soft pillow, and baby Sarah was held captive. "A pen for Mary's little lamb," laughed James.

Unlike the tears of unhappiness caused by the crib, Sarah loved the pen. She no longer had to struggle out of her parents arms to get on the floor, to her it was freedom. With the baby safe, Mary could relax in the kitchen, and now enjoyed talking to the child and allowed her to hold various kitchen utensils. A wooden spoon was her favourite, she banged it on the bars, causing her father to be convinced she was going to musical. Unfortunately Sarah also bit the wooden bars, with her tiny teeth, leaving strange little patterns on the wood. She was now speaking a few words, Mama, Dada, Enny, for Jenny and Aine for Jane. Jane kept saying, "Grandma, Grandma, Grandma, say it for Grandma, sweetheart," but to no avail. Sarah was very intelligent, when she shouted, "Aine," Grandma came so why bother with the difficult Grandma word!

The bars of the pen also had another use, so Sarah soon found out. She held on to them and pulled herself to her feet. Mary was horrified, and imagined that she might damage her legs. She had seen children with bandy legs, but Jane assured her that the bent bones of those poor children, were the result of a disease called rickets, caused by lack of good food and fresh air. "Not something Miss Sarah will ever have," she chuckled as she looked at the baby's rosy cheeks, and stroked her pretty, curly hair. "If her brain is ready to allow her to do such things, you can be sure that her body is ready also."

Jenny made the child a toy lamb, from some scraps of cream flannelette. It was a simple shape, with a long tail. It's ears and a smiling mouth were made of pink woollen cloth. Sarah loved it at once, and shocked everyone when her father came in, by holding it up to him and saying quite clearly, "lamb!" "Well Mary," James laughed, "two lambs in your pen now, what next, a flock?"

All James' business ventures brought success that year. His flour, milled from his own corn at the mill, was fetching a high price, and the mill itself business was brisk. The sale of the sheep had gone well, and his cheese was in great demand. The toll road was progressing well, and return for that investment was coming near. Someone had even sent a violin to him from across the river, to be repaired, on the parson's recommendation. "He does have his good points," James said, as he sat happily and patiently repairing the instrument that evening, but Mary was not so sure. The parson's sermons were becoming more fearsome each week and she was beginning to doubt his sanity, but as James was content, and life was good, she said nothing about this, instead, she went over to her husband and kissed him.

She would voice her concerns about the parson another time, but never could she have guessed the extent of sick depravity in the mind of their man of the church.

Chapter Five

Martin, James' new labourer worked very well. He was not a country boy, but adapted and seemed to be able to turn his hand to anything. After the sheep were sold that autumn, James sent word for Martin to go up to the farm to see him.

This was the moment Martin dreaded. With the sheep gone, he expected that James would no longer need him. He thought of his father and tried to be cheerful, but his feet dragged as he made his way up to see James. Even the beauty of the changing autumn leaves could not cheer him.

It was such a relief to hear, that far from letting him go, James wanted him to stay, and even gave him a generous bonus. The sheep were in such good condition, that they had fetched the best price at the market that day. James explained how he would buy more sheep in the spring, but until then, Martin could continue to look after the cows, and also lend a hand at the corn mill.

He returned to his hut that afternoon, singing with joy, and with money in his pocket. Now he need no longer hold back for he was desperately in love. His heart was lost to Jenny, on the first day he saw her. Shiny hair, held in such an unusual pretty way, and shy smiles which captivated him. At first he thought that she was related in some way to James' family. She had Mary's gracious ways, and often displayed James' patient tactfulness. She also, seemed very knowledgable, always discussing with Jane, remedies of some sort or another. He was very surprised to discover that she came from just a poor family in the village. She always looked so sweet and refined, and oh she smelled so good, just faintly of lavender and roses. Martin so far, made no approach to her, despite his feelings, as he had not expected to be kept on when the sheep were sold, he felt that it would not be right.

Now all was different. He had of course always been his normal, friendly, charming self to Jenny, but no more than with the rest of the family. "I must think of ways to win her attention, and I will now save my money. I have no need to go to the alehouse in the village, now that I have hope in my heart," he thought. "When I have enough money, I will go to the market, and buy myself some decent clothes, then I will be able to accompany her to church on Sundays, but first I will buy her a green ribbon for her lovely hair, to go with her hazel eyes."

Before going home to his hut, he called at the mill to tell George of James' good news. George was not surprised, as James had already discussed the matter with him, but congratulated Martin all the same. He was a hard worker, and a likeable lad in the bargain. Emily gave him his loaf and jug of milk, and also today two eggs and a pot of pork fat. He was disappointed that Jenny was not at the mill, but happy at the prospect of being able to court her in the future. Of course, he said nothing of this to George and Emily, but waved goodbye and set off for home.

As he walked along, he came across some mushrooms. "What luck," he thought, "I will have fried bread, eggs and mushrooms tonight, a feast indeed." He picked as many mushrooms as would fill his cap. "Horse mushrooms, I think Emily calls them," he said to himself as he picked the slightly yellow topped mushrooms, with pink gills, "I will pick more tomorrow and take her some. It's a wonder she has not seen them growing here."

As he reached the hut in the field, where the sheep grazed before the sale, a small animal darted out to greet him. "Oh no you don't," he laughed. "You little egg stealer, you are not having these eggs." The animal was a slender creature with a long tail. Its coat was a dark brown and face marked with white. It wrapped itself about Martin's legs, so balancing his food, he bent down to stroke it.

In June he had found it, in a tree hollow with three others, already dead. A little white coated animal then, with beady black eyes. The mother had obviously met some dreadful fate, so Martin carried it home. At first it either cowered away from him, or bit him with its sharp little teeth. He fed it with bread and milk, and whatever he had to eat himself, and somehow it grew into this wild but affectionate creature, about a man's arm length from nose to tail. The animal did not like to climb, but amazed Martin with its ability to swim and dive. Now fully grown, it caught mice, frogs and even small birds, but it loved eggs, and seemed to be a natural egg thief. Its prey was brought home to be devoured alongside Martin, and although this was rather off putting at times, he could not help loving the animal. He mentioned it to George, who said that it was probably a polecat, and that if it came near Emily's hens, it could look out! George also told Martin that such animals could be used to catch rabbits. The polecat, put down a rabbit hole would chase the rabbits out, and if a net was placed at the other end of the burrow, one could be easily caught. Martin experimented, and the result was many a rabbit, roasted on a spit, outside his hut, shared by Pole, which seemed a natural name for the animal.

He made a fire with dry tinder wood stored inside the hut, and in a very large frying pan, the only legacy from his mother, he melted some of the pork fat. He took two thick slices of bread and put them into the hot savoury fat, then cut up some mushrooms and added them along with the two eggs. The fire was warm, so he hung up his coat on one of the pegs hammered into the wall inside the hut.

The meal was soon ready, the hot pork fat added flavour to the food and everything was delicious. Martin was hungry, and ate heartily, but strangely, the animal refused to eat anything at all. "Been a'hunting, eh!" he laughed as he stroked its fur. He washed the meal down with a cup of milk, and offered some to Pole. The creature drank enthusiastically. "Fussy tonight are we? You will not be getting any of my breakfast," he playfully scolded as he put the remaining bread and mushrooms away for the morning.

The nights were getting shorter, and it was now dark. Martin sat by the fire, thinking happily of Jenny and how he would woo her. Gradually he became aware of a pain in his stomach. The pain rapidly increased, together with a great nausea. He stood up and ran to the pit dug at the back of the hut. His mother had always instilled the need for cleanliness on the family, he remembered and dug a new soil pit each week. He was violently sick, but the pain increased. He almost crawled to his bed of straw, and lay in agony before passing out. The little animal crawled over to him and licked his face. There was no reaction, so it positioned itself at the bottom of the bed.

Next morning at the mill, Jane was irritable, as Martin had not turned up to milk the cows. She and Emily left their chores, and tackled the milking, making them late for the rest of the day. Jenny arrived to help with the cheese, just as Jane was grumbling. "Worthless good for nothing, why does he have to be late this morning?" George overheard and was concerned. "Never been late before, you know, could be something wrong." Emily suggested that perhaps Jenny should go to find out, so the girl set off across the fields.

Martin's hut was built from wood and stone, and it seemed to be thatched with bracken. It was the first time Jenny had been there, and it filled her with sadness. Such a pleasant young man, but this dwelling was only fit for an animal. The rough door was open and she walked in. Her heart almost stopped, Martin lay motionless on the bed. She bent down to feel his chest, and saw that his breathing was only shallow. Tears welled into her eyes as she failed to wake him. Then she was aware of a creature with tiny black shining eyes looking at her. She felt a horrible tingle at the back of her neck as she faced it, but it came over brushing its soft fur against her hand, as if asking for help. She knelt by the straw mattress, transfixed for a while. She was in love with Martin, but he had never shown any interest in her, and now he was here, with his strong arms limp, and his mouth without a smile, on the verge of death. Forgetting the animal, she lifted her skirts and ran like the wind back to the mill. Brambles tore at her bare legs in her flight, but she did not notice, knowing she must to reach Jane for help.

Jenny burst into the mill. "He's dying, he's dying," she sobbed. Jane reached for her coat, "Come child, tell me what is wrong," she coaxed. Jenny stammered out all that she had seen and Jane was most concerned. "George and I will go and see, and I will send him back to you if I need any medicines. No, you stay," Jane commanded as the girl turned to go with them, "let Emily bathe your legs with some warm salt and water. Jenny looked down, she was still clutching her skirts, her hands were clenched into tight fists, and blood was trickling from the vicious bramble scratches.

"Sit down my lamb," Emily soothed as she poured boiling water onto some cooking salt. She also made some camomile tea to settle the poor girl's nerves. What Emily's experienced eyes saw on Jenny's face was not just distress, but love. "Only a matter of time my dear," she thought, "You have become such a lovely girl." Emily knew better than to voice such thoughts, but just made sympathetic noises as she bathed the wounds.

At Martin's hut, Jane examined him for injury, but found none. He was unconscious and hot, so she looked around for other causes. The polecat fled to a dark corner as they approached, but watched quietly with secret black eyes. George could see nothing wrong either. Martin's supper things were neatly stacked away, and he had put food aside, apparently for breakfast, but the poor lad looked very ill indeed. Jane was beginning to despair, until she spotted the mushrooms, "Yellow stainers!" she exclaimed. George thought that they only caused stomach ache, but she explained, "Some people react badly to them, and it looks as if Martin is one, but luckily most recover in a few days. He must not have known about the obvious yellow stain on the bottom of the stalk, and mistaken them for horse mushrooms. I would say he ate quite a few of these last night, it is little wonder that he is so ill."

Back at the mill, Jenny allowed Emily to see to her wounds, and sat like a child, staring at the fire. Emily gently wiped the poor girl's tear stained face, and brushed her silky hair. "Heartbroken," Emily thought, but said kindly, "There my dear, now sip this tea, and stop worrying, Jane will do everything she can."

For the two women left behind, it seemed such a long time before George returned with the news. Jenny came back to life, and thanked Emily graciously for her kindness. She packed together the required medicines to take for Jane, a decoction of melissa, Mary always called it lemon balm, but by now Jenny knew Jane's terms for medicinal herbs. Added to this, according to Jane's instructions was a pinch of preserving salt, which they used for the cheese.

There was still no sign of improvement when Jenny arrived at the hut with the medicine, but Jane explained that this was the way with such poisons. She wondered about the human body. How strange she thought that a strong young man, apparently resistant to the terrible disease diptheria, should succumb so badly to poisonous mushrooms.

"We will bathe his neck and wrists with the mixture, as some of it will enter his system through the skin," Jane instructed, as she took the jug from Jenny, pouring a little of the fragrant green liquid into a bowl "When he wakes he must take sips of it as often as possible." "I will stay with him," Jenny volunteered, "If you think Mary could spare me today." "Of course, but he should not be left tonight, it could be a while before he regains his senses," Jane replied. "I will stay as long as it takes, it is not Friday, so my parents will not miss me," Jenny said absently, with an edge of pain in her voice. Jane understood the implication for Jenny always received her money on Friday, and this confirmed the sad situation of Jenny's homelife, which Jane had long suspected.

They lit the fire outside the hut with dry tinder wood and used some of the logs piled up at the side of the hut. Jane left Jenny to administer the medicine, and headed off back to the mill, promising to send George over later with some food. Jenny sat patiently beside Martin, bathing him as Jane had instructed, and kept the fire burning. She looked around the hut. It was surprisingly neat and clean. Martin's few possessions were hung from pegs, arranged around the walls. The bracken on the floor, and the straw of the mattress was obviously fresh, a cared for little dwelling. George arrived with a basket of food, some cold meat, a fresh loaf and a jug of milk. Jenny's stomach felt in a tight knot and she could not eat anything, but thanked him kindly and was glad for him to stay a while. "You're a good girl," he said as he left, "See you tomorrow."

It was becoming dark now, and as she sat gazing at Martin with such sadness, something suddenly jumped onto the bed. Badly frightened, she stifled a scream, but then realised that it was the strange animal. She had forgotten about seeing it earlier, but it seemed to remember her. It was carrying something in its mouth, and dropped it onto Martin's chest. "It is an egg!" she whispered, "You brought us an egg." It allowed her to stroke its smooth fur. "I am sorry, but Martin can not eat it, perhaps you would like it for yourself," she said and gently placed it on the floor. The animal skilfully bit the egg with its sharp white teeth, and soon devoured the contents, leaving two clean halves of shell on the floor. "You clever little thing," she laughed, and clapped her hands.

"Jenny, oh how many nights have I been alone, wishing you were here," Martin whispered. She spun round to face him. His eyes were glazed and somehow unfocused. "I have always loved you Jenny," he reached out to her, his voice scarcely audible. "I don't know what to say," she murmured, her eyes lowered in embarrassment. There was silence, except for the sound of his breathing, no longer so shallow, and when she looked at him again, his eyes were closed and there was no sign of movement. Had she imagined it? Could it perhaps have been just something she had wished could happen? There was no answer. She tried to wake him, but there was no response, so she decided to put it out of her mind.

Jenny watched Martin, by the light of the candle for a long time. She bathed him with Jane's mixture, and eventually fell asleep. She woke with a start, for she had slept, with her shawl around her, and her head resting on the straw mattress. Now she felt very cold and stiff. The fire outside was only embers, but the supply of tinder wood soon got it going, and she put on a pan of water. She washed the sleep from her face with a little of the warm water, and left the rest to boil. In the hut, she found a comb, and was standing by the door, combing her hair, when he called to her.

Chapter Six

"Jenny," he called, "are you really with me?" She dropped the comb, and with her long shiny hair flowing loose around her shoulders, turned to look at him. Relief wiped away all the embarrassment, as she ran to his outstretched arms. He held her so tenderly, hardly able to believe that this was not a dream. They remained embraced as time stood still. Jenny, who had never been held before, loved before, wanted before, felt she might die if he let her go now. The strength of his arms and the closeness of his body intoxicated her. He kissed the top of her head, inhaling the faint lavender fragrance of her hair, and took her face in his hands.

"I had planned to woo you, to somehow gain your interest. How can this be? Have we been bewitched? Do you feel the same for me? Can it be that you love me?" Martin whispered, never taking his eyes from hers. Shyness suddenly returned, and she lowered her eyes, "I have always loved you. My heart has leapt every time I have seen you, but I am being too forward," she sighed regretfully. "No, no," Martin almost shouted, fearful that she might slip away from him, "You being here this morning is the answer to my prayers." He kissed her tenderly, Jenny's first kiss, which raised love and passion inside her, beyond her wildest dreams. Forgetting the shyness she returned his charming smile. He gently stroked her smooth cheek, and brushed her hair from her face with his hand. "Your hair is so beautiful, I have never seen it like this before, what has happened here?" She explained, as he held her hand, almost afraid to let go. "You have been very ill, in fact unconscious for a day and a half. Do you remember the mushrooms for supper? They poisoned you. Jane and George have been here, they could not find what was wrong at first, but rest now, I should give you some of Jane's medicine." She poured some of the green liquid into a cup and asked him to sip it slowly. "Jane said that you had a particularly bad reaction to the mushrooms, but she was sure that you would recover. I have been with you since Tuesday morning, it is now Wednesday." Martin was horrified that he had missed a day's work. "James," he exclaimed, "I have let him down." "No, no", Jenny interrupted, "he understands. Please do not worry so, he even sent this pillow and blanket for you from the farm." "Well I must go today," Martin insisted, but felt dizzy when he stood up. "Be quiet, or Jane will be here to scold you for being a bad patient," Jenny giggled, "but do not fret, you will soon feel strong again." Pacified, Martin leaned back against the pillow, and watched enchanted as she picked up the comb from the floor and began to braid her hair.

She warmed the milk, and added some of the bread for their breakfast, suddenly she felt ravenous. "We could have had an egg yesterday", she said, "A friend of yours, some kind of animal, not a stoat, brought it, but then ate it itself. I was scared the first time I saw it, but it seems very friendly. What is it?" Martin told her all about the polecat, and how it helped him to catch rabbits. Jenny was impressed, "but I am afraid that the egg was a hen's egg, I hope it wasn't one of Emily's." "So do I," laughed Martin, "or we will have George here after the three of us!"

Martin's strength increased, and by mid-morning he was outside, stretching his legs, as Jane arrived. She was relieved to see such an improvement in her patient. He thanked her kindly for her attention. "You must take it easy today," she instructed, "Jenny will come to the mill with me now, but I will send her back with a meal for you tonight. She pretended not to see their parting look, but thought, "Emily was right." Jane was pleased for Jenny. She had become a pleasant, surprisingly intelligent girl, all she had needed was a little attention, she deserved some love in her life.

Jane kept her thoughts to herself as she told Jenny that Mary needed her on the farm, but planned to prepare a good meal for the young couple that night. Thanks to Emily, Mary was also aware of the situation, although tactfully made no comment. Sarah was delighted to see Jenny and put out her arms to be lifted from the pen. The little girl gave her a big hug, and did not want to be put down. Mary smiled at her happy child, "She has missed you, and she has not been down to the mill." "Missed Jenny," Sarah said, in a most grown up way, "Go and see cows now." Her speech was quite remarkable for her age, and she was now almost walking unaided. "For someone who was so delicate, you are becoming a real little miss, and anyway you saw Rosie this morning. When your father milked her, I sat you on her back, but I expect that does not count!" Mary laughed, tickling her little daughter, then putting her back into the safety of the pen, with a crust of bread to keep her quiet.

Mary was pleased to hear about Martin's recovery, and kindly told Jenny that she need not go to help with the cheese that morning, as it was getting late. Jane and Emily would be willing to manage for another day. Mary directed Jenny to the scullery. "There is warm water, you can wash and change now, I have ironed your apron." She felt, so glad to see the glow on the girl's face, which she knew to be love and delighting in her happiness. How sad that circumstances had forced this beautiful girl, to take so long to emerge from her dull and shabby chrysalis.

Jenny kept her few new clothes and aprons at the farm now, always washing and changing there in the morning. The first time she took a new dress home, caused such trouble with her parents. It had taken much time to make, being her first attempt. Although only a simple garment, with Mary's guidance, all the stitches were neat and small, and she was very pleased with the result. Her mother flew into a rage, when she saw it, accusing her of selfishness, and of squandering money, which could be better spent. Her father, in one of his more lucid moods, joined in, and lashed Jenny across her arm and back with his belt. The next day, defiantly wearing the dress, she set off to work, sore and stiff. Mary could not help but notice the large ugly bruise on the girl's arm, and Jenny broke down, crying when questioned about it. Promising not to tell a soul, not even Jane, Mary coaxed the whole story from Jenny, and was saddened to learn just how little money she kept for herself from her wages. "How could they hit her?" she thought angrily, "They want to keep her down. Here she is striving to improve herself, and still giving them nearly all her money each week." From then on, everything new Jenny made was left in Mary's care. Mary also suggested that she should always have her evening meal with them at the farm, or with Jane at the mill, wherever she happened to be.

Jenny gratefully took the water to the scullery for her wash. She also washed her hair, rubbing it as dry as she could before braiding it. "How kind of Mary to iron my apron," she thought.

The morning passed by quickly as she helped Mary with the cooking and cleaning, and then in the afternoon, joined the excitement when James arrived home. He had met the ferry at Eastham to collect some cloth. Mary was going to make new clothes for Sarah and the children at the mill. There was dark blue woollen cloth and lining to make coats for Emily's boys and for Sarah, the same in red, together with a length of muslin and flannelette in a delicate cream colour. A separate little box contained a bobbin of matching cream lace, and thread for all the colours.

Sarah sensed the excitement, and became fractious, not even satisfied with her father's attention. James decided that a walk down to see Grandma would be a good idea, he needed to call on George anyway, and he also wanted to see how Martin was progressing. Mary suggested that Jenny might leave early to go with them, knowing of Jane's plan to send her to Martin with supper.

Sarah's mood changed immediately when she realised where she was going. "I think she is growing another one of those pretty little teeth," Mary said, touching one of the baby's pink cheeks. "No fever though, see what Grandma says." Sarah wriggled as her mother tied her bonnet over her short brown curls, but then put her little arms round Mary's neck for a hug. "She has got us all around her little finger," Mary smiled, and kissed her little daughter goodbye.

As the ground was dry, Sarah was allowed to walk, holding hands with Jenny and her father for part of the way. She wore little soft leather slippers, made by her mother, but it was now nearly time to take her to be fitted with real boots, soon she would be running around by herself. She became tired, and allowed herself to be carried on James' back, laughing and giggling, holding his hair as they went along. "How she has come on," he thought, "and how time flies."

Jane was not at her cottage, but next door at the mill with Emily. Sarah was most pleased to be with Emily's children. She gave Jonathan a big kiss when he picked her up, and with a smile for his little brother, Roger, they all went off to play.

"She is teething," James told his mother, "Mary says will you have a look," in the distance they could hear the children laughing. She shrugged her shoulders, "Nothing a drop of camomile won't cure, she seems happy enough now. Teeth have to come through, you know,"

Jane took Jenny back to the cottage, "Emily will keep an eye on the children, so we will leave you to your business," she told her son, "We have cooking to do." In Jane's oven there was a pot with mutton cooking slowly in some stock, "This is for Martin," she explained. "You peel some vegetables and add them to the meat with some herbs. Later on we will thicken it all with some butter and flour. I have made plenty, perhaps you would like to share it with him tonight?" Jenny was delighted at the thought of sharing a meal with the man she loved, and it showed on her face when she said, "yes thank you," as calmly as she could manage.

James walked with Jenny to see Martin, and carried the basket of food. He smiled to himself when he saw a half full bottle of Jane's red wine inside. "What is my mother up to?" he thought, but he had long ago decided that the ways of women, were not a man's concern, especially if his mother was involved!

Martin assured James that he would be back at work tomorrow, and was heartened by his sympathy. "Get Jenny here to show you some real horse mushrooms, that is if you can ever face a mushroom again," James joked.

"See you both tomorrow," he called as he left the young couple, and headed back to collect his baby daughter. "The little scamp will be tired out by now. How she loves to play with Jonathan and Roger," he thought.

With James gone, Martin looked into Jenny's hazel eyes. "Still feel the same?" he questioned, almost fearfully. She did not speak, but put her arms around his neck. They kissed passionately, until interrupted by the furry little animal, twisting itself about their legs. They looked down, and both laughed as Pole disappeared nose first into the basket of food, which was still at Jenny's feet. "Bad animal," Martin scolded gently, pulling it out by its tail, "Come out of there and be introduced properly to my love."

It was a wonderful supper, eaten by the fire, outside the hut. "I have never been so happy," Jenny murmured, "Tell me all about yourself." Martin told her how all his family had worked in the coal mine, his father, mother and even his little sister of four years, as well as himself. It was hard, and dirty work, but his mother always insisted that they all wash at the end of the day, and kept clothes just for work. She was a strong and determined woman, managing the money and keeping the family in order. They lived in a small rented house with two small rooms at the top, and a large kitchen on the ground floor. It was good accommodation for a miner's family, and his mother always made sure that they had the money for the rent. His father was not allowed to squander money at the ale house, as many men, and indeed their wives often did, but he always seemed happy enough. His mother worked as hard as a man in the mine, but still found time to cook good food, and wash clothes once a week. She also taught Martin to read and write. The only book they owned was a bible, so Martin knew all the bible stories. Both his mother and sister fell sick at the same time. He had never known his mother to be ill before, and it filled him with fear. They paid for a doctor but he just took their money, and said that he must bleed the patients. He applied horrible leeches to their skin, and they became weaker and weaker. The fever was alarming, but the membrane growing in their throats was horrifying. They choked to death, within an hour of each other, while Martin and his father stood helplessly by.

His father went mad with grief, raving that they must have a proper funeral, and that his wife and daughter would not have a pauper's grave. Martin could only stand by while his father sold almost everything they possessed, and arranged the funerals. Martin thought it was wrong, but had not dared to say so. He loved his mother and sister dearly, but what was being buried were no longer the people he had loved, they were no longer in those corpses, and his father was leaving them with nothing, so that he could pay for the fancy funerals.

They could no longer afford to live in the little house, so they rented a small cramped and damp room, with a tiny window which would not open. His father spent most of his time and all of his money in the ale house, with a broken heart, leaving Martin to cope for both of them. He kept up his mother's standards of cleanliness, but his father refused either to keep himself clean, or even allow his son to wash his clothes.

Martin paid the rent and bought the food with his own money. His father would only join him for a shift at the pit when he ran out of funds for the mind numbing alcohol. It was one of those times when the accident happened, and Martin was left alone with only his father's last words to comfort him. "He was right though," Jenny interrupted, snuggling closer, "You do have a beautiful smile."

"What I did then was not so beautiful," Martin confided guiltily. "When they dug me out of that mine, leaving my father dead, I went straight back to our room. I washed myself down, put my few possessions into a sack, left my mining clothes behind and left. Jenny, I just took to the road and didn't look back. I did not bury my father, just left his body to the mine bosses, and a paupers grave. I had said goodbye to him in the darkness of the mine, and that broken body under the wooden beam, was no longer my father. It still does not seem wrong, but does it change your feelings for me?" "Of course not," she reassured him, gently stroking his hair with her hand, "You were lucky to have grown up surrounded with love, I know your father would not have blamed you." "Well," he continued, "after many weeks on the road, with small jobs along the way, I arrived here, and lost my heart to a beautiful girl," he smiled and took her in his arms.

Jenny did not go home that night, both tired by the events of the last few days, and warmed by the red wine and good food, they fell asleep in each other's arms, the deep and blissful sleep of those in love.

Chapter Seven

Emily told George of the situation between Martin and Jenny. He was most concerned, "Women, what is the matter with them?" he thought angrily. "One sniff of romance, and all good judgement vanishes. I might have expected it of Emily, and perhaps Mary, but Jane should have more sense. Surely they can see the consequences of such a match? What has Martin got to offer Jenny? Poverty, that is all, I must speak sternly to the lad.

The young couple looked radiantly happy that morning, they arranged to meet after work, and Jenny went cheerfully off to the farm. She was still there with Mary, when George called Martin. They were well into the morning's work and due for a break. Emily brought in some cake and nettle beer, but George told Martin to leave it for now, and to step outside. They walked over to the grazing cows, near to where the poisonous mushrooms grew, out of earshot of Emily and Jane.

"Now lad, I must have a serious talk with you. What are your intentions towards Jenny?" George asked sternly. Martin had not expected this, and was taken aback, "I am going to marry her," he replied shakily.

"Have you asked her? What have you got to offer her, but a shepherd's hut and a life of poverty, is that what she wants?" questioned George.

Fear that Jenny might reject him, filled Martin as he answered. "No I have not asked her yet, but I will save every penny I earn, and eventually we will buy our own little house. I will look after her, we are very much in love." George's attitude softened. "Yes lad, I can see that your intentions are good, but in that case I must speak even more frankly to you. What if she becomes with child?". Martin blushed to the roots of his hair, "I have not laid a hand on her," he replied hotly, "I said that I must speak frankly," George calmly replied. "You are not made of stone, and neither is she. Oh yes, she is shy and demure, Emily was the same when I met her, but just you wait, the passion, once aroused in such women can be incredible. Also never forget, women in love are like broody hens, they want babies. Emily would fill the house with children given the chance, but that is the way to poverty. Remember lad, you are not a tup in a field of sheep, if you empty your balls inside her, you will have her pregnant in no time. Don't look so embarrassed lad, I am talking straight to you, just as I will to my own sons. What is your experience in such matters? I would guess, a couple of miner's whores on a Saturday night," George went on as Martin gulped and nodded. "Well this is different altogether. First I think you can be sure that she will be like my Emily, never had a man before. You must be patient and gentle, be frank with her. Although she is shy, touch her, and ask her to touch you, ask her what gives her pleasure, and tell her what is good for you. Explore gently with your hands first, move at her pace, however long it takes, and she will love you for ever. As for avoiding babies, just pull out before you climax, you can please each other after if need be, but you will soon know each other's needs. Live happily with your plans, and you will have my blessing, condemn her to a hut full of brats and poverty, and you will have my wrath, understand?" George held out his hand to Martin, who mortally embarrassed, appreciated the wisdom of the advice, and shook hands heartily.

Emily returned to find the cake and beer untouched, and saw the two men in the distance by the cows. Tonight she would find out what was going on, but she knew better than to question such a situation now.

Jenny spent an enjoyable, but hard working day with Mary, who seeing the good drying day, decided to do the wash. Washing was a hot steamy affair. Water was boiled in a huge cauldron, and with the soap added, white clothes were washed first, darker ones last. The washing was pressed down by a stout stick, with three feet on the end called a pauncher, because it stabbed the air from the clothes and pushed them back down into the soapy water. More delicate garments were carefully washed in a bowl by hand, and everything was rinsed twice in cold water, with a few drops of lavender in final rinse. For the linens, they added a little boiling water to some amylum, a fine white powder, which turned to a translucent jelly, and was used to stiffen the fabric.

Sarah, in the pen with her toy lamb, watched the washing process with interest, and occasionally, Mary blew bubbles with the soap, through her fingers. The little girl laughed as they floated over to her, and burst as she tried to catch them. By lunch time, all the clothes were drying outside, and the two women sat down with a drink of birch tea, before preparing lunch for James. Sarah had fallen asleep on her pillow, with her thumb in her mouth. "She is so sweet," Jenny thought as Mary covered her with a blanket.

Mary tactfully asked about Martin, as they sipped the hot refreshing tea. Jenny, calmly said that he was recovering well, but then blurted out. "Oh Mary, he loves me, I am so happy, I could burst." Mary laughed, "Well in that case, how about taking some food to eat with him tonight, instead of your meal with us?" She did not say that she knew full well, that Jane had done the same the night before. "You are so kind, my life has changed so much in the last year," Jenny replied gratefully. "Well my dear, I know you work for me, but you are also my friend, and if you are happy, then so am I, but enough of our gossiping, let us set the table before my hungry James arrives."

James was full of news regarding the toll road. About to be opened, it was soon be linked to others, incredibly forming a good road route all the way to London. It was looking to be a fruitful investment. "We will have much more news, and interesting people to meet," he enthused, filled with his late father's desire for new ways and inventions.

In the afternoon Mary played outside with Sarah, while Jenny took in the clothes from the washing line. It was so much better on a day like this, to wash and get everything dry in one day. The two women set upon the ironing. They sang nursery rhymes to Sarah as they worked, to keep her happy, and the child joined in, in her own little way. Mary's flat irons were a set, ranging from very large, for linens, to tiny for lace or pleats. Sometimes Mary allowed Sarah to play with the tiny iron, and she would copy her mother pretending to press a handkerchief, but she soon became dissatisfied when she realised that hers was not being heated on the stove, like her mother's and Jenny's. "She misses nothing," Mary sighed, the baby's energy making her feel tired as they ploughed through the ironing.

James was surprised that Jenny was not staying for the evening meal. He smiled knowingly when Mary explained, now he understood what his mother was up to yesterday. It was not like her to indulge in match making, but then she often did things which surprised him.

Jenny set off with a fond, "goodnight," to Mary, who had provided some cold pie, a piece of cheese and some apples in a basket for supper. Carrying the food, the tiredness of the day vanished as she walked down towards the mill with a spring in her step. Martin was not quite finished work as she arrived, so she waved to him and went to chat with Emily. Being a natural gossip, Emily tried to find out how things were going, but Jenny made herself outwardly calm, and answered her enquiries in a matter of fact way, but when she saw Jenny join Martin and walk away hand in hand, she smiled to herself. "All is well, I see," she thought.

Pole appeared from nowhere when they arrived at the hut, and Jenny broke off a piece of bread from their fresh loaf for him. She knew now, not to put the basket down, or he would be inside it, eating the pie in no time.

Martin lit the fire and put water on to boil. They chatted as Jenny laid out the meal, sitting in front of the fire to enjoy it. The pie was delicious, made from pork, with whole hard boiled eggs inside, and the cheese, matured perfectly, was delicious eaten with the tartness of the crisp apples.

"Can I talk to you most seriously?" Martin asked, with an undertone of fear in his voice, as they sat contentedly watching the fire. She looked into his eyes, feeling startled. Perhaps he had changed his mind, could it be that he no longer wanted her?

He took her hand, "I have very little to offer, except all my love, but I will work hard, and look after you if you would marry me!" "Oh," Jenny cried, tears shining in her lovely eyes. "Of course I will marry you, I love you more than life itself." "Then we will see your parents tomorrow," Martin said eagerly.

Sadness clouded Jenny's face, "I must explain about my parents." She told him candidly about her life. There was no hostility in her voice, as she described the lack of love, neglect and verbal abuse. She explained how she had become Godmother to Sarah, but not about the stillbirth, no one, not even the man she loved would ever hear of that from her. She told him firstly of Mary's kindness and then of Jane's, about her father's addiction to laudanum, and how she had fought to improve her life. For all this she seemed to bear no malice, just a resigned sadness, which caused Martin such pain. "They are my parents, I cannot change that. I give them most of my money each week, to pay the rent on their house and to keep my father supplied with his medicine. I have five brothers, who are long gone. They left before I was born, so the responsibility is mine alone," she sighed. "No," Martin cried, "you will never be alone in any way again, we will always be together. We will see your parents after work tomorrow, they will be expecting you with the money as it is Friday. You must continue to pay them, and we will try to look after them, but they will not hurt you with words or actions again, with me by your side. I want you to have a wonderful life Jenny, and for you to have the best I can give. I want to save my wages to buy a small plot of land, then build a house of our own, which, however modest, will be our security for the rest of our lives. I can see we have two choices. To save for our own house will take a long time, and we could postpone our wedding until then, continuing as we are, or, we could live here in the hut."

Jenny interrupted, forgetting that when she first saw it, she had thought it only fit for an animal.

"I do not care, I would rather be here with you than in that loveless little bedroom in the house of my parents."

"That is what I had hoped, but it is a poor start, not what I want for you. The weather is still kind for late October, but when winter sets in, how will you feel then?"

"We could improve the hut, build a chimney for an inside fire. There is stone and broken brick around to do just that, and there is slate down by the stream, we could line the floor with it, under the bracken, to help keep out the damp."

"My wonderful Jenny, we will make ourselves a home. I will put by all my earnings, but I want you to keep what little you have left each week to buy pretty things for yourself. Pole will help me to catch rabbits, and we will have Emily's bread and milk each day."

"Don't forget we could pick mushrooms."

"You wicked girl! Let us be married as soon as possible."

They kissed passionately, and she felt a thrill as his manhood swelled against her. She pulled away, concern on her face.

"I had not thought. What if we were to have a child? How can we live together here and wait that long? It would be irresponsible to bring a child into the world here."

"My love, when the time is right, there are ways of avoiding pregnancy, gentle ways, which will not spoil our pleasure."

"Oh, I am so glad that you know of such things, but I think the time is right. You stir inside me such feelings of desire, I have never been with a man, but I know that I want you."

He picked her up and carried her into the hut which was to be their home.

"We must be open and unreserved with each other," he whispered, silently but eternally grateful for George's advice. "We must take time, you must not be shy. Tell me what pleases you, and if anything does not. He gently took off her dress, leaving her standing in her shift. She unbuttoned his shirt, and sighed with pleasure as she pressed herself against his bare chest. He caressed her breasts, so small and firm, and felt his desire heighten as her nipples hardened beneath his touch. To his surprise, she pushed the shift from her shoulders, and let it fall to the floor. "Oh you are more beautiful than I ever could imagine," he almost sobbed. Gently putting her hand on the bulge in the front of his breeches, she whispered shyly. "Can I see you?" Martin gulped, how right George had been about such women, once aroused. "It might alarm you," he warned, "but I will give you such pleasure when we eventually come together." To his utter astonishment and delight, Jenny was so full of desire, she dropped to her knees and kissed and caressed him. He lay her on the straw mattress, and she clung to him as he kissed her. He slid his hand between her legs and she moaned with pleasure as he gently stroked her. "Does that please you too?" she gasped. He put his hand to his lips, tasting her wetness. "Such pleasure, this is your desire for me." "Please let us not wait," she begged caressing his erection and the delightfully laden pouches beneath. He was very gentle, as she gasped, not with pain, but with ecstasy as he entered her. She moaned and clung to him as they made love for the first time, crying out as he withdrew to climax, but thanks to George's advice, Martin brought to shuddering satisfaction with his hand. They remained entwined, until the chill of the night air brought them to their senses. Martin brought the blankets over, "I did not hurt you, did I?" Concerned now, as he had intended to take it all more slowly, but she just smiled and kissed him. "So happy I could die," she whispered, snuggling into his strong embrace, "Everything is wonderful."

Chapter Eight

Jenny's stomach churned as they went to see her parents that Friday night. Holding hands, they entered the house. Her father was slumped in a chair, apparently asleep, with an empty bottle of laudanum by his side. Her mother almost jumped to her feet, hand out for the money, before noticing Martin.

Politely Jenny introduced him, "This is Martin, we are going to be married." "Married, you selfish and stupid girl," her mother yelled, "and to him. He is the shepherd isn't he? He has not even got any sheep to tend now. What about our money, your duty lies with us, just look over there at your sick father."

"I know all about that medicine," Jenny said calmly. "His illness is his own doing, it is opium, made from poppies, and it is rotting his brain!" Her mother's face contorted into a malevolent mask, and she flew at her daughter with amazing agility for an old woman. She lifted her hand to strike Jenny, but Martin stepped in front of her and took the blow on his chest. He firmly took the furious woman by the shoulders. "Jenny, my love, please go outside for a while, I will not be long," he insisted. Shaking, Jenny slipped out through the door, leaving it slightly open. Her mother started ranting in a high pitched voice, but Martin knew just how to stop all this. The situation was worse than he had expected, but he had given it much thought that day, and was prepared. "Stop," he shouted, "or there will be no money." It worked, as he knew it would, and she stood quivering with rage before him. "Now, we will be getting married," Martin growled, "and you will give us your blessing. I cannot buy your love for Jenny, but I can buy respect. You will never speak harshly to her again, if you do, you will get no money. If you ever physically hurt her again, I will come and kill you. That is no empty threat, and you will make your husband understand. Behave and we will look after you. We will live on what I earn, and Jenny will give you the same amount as always. We will visit the parson, to put out the banns, and should be married within a month." An ugly smirk spread across the old woman's face. "No," Martin said confidently, "we are not going to have a child, if that is what you think. Our children will come into the world, only when we have the best to offer them, and they will have the love and happiness from us, that you have denied your daughter. Now, have I made myself clear?" She just nodded, and looked over to her husband, drugged to a useless stupor. Martin almost felt pity for them, but then called to Jenny.

She tiptoed through the door and handed the money to her mother. Astonishment replaced fear as the old woman spoke. "Thank you, and you have our blessing for the wedding." "We will be back next week with the money, and news of our arrangements," Martin called as he ushered Jenny out of the door. She was visibly shaken, but recovered as Martin kissed her. He took her by the hand, "Now to see the parson, no time like the present!"

"The parson does not like me," she whimpered. "Come, come, Jenny this is not like you. From what I have seen, he does not like anyone who is not a big landowner. What has my sweetheart done to deserve his special wrath?" Jenny told him of the day that the parson had blessed Sarah, and how Mary had spoken up for her, insisting that she remained Godmother to the baby. "That was the day I started to get my life together," she sighed. "Well," Martin laughed, putting his arm around her waist, "It looks as if we are in for another bad reception, but at least he will not hit me, unlike your mother!" Jenny could not help but giggle. "That's my pretty Jenny," Martin smiled, as he pulled her towards the parson's house.

It took a long time for him to open the door. Parson Richardson was a tall thin man, in his early thirties, whose crow like features were not helped by his long black cassock, a straight full length garment with a standing collar, buttoned from neck to hem. "Yes," he bellowed, making Jenny jump a step backwards, but Martin stood his ground and explained that they wished to be married, and to start the reading of the three week banns as soon as possible. Leaving them standing on the door step, he shut the door, and disappeared into the house for a piece of paper to take down their full names. "Banns will start a week on Sunday, wedding four weeks on Saturday at mid-day, short ceremony, no orchestra, no choir," he said when he returned to write down their names, and, giving them no choice in the matter, shut the door again.

"Do you think he is human?" Martin laughed, "he has no personality at all, but we are to be wed, and that is what matters. Do you agree?" Jenny nodded, relieved that they had not been on the receiving end of one of his vicious, 'sins of the flesh' sermons, which seemed to be getting more ferocious each week.

They were tired now, and it was dark as they made their way to the hut, which had become their love nest. "Only simple bread, cheese and milk tonight my love," said Martin. "Riches beyond my wildest dreams," she laughed."

Mary was delighted at the news of the wedding, but frowned when she was told of the parson's reception of the young couple. She spoke to James about the matter, and found that he was most concerned about the parson's attitude in general. "He terrifies the young people in the junior orchestra," he confided, "I have to tell them to pay no heed. If Jenny wants a short ceremony, so be it, but I am in charge of the orchestra, and we shall play for her on her special day, whatever parson Richardson says."

Mary thought about her simple cream silk wedding dress, stored away with sprigs of lavender, in a trunk for four years now, and offered it to Jenny. Tears of happiness filled her eyes, as she touched the fine fabric, and thanked Mary for her kindness. "It is very plain, because I married so soon after the family deaths from the typhoid epidemic," she explained, "but we have that bobbin of pretty cream lace, for

Sarah's Christmas clothes. There will be much left over and we could sew it onto the dress."

Preparations were under way, and Jenny was excused from her cheese making duties, with the blessing of Jane and Emily, but James kept up her wage just the same. Jenny missed seeing Martin during the days that she was not at the mill, but sewing with Mary, was delightful, and blissful nights with him made up for everything. "You must have some new clothes for the wedding," she insisted to Martin, who was loathe to spend any money on himself. "They can be for Sunday best, afterwards."

Armed with two weeks wages, and the bonus from James, Martin reluctantly set off with George, carrying the flour in the horse and cart, and chatting amicably along the way to the market. The wedding was to be a small affair, the guests comprising of only Jenny's parents, James, Mary, Jane and Sarah, George and Emily and the two boys. Martin confided that he would be for ever grateful for George's sexual advice, and asked if he would stand for him at the church. They arrived in a jovial mood, then Martin left George and went off to the other side of the market.

By mid-morning, Martin's purchases were complete, and he was well pleased with his bargains. He bought a fine new muslin shirt, a matching neckcloth, and a pair of breeches. He found a very good pair of boots and a smart jacket, which although not new, were very presentable and saved him a great deal of money. Once the necessary items were bought, he went to the goldsmith's stall. Jenny had not mentioned a wedding ring, and he suspected that she would be willing to make do with a band of cheap brass, which would turn green on her finger, as did many other labourer's wives. "Not for my love," he thought fiercely, "She will wear my ring for life, and when our circumstances are better, I want her to still be proud of it." He bought a pretty little gold ring, hoping that he had judged the size correctly, and with the last of his money, bought a length of ribbon, the colour of sweet chestnut leaves in summer, and tied it through the shining band of gold.

Jenny was waiting with Emily, like an excited child, when they returned, and much admired his new outfit, but it was by candle light, as he held her in his arms, when he gave her the beribboned ring. "Green to please your lovely eyes, and gold to please your heart," he whispered, kissing the soft warm skin between her breasts. He tied the ribbon with the shining ring around her neck. "Soon it will be on your finger, and the world will know you are mine," he sighed as they made love, with a delightful passion, that Jenny had never thought possible.

Chapter Nine

Parson Richardson was not pleased. James had visited him concerning Jenny's wedding, and insisted that the orchestra be present. Not only was James leader of the orchestra, his farm was rapidly expanding, and to own land was to have power, so the parson felt it his duty to respect his wishes.

"Why does a man of his status act in such a way," the parson bewailed to himself after James' departure. "To make such a fuss of a labourer, and that upstart of a servant girl. First made her Godmother to his child and now she is dressing like a lady, and sitting at their pew with them. It is so wrong to give such lower classes ideas above their station, all labourers should always sit at the back of the church. Their wives were always obliged to curtsey to the parson's wife, when I was doing my training. People are losing their senses. I have heard of that stupid Welshman, Robert Owen, building houses for his factory workers, and educating their children indeed. If his ideas spread, society will be destroyed. I believe he will not even allow children to work at all, gives them full time education. It is the devil's way, they will rise up and cut the stupid man's throat one day, leaving us with a country full of hooligans. I must pray to the Lord to stop it." He paced around his dismal house, with his thoughts, and his eyes flashed wildly as another intimidating sermon began to form in his mind.

James also approached Martin about living in the hut after he and Jenny had wed, and was impressed by the lad's ambitions. "It will take many years to save, even to build a small cottage," he commented. "What if I were to build it and then rent it to you?" Martin thanked him for the kind offer, but explained that he could not accept. "I am willing to wait as long as it takes, so that I will have the security for my family, which my father had not." James frowned thoughtfully, "We have become very fond of Jenny, and you have proved yourself to be an excellent worker. What if I can help in a different way? What if I were to build a one storey cottage, and include a garden plot, like my mother's? Instead of paying rent, you could buy it from me in instalments from your wage each week. I would have papers drawn up to make it legally binding, but you would have to be bonded to work for me during that time. It would be beneficial to us both, as I intend to keep extending the farm, and will need reliable help. Could it be that we have a deal?" James asked, seeing the delight on the lad's face, and holding out his hand. Martin shook his hand, "Indeed we do, I can't wait to tell Jenny!"

The wedding was soon to be upon them. It was now late November, and the weather turned typically wet and cold. The chimney for the hut had been completed, but despite the fire, it was cold and draughty. For all that, Jenny was happy, it was worth any amount of cold to be able to fall asleep at night in each other's arms. Mercifully, the sun shone on the Saturday of the wedding, and the day was dry and unseasonably warm.

James and Martin waited in the kitchen of the farm, keeping an eye on Sarah, while Jane and Mary, fussed upstairs, over the bride. With Jenny out of earshot, Martin was able to broach the sensitive subject of her father, to James. He explained about the old man's laudanum addiction, and that he was afraid that his future father-in-law might not be in a coherent enough state to give Jenny away at the wedding. Her parents had simply said that they would do their duty, and be at the church at the allocated time. Martin asked James, if there should be a problem, would he stand in for Jenny's father. "Of course lad," James said, slapping him on the back in a friendly way, "we will make sure that nothing spoils your special day." Martin was uneasy, as he had sensed more than a feeling of malice on their last visit to Jenny's parents, who really wanted nothing to do with the wedding. To relieve his tension, and to stop himself fiddling with his neckcloth, which Jenny had tied so beautifully, he started to play with Sarah, who was intent on removing her new boots.

James and Mary had taken their little daughter to be fitted for her first real footwear. Mary chose soft red leather, and the resulting boots looked so very comely on the child. Sarah had other ideas, oh, she loved the colour, but those nasty heavy things on her feet, were something she tried to avoid. She had at first cried, and then kicked, in a most uncharacteristic way. Then, being an intelligent little miss, she found that she could undo the laces, and triumphantly threw one of the offending, and hated things across the kitchen. Mary would not give in, and tied the red laces into a double bow, which for now had the child bemused. She forgot about the boots, when Martin started to play 'peep' with her, hiding her toy lamb behind his back, and then popping it over his shoulder. "George told me that women in love are like broody hens," he thought, "but he did not tell me that I would feel the same. We might have to wait a few years, but it will be wonderful when Jenny and I have a child like this." Mary had made for Sarah, a little high waisted dress from the fine cream muslin. It was mid calf length, and underneath she wore ankle length pantalets. The whole outfit was lined with warm matching flannelette and trimmed with pretty cream lace. Her brown curls were tied up with a bow of the fine muslin, and she looked as pretty as a picture. He was so enchanted with her giggles, that he did not hear the women coming down the stairs.

"Martin," Jenny called, he turned to see a vision of loveliness. "She could be a princess," he thought, his breath almost taken away. The simple lines of the dress showed off her figure, and in her shining hair, was braided his gift of green ribbon.

"Come on," Jane commanded, breaking the silent magic between them as they looked into each other's eyes, "We have a church to get to." She felt a lump in her throat, as she remembered her own wedding, and her dear late husband John. She had not realised how much weight she had lost in the four years since his death, until she had tried on the black silk outfit, which Mary had made for her when she and James wed. Eating now she thought, just provided fuel for her body. Before, she and John had looked forward to their meals together, when they would eat, and enjoy discussing his many plans for the future. Mary took in the seams of the outfit drastically to make it fit again, but she could not take away the memories of pain, from the last time it was worn, so soon after John's death. Jane shook her mind from the sombre thoughts, and busied herself with the bride, giving her own fine white shawl to provide warmth over the wedding dress.

George arrived with the horse and cart, Emily and the boys had gone ahead to the church. Just as they were ready to go, James led out his own horse. It was a solidly built animal, strong enough to pull the plough and seed drill, but fine enough in looks and temperament for any country gentleman to ride. Its bridle was festooned with white ribbons, and Mary threw a white embroidered tablecloth across its back. James picked up Jenny and placed her side saddle on the horse. "There," he smiled at Martin, "take my lady to the altar." They made quite a procession on their way to the church, with Martin almost bursting with pride, as people stopped to wish them luck.

The parson was waiting by the door of the church, his usual unsmiling self. As they arrived, Jenny's parents appeared from inside the church. Jenny was rigid with shock, she had never seen her parents this way. They were clean, to the point of being scrubbed. Her mother's usually lank grey hair was scraped severely into a tight bun under an elegant hat, and her father's was slicked back with some kind of grease, but the reason for the shock was their clothes. They were both outfitted in obviously expensive new clothes, right down to shiny boots and shoes. Jenny could not imagine how they could have paid for such outfits, but felt so proud that they had somehow done this for her.

"Thank you father," she whispered as they walked down the aisle, but he neither looked or spoke to her. The wedding ceremony was short and precise, but the orchestra played beautifully. Both Mary and Jane noticed the expression on the parson's face. His dark beady eyes darted about, and as James remarked later, he had the countenance of a trapped rat. At the end of the service, when the guests were throwing rice at the young couple, Jenny's parents simply walked away from the church, without a word to their daughter, and went home. Martin's kisses healed the hurt. "After all," she thought. "They have never been any different."

The days passed happily. James suggested building the house near the hut, so that Martin could help when he had the time, and it was growing rapidly. He also insisted on strong foundations, with a slate and tar lining on the floor, to prevent damp. Work went very well until the week before Christmas, when the snow closed in for two weeks, and Sarah had a blizzard on her birthday once again. "What is it about you and snow?" James teased, tickling his little daughter's tummy. "Is it always going to snow on your birthday? Perhaps we should have called you Snow White. Mary, she even looks like the child in the story, Snow White, Rose Red. She has the dark hair, pale complexion, and rosy red lips." "Ah, but would such a story book child, bite the bars of her pen, and throw her boots across the kitchen," she laughed. The little girl was walking on her own now, and actually, the once despised footwear had become part of her life.

Sarah loved to hear stories, and to listen to songs and nursery rhymes, for twelve months old, she seemed very advanced. When Mary made her the red balandrana style coat, with a hood, her father said, "my own Red Riding Hood," and bounced her on his knee, telling her the story, without making it too frightening. Jenny helped to make the coat, and they also made two similar ones for Jonathan and Roger, from the lovely blue woollen cloth. The younger, Roger, jumped about in his, but solemn, and so grown up Jonathan, just asked if he could take Sarah for a walk outside with their hoods up. To the amusement of everyone, with her lamb, in its red coat, her most prized possession, under her arm, she took his hand firmly, and went out into the snow to watch the flakes whirling round. "As old as the hills, they look," Emily laughed.

It was May before the house was complete. Martin and Jenny watched enthralled as a pair of swallows made a nest in the eaves. "They will come back to us every year now," she told him. "Did you know that they hardly ever land on the ground, except to gather the material for their mud nests? Swallows always make a cup shaped nest, and you can tell it is a swallow by the chestnut coloured patch under it's throat. People say that they disappear into the mud in the winter, but Jane thinks that they fly over great seas and vast lands to a place where it is always hot. It gets too hot for the birds there in the summer, and that is why they come here."

That year they watched the birds rear their family. The crafty polecat eyed the birds intently, but despite every effort, failed to get either a bird or egg. "Go and find yourself a frog," Jenny would often say when she caught him sneaking about under the nest, but at the same time she always stroked his fur, and gave him a titbit to keep him happy. After harvest time, as the nights lengthened, they watched them fly away. "Leaving us to ourselves, in our nest," Martin whispered that evening, "but one day we will have our own babies." Jenny smiled wistfully. "Not yet, my lady," he laughed, "I have other plans for you, come to my bed and let me show my love for you." He carried her inside, pushing the door shut with his foot, and kissed all over her body, until she cried out for his lovemaking.

Chapter Ten

It was the summer of Sarah's fourth year when Parson Richardson introduced his niece to the congregation. One Sunday, she appeared, sitting on a chair by the pulpit, shy and quiet, with her hands folded onto her lap, and eyes downcast. Before his sermon, he introduced her, "This is my niece, Elizabeth," he told them, "She will be staying for a while." She stood up, a petite girl, no more than eighteen, with the lightest of blonde hair. Although she smiled at her introduction, there was something strange about the expression in her large blue eyes. "Fear," Jane said afterwards to Mary, "I feel sure she is afraid of him, and who could blame her, he becomes more eccentric every week." "That sermon at least, was more subdued," James butted in. "Perhaps his niece will have a calming affect on him, and he has respected my wishes about the junior choir and orchestra. In fact he ignores them altogether, after my threat to resign."

The incident with the juniors shocked James. He had been late for rehearsal, and as young people will, they had started to play about. A talented boy from the village, only eleven years old, and a magical player of his wooden flute, accidentally knocked over a heavy candlestick, just as the parson walked in to see what was going on. He threw the terrified child to the floor, and proceeded to beat him with the candlestick, breaking the fingers of the hand the poor child put across his face to protect himself. James had to drag the demented clergyman off, as he laid into the child with the bloodstained weapon, ranting about the devil and all his works. He stared at James, with terrifying hate in his eyes, then turning on his heels, walked calmly back to the house. Jane did what she could for the injuries, but the fingers were so badly broken, that he never played the flute again, and remained with a crippled hand. "How can he call himself a Christian, when he terrifies little children," she scowled, but other than the warning from James, there seemed little that they could do about the parson's attitude. Sarah did not like going to church, and wished that she could be with Jenny, who now sat at the back with Martin, but she was to take her place on the front pew between her father and grandmother, with the threat of, "no nonsense, young lady," from Mary.

James continued to buy more land, his property now covering a large area. His main concern was the growing and grinding of corn, but he carried on with the specialised cheese making, and limited sheep farming. His latest acquisition being land belonging to an old couple, whose two sons had left the farm to work at the ironworks in Shropshire. As usual James paid a fair price for the land, and left the old couple with the small house, garden and limited grazing for a house cow. The old man had grown corn, and sometimes reared pigs and sheep for as long as he could remember, but now he looked forward to an easier life and his wife could have the house cow, she had always wanted. Now she would have time to make butter and cheese, and earn some money selling it at the weekly market.

Unfortunately the in-calf cow, bought for this purpose, although a bargain in price, was not doing too well. It had looked rather bony, when they bought it, but the wife was sure that some good food would soon put it right. It had given birth easily enough, to a female calf, but mother and daughter were becoming increasingly sickly. Knowing of Jane's skills, the old lady had sent word to the mill, to ask if she would call sometime to see the animals.

As the weather was so kind, Jane thought it would be a good idea to make a day of the trip. It was a long way on foot, but it would be a good day out for the children. She explained that she would take some baskets of food, eat along the way, then collect plants on their return. Mary knew all about Jane's herb gathering, it certainly would take all day, as she would explain the virtues of each plant she picked. Although Mary used her mother-in-law's preparations, she had no interest in their ingredients, and besides the thought of a peaceful afternoon, sewing in the garden, was much more appealing.

"Perhaps Jenny would like to go instead, she is interested in your medicines, and is so good with the children. Tell Emily I will come down in the morning to help instead of Jenny. We will enjoy a good gossip, while the men are out of the way, you know how she is, always with a good story to tell."

So it was settled and next day they set off early. Jane packed some tasty potted meat, made with bacon, pork, herbs and seasonings, fresh potato cakes, a deep crisp rhubarb pie, some nettle beer, and a large bottle of elderberry cordial for the children.

Jenny's excitement matched Sarah's as they left, Martin smiled to himself as he watched her skip off with the children, and blew a kiss to her as she turned to wave to him once again in the distance.

Jonathan carried one of the baskets. He was now ten years old, and although a charming child, was more serious than ever. A complete contrast to his younger brother Roger, who full of mischief ran along ahead of everyone. Jane noted and pointed out to Jenny, herbs which they would gather on the way back. It was a delight to have someone so interested, and she hoped that some day her little granddaughter would be the same. Sarah ran, skipped and scampered as they went along, eventually becoming tired. "I told you not to run," her grandmother scolded. "It is early in the day and you are worn out, and look at your shoe laces, all undone. For someone who is so forward in everything else, you should be able to tie a bow by now." Jonathan came to her rescue, and tied the offending laces, something which Sarah genuinely somehow was unable to master. Asking Jenny if she would mind carrying the basket, he lifted up the little girl and carried her piggy back. She put her arms around his neck tightly, and snuggled her forehead into his hair. "Thank you Jonathan, I do love you," she said.

They stopped at lunch time, almost there, to eat the meal under a shady oak tree. They were all hungry, and the freshly made food was delicious. Despite Jane's plea to eat slowly, the children demolished the food at amazing speed, and drank up all the elderberry cordial, leaving none for the return journey. The sweet, slightly smokey red drink, was so good that they did not care. "Well it's water for you later, and you had better not complain," she warned.

The old woman with the sick cow, made a great fuss of the children, and entertained all three while Jenny and Jane went to see the animals. Both cow and calf were a sorry sight. The calf had now developed diarrhoea and both were emancipated. Jane sent Jenny off to ask if there was a hazelnut tree around, and meanwhile administered a drop of camomile oil diluted in milk to the calf. Jenny returned with a bunch of leaves, to aid the cow's digestion, and was sent off again, this time for a bucket of very hot water and a cloth. More camomile oil went into the bucket, and they bathed the poor calf's stomach with the hot cloth. "Worms are the main problem," she told Jenny, putting a few drops of thyme onto the hazelnut leaves for the cow. "Both will recover, but it will take time. Luckily the owner seems to be a kind and patient woman." She found some lemongrass in her basket of medicines, and putting a few drops onto a cloth, instructed Jenny to wipe the heads of both animals with it. "This will keep away the flies, and make them feel better," she explained. Leaving Jenny in charge of the fly repellent, Jane went back to the house to get the children. She had noticed that the cow had cowpox. It was not serious, but a nasty sore on the udder. Jane's family had long known about cowpox. It was treated with tormintil root, mixed with Pellitory of Spain and alum, but this was something she did not have with her. She assured the old woman that the animals would recover, and that she would ask George to drop off a pot of tormintil mixture next time he went to market.

Jane knew that anyone who had been infected with cowpox, would not get smallpox. To be sure, cowpox left an unsightly scar, the one on her own hand and that of James, bore witness to that, but she considered it a small price to pay to avoid the terrible killer.

She explained about the cowpox to Jenny, and why she was going to deliberately infect the children with it. "You should have it too, and if it develops you should pass it on Martin, it's worthwhile to keep you safe, smallpox is a terrible way to die." Jenny agreed, but looking at the scar on Jane's hand, suggested that perhaps it could be done on her leg instead, so it would not interfere with her cheesemaking. Jane had not thought of this. Cowpox was always on the hand, usually caught from milking the cow. "Good girl, I do not see why we should not try that." she said, breaking off a thorn from a nearby hawthorn hedge. She made a small scratch on the legs of Jenny and the children, explaining why as she went along. Sarah's eyes widened, as she decided this was something she did not like, but Jonathan told her, to be brave like him, so she allowed it to happen. Jane broke off some of the cowpox scab from the cow's udder, and rubbed it into the scratches. "There all over," she said cheerily, knowing that it was not. If it took, there would be an uncomfortable itchy patch of skin to be endured. "Now, on the way home, I know where some late strawberries grow, we will eat them as we walk along, and rub our teeth with them to make them extra white!"

It was late when they returned to the mill, all tired, with gallant Jonathan carrying Sarah on his back. Emily laughed to see the children, who had set out full of life and spotlessly clean, now so dusty and sleepy. Jenny went home to Martin, who had caught a rabbit with the help of the polecat which sat patiently beside him as the meat roasted on a spit outside. "Just like old times," Martin said as he took her in his arms.

Sarah was too tired to eat, and as soon as she was washed, fell asleep until next morning. "She has been eating all day," Jane assured her worried parents, "and we have all had a lovely time."

Two weeks later Mary was furious when Jane explained about the mysterious sore developing on Sarah's leg. She explained at length the reason for it, and that George, Emily and Martin had also now been protected by the infection. "You should also have it," her mother-in-law reasoned, Mary was not pacified. "You are not doing that to me! Oh poor Sarah, it will leave a terrible scar," she wailed to James, who was trying to keep out of the argument, although sure that his mother was right. He knew that Mary had other reasons for being weepy. She longed for a son, a brother for Sarah, but this month, two weeks after raised hopes, she was again disappointed. She promised to speak to Jane about it but had not yet done so, and her mother-in-law, although feeling there was some deeper problem, did not understand Mary's unreasonable behaviour.

It was James who eventually confided in his mother. Jane had every sympathy for Mary. Her own situation had been similar, for some reason she also only conceived once, making James an only child. She blamed herself in some way, although she had always been in perfect health. Now she began to wonder if perhaps it was something to do with the male line. It could be that James and his father, although showing no sexual problems, had only a limited fertility. Such things could do so much damage to a man's pride, that she decided not to mention it, instead blaming the problem on the circumstances of Sarah's birth. She told Mary not to be despondent, and to count her blessings for having such a delightful daughter. Mary did indeed settle down into a happier attitude again, and Jane unfortunately thought it prudent not to mention cowpox for the time being.

Chapter Eleven

Mary gave up all hope of having another child. Sarah would be six at the end of the year, was wonderful company, and had developed many talents. James made a wooden flute for her, and she played amazingly well for her age. He was so proud, hoping that she would play with his junior orchestra, but she cried so pitifully at the mention of it, that he hid his disappointment and dismissed the idea. "I don't like it in church," she wailed, "and that nasty man will beat me." Nothing could reassure her, and James felt real anger against the parson, whose humour had not improved, even with the reappearance of his niece, who had been away for the last six months.

"Sarah, let's have a story", he said to distract her, knowing that would make her happy. James now took regular trips to various towns, along the new toll roads, gaining knowledge all the time. He always returned with some pretty cloth for Mary, or some unusual buttons or ribbons, and a new story book for his daughter. She happily sat on his knee, and soon knew each story word for word.

She also loved to draw, inheriting her father's artistic flair. She drew flowers on some cloth, and Mary showed her how to embroider over it, with surprisingly beautiful results. It was such a pleasure to sit sewing in the garden, with the little girl watching and trying to copy each stitch.

Mary decided to begin Sarah's formal education. Being the only girl, and the baby of her own family, Mary's parents had gone out of their way to educate her. Now Mary could do the same for her own child, but she would teach Sarah herself, and was looking forward to it. Sarah was so intelligent, Mary felt sure that she would be a joy to teach.

How wrong she was. Sarah already knew her alphabet, in a singsong way, and could recognise the printed letters. Mary began with the child's name. She showed her each letter in order, and asked her to copy them. The effort was disastrous, with the S and the R always written back to front. However she tried the result was always wrong, and Mary became exasperated. "You can draw so many things with your father, now write these letters properly. The way you write R and S are the way they look in the mirror." Sarah could not understand, they did look right to her, and so her education began with much unhappiness.

Counting was equally traumatic. Again in a singsong way, she could count to ten. To Mary's dismay, when she put ten nuts on the table for Sarah to count, the result was always the same, 1,4,5,6,7,8,9,10. "Why are you missing out 2, and 3?" she asked, you can count to ten as a song, now take each nut and count slowly." The same thing happened each time, 1,4,5. with Mary's patience sorely tried, and Sarah reduced to tears.

Day after day Mary tried, and each day Sarah became more upset, she could not do what her mother wanted. It was like tying bows in her laces, they just would not tie. She sat pen in hand trying to copy her name. "Just do it," Mary scolded, "I think you are being naughty." The frustration was too much to bear, Sarah threw the pen across the kitchen, and fled through the door, past her astonished father, along the path to the mill.

"Leave her go to my mother," James reasoned with his wife, "I can not have you both getting into such a state. Tonight when she is settled, I will have a quiet word while she is on my knee and perhaps I might be able to solve the problem."

Sarah did not go to Jane's house. She pulled off her boots and sat by the stream with her feet in the water. As she became calmer, anger gave way to tears, and she wept as if her heart would break.

Jonathan found her, and at first thought she had been hurt. "What on earth is wrong?" he asked, trying to stop the tears from flowing. Her eyes were bloodshot and her face was puffy. He worried what terrible event had happened to make her so upset. She sobbed out her story. "Is that all, I thought something awful had happened to you," he said, relieved. She stood up, stamped her little bare feet on the grass, and glared into her friend's vivid blue eyes, "Even you don't understand!" He watched in despair, as she picked up her boots and stomped off angrily to her grandmother's cottage.

Jane was very careful with the child, and listened intently to her story. Mary had already told her that she was having problems with the teaching, but Jane had not realised to what extent. She warmed some milk and honey for Sarah, and bathed her face with some soothing water and witch hazel. Then she brushed her springy curls until she calmed down. "Now," she said, "without getting upset, tell me honestly if you are being naughty." Sarah shook her head, tears brimming again. "Hush, hush, I will speak to your mother, now let us go into the garden."

Sarah helped her grandmother pick some fresh herbs, she already knew their names and their uses, and loved to watch Jane prepare them into medicines or preserves. There could be no doubt of the child's intelligence. She suddenly felt tired, and sat down on a log to watch her grandmother.

"Why do you always wear black Grandma?"

"Because your grandfather is dead, and I miss him."

"Did he like black? Did he want you to always wear it?"

"No, he liked me to wear blue, like the sky on a summer's day."

"Well, let's make you a lovely blue dress, and I will embroider some cornflowers on it, and it will make grandfather happy."

"Oh child, you know he is dead and gone."

"Grandma! You know death is not the end, Martin tells me bible stories. Jesus died so that we would all know just that. I will ask father to get you some blue material as soon as he can."

Jane was astounded by Sarah's train of thought, and by the fact that in her childish way, she was right, John had hated black, she would think about a change.

Jonathan came shyly into the garden, "Are you better?" he asked cautiously, "I have thought of a rhyme to help you." Sarah smiled sheepishly, and allowed him to hold up her hand. He counted each finger saying, "one, two, three, four, five, once I caught a fish alive, which finger did it bite, this little finger on my right," wriggling her little finger, and making her laugh. "Pretend the nuts are fingers, and say the rhyme to yourself as you count." They practised together as Jane went into the cottage to get them some elderberry cordial.

That night James attempted to show Sarah each word in their favourite story book. She knew the story, and could tell it with her eyes shut, but when her father pointed out certain words by themselves, she began to get agitated. "You know what the first line says," he tried to persuade her, "Just look at each word as you say it." She began to panic, her eyes filling with tears which ran down her cheeks as she became hotter and hotter. "I can't," she cried, "they jump about." This reaction was worse than he had expected. "What jump about? Tell me what is wrong, then I can help you." "The letters in the lines of words, see," she pointed sobbing. "They don't keep still when you look at the line." She became so upset, that he put the book down, and cuddled her instead. "Now," he said, "if you give me a smile, I have something for you." He stood her on the floor, and she felt sick and giddy, but smiled weakly. James took his gold chain and crucifix from around his neck, and put it over her head. "When you were born, I promised this to you, and now you are old enough to have it. You will always be my precious baby, but you are also a big girl now, and I do not want any more upset between you and your mother, there will be no more lessons." The joy on her daughter's face touched Mary's heart, and she came across to hug her. "Tomorrow we will do some sewing instead," she said as she kissed her hot little cheeks.

James discussed the problem with his mother, concerned that the child's eyesight may be at fault. "I think not," she said, "Look at how she can draw and sew, and as for intelligence, she has always been so forward. No, I believe that Sarah's mind just works differently to ours. Your father once knew a man called James Brindley, he was a brilliant engineer, and built the canal to carry coal to Manchester. He said Brindley was the most talented and intelligent person he had ever met, but do you know, he was never able to read or write. I think Sarah will be the same, so we must encourage her talents. Tell her stories of Shakespeare's plays, and later on read them to her, keep buying her story books, but read her poetry too, and make her interested in anything new you see on your travels. If we do all this, I feel sure she will grow up happy and well balanced. Perhaps she may even pick up a little reading and writing along the way.

Chapter Twelve

A week later, Sarah had another upsetting experience. She set off to the mill with Jenny to play with Jonathan and Roger. They would be helping their father, but she knew he would send them to play when she arrived. Jenny told her that Emily was going to make seed cake today, and Sarah's tummy rumbled at the thought. Emily always gave the children cake and buttermilk, but seed cake was Sarah's favourite.

Jenny went to help with the cheese, while Sarah skipped off to the mill. As she rounded the corner, she bumped into Roger, who was carrying something horrible and bloody. "Sparrow heads," he said, triumphantly holding them up, "four sparrow heads for the parson." Sparrows were nesting in the bell tower of the church, and the parson had long had a bounty on their eggs. Now he had taken it further, and was paying for their severed heads. Roger could not understand Sarah's reaction. "You wicked boy," she sobbed, "You can't kill animals just because they want to go into God's house." "Well, the parson said to do it," Roger replied, bemused. "I hate him, and you, it's wrong to kill animals for nothing," she yelled as she ran from him, straight into his brother, who was coming to see what all the shouting was about. "I suppose you knew all about this," she shouted angrily, pointing at Roger's bloodstained hands, "How many have you killed? I hate you both!" Roger, ignoring the outburst, strode off to find the parson, but Jonathan was stunned. "What is the matter with you now?" he asked, as she sagged despondently to the floor and began to cry. "These past few weeks you have cried more, than in all the years I have known you, and remember I knew you when you were a baby, carried about in your father's shirt." The anger and tears faded from her eyes, as she, the mollycoddled baby, had always been a joke between them. She told Jonathan about the horror of the birds, and he frowned, "I wonder if our parents know about this?" he thought out loud. He took her little hand in his, "Please do not hate my silly brother, I will talk to him. He must have only been thinking about the money, I am sure he will see how wrong it is when I explain." They sat for a long time on the grass, and he stroked her hair, until she calmed down before they went to see his mother. "Oh, trust Roger," Emily sighed when she heard the tale, "always thinking of money. That parson is a bad influence on a boy like him, the man is becoming quite insane. Don't you go a'worrying Sarah, George and your father will sort it out. Now, I was wondering where you had got to, there is a fresh seed cake here, how about a piece?" To Jonathan's relief, Sarah cheered up, he did not like to see her so emotional, and to keep the good mood going he sat and made plans for the rest of their day.

Jane was worried about the parson's niece, Elizabeth. Since she had been away her appearance had worsened. Oh, she was smartly dressed, and her hair neatly arranged beneath her bonnet, but she was so pale, and dark shadows had now appeared beneath her haunted eyes. She took a chance and approached the girl, who appeared only in public at church services. "Elizabeth, my dear, are you well?" Jane enquired. Before she could answer, the parson was at her side. "My niece is in the best of health, thank you, and if there was any cause for concern, I would pay for a visit from a professional doctor." Leaving Jane snubbed, he whisked the girl away.

At the following Sunday evening service, Parson Richardson began his latest sermon. It was the story of Jesus and the loaves and fishes, but he twisted it into a fearful lecture about a master's power over the poor. Sarah sat listening in the front pew with her parents and grandmother, until she could bear no more.

She stood up shouting, "No, you are wrong, you bad man!" Shocked silence filled the church, as she carried on, only Jonathan stood up at the back of the church willing her to be silent. "That story is about how Jesus taught people to share. He shared the loaves and fishes with as many people as he could, and everyone else followed and shared what they had too. He didn't do magic tricks to frighten people. I know, Martin has told me all the bible stories, and Jesus loved animals, and would not cut off their heads for coming into his church like you do, or break the fingers of little boys who played music for him." Elizabeth fearfully turned to face the angry little girl in the front pew. For a heart stopping moment, their eyes met and their minds linked. Sarah quite plainly heard Elizabeth's unspoken plea in her head. "Stop little girl, he will hurt you, like he hurts me, he has killed my baby." Sarah hysterically carried on, "and her hurts Elizabeth and he has killed her ...." Before she could finish, the parson was before her, grabbed her by the shoulders and hoisted her over the bench in front of their pew. James pushed his way past Mary and his mother to reach his daughter, but Jonathan got there first and gave the parson a resounding kick on the shin with his heavy boots. James reached out his hand just in time to stop the blow from the furious man's hand from hitting Sarah's face. "Do not ever raise your hand to my daughter, her childish behaviour was wrong, but yours is inexcusable!" James was shaking with rage as he picked Sarah from the floor, obviously shocked with her eyes wide with terror. "I will be writing to your superiors about this," he growled into the parson's face, but he simply looked at the shocked child with an expression of disgust, and turned on his heels. "Come Elizabeth, let us leave these devil's disciples." Martin, now by James' side, restrained him, more violence was not the answer. As they reached the door, he turned and stared at Martin, with evil black eyes, "Vengeance will be upon you. Who are you to preach the bible?"

James gently carried Sarah home, with Jane supporting Mary in a very distressed state. Sarah seemed almost vacant, with her eyes unnaturally wide. She did not speak as Jane washed her face, "Perhaps you should try to sleep," she suggested. Sarah jolted, "No Grandma, please no, not in my room, all by myself, not in my own bed. Can't I sleep in mother's room? I will be safe there." Mary's heart sank, it had taken them four years to persuade Sarah to sleep in her own bed, and another year again to get her into her own room.

Jane carried her up to the big double bed, and persuaded her to sip some camomile tea. Suddenly she clutched her grandmother's hand, almost spilling the hot liquid.

"I am afraid Grandma."

"Hush child, he can not hurt you now. Do you think your father would let anyone hurt you?"

"No it's not that, I am afraid of what is in my head."

"What do you mean? tell Grandma, and I will make it better."

"When I was in the church, I looked at Elizabeth. She didn't speak, but I heard what she said in my head, and that frightens me."

"Child that happens to me all the time, it is a gift, you must not be afraid of it, it just means that you are like your old Grandma."

Sarah began to cry.

"I don't want to have that gift, Elizabeth tried to help me, but it was too horrible. He hurts her you know, and he killed her baby, and the birds, Grandma. Did you know about the birds, he pays people to cut their heads off."

"Now calm down, sweetheart, you are very confused and all this has been too much for you. Try to forget those nasty thoughts, your father will sort it out, you will see, it will all seem better tomorrow."

Jane tried to be reassuring, but it was not how she felt. She was most disturbed about Elizabeth, there had been fear in her eyes, she always thought, but for Sarah to say such a thing about a baby, chilled her to the bone. Such flashes of thought were common to her, but she had never experienced anything so harrowing, and Sarah had said it with such innocence and conviction. For the moment, she felt it best to say nothing, for her granddaughter's sake, but the implications were to stay foremost in her mind.

James wrote that very night to the bishop in Liverpool, including great detail about the parson's behaviour. What he did not know, was that the parson was the bishop's nephew, and that he had already set off post haste, to see his uncle. Before the following Sunday, a special messenger delivered a curt reply stating that the matter was in hand. The parson had been reprimanded for his over enthusiasm, but that the behaviour of unruly children could not be accepted in the church! James was furious, "I will resign from the orchestra," he shouted, his hand shaking as he read the letter to Mary. She had other ideas, "If you resign, he will have won, the orchestra will disband without you. Then what will we have? We will be left with nothing but a parson who is losing his mind. We should go to church as normal, and just sit facing him calmly, he will not be expecting that. One day we will catch him out and even the bishop will not be able to defend him. Sarah, on the other hand should sit at the back with Emily, if there is to be a battle of wits, there is no place for a child."

James agreed, "How lucky I am, to have such a wise and beautiful wife," he said as he kissed the special place on her neck, which always made her wriggle with pleasure. "Our poor little Sarah has had an unhappy time lately, let us make sure that she never gets so upset again." "About that, I have an idea which may help," she suggested. "I think the final straw for her was the beheading of the birds. Perhaps we could provide a net, and get George and Martin to fix it onto the bell tower, to stop the sparrows from flying in."

So it was done, there was no more beheading of birds, and Sarah sat in what she felt was the safety of the back pew next to Jonathan. Parson Richardson was sullen, and sarcastically polite, but Elizabeth's state of health was deteriorating. Eventually, she disappeared for another six months, presumably returning home to visit her parents, as she had done the previous year, but she was not the only one to go missing. Martin's polecat could not be found.

Jenny was distraught about the animal, he had been so much a part of their lives, from the beginning. She felt sure that the parson had taken revenge upon the poor animal and Martin tried to console her. "Perhaps he has found a mate, a good woman like I have," but he failed to cheer her. George suggested that perhaps the polecat had taken ill. "A sick animal in the countryside, will often go to hide under a hedge to die. It is nature's way, you must not grieve so."

Nothing could convince her, and she did grieve for a long time. Their lovely little house seemed empty without Pole, and through the rest of her life, she would never lose the love she felt for the crafty little creature.

Chapter Thirteen

After the loss of their pet, Martin and Jenny thought even more about having children of their own. The problem was of course, her parents, who expected almost her full wage each week, but they found a way. It had been a long term project, but now at last it was about to pay off.

James' sheep were flourishing on a small scale, with his high quality lamb equalling the popularity of his excellent cheese. He had visited a model farm, in Dishley, Leicestershire, run by Robert Bakewell who specialised in selective breeding. With these methods in mind, good buying and regular change of rams, James' flock was now of Bakewell's excellent calibre New Leicester sheep, each animal producing far more meat than the old breeds.

Every year for the last five years, Martin and Jenny bought a lamb from James, who appreciating their problem, allowed them free grazing along with his own flock. This year they now had five sheep in lamb, and their offspring and fleece would pay enough for Jenny's parents. Martin proved himself to be an exceptional shepherd. The sale of the sheep would now provide an income for his in-laws on an annual basis, and James was happy with the situation.

They saved carefully, furnishing their cottage very comfortably, paid James back his loan every week, and even managed to put a little aside for any emergency. Although they planned for the time that they would be able to have their own child, Jenny was surprised and delighted at the new dimension to their love making.

One night during their passion, he withdrew early, moaning with pleasure as she skilfully took him into her hands, but said, "no, let us make a baby." "Oh Martin, now, should we?" she whispered almost fearfully. He did not answer, but glided back inside her, and aching for each other their climax was shattering. She cried in delight as he shot his seed deep inside her, and wrapped her legs around him, as if to make the moment last for ever.

Despite their frequent sexual expressions of love, there was disappointment, for Jenny was still not pregnant. It was not until the following March, with October's sheep sold, and the next year's stock about to lamb, that she began to feel ill.

She had not even reached the week due for her monthly courses, when she began to be sick. It was a debilitating nausea, from morning to night. She could hardly eat, and the very smell of the cheese sent her running outside. Jane looked at her carefully, "You might be with child, my dear," she said. "It is too early," Jenny complained wretchedly, "It can not be that, it is not my date until next week, and I feel so ill." Jane explained, "Perhaps it is unusual, but babies are strange creatures. They will settle into your body, and put themselves right, no matter what affect it has on the mother. In fact it could be said to be a sign of a healthy baby, as mothers who are so ill at the beginning, often have an easy delivery. Let us wait and see, I have a feeling about all this, I think that you and Martin are going to have a very special Christmas gift this year." Jenny was cheered by the thought, but did not dare to be as confident as Jane. Of course, she was right, Jenny was indeed going to have a baby, but the nausea continued to the end of May, and by then she could not imagine feeling well again. One morning as Martin woke her gently with a cup of weak peppermint tea, which was supposed to calm the nausea, she sat up cheerfully, drank it and smiled. "Oh, how wonderful, the sickness is gone, Jane said it would go but I didn't believe it." Martin was even more relieved, he had felt so guilty and helpless during the past three months.

By late June she was blossoming, back to her normal self again, and with a rosy glow about her. Sarah, eleven years old now was excited at the prospect of a new baby, and was fascinated by the growing shape of Jenny's previously flat tummy. Being very fond of the little girl, she involved her in the making of baby clothes, and the discussion of names. The baby was due around the end of December, and as Jenny told Sarah, it might even arrive on her birthday. James overheard. "Oh no, not another Snow White, born in a blizzard, and would not sleep in her own bed!" he joked, making his daughter laugh until she was racked with hiccups.

Jane had also been right about Sarah, she developed into a happy well balanced child, and to her grandmother's relief, showed no more signs of the inherited insight that she found so frightening. She was bright, and interested in all new things, just like her father. She eagerly waited to hear about every new discovery made by James on his travels, and loved stories, poetry and plays brought home by him. She could now sew as well as her mother, watched Emily cook, and could nearly make bread as good as hers, but was happiest with her grandmother, learning about medicinal preparations, and tending the garden.

Reading and writing remained a problem, but Jonathan managed to teach her to write her name and to read a little. Although nearly five years older than her, a young man of sixteen, he always had time for Sarah. He was a great help to his father, but was quiet and studious. He took very seriously the fact that his parents could not read or write, and had lost their property because of it, all those years ago. He asked Martin to teach him, and became an eager pupil. Sarah was envious of his abilities, but he told her not to worry. "You will have a good strong husband to look after you one day, and you will never have to bother your pretty little head about such things."

Sarah was fascinated by Shakespeare's plays, loved the horror and the superstition of the Scottish one, which she refused to call by name, in true acting tradition. She cried at the deaths of Romeo and Juliet, although calling them a silly pair, but her favourite was Midsummer Night's Dream.

One day when James was at the mill with George, a band of travelling players arrived, asking to buy milk. He was thrilled to hear that they were Shakespearean actors, planning to set up a show at the ferry house. It promised to be an excellent show. The leader told James about how they had come across a trunk of costumes in a market two weeks before, at a ridiculously low price, which would add authenticity to their play. He seemed a well versed man, and James talked to him for a long time, while Emily fidgeted disapprovingly. To her, they were a band of dirty people, who she did not want near her dairy or kitchen, and she was glad when they left with their waggons, after buying the milk.

They spent their lives travelling the country, and were, after the next show, going to take the ferry to Liverpool, where there would be rich pickings. Not only did they act, they also sold potions and confection. The potions were coloured water, which they would claim to cure various ills, and the confection was a kind of fudge, made from sugar and milk.

"Keep that brat quiet," the leader snapped at his wife. "She has been whimpering all week." "This is your daughter you are talking about, not one of the donkeys," she retorted. "The poor child is sick, and I am trying to make the confection and look after her. Just look, she has a fever, and red weals across the back of her neck." The man showed no sympathy, "Well keep her out of sight, there's nothing like sickness for keeping an audience away." He sauntered off to the company of other members of the troupe to get drunk, leaving his wife to cope with the child, who coughed and sneezed as she poured the sweet sticky confection onto trays to set.

"Midsummer Night's Dream", shouted James as he reached home, and told Mary and Sarah about the travelling players. "On Saturday, at the ferry house. We will make an afternoon of it, and we will all go, Emily, George and the children, Martin and Jenny, even her parents, if they want to go, we will have a holiday!"

Jenny was not too sure about taking her parents on such a family event. They had shown no interest in her pregnancy, except to make it quite clear that they still expected the money. When Martin explained the arrangements, they had quietened, but not once did they offer their congratulations. Nevertheless, on Saturday, they were waiting to be picked up in the horse and cart. Her father quite lucid, and both were dressed in the same clothes worn for Jenny's wedding. They allowed themselves to be helped into the cart, but otherwise paid no attention to their daughter or son-in-law.

Jenny seated them comfortably at the show, and James bought what his mother said later was a disgusting amount of fudge for everyone. The old couple devoured it at such speed, that Martin and Jenny also gave them theirs. Their ingratitude and greed, was so comical that neither Jenny or Martin could keep a straight face, and moved away for a while so as not to cause offence. Jane sat watching all this with distaste, the poor girl did not deserve such awful parents, but she said nothing to spoil the day and sat looking remarkably attractive in the grey-blue dress, with embroidered flowers, made by her granddaughter. It had taken Sarah a long time to persuade her grandmother to wear anything of such a light colour. Although she had been successful with dark shades of green and blue, she had never been able to make up the pretty sky blue cloth, her father had once bought, into anything for Jane.

The production, when it eventually started was superb. Even Emily could hardly believe that the talented actors in such rich costumes, were the same dirty people, who she had felt sullied her kitchen a few days earlier. Sarah had explained the story to Jenny, the previous day, and they sat together laughing and clapping at the antics of Bottom, with his asses head. Even the parson and Elizabeth seemed to be happy that day, both smiling, and she looking a little less pale.

Everyone was tired at the end of the day. Jane became grumpy because of the sale of the miracle medicines at the close of the show, and Jenny's parents were returned to their home, without even an acknowledgement, never mind a thank you from either. Sarah, Jonathan and Roger re-enacted the play on the way home, to shrieks of laughter, but Sarah became so tired that she fell asleep with her head on Jonathan's shoulder by the time they reached the mill.

The players packed up ready for their journey in the morning. Now the leader's wife and sister also had the fever, with chills and nausea. The little girl was extremely ill. The red weals had spread to other parts of her body, and had now become raised pus filled blisters. In another day, she would be dead, leaving the legacy of a terrible disease behind with her father's audience of that afternoon.

Chapter Fourteen

Mary's head was aching so badly that Jane put her to bed with a lavender ice pack. James had planned a trip to Liverpool, to collect some musical instrument parts, so he decided to take Sarah along with him. She was thrilled at the thought of a ride on the big ferry boat. "Can't we take Jonathan and Roger too?" she asked excitedly. Her father could hardly refuse, the boys were like brothers to her, and he was pleased that she was unselfish enough to want to share the treat. Unfortunately George was very busy at the mill and needed help, but Roger uncharacteristically volunteered to stay, allowing Jonathan to go. Roger's plans for the afternoon, did not include a trip to Liverpool. Although only fourteen years old, he already had an eye for the ladies, and had a secret meeting arranged, with one of the girls from the village. Jonathan, not knowing anything about this, slapped him on the back and thanked him for working in his place.

James, now with Jonathan and Sarah in tow, could not take his horse, as was usual, so they caught the coach and four service, which ran along the road from Chester to Eastham. Although their journey was only along part of this road, it was exciting because neither of the two young people had ever been in a coach before, and how very different it was from the horse and cart. Jonathan looked very smart in his best breeches and a muslin shirt, which Sarah knew was his father's. Sarah wore her latest outfit, recently finished with the help of her mother. It was really fine, an empire style dress of pale blue, with a Caroline Spencer jacket. This was a black velvet jacket, lined with blue satin, in the style worn by the King's wife Caroline, and Sarah felt very grown up indeed. James smiled proudly as Jonathan helped her from the coach, "A real little lady," he thought.

The steamer was a new, impressive vessel called the Princess Charlotte, and looked very large to the inexperienced eyes of Sarah.

Suddenly someone shouted, "look there's the Safety." "What is that?" she asked. James did not know, but having a little time to spare, took them over to see.

The Safety was a ship, but it was not powered by sail or steam, it was powered by horses! They were forced to go round and round the boat, like a threshing mill. Jonathan's heart sank for he was remembering only too well Sarah's reaction to the parson's beheaded birds, he dreaded to think what she would do about this mass cruelty. James was way ahead of him. Before she could say anything, he was demanding to know the name of the Safety's owner. "It is a disgrace, in this age a achievement and invention, to abuse animals in such a way, I shall be writing to the port authorities to have it stopped." Behind Sarah's back, he winked at Jonathan.

Actually weeks later he remembered the incident and did write a letter of complaint. Whether it was that, or the impracticality of the Safety, the service was soon abandoned, and the horses sold off, hopefully to a better life.

The ferry ride on the Princess Charlotte was wonderful, and Sarah, despite her sophisticated outfit, bounced about the boat, wanting to see every part of it.

Liverpool was a crowded, busy place, and neither Sarah or Jonathan liked it very much. Everything seemed so dirty and, smokey to the young people who had never before left their village in the countryside. James threw a half penny to a beggar, as they boarded the coach and pair to take them to the centre of the town. He was a horrible sight, with dark swellings all over his skin. "He has scurvy," Sarah said with an authority that shook her father. "Grandma told me all about it. Sailors often get it because they do not eat enough fresh food. The swellings are caused by blood escaping from the veins, and congealing under the skin." "Poor man," said her father, intending to check these facts with his mother when they reached home, and wondering what his daughter would surprise him with next.

The day went well. The musical instrument shop was similar to the one once owned by James' father, and he had become very friendly with the owner. Sarah was fascinated with the contents of the shop, and he bid her look around as much as she wished. Although Jonathan had no interest in such things, he was happy enough to read labels to her, and to pass things from shelves which she could not reach. Her happiness was always enough to keep him content. The owner's wife gave them a wonderful lunch of cold lamb, fresh bread and pickled onions. Jonathan was allowed a glass of ale, but Sarah had to make do with barley water, which did not taste the same as she was used to at home. It made her cross because James usually allowed her to have a glass of wine or nettle beer, but her annoyance faded when a large bowl of strawberries arrived on the table.

It had been a long day for all three, and James looked forward to the evening at the farm, relaxing with his wife, and his precious, but chatty little daughter tucked up in bed. When they dropped Jonathan off at the mill on the way home, Emily appeared at the door looking agitated. "It's Mary, Jane is with her, she is very ill."

Jane was anxious. "She has a fever, headache, and aches in her bones. I will stay tonight to be with her. I do not know what it is, but Jenny's parents are ill too."

Jenny had been called to her parents house that morning. The old couple had seemed so ill that she suggested that Jane should to come to see them. Her mother snarled, "Wicked girl, you are our daughter, you must stay here to look after us, I am not having that Mrs. Brand coming into my house with her critical eyes." Martin was concerned for Jenny and their unborn child, but as she pointed out, there was no one else to look after them. He reluctantly agreed, and went after work that night to join her. By then, red weals had broken out across her father's neck and all over the old woman's body.

Her father slept fitfully, his nightly dose of laudanum probably keeping him quiet, but her mother was delirious. Martin sent Jenny downstairs and took over, with the old woman cursing and swearing when she realised that it was him wiping her brow with a cool cloth. He could not remember falling asleep, until Jenny came up at first light. She had been so exhausted that she had fallen asleep in a chair, and was now sore and stiff. Her scream jolted Martin awake. The old woman lay dead, eyes grotesquely staring at the ceiling, and skin covered in raised, pus filled blisters. Her father did not wake as they covered her with a sheet, and Martin carried the disease ridden body into the tiny room that had been Jenny's. "I will have to bring Jane, we must find out what this is, and I must find the parson," he whispered so as not to wake the old man.

He was to be gone a long time, not expecting Jane to be up at the farm, and filled with fear when he heard that Mary as ill too. The old man woke, shocked to find his daughter at his bedside. As kindly as she could, she broke the news about her mother, and to her horror, he began to cry pitifully. Other than anger, she had never seen any emotion from either of her parents, and felt shocked beyond feeling. Not knowing what to do, she sat patting his old hand, the hand that had never held her, never loved her, only hit her in temper, and tears fell down her face, making a damp place on her dress where the baby bulged.

After a while he fell silent, and looked at her, "God help me, she has her father's looks," he thought and he was filled with guilt. How badly they had treated this beautiful girl, and despite their neglect she had made a good and happy life for herself. She was so proud telling them about the baby, yet they just snubbed her, only interested in the money. She asked if he wanted his laudanum, but he shook his head. "Just a drink of water, I must speak to you while I am still able."

Unbelievably, he took her hand but he was very hot and the red weals were beginning to spread. "I am sorry child, your mother was too old for another pregnancy, and I must admit you were not wanted, but I will make it up to you, now that my life is at an end." She jumped, "No, you will not die, Jane is very skilled, and she has taught me, we will be able to help you."

"I must tell you Jennifer," he gasped, "We took all the money from your brothers, just as we have done from you. They worked hard and resented it. They left home one by one, as soon as they could. This house is not rented, as we led you to believe, it is paid for, and it will be yours. Also, under the bed there is a loose board, all the papers are there, and money too, use it to give your child a good life, and try not to think too badly of us." He spared her the most painful part, that he was not her father!

His youngest son, the last to leave home, had been the worst treated. He represented their income so they restrained him as much as possible. His resentment grew to boiling point, then one day, instead of going straight home with his pay, he went to the alehouse and got drunk. Never used to alcohol, he went mad, stormed into the house and announced to his mother that he was leaving, like his older brothers before him. She flew at him, only making his anger worse, and in his drunken madness, he knocked her to the floor, kicked her, and raped her. Jenny was the daughter of her own brother!

Conceived with hate right from the beginning, her mother had never been able to love her, her father could not cope with the shame, and had taken to the laudanum, but he would take this secret to his grave.

Jane, with Mary at the farm, listened in horror to Martin's description of his mother-in-law's death. She felt sick with fear, "Smallpox," she whispered to Martin, "I have not heard of a case for a long time but it sounds like smallpox, and Mary has the same symptoms, I must speak to Sarah."

Sarah looked so small and vulnerable as Jane told her of the situation. "I need your help," she explained, "Do you remember what Culpeper recommends for smallpox?" She nodded, she did remember, and could make up the potions with no problem, but she also knew all about the disease, and had not realised how much she loved her mother. She cried all the way as she ran to a rocky piece of land just outside the woods, armed with a small trowel. The tormentil was easy to find, with its little yellow flowers, and leaves with toothed edges. It was the root she needed, and she dug up the plants ruthlessly, without the selection and care for conservation that she had been taught.

At Jane's cottage, Sarah crushed the root, and mixed it with some Venice treacle to be taken as a medicine. Then, to apply to the sores, she mixed some more with Pellitory of Spain and alum. She did not remember running all the way home, not being able to think of anything but the fact that she might lose her mother. Jane entrusted the application of the medication to her granddaughter, confident that she would be able to tend to Mary, and left with Martin to go back to Jenny. The old man's condition was far worse than Mary's. She gave him some medicine and applied the ointment to the fast erupting blisters. It was surprising how quickly his wife had died, and he was so old and frail that she did not hold much hope for him. His wife's burial was now an urgent requirement, so Martin set off in search of the parson.

He was in the church when Martin found him, arranging candles. He turned pale with horror at the mention of smallpox, but agreed to arrange the funeral the next morning.

Parson Richardson did no funeral arranging. Instead he bought food supplies, and locked himself and Elizabeth in his house. "It is not for me to expose myself to pox ridden bodies," he ranted wildly to her, "You will not unlock the door, or go near any window, until the pestilence has passed." He placed the heavy door key into his pocket, "Get me a drink, Elizabeth, my head is thumping, and every bone in my body aches. Why am I plagued with such un-Godly parishioners?"

The parson could not be found. Martin and George dug the grave for Jenny's mother themselves. Other people in the village, and round about were falling sick, but there was no man of God to comfort them in their last hours. Her father lasted for another two days, and then they buried him alongside his wife.

Mary held out, delirious most of the time, and James would not leave her side. The weather had been hot and the harvest was ready. George and Martin gathered the few available men, and set to getting in the crop. Roger and Jonathan joined them, along with Sarah, dressed in an old shirt and breeches that once had been Roger's. Jonathan hated to see her doing such rough work, her pale skin burned in the sun, and her hands bled as they all worked and sweated in the heat. That was not the worse thing, sometimes he would find her sitting in the field crying her heart out about her mother. He would hold her and let her cry, her sobs shaking his body along with her own. He felt so helpless, but could only kiss away the tears, and give her words of encouragement.

The fever slowly abated, and Mary began to regain her senses. The blisters had turned to horrible sores, despite the ointment, guaranteeing to ruin her beautiful skin. She managed to take a little soup and Sarah felt very relieved. For the first time in many nights, Sarah slept deeply, but was abruptly woken by a dream. She was sharing her bed with Jane, who would not leave Mary, and sat up screaming, "Grandma, Grandma, it's happened again." Jane lit the candle to see terror on her granddaughter's face, "Hush sweetheart, it was only a dream." "No," Sarah screamed, "It is real, in my head like last time. It is Elizabeth, he has locked her in with a dead animal!"

Chapter Fifteen

Elizabeth awoke in the big bed with the hard mattress that she had shared with the parson for the last seven years. He was moaning loudly and thrashing about, so she lit the candle and timidly shook him. He came to his senses, hot and nauseous, "Pass the chamber pot quickly Elizabeth," he ordered as he retched, her own stomach turning at the sight. She poured him a drink, but he would not settle. "Light another candle and read to me from the good book," he said angrily. In the dim light she read until early morning. He looked more frightening than ever, the sickness drawing his face into an even meaner than usual mask, and strange red marks appearing across his neck. By morning she was cold and tired, but he seemed to have recovered a little. Putting on his robe, he bid her help him downstairs. Taking a basket, he packed it with food, bread, now stale, cheese, and four jars of fruit preserve, together with a bottle of wine. He filled two jugs of water and told her to take them upstairs.

When she was gone, he unlocked his desk and took out a manacle. It consisted of a chain with a shackle and lock for both wrists. Tucking it inside his robe, he called for her to hurry. She had to help him back to bed, as dizziness was overtaking him. When settled, he asked her to see to his pillows, but clutched at her hand with an iron grip. He slipped the manacle onto her wrist, snapping it shut and quickly attached the other end to the top of the iron bedstead.

"Ha, now I have got you," he cackled, "You will not get away. If I have caught the pestilence, you will have to look after me. If I die, you will die with me, and no-one will ever know your wicked secrets! There is no key for you to find for I threw it out of the window. Your only hope of salvation is to pray for forgiveness and to nurse me until I am well." She had placed the water jugs near the bed, but he had deliberately put the basket of food out of her reach. Later he crawled from the bed and carried back from the basket some bread, cheese and the bottle of wine, which he shared with her. The strange red marks were turning to blisters, but she said nothing for fear of raising his temper. He lasted for two more days. Elizabeth could not reach the chamber pot, and he did not have the strength, so he soiled the bed and she had no means of cleaning him up. He died as he had lived in his last years, ranting madly about mortal sin, and left Elizabeth to perish shackled by his putrid corpse. She covered him as much as possible with the sheets and blankets, but flies came from nowhere, and she could hear them buzzing under the covers as they attacked the rotting body.

She tried to make the water last, but after four more days it was gone. Her mouth became so dry that her tongue began to swell, and even when she cried, tears no longer fell. The heat during the day and the smell from the corpse was unbearable but mercifully she lost consciousness for part of the time.

Somehow she fought death, she could not let herself die like this. No one would know what she had been through for the last seven years. Her wrist was rubbed raw by the strong iron shackle, but although now pitifully thin, she still could not free her hand.

She looked over the bed at the cross on the wall, Jesus, with bowed head, did not seem to care about her. "I am not wicked," she said to him, in a rasping whisper. On her knees now, she looked at the wall. The crucifix was fixed there by an ugly black nail, and next to it was the pelt of a small brown animal, with a long tail and a white face, a shaft of moonlight caught its little white teeth, and it looked as if it was screaming. "Poor dead animal," she thought, "Oh please, someone help me!"

Sarah could not be consoled, and would not sleep for the rest of the night. When Jenny arrived in the morning, Jane told her the entire situation. Not mentioning it to James, she asked her to go straight for Martin, and to check the parson's house. "Break the door down if you have to, you must trust me, this insight is something which Sarah and I share, and her father has enough on his mind with Mary."

Jenny was sceptical, surely they could not be still at the parson's house, they had not been seen for two weeks. Nevertheless, trusting Jane's judgement implicitly, she went back to the mill and explained to Martin.

The house seemed deserted. They banged on the door, but there was only a hollow silence. "Jane said to break the door down if he didn't answer," Jenny said fearfully. Martin considered for a while, and decided that it would do less damage, if he forced a window. He broke through the scullery window, and finding the front door locked and with no key, he slid the bolts on the side door letting Jenny in.

The house was dark and musty, with curtains pulled against the light. He called but there was no answer. Taking Jenny's hand, they cautiously climbed the stairs, in no way prepared for the sight behind the door to the right at the top, where a sickly smell greeted them. They were nearly overcome by the stench when the door was opened, and slumped on the floor, Elizabeth looked dead. Before he could stop her, Jenny ran over to the poor girl. She turned to Martin, "Oh look, she is chained to the bed, but she is still alive, we must help her." It was only too obvious that the bed contained a rotting body, so Martin did not bother to investigate. Leaving his brave wife to support Elizabeth, he ran down to get the hammer which he used to force the window. With one blow, he broke the chain, and carried the almost lifeless Elizabeth downstairs. Jenny wiped her face with a cool cloth and dropped a little water between her cracked lips. She began to revive, but her mouth was now so dry and swollen that she could not speak.

Martin carried her back to the mill to a horrified Emily. "Jesus help us, poor mavournin*, she is nothing but bones," she cried. In her lovely motherly way, she washed and soothed the girl, allowing her sips of water and talking all the time in her lilting accent, which was

---

Mavournin - Irish term for darling

always more pronounced with her sympathy. George and Martin dug a hasty grave and dragged the parson's body into it without removing its rancid sheets, and without any sympathy or ceremony, locked the house of death and left it to its secrets.

It was many days before Elizabeth came back from the brink of death. Despite her ordeal, she showed no sign of smallpox, somehow she had not caught it. Nowhere on her body was a scar from cowpox to protect her, the only scars Jane found were those of past beatings, those of a leather strap or belt having cut the skin on her back.

Although recovering physically, she remained quiet and withdrawn, until one day she began to cry. Emily took her hand. "There my lamb, don't take on so, it is all over now, see, you are safe in my kitchen." Her haunted eyes met Emily's, "I am not wicked or evil, I think he was mad, he said they were the devil's spawn, and it was my fault that he must kill them." She could hardly speak for sobs, and Emily's stomach twisted into a knot. "Who did he kill love? Tell me what you mean." Elizabeth swallowed hard, "My babies, my poor little babies, he strangled them when they were born. Five babies, he forced himself on me night after night, and when I became pregnant, he said that I had consorted with the devil, and locked me away until they were born. They were innocent babies, his own flesh and blood, but he killed them as if they were rats, and then beat me for giving birth to them. He kept their bodies in his dresser in the bedroom to remind me of my sins." Emily was lost for words at such horror, but let Elizabeth cry in her arms until she fell asleep.

Martin and George went to the parson's silent house, this time prepared for the horror they were to find. The smell of his rotting corpse was still in the air as they entered the bedroom. This time Martin looked around the room, and jumped backwards as he saw what was nailed to the wall. It was Pole, or at least the pelt of his beloved polecat. Gently he pulled down the stiff fur, and George realising, put his hand on his shoulder. "So Jenny was right," he said gently, "This was no man of God Martin, he must have been as insane as old King George."

The dresser was there just as Elizabeth described, and the two men steeled themselves to open the drawer. Even though prepared, the pitiful sight turned their stomachs. The bodies of five new born infants, partly mummified, and in various stages of decay, were neatly lined up in the heavy top drawer. A narrow piece of cloth was around each tiny neck, obviously used for strangulation.

In the clean white linen from Jane's house, they wrapped each tiny body. Without speaking they dug yet another grave and buried them together. Tears ran down Martin's face, as they threw the soil on the top, thinking of his own child, which was to be so much loved. "May your father roast in hell," he whispered as they left the graveside, "Poor innocent little mites."

Elizabeth's family lived in Shropshire. She was the third daughter of five, and her parents had wanted the best for her. They met Parson Richardson, and found him polite and charming. He explained that he was looking for a wife, to work with him in his new parish. She must be quiet, reserved and virtuous he said, and Elizabeth was brought forward. Her parents were thrilled with the match, thinking that their daughter would now have a good life, with a man of the church. She made no protest, knowing how difficult it had been for her parents to make ends meet. The day he came for her, he brought a collection of dresses and bonnets in delightful pastel colours. "You will be a lady of position now," he said, "You will dress smartly. You will smile and be polite, but I do not want you to mix with my parishioners." This was not what he had told her parents, but she kept quiet, because as they left he gave them a large sum of money for goodwill. She just smiled bravely and waved goodbye. There was no mention of a wedding when they arrived at his house. He took her to his bed that very night. She had no sexual experience, and he hurt her badly. His lust satisfied, he then turned upon her with his belt. "You will always be obedient," he scowled, "and remember, I will introduce you as my niece."

All this she told Emily, who sickened and shocked, nursed her back to something like health, and when she was strong enough, George took her home to her parents, who wept on their knees when they heard the story.

Chapter Sixteen

Mary continued to recover, but slowly. The hideous sores began to fall away, leaving great pink pits in her skin. Jane applied carrot oil to the scars and tried to reassure her that they would fade. As her health improved, she realised the damage to her looks, and even worse, her eyesight was now impaired. No longer able to see well enough to read or sew, she fell into a deep depression. James rarely left her side, not seeing the scars, loss of weight and dull hair, but loving his wife more than ever, and now fighting her for her own recovery. Martin and George kept the farm and mill running smoothly, as James could think of nothing but Mary.

At this time Sarah suffered more than most. Jane, Emily and Jenny tried to comfort her, but she needed her parents, who under the circumstances could be forgiven for not realising.

The horror of Elizabeth's torment had shaken her. Jane tried to spare her the full story, but she already knew every detail from her grandmother's mind, and could not be shielded. She was almost twelve years old, and had lost her childhood that year. "It started in January with the King's death," she thought, "Poor old farmer George, people said that he was completely mad, and then his horrible son wanting to divorce Caroline. Beautiful, fashionable Caroline Spencer. Why doesn't he want her? She would make a lovely queen and everyone loves her. John Keats has gone away too, to Italy for his health. Grandma says he has got consumption, he is going to die, now there will be no more of my favourite poems. Oh, I will always hate this year!"

The only shining light in her darkness was Jonathan. Always there to listen and love her, she began to understand that their love was something special. It hurt him to see the change in Sarah. Time after time he would hold her as she cried. "My mother has no will to live, what can I do?" She took over the house, washing and cooking with Jenny, but the spring in her step was gone, and there were no enjoyable evenings with her father, reading plays and poetry or playing their music.

There was still no man of God in the parish to console the people, or even bless the hasty graves. Jonathan realised that probably no-one had notified the parson's superiors of his death, or the situation of the parish. He thought about it carefully and was determined to approach both James and Mary. Not telling his father, who he knew would disapprove, he called at the farm one day, when he knew Sarah was out of the way at the mill with her grandmother.

He stood in the doorway of the bedroom, reminding James of the first time he had seen George, so tall, strong and dignified. "I must speak to you both," he said trying not to notice Mary's haggard looks, "I hope you will not think badly of me, but I feel I must speak my mind. We have gathered in the harvest, and kept the mill and the farm going, and indeed we would all gladly work twice as hard again for you if it were called for, but now we need your guidance for our community. Has anyone informed the bishop of the parson's death? A man of the church is sorely needed here. We need your decisions on the farm and mill, we do our best, but we are no businessmen or negotiators. More than all this is Sarah. Oh yes, she quietly helps with everything, and is so capable that you have not realised her hurt. Your daughter needs you to give her hope, I know, Mrs. Brand, that your eyesight is now not good, but please think of Sarah. If only you would sit in the garden with her again. She knows so many plays and poems, you could recite them together, and I am sorry that you can no longer sew, but it would make Sarah so happy to sit, and perhaps make something pretty for you. Do you understand what effect her strange gift of insight has had upon her, and the horror of what happened to Elizabeth? It has frightened her badly. She needs you both so much."

James and Mary were shocked. "Thank you lad," he said, "If you would leave us now." Jonathan left with heavy heart, thinking that perhaps he may have caused his father's worst nightmare, that he would lose his position at the mill, and all through his son's interference. Later James was to thank Jonathan, but he was not to know that as he walked home with only his conscience for company.

"Jonathan is quite right," Mary said, "I have lain here, full of self pity, making both you and Sarah suffer. You are the best of husbands, James, I know it is only your willpower which kept me alive. If you will help me up, I will dress and be in the kitchen when Sarah returns." She was pitifully weak, and her clothes hung from her once shapely frame. She did not care, but smiled at James, "You have looked after me, now I must make myself into a wife and mother again."

Sarah cried with delight when she found her mother in the kitchen with Jenny, and from then on Mary strove to regain her strength. Her long fair hair, now dull and lifeless, did nothing for her appearance, so she allowed Sarah to experiment with it. Filled with apprehension, she sat as her daughter, who now seemed so grown up, chopped the hair to chin length, and cut a long fringe, which was to cover the worst of the scars. She massaged egg yolk and olive oil into her scalp, then applied the egg white, beaten together with a drop of geranium oil to her face, saying, "Now you must sit still for ten minutes. We will have a game, I will recite some funny poems, but you must try not to laugh, if you do, you must pay me a forfeit!" Mary did laugh, and joining in the fun, promised to do several outrageous forfeits, making Sarah laugh until she cried. They were still giggling when she washed off the egg mixtures ten minutes later with a mild soapwort solution. She borrowed a strange looking curling iron which had been hung up unused in Emily's kitchen for as long as she could remember, and set to work curling her mother's hair. She used the iron gently and with great care, testing it each time it was heated on the top of the range. Emily had given her the dire warning, "It is a long time since

I used it, but I saw many a curl burnt right off when I was young!" Mary found the process relaxing, with Sarah's gentle touch, and was amazed at the beautiful result. She never before had curls in her hair, but the person who looked back at her in the mirror, looked so much better than the poor careworn Mary who had nearly died from smallpox. Sarah had made her a dress from the beautiful sky blue material, originally bought for her grandmother long ago. On it she had stitched little buttons and embroidered flowers. When James returned that lunch time, it delighted him to see Mary's shining curls, pretty dress and happy smile, not exactly her old self, but looking remarkably attractive and content.

He was now giving his businesses full attention again, and was very grateful to George and Martin for all their efforts. He wrote to the bishop to inform him of the parson's death from smallpox, but saw no point in going into the horrendous details of his misconduct. He did however explain how badly hit the parish had been, with so many deaths, and requested a replacement clergyman of more mature years.

As normality began to return, Jenny and Martin decided to tackle her parents house. There had been no time to take her father's story too seriously, but as there was no demand for rent, they went to investigate. All bedlinen and mattresses had to be burned after smallpox, as the disease could linger on bedding and clothes. They dragged the feather mattress outside, leaving the empty wooden bedstead. Sure enough, just as her father had said, a loose board was under the bed, but they were not prepared for the secrets beneath it. There were papers showing that her parents really did own the house, which would now be Jenny's, but the amount of money astounded them. Gold coins, neatly stacked in piles, hoarded by the old couple from their children's wages over all those years. More than enough to pay back the loan from James, enough in fact to build another storey onto their cottage, making it a substantial home in which to raise a family, and Jenny's pregnancy was progressing well.

It was late August when parson Henry Jones arrived on the scene. With no notification, he and his wife turned up at the parsonage, to find it and the church locked and deserted, and were directed up to the farm to see James. Sarah was busy preparing dinner, while her mother rested in the garden. Apple haddock was one of her favourites, learned from her grandmother. James bought the fish, really enough for two meals, and took delight at Sarah's enthusiastic pleasure in preparing it. She skinned and boned the haddock placing it into an earthenware dish, then she added sliced onions, sour apples, some of Jane's cider, salt, pepper and a fresh bay leaf from the large plant in a pot, which was allowed to live outside in summer. The covered dish was cooking in the oven when the parson called.

He was not the mature man of James' request. He was no more than twenty five, younger than Martin, and newly married. He had hoped for a missionary post, but hid his disappointment, when told of this parish in great need. He introduced himself as parson Henry Jones and his wife Rebecca. James was astonished, it was as if his wishes had been deliberately dismissed. Regaining his composure, he invited the couple in, introducing them to Sarah and Mary.

For some reason Sarah took to them right away and suggested to her father that they might stay for dinner. "Father always buys too much fish," she smiled, with an air older than her years, "We would be happy for you to stay." It was almost cooked, so she took some breadcrumbs mixed with grated cheese to sprinkle on top, and brown in the oven. Rebecca peeped over her shoulder, "How lovely it smells, please tell me what is in it." Sarah explained the recipe, "Haddock, St. Peter's fish, with his finger and thumb prints on their necks, cooked with apples, onions breadcrumbs and our own cheese, we must have known that you were coming." Henry looked over to his wife and Sarah and laughed, "I am sorry my dear, we should not laugh, but it is the story of the haddock." Sarah was intrigued, and unselfconsciously sat on her father's lap to hear more.

"Well it is a fine story. How St Peter picked the fish out of Lake Gennesaret, leaving his fingerprints, but whoever made it up did not think. The lake would be fresh water, and haddock are salt water fish!" Sarah clapped her hands, "Oh how clever of you, I wish I had thought of that."

Sarah was complimented on the meal, and she cuddled down by Mary, as her father told the parson the whole story, of parson Richardson's madness, Elizabeth, and the smallpox. Young as he was he had a remarkable sympathy about him. He showed shock, but no anger, not even resentment against the bishop for not informing him of the situation, but simply said, "We must look to the future, I can see there is much pain here to be healed. Perhaps we could start with a special service for the dead on Sunday, and I could bless the graves. Then we will try to restore the faith of those left behind."

Suddenly Mary thought of the parson's house. Other than burning of the bedding, it had not been cleaned. "Oh dear, you cannot stay in that house, it is still soiled by the smallpox, and will for ever be contaminated by the parson's deeds." Rebecca smiled and took parson Henry's arm, "Please do not worry, we will soon clean the house, and it will hold no sin with God's love in it. James promised to help in any way, he could not help but like this young man, in whose eyes nothing seemed impossible.

Chapter Seventeen

Parson Henry, as he was usually called, wove his magic around the community. With no complaint, he and Rebecca set to work, scrubbed out the house, and cleaned the church. Villagers called out of curiosity, and charmed by the attitude of this new clergyman and his wife, lent a hand, baked cakes, and generally made them welcome. His first service was very different to those of parson Richardson. Before the hymns, he thanked the orchestra for attending, and his sermon was also most unusual. He expressed his sadness for the loss of so many lives, and for the deeds of his predecessor. "We must understand that his mind was more diseased with insanity, than his body was of smallpox. Please let us not dwell on the past, let us make this church a joyful place again. I see little children placed in the back pews. When they feel more confident, let them come forward. Let them come to the front and sing. Every parent knows that the voice of their child, however out of tune, is as sweet as a nightingale's. God will feel the same, and bring your babes in arms. So what if they cry in the service, that is how they express themselves, and if their mothers become weary, there will be plenty of friends only too pleased to rock a baby in their arms for a while. For as long as we can, I would like not to use the collection plate. Instead of giving money, I would ask you all to do just one good deed for a neighbour. Even if it is only a smile to someone who is usually unfriendly."

The collection was normally used to supplement a parson's meagre wage, but Henry and Rebecca were determined to manage without taking from the people, and would only start a collection for the needs of the church. They had expected to be provided with a fully furnished house, but because of the smallpox, there was no mattress or bedlinen. Rebecca had received, as a wedding gift, a set of fine sheets and pillowcases, so she set to work, stitching them together to make a bag, which they filled with clean straw, and did the same with the pillowcases. They took down and washed the heavy curtains to use as blankets, and said nothing to anyone about the linen problems. However, Jenny remembered how they had burnt the bedding, and approached Martin about it. As they now had some money, to spend on alterations to their house, starting in the following year, after the birth of their child, they felt they could spare the price of a new soft feather mattress, pillows and blankets. James sent an order for them to Liverpool, and Jenny and Martin were to take the horse and cart to the ferry to collect the much needed goods a week later.

Parson Henry had met Rebecca in Scotland, when he was finishing his training at Perth. Her accent was as Scottish as his was Welsh. He came from a well-to-do family in Newtown, Montgomeryshire, and the pair made a strange combination for a quiet Cheshire parish.

Rebecca, her parents and brother had moved from Perth to work in the cotton mills at Lanark, on the banks of the Clyde, near Glasgow.

Henry's family were acquainted with the managing partner of this cotton mill, and being a fellow Welshman, from Newtown, Henry went to visit. Rebecca's relations left behind in Perth, heard of his planned journey, and asked him to look up the family to pass on their greetings.

He was amazed at the conditions of the workers. Everything was provided for their welfare, from housing to education for the children. No small children were employed in the cotton mill, and everyone was treated with respect. The name of this foresighted man in charge, was Robert Owen, the very man about whom parson Richardson had constantly berated! There Henry met Rebecca, and their two years of happy courtship had resulted in marriage.

Henry possessed a gift for sensing people's fears, and therefore was soon able to gain the confidence of his parishioners. Even Jane, notoriously difficult to get on with at first, was charmed. He asked her advice on many things in the beginning, which was, as James remarked to Mary, the only way to win her round, and very perceptive of him.

He talked at length to Sarah, who he found to have a refreshingly enquiring mind, and different outlook on many things, including the bible. He was horrified at the 'loaves and fishes' incident of Sarah and parson Richardson, and realised after hearing the story, why the children of the community cowered at the back of the church. "You agree with me about that story, don't you?" she asked, "I know because of what you did about the church collection, you asked everyone to share, and be kind to each other, and that's what Jesus was saying." He had to agree. What a deep thinking little girl she was, and what a pity her thoughts about the bible had met with such hostility from his predecessor. She also told him of her power of insight, and how it frightened her. He thought for a while, and said, "Your grandmother is right, it is a gift, but if it frightens you so much, you can put a stop to it. You can do it with the power of your own mind. Stop the fear, just say to yourself that your mind will not let it happen any more. It will work, believe me, I have a friend who was a missionary in Africa. He heard a story of a woman who came to a priest, saying that her daughter was dying from a black magic spell. Do you know what black magic is?" Sarah nodded, "Yes Grandma told me about witch doctors in Africa." "Well he went to see the girl, and she was dying, for no apparent reason. He said to her that the only way to break the spell, was to let him burn her back with a red hot knife. He heated the knife to red hot, but behind her back he had a glass rod in cold water. When she was ready, he took the ice cold rod and said to prepare for the pain of the burn which would save her. When he drew the cold rod across her skin instead of the hot knife, she screamed, and to his horror, a line of blisters appeared, just as if it were a burn. She jumped up, shouting with joy that she was cured, and was still alive and well when he left for another posting. You see, she really believed, in her mind that she would be burnt, so much so that her body reacted as if it had happened. It is the power of the human mind, so you see, you can control your flashes of insight, if you are determined to do so." Sarah frowned, then smiled, "Yes, I see, I have to believe that I can do it, I can't wait to tell Grandma." Henry was not sure how 'Grandma' would react, but resolved to have a word with her himself later. To his relief, Jane was pleased, "She seems much happier now," she said, "It was unfortunate that one so young should have been exposed to such horror."

As the weeks went by, the community became settled again. Rebecca was embarrassingly grateful for the mattress and bedding, making Jenny realise that it was the first time that she had been able to give anyone a real gift. Being of around the same age, the two women became great friends. Rebecca wanted to know every detail of the progress of Jenny's pregnancy, and confided that she also longed to have a baby, and hoped that she would not have to wait too long.

Parson Henry organised many church events. Nothing on a grand scale, but just enough to make the church a happy place to be, and to re-establish it as a focal point of the parish. Sarah was an enthusiastic helper, and Henry, noticing a resentful glance from Jonathan, said nothing, but involved him too. Jonathan showed him Sarah's crucifix, and asked him about the inscription on the back, which had long been a puzzle to them both. Neither Jane or her father could make out what it stood for, so they were delighted to find that parson Henry knew all about it. He turned it over in his hand, "This must be very old. It is what is found on amulets worn by early Christians. The inscription, Ichthus, stands for Iesos CHristos THeou Uios Sotei, Jesus Christ, Son of God, our Saviour. Sarah and Jonathan were impressed, and from then on he taught them snippets of Latin for fun. Sarah's favourite was Contra bonos Mores, meaning, not in accordance with good manners, and she teased Roger for weeks with it before he found out what it meant.

At this time Henry and Rebecca gained a donkey. A woman from an outlying farm, whose husband and two sons had met their deaths from smallpox, sold her farmland to James and bought Jenny's parents' house. She came along to the village with her thirteen year old daughter, and the donkey. As there was nowhere to keep the animal, she made a gift of it to the parson. It was all rather difficult, as Henry confided to James. There was no way that he and Rebecca could afford to feed a donkey, even if it lived in the overgrown garden of the parsonage. Mary thought of the solution, if Henry kept it, people could contribute a little here and there for its food, and James always stored hay and turnips, if the poor creature was starving. It could be a village donkey. If anyone needed it to make a journey, the donkey could be borrowed, and this would make life easier for many folk. So the donkey stayed. It was a strong but gentle animal, for some reason called Manfred. It not only saved the legs of many of the older parishioners, going to market, but gave rides to the children after church on Sunday evenings during the summer months, and was loved by everyone.

As the nights began to lengthen, Henry wrote to the bishop to ask for funds for a church stove. The days were getting cold, and he could see that the church would become an uncomfortable place for his parishioners to sit. To his, and to James' amazement, word came that the requested stove, awaited collection at the ferry house, having been sent across the very next week. It turned out to be quite new, but a large awkward, bulbous piece of equipment, made from cast iron, complete with what seemed to be endless lengths of pipe to form a chimney. Henry's initial despair at the thing, vanished when George examined it. "Easy," he enthused, "We'll have it up and running in no time." Gaining great admiration from Henry, George dragged it into the church, and started to assemble the monster. Henry could not thank him enough, it seemed a daunting task to him. George smiled to himself as he put the pieces together, "How can he wear that cassock, and yet be so different from parson Richardson?"

Now the winter services were no longer dreaded by the elderly parishioners, whose bones suffered from sitting in the cold. James provided coal for the stove and it contentedly glowed every Sunday, not looking in any way out of place. Christmas was approaching and plans for a Nativity play were afoot, parson Henry by now having won the trust of all the children. Bits of material were collected and miraculously transformed into fairly believable costumes. Henry refused to let the donkey take part, but Sarah still had her toy lamb, and insisted that it must have a place by the crib, making Jonathan howl with laughter. Realising that Mary would be sad, not to be involved in the sewing, Henry somehow cajoled her into organizing the play, causing Jane to comment, "That man has a knack of making everyone happy." Which was quite a compliment coming from her.

Jenny's pregnancy continued to progress, with her in perfect health, although now feeling rather heavy. The only problem was Martin's plan for the birth. With Jenny's agreement, he was determined to be with her right through labour, and to see the baby being born. Jane was disgusted, and commented harshly, "She is not one of your sheep, for heavens sake have some dignity. A man's place at such times, is pacing the floor outside, and with some men they are better off at the alehouse!" Martin and Jenny were not to be put off, and pointed out that James was with Mary when Sarah was born. Jane was exasperated, and retorted that Sarah had just arrived at the wrong time, and that Jenny knew quite well that it had not been his intention to be there at her birth. Not having any success, she left them, and hoped that Jenny would go into labour whilst Martin was at work.

Two weeks before Christmas the baby started to come into the world, on a gentle Sunday morning, with no blizzard or storm. To Jane's annoyance Martin held Jenny's hand all the way through, echoing her midwifery instructions, so much so that she almost felt not needed. It was a remarkably short and easy first labour. By two o'clock, a beautiful baby boy was in Martin's arms, and even Jane could not help but be happy. Parson Henry was able to announce to the congregation that evening, the birth of baby John George, and that mother and baby were doing well.

Sarah was thrilled, as the baby was beautiful, with tiny hands, chubby cheeks and a rosebud mouth. He was in the crib, which had once been her own, next to Jenny's bed. "Oh, a good baby, are you John?" she giggled, "Not naughty like me. I would not sleep in there when I was little." "Stop giving him ideas, and give me a hug instead," Jenny laughed. The family were so happy. Sarah realised then that this was what she wanted, a husband and baby, "How long will I have to wait," she wondered.

Next morning she went to see Emily to help make a cake for Jenny. Jonathan was there in the kitchen with a bandage on his hand. Sarah was most concerned, but he just laughed, "It will heal, it is deep, but clean. Your grandma says to sit quietly this morning while it knits together. It is good, because I can sit and watch you two making the cake, and I can lick the dish! What kind of cake is it anyway?" "Groaning cake", Emily replied, quite seriously, causing screwed up faces from both Jonathan and Sarah. "Don't like the sound of that," they both said at the same time. "Really you two are like a pair of pirate's parrots," she scolded. This resulted in howls of laughter from both of them, as they looked at each other, giving their impressions of a parrot's face.

Emily felt good to see her eldest son so happy, most of the time he seemed far too serious, so unlike his brother who was always up to some mischief. She patiently explained that the cake would contain, dried fruit, nuts and spice, but that any cake could be a groaning cake, if taken to the mother of a new born baby. "It is given to guests who come to see the baby. Do you understand now?" They both nodded, but were more interested in the ingredients. They actually made two cakes. Emily knowing quite well that her menfolk, and her little guest, would be after a piece as soon as they smelled it cooking, made sure that the extra one would keep everyone happy. Of course, she was right, and by the time lunch was over, the spare cake was almost eaten.

As Jane decided that Jonathan should not work for the rest of the day, with his cut hand, Emily sent him off with Sarah to deliver the cake. He was enchanted with the baby, and amused Jenny by asking to hold him. "Oh, look at his little hands Sarah, he is so beautiful. I remember when you were like this." Jenny laughed, "Jonathan, you fibber, you were only five when she was born, you would not remember," but he only smiled and looked at Sarah. "No I remember everything about her." Then changing the subject, congratulated Jenny, and explained to her about his mother's cake. "We can recommend it," Sarah interrupted, "Emily made two and we have almost eaten all the other one!"

Jonathan was quiet as they walked home. "Is something wrong?" she asked, gently taking hold of his injured hand, "Is it hurting?" He smiled, "No, I was just thinking, how wonderful it must be to have a child with someone you love." He kissed her forehead, "Come on, I will race you home."

Chapter Eighteen

Sarah was out early, armed with gloves, scissors, and two baskets. It was a fine April morning and she was looking for nettles. She knew they must be gathered young, as they became too strong later in the year, and this was an ideal day. Some were to be dried for herbal tea, which was both refreshing and medicinal, being helpful for wheezing of the chest. Jane told her how the leaves could also be smoked, to help chest complaints, but she had not actually seen anyone do it. For once Sarah thought that her grandmother must be mistaken, surely anyone with a wheezy chest would not want to inhale smoke of any sort, but she knew better than to argue with Grandma. Jane would later make some of the nettles into nettle beer, which was delicious, and Sarah looked forward to helping with that, not intending to upset her in any way. All this was not the main reason for the nettle gathering, for Sarah wanted some for Emily. She intended to make her a Nettle Champ for lunchtime. This she knew, was one of Emily's childhood favourites. Potatoes were to be boiled with their skins on, to keep in the goodness, then onions boiled for the last five minutes with the potatoes, which were skinned when cooked. The potatoes and onions were mashed together and left in the pan. The tender nettles were chopped and boiled in a little milk, until it curdled, salt and pepper added, then mixed together with the potatoes and onions, and put on a slow heat to dry out slightly. It was served on hot plates, with a large lump of butter on top, and all washed down with a glass of buttermilk! Sarah had many times shared such a meal with Emily's family, and now she would cook it to try to make her happy.

Emily had not been herself for a while now. Beginning early in February, she felt overcome with debilitating tiredness, which worsened as the weeks went by, and she had now fallen into a deep depression. She was becoming withdrawn, and would hardly speak to George or Jane, who were most concerned. How could she tell them what was wrong? She remembered how the same thing had happened to a friend of her mother. A tumour inside her, that is what they had called it. She, like Emily, had become tired and listless. The tumour grew inside the poor woman, sucking away all her strength, and grotesquely swelling out her stomach. Emily fearfully looked at her own stomach, and sure enough there were the tell tale signs. Her stomach had not been exactly flat after having the children, but now there was a growing bulge, where the disease consumed her from within. She was filled with fear, knowing that nothing could be done, and that she would soon face an agonising death. How could she tell anyone, and burden them with that torturing knowledge.

Jonathan knew of Sarah's plan for lunch, and hoped that perhaps it might just raise a smile from his mother. The meal usually provoked tales of her childhood in Ireland, and lots of good humoured teasing from his father, who she would say was as English as Cheshire cheese! Dear sweet Jonathan, Sarah thought as she walked along. It hurt her to see his sadness, and she remembered how he helped her, years ago, when her own mother seemed to want to die after the smallpox. She reached Jenny's house, to call for John-George. He was now a bright little boy of three years, with Jenny's light brown hair, and Martin's smile. She loved to take him out, such a happy child, he would spend the morning with her, visit Grandma, who would give him a piece of barley sugar, and have lunch with Emily. John-George had somehow got stuck with the double barrelled name. Just John, did not suit his personality now, and John George was what he called himself. He also adopted Jane as his grandmother, for in his little mind, if she was Sarah's Grandma, she was his too. Jane was not unhappy about it, so Grandma, she stayed.

The meal failed dismally, Emily's attempt at cheerfulness was painful, and when John-George innocently asked, "are you sad, Aunty Emily?" she ran from the kitchen in floods of tears, leaving her family stunned, and the child upset. Sarah took John-George home and then returned to visit her grandmother, hoping for some advice. "This is the last straw," Jane shouted indignantly, "To upset the child like that. What is she thinking about? I will go round this minute and get to the bottom of it all." Her mouth was set in a hard line, and a little frown appeared between her eyebrows. Sarah knew these were signs of a bad humour, and decided not to wait about for the outcome, but headed for home out of the way.

George and the boys were still at the table when Jane entered the house. George held his head in his hands, a picture of despair, with Jonathan trying to comfort him and Roger standing helplessly by. She put her hand on George's shoulder, and he looked up with tears in his eyes. "This had gone on for too long, I will sort her out," she said briskly, as she stomped upstairs.

Emily lay on the bed, staring at the ceiling, seemingly unaware of Jane's presence in the room. She sat on the edge of the bed and took her hand, all the previous anger evaporating. "Emily, you must tell me what is wrong. You are hurting yourself and all your family. Whatever it is, it can not be so bad that you have to get into such a state, and for so many weeks."

"Oh, it is that bad," she sobbed, "I am dying. How can I tell George and the boys? How can I let them watch me swell, and rot and die screaming."

"Emily! Listen to me, who said you were dying?"

"I don't need anyone to tell me. I know all the signs, just like my mother's friend. I have a tumour growing inside me, it is growing fast now, I can see it bulging and it is sapping my strength. I lie awake at night, staring in the darkness and feeling it growing inside me."

Jane was horrified, but did not show her feelings. She questioned Emily about her general health. She certainly was gaunt and pale, appeared to be eating almost nothing, and sleeping little. There was no pain as she gently examined the bulge in her stomach. "What about your monthly courses?" she asked, and Emily tried not to cry.

"No monthly courses, that is another sign, the tumour blocks that. Oh Jane, what am I going to do?"

"I will tell you what you are going to do. I will bring you a bowl of hot water, and you will wash your face and brush your hair. Then you will squeeze into your best dress and go down to see your husband. You are not going to die from a tumour, it is a baby you have got in there!"

Emily sank down onto the bed with a thud, her eyes as wide as a cat's in the night. "No, how can that be? I know how it feels to be with child, it is not like this, and George, well, he always makes sure his seed comes outside me." Jane shook her head, "Now think back my dear, George must have made a mistake, and around the beginning of January, I shouldn't wonder!" Emily closed her eyes, head swimming. "The elderflower wine," she almost shouted, "In the new year I was cleaning and found a bottle behind some storage jars. It must have been there for a couple of years. Jonathan and Roger were up at the farm helping James and stayed late for dinner. George and I had our meal by ourselves, we have never done that before. I remember, we ate jugged hare, with a rich red wine and cranberry sauce, and we drank the bottle of elderflower wine. It was very strong, and I am afraid to say that we became quite drunk, but Jane, we made love like a couple of sweethearts!" "Well there is the answer then, and now you must start to look after your health. You are pale because you have not been eating well. You must eat lots of fresh vegetables, eggs and meat. I think you will find that your appetite will have returned now that we have solved the problem. The tiredness is a sign of pregnancy, which some people have. If this time you feel so very different than when you carried the boys, this one could well be a girl." This seemed to jolt Emily back to reality, "Oh, my goodness, the boys, Jonathan and Roger are young men, what will they say?" Jane chuckled wickedly, "You just come down and find out."

Of course the news was greeted with great joy, and George found himself congratulated everywhere he went. He had never been so happy. His own dear Emily was back, with a smile on her face, and a blush to her cheek. Life was settled, good and secure, so what more could a man want from life?

Sarah and Jonathan's love for each other blossomed as surely and gently as the poppies which grew every year amongst the corn. The difference in their ages, she coming sixteen and he twenty, did not seem to matter. After one day late in August, Jonathan had taken the horse and cart for his father to market. He was to sell some flour, and to collect some very fine cloth ordered for Emily. Sarah was going to make some beautiful nightgowns for her when she had the baby. "This is a very special baby," she whispered to Jonathan, "and she deserves to look stunning when it arrives." He was pleased to go along with her surprise, and delighted to have her company for the day.

She packed a meal to eat on the way, but refused to let him peep inside the basket, or to tell him about the contents.

They arrived at the market early. Jonathan went off with the flour, and Sarah bought the fine white lawn fabric, some pink ribbon and matching lace. "Emily will look like a princess," she thought as she headed back to where the horse was tied. Jonathan was waiting, and as the sun was becoming hot they decided to leave the market without looking around, preferring to find somewhere cool and shady to eat. Jonathan knew just the place, it was a small wood, not much more than a few dozen large trees, with a stream running through. The old horse was thirsty, and drank greedily from the stream, then, released from his harness, pottered about happily grazing here and there. He was a contented animal, well used to Jonathan and Sarah, and knowing that he would not wander away, they left him untied.

Sarah set out the meal as Jonathan hovered about trying to see the contents of the basket. "I have a surprise too," he teased, but you have got to take off that bonnet first." He hated to see her curls trapped inside that thing, but she had insisted on wearing it, to keep the sun from her face, and remembering how easily she burnt, he could hardly argue. The bonnet came off, with no chance of sunburn under the shady trees. "Now tell me what you have got," she demanded. He pulled something from the cart, "A bottle of wine, to go with the meal." She started to laugh, "Oh, I hope it's not your mother's elderflower wine, funny things happen to your stomach if you drink that!" This had become a family joke since Emily's pregnancy, and laughing himself, he jumped at her. "You wicked girl, my poor sister or brother will never be able to look at an elderflower, when it grows up. Anyway, it is last year's broom wine, just ready to drink, and your favourite." He was right of course, it was her favourite, in fact she had helped to make that very batch, and it was lovely, fragrant, pale yellow wine.

He sat beside her, "Look at your hair, it is all damp with the heat of that bonnet. I love the way it curls when you get hot," he said absently, and twisted one of the curls around his finger. The silent enchantment of the woods surrounded them, as he looked into her grey-blue eyes. Without conscious thought, she put her arms around his neck, saying, "I love you Jonathan," as they kissed as man and woman for the first time. Their passion inflamed them under the protection of the trees. He unbuttoned the front of her dress and kissed her beautiful firm white breasts, with dark erect nipples. He thrilled as he felt the moisture in that special place between her legs, and heard her cries of desire for him. They made love, slowly, gently, cherishing every precious movement. It felt so wonderful to have him inside her, making them as one, and causing such unbelievable pleasure. He called her name over and over, "Oh Sarah, I have always loved you, I have waited all my life for you, I love you, this is how much I love you." To his surprise and delight, she reached her climax first, making strange little sighing noises and clinging to him, just before he came inside her. They lay entwined, in the blissful state known only to true lovers, until suddenly disturbed by the horse, which had developed an interest in the food set out for lunch and forgotten in the heat of passion. Jonathan tied him to a tree, but gave him a piece of cake as an apology. He took Sarah's hand, her cheeks were flushed and she looked prettier than ever. "Shall we get wed?" he asked, "I have money saved, and a bonus due after the harvest, we could ask your father then". "Oh yes, I want to be with you for ever," she sighed.

They splashed in the stream and eventually got around to eating the food. Appetites sharpened by spent passion, the food and wine was extra good. He appreciated the trouble she had gone to, with tiny sugar iced cakes, and short pastry envelopes filled with savoury meat and apple.

It was a happy couple who returned to the mill that afternoon. George mistook Sarah's flush of happiness, for her plans of her secret surprise for Emily, and thought no more about it, but Roger knew better. He knew from the way they looked at each other, that something had happened, and with Roger's sexual experience, he did not have to guess what. He felt a deep burning jealousy. Why had Sarah always loved his brother, even before she could walk, she had loved him best, and now she was his, he could tell, it was so unfair.

For the next two weeks the young couple met as usual, but managed to steal away to be alone, and to make love in their deliciously gentle way, each day, without giving rise to any suspicion from anyone but Roger.

George many a time lectured his younger son on sexual matters. He had been spreading his favours for a good few years, with any young lady of easy virtue he was able to find. One morning, when in the village, George was accosted by the father of one such girl. "Your son has got our Jilly with child. He must take his responsibility," he shouted. George was furious, went straight home and yanked Roger by the scruff of the neck from the mill, into a quiet place, away from Emily. "You stupid boy," he yelled, "you've got the morals of a farm cat, and after all the times I have warned you. Now there's a girl in the village, Jilly, her father said, with your brat in her belly!" Roger was taken aback, he had never seen his father so angry. "It can't be mine, father, I always pull out, like you told me. It can't be mine. Anyway haven't you heard about Jilly, she has given more rides to more people than the parson's donkey! You should know that I can take care of myself, and as for farm morals, you should speak to Jonathan and Sarah." He had not intended to say that, and felt sick as the words tumbled from his mouth.

Chapter Nineteen

Roger stopped, horrified at what he had said. His father turned ashen grey as he demanded more details. "I didn't mean it like that," Roger stammered, "It's just that they are in love." At this point his mother appeared on the scene, having seen even from a distance that harsh words were being spoken. She fainted when she found out what was going on, reviving as they helped her back to the house. Both she and George could see their secure future disappearing before their eyes. Surely James would throw them out, his precious daughter defiled by their own son. Emily clutching at straws, tried not to believe it, "No," she said, "Sarah is but a child." Uncharacteristically, George rounded on her, "A child, she is not a child. She is the same age you were when the squire brought your father over from Ireland to be blacksmith. You and I fell in love then, but remember how he guarded you. I would have had you in my bed long before we wed, if it hadn't been for that great Irish blacksmith, waving hot irons at me. Widow Blake's son, from that little cottage, making a living from a scratch of land. I know he thought I was not good enough for you, and what did he do when the squire stole my land? Let my old mother do his washing, and turned us out on the road with two babes!"

Roger could bear to hear no more, he had destroyed everyone he loved in the world, with just one flash of jealousy. He ran from the house until he reached the woods, where he was first physically sick, and then sat hugging his knees and crying like a baby. George looked at Emily, so hurt, frightened and vulnerable. "Oh forgive me, my love, forgive me, I had no right to speak like that. We must be calm and think this out. I will speak to Jonathan, and if it is true, he must go away, and we will have to pray that it all blows over." Emily nodded, knowing that George was right, but how could she bear to send dear Jonathan away.

Jonathan was helping at the farm that day, and he and Sarah enjoyed a wonderful afternoon, making love in the hay barn, and stealing secret kisses here and there. She waved goodbye as normal as he set off for home at night, thinking of what pleasures tomorrow may bring. James smiled indulgently to himself, "How soon before she tells me?" he thought, "I know they are in love."

Jonathan could not believe his father's anger. George practically jumped at him as he entered the door. Challenged, he readily admitted, "Yes we are in love, and after the harvest, when I am paid my bonus, I will ask James for her hand." "Have you no sense?" his father barked, "You will be the ruin of all of us. James will expect Sarah to marry into a good family, not the son of one of his employees. He will turn us out with nothing, and we have no property of our own, it will be as it was before. We lost our house and land as you well know, when Roger was a babe in arms and you were like a lamb at foot. We were young then, but it nearly killed your mother. How would she survive now, at her age and with a child on the way? No lad, I am afraid there is only one way out, you must go away and never return. You must go tonight." Jonathan pleaded, but his father would not be moved until he realised that this was the only way to save his family. He knew he must leave without even seeing Sarah, as she would never let him go.

Understanding her trouble with reading, he wrote a simple note for her, and left it on his bed before he left. His feelings were now dead, his body moved with no soul, so he took what money he had saved, a simple change of clothes, and left. Without Sarah, life held no meaning, and he walked on with no purpose or direction. Early next morning he took the ferry and found himself on the docks of Liverpool where he stood vacantly looking at the ships.

"Want to be a red shirt yankee salt, lad?" a voice behind him asked. "Want a job on that ship? Could do with a strong lad like you, we're sailing home to Boston this morning with a hand short. Know anything about sailing?" Jonathan turned fully to look at the man, and with a half smile thought that he could be Sarah's Ancient Mariner, she could recite that strange poem from beginning to end. "I know you navigate by the loadstar," he said vaguely, thinking how Sarah once told him that it was the leading star to guide mariners. That had been when he had been the real Jonathan and happy, not this empty shell which was all he had left of his life. Just like a ghost in that poem,

"The body of my brother's son
Stood by me, knee to knee:
The body and I pulled at one rope,
But he said nought to me."

The old sailor interrupted his thoughts, "Loadstar eh, that's good enough for me. Come on you've got the job."

The ship was of a new breed, an American steam ship. It used sail, but also steam engines for part of the trip for speed. It could not carry enough fuel for the whole journey, but with the benefits of steam and sail, the journey from Liverpool to Boston would take only twenty seven days. No Ancient Mariner's ship this, it would never be becalmed. He could hear Sarah's voice in his head,

"Day after day, day after day,
We stuck, nor breath nor motion;
As idle as a painted ship
Upon a painted ocean."

"Sarah would have been impressed with this vessel, so interested in all things new," he thought. "If I die on the journey, it will not be too soon. How can I live without her?"

Sarah, unaware of the tragic events, rose early to pick some wintergreen from the woods. She knew exactly where it grew, in a damp, shady place between the trees. It was a small plant, something like lily of the valley, with little bells growing on a long stem. The leaves pressed, would produce a fragrant oil, which when made into a paste, would be used to rub on the neck and chest for winter colds. She carefully picked the leaves, making sure not to destroy the plant. The pungent fragrance stained her hands. She looked forward to making the ointment with Jane that morning, and of course she would then be close to Jonathan. Just about to leave, her heart leapt with fear, for crouched under a distant tree, she saw a figure. Shaking, she called out, "Who is it, are you ill?" It was Roger, looking like a ghost, with a white face and red swollen eyes, he had been there all night.

"Oh, Sarah, can you ever forgive me!" Having no idea what was wrong, she kindly took his hand, "Whatever is wrong, Roger?" Fearfully he told her everything. She dropped the basket of wintergreen leaves, and still clutching his hand cried, "Quickly we must not let him go, I can not live without him." They ran to the mill, she almost dragging him. George was at the door holding Jonathan's letter, "He's gone Sarah, it's for the best," he said quietly. "Best," she screamed like a banshee, "Father loves Jonathan, he will give us his blessing." She snatched the letter, and pushing it down the front of her dress, ran uphill to the farm. She ran so fast that her heart banged in her ears, and her throat constricted until she could taste blood. "Oh Father," she sobbed, almost knocking him over, "You must bring Jonathan back."

James sat his daughter down and Mary brought her a glass of brandy, making her sip it, while she hysterically poured out the story. "Whatever gave George such ideas?" James asked, "Your mother and I knew that you were in love, we were pleased for you, and just waiting for you to tell us. I will go to see George, and we will both search for Jonathan. Now, stop crying, my pretty Sarah, we will find him how could he get far, in such a short time?"

She watched with a sense of dread as her father saddled up his horse, knowing in her heart that her love was lost for ever. George saw James riding towards the mill, his horse kicking up the dust on the track. "The moment has come, all too soon," he thought. Emily broke down, when she heard what James had to say. They had sent away their first child, and broken his and Sarah's hearts for nothing. James ordered George in one direction with the horse and cart, sent Roger to find Martin to join the hunt on foot, then set off himself in a different direction. At the ferry, James found that Jonathan had crossed early that morning, and rode back with the news. He changed his clothes, and took some money. "Jonathan does not know Liverpool very well, other than the musical instrument repair shop, I will start there. Be patient, I will stay for a week if I have to, but I will find him.

His friend at the shop had not seen Jonathan, but because he remembered him well, shut up his business and helped James with the search. Of course it was all in vain, and it was with a heavy heart that James returned eight days later. Sarah had hardly, spoken hardly eaten, hardly slept. She just sat holding Jonathan's note.

"Sarah, I will always love you, Jonathan"

That was all she had left now, a few simple words. She remembered how he had managed to teach her to read, even though it was just a little, and how he taught her a rhyme, because she always counted 1,4,5. missing out two and three. Now there was just this piece of paper, impregnated by the smell of wintergreen from her hands that morning. For the rest of her life that smell would cause her pain. "Why did we not see how George would feel?" she thought, "Yes, love is blind and lovers cannot see, the pretty follies that they themselves commit."

Each night she lay in bed with hands clasped across her stomach. "Please let me have his child," she prayed, "There must be a chance, it is my only hope to keep a part of him." She was disappointed, her monthly courses arrived on time, bringing even deeper depression. As the days dragged into weeks, she did not improve, with no interest in anything, and breaking her poor father's heart.

James now realising George's insecurity, made plans at least to put that right. He could see now, how when Martin had used money from Jenny's house to buy a partnership in James' lamb project, it had reminded George how vulnerable his position was. "You have worked so well and for so long for me, George," he said, "that I want to give you a partnership in the mill. Without you, the mill would not have thrived, and I want to make sure that you will not leave us." It was his way of giving the gift of security, without causing offence, and George was delighted, but it failed to cheer Emily.

Soon after, she gave birth to a baby girl, not a difficult birth, but she remained depressed, with no interest in the baby, not even wanting to name her. In her mind, the baby had been the cause of Jonathan's departure. If she had not been pregnant, George might not have acted so hastily, so she turned away from those who loved her, and sank into the same blackness as Sarah.

It was Rebecca who made the breakthrough, as she insisted on seeing Sarah. "I am going to talk to you," she said firmly. "Look at me Sarah." She looked at the parson's wife, with blank eyes, no tears now, just devastating bleakness. "Sarah, have you looked at your father? You are breaking his heart. I am sorry that you have lost your love, but you are hurting others. Your parents are sick with worry, and you know your mother is not strong, you must stop this. Where I was born, we believe in destiny. If Jonathan has really gone, and it looks that way, he was not your destiny. We have a story in Perth. It was the year of the great plague, 1666, I think. Two young ladies, Bessie Bell and Mary Grey, hid in Mary's country house to avoid the plague. A young man, who was in love with them both, took them some food, but he also carried the plague. They both died, buried at

Dornock Hough, you can still see the graves. You see, they could not escape their destiny, and look at me. Who would have thought that a parson from Wales would find a little Scottish girl like me, working in a cotton mill at Lanark. It was my destiny, and yours will catch up with you one day. In the meantime I need your help with Emily's baby. "Baby," Sarah repeated sadly, "Mother said Emily had her baby. I prayed that I might have Jonathan's baby, but I was denied even that." Rebecca ignored her sadness and carried on, "Emily has a little girl, the daughter she always wanted. A lovely wee girl, with blue eyes and light sandy hair, yes like Jonathan, but Emily blames her for the trouble, and just sits in bleak despair, as you do. Sarah, she will not even name the child, please go to see her."

As if waking from a deep sleep, with a nightmare lurking close to consciousness, Sarah pulled herself together. She washed her hair, put on her father's favourite dress, kissed her parents, and went to visit Emily. The baby, with Emily's colouring, was so like Jonathan that it made Sarah cry. She would not leave Emily, but made her listen to everything. How she loved Jonathan, how she was hurting, how she had prayed that she might be carrying his child, but most of all, how they must stop causing such pain to their families, and must help each other. Emily looked at the baby in Sarah's arms, and saw her for the first time. She had been feeding her, changing her, and nothing more. There had been no love until now. The baby became a great comfort to both women, the daughter Emily had longed for, forever to remind them of dear Jonathan. Sarah now became Aunty Sarah, and they called the little girl Joanne.

Chapter Twenty

Part Two

SARAH - JOSEPH AND COL D'ARBRES

"Aunty Sarah," Joanne wailed, "John-George is teasing me." She took the little girl onto her knee, and sighed as she kissed her light sandy hair. She looked just like her oldest brother, who she would never know. Her hair was getting long now, but the way it curled at the nape of her neck, and always parted to the left, no matter which way they combed it, together with her vivid blue eyes, tugged at Sarah's heart. Three years had passed since Jonathan left. She got on with her life, dedicating herself to her parents and to the children of the village. John-George now had a new baby sister. Although very proud of her, he secretly whispered to Sarah, how disappointed he was that she did not do much. Jenny and Martin laughed when she told them, saying, "just wait until she starts to crawl!"

Parson Henry and Rebecca had two little boys, of four and two. Although she had looked forward to having a family, Rebecca confided to Jenny that she was afraid that they might fill the parsonage with children, and starve to death in the process! She was surprised and intrigued when Jenny told her how she and Martin limited their family, and instructed Henry in no uncertain terms, with success, as they remained a happy family of four.

All the children loved Aunty Sarah. She always made time for them, trailing them around, gathering flowers, and making little treats.

She sewed many children's clothes, and was delighted when Jenny produced a baby girl, because she loved making little dresses best.

Mary's eyesight further deteriorated, and she now could see very little, but took great comfort from her attentive daughter. James often took Sarah on trips with him now, leaving his mother to care for Mary. They would always return with beautiful material, and up to date ideas of fashion, which Sarah would transform into clothes for herself and her mother. They went to see plays and bought new books of poetry and verse, which James would read, and Sarah would learn, but she always loved the old favourites best, Keats and Shakespeare.

Many young men sought her attention, but she had no interest. James tried matchmaking, inviting various young businessmen to dinner. The result was always the same. Sarah was beautiful and charming, but always cold to any advances.

A friend of parson Henry, called at the parsonage, one day towards the beginning of autumn. Joseph was a striking young man, just a little older than Henry. They met in Scotland, and he had been a guest at their wedding. He was something of an inventor, but generally repaired scientific instruments for a living. Originally from London, he travelled all over the country, earning here and there as necessary, and absorbing everything new. "You must meet James," Henry enthused, "You are two like minds to be sure, and his daughter, Sarah, is the same, a thirst for knowledge I call it."

After arranging dinner for that night, Henry sent Joseph off to investigate the mill and to wander round the village. Rebecca flew into a panic. "A dinner tonight for James, Mary, Sarah and Joseph. What am I supposed to give them?" Henry smiled infuriatingly, "I hadn't thought of that. Let's see, my canny little wife, I am sure we can gather something together.

They hunted around the fields and gathered, blackberries, elderberries, field mushrooms, apples, a few ripe hazelnuts and some wild marjoram. From the tiny part of their garden, guarded from the donkey, they picked the last cauliflower and some runner beans. In the larder, Rebecca found cheese, milk, eggs, potatoes, onions and bread, no meat at all. Shooing the children out to play, Henry put on one of her aprons, saying. "Let's get started, and see what we can do with this nature's bounty."

He often called Rebecca, canny, in a loving but teasing way, and when it came to food, she could manage to make a meal out of nothing. He watched her glow, as she set about an almost impossible task, with his help as kitchen maid.

Joseph, with instructions to seek out James at the farm, called first at the mill to inspect it. He introduced himself to George, but did not endear himself by wanting to poke about the workings, and holding up the work. Emily tactfully pointed him towards the farm, saying how pleased James would be to see him. On the way up the track, he saw Sarah heading home from Jenny's house, with a basket. He trotted his horse up to her, just before they reached the farm, and quoted,

"Where are you going, you Devon Maid?
And what have you there in your basket?
Ye tight little fairy, just fresh from the dairy,
Will you give me some cream if I ask it?"

Her reaction shook him. "How dare you. Using Keats poetry for your own ends, I am no ignorant country girl."

"You'l not hang my shawl on a willow,
or kiss me on a grass-green pillow,"

she quoted back. "Now I will bid you good day!" Her grey-blue eyes flashed mockingly, and her dark curls bobbed as she turned her back on him.

Absolutely smitten, he was for once lost for words. What was this beautiful girl, with such poetic education, doing in Henry's little parish? He kicked his horse on to go ahead to the farm, but his heart sank as he saw she followed him. "Oh no," he guessed, "She must be Sarah and now she hates me. What is it going to be like at dinner tonight?"

Joseph introduced himself to James and Mary before Sarah arrived, and offered Henry's dinner invitation. He made an immediate impression upon James, with ideas for the mill, and tales of new inventions in different parts of the country. When Sarah arrived, James introduced his new friend, and was shocked at her reaction. "We have already met Father, and in my opinion he is Contra bonos Mores." Quoting the very one of Henry's Latin quotations, which Joseph happened to understand, she flounced inside.

James stood wide eyed. "Not in accordance with good manners, I think, whatever did you do?" Joseph explained how he had introduced himself with some of Keats poetry. "A bad mistake I think," James winked, "Do not be too sure, it would seem that you and Sarah have much in common."

Rebecca prepared a feast, with a little help from Henry, and they were glad to find that there were three bottles of rhubarb wine left over from last year. They fed the children early with bread milk, and apple puree, and put them to bed, bribing them to stay there, by promising to make barley sugar the next day. Not knowing of Joseph's encounter with Sarah, Henry sat them together at the table, wondering why she seemed so upright and frosty. The meal was wondrous. Large flat mushrooms, stuffed with seasoned breadcrumbs, cheese and onion. Runner beans, cooked with garlic, olive oil, and wild marjoram, cauliflower and hazelnut bake, made with eggs, cheese, nuts, onion and seasonings, baked to a golden brown. All this was served with apple puree, and an elderberry sauce, made spicy with brown sugar, black pepper, dried juniper berries, and nutmeg. Instead of bread, Rebecca produced, hot from the oven, a tray of potato cakes, cut into tiny triangles. The combination was delightful, and the rich rhubarb wine complemented it all beautifully.

By the time they were ready for dessert, Sarah had thawed out a little, and was more relaxed as they ate the delicious, light blackberry tremble. Although Joseph stirred hostility within her, she had to admit to herself that there was something more. Older than her by perhaps as much as ten years, she found his maturity attractive, and she could not help noticing the way he dressed. Not only did he know all Keats poetry, he looked exactly how Sarah had imagined her favourite poet to be. He wore his dark hair slightly long, waving over his ears. His shirt of soft muslin, had an unstarched collar, worn with a long silk tie, and on the shirt were the most exquisite mother of pearl buttons. His coat was of a soft look fabric, of chamois colour with wide lapels. Even his boots were different, a sort of half boot, sides laced together over the tongue. He was later to tell her they were called Blucher boots, because they were invented by Field Marshall Von Blucher, commander of the Prussian forces at Waterloo, and to comment laughingly. "Thank God there is something you do not know!"

After the meal he thanked Rebecca graciously, "I was going to say something about autumn's mellow fruitfulness, but I fear Sarah's reaction if I do." He looked straight into her eyes, his wickedly twinkling somehow, and making her catch her breath. Henry looked at Rebecca as the couple's glance held transfixed. Sarah suddenly laughed, "Very well, I apologise, but you were very impudent, you did not expect me to understand the implications of the poem, did you? Keats has always been my favourite." The conversation warmed immediately, as he explained the incident, making it sound so funny, elaborating on his dented ego.

Next morning Joseph was to leave, having business to attend in York. He waved goodbye to Henry and Rebecca, but rode off to the farm to see Sarah before he left. James was delighted to see him, but Sarah had gone to the mill to help her grandmother. It was now becoming late, but he kicked his horse down the track to the mill, determined to see her.

Her heart leapt as she saw his chestnut horse in the distance. She was feeding the pigs, as he arrived. "Is there no end to your talents," he laughed. This morning there was no animosity between them, and she smiled happily as he led his horse up to the sty. "Oh, delicious roast pork," he said wickedly, peering at the two large pink and black spotted pigs. "Take care of what you say," she teased, "Pigs can be dangerous." "Sarah, these pigs are as tame as pussy cats, they are not in the least dangerous." She tossed her head, curls bouncing in a provocative way which was to stay in his mind, ruining his train of thought during his business meetings in the coming week. "Do not underestimate pigs. One killed a king once. Haven't you heard of Louis the fat? Actually Louis V1, he fought Henry 1 of England, and repelled a German invasion, but how did he die? A pig ran under his horse, it stumbled, and killed him. So be careful what you say to my Grandma's pigs!" "Sarah, where have you been all my life," he laughed, "I have travelled far and wide, and never met anyone like you." To her surprise, he kissed her cheek, leapt on his horse and waved goodbye. "I will be back," he called as he galloped off towards the village.

It was not love, not like the love she felt for Jonathan, but some kind of deep excitement. She put her hand to her cheek, where she still felt the kiss, and stood watching, until the dust from his horse in the distance could no longer be seen. Jane watching through the window, smiled.

Jonathan, on the other side of the Atlantic, had not died on the voyage, as he had hoped. He found solace in work and sleep. His fellow shipmates had teased him at first, being a raw 'limey' recruit, but soon recognised the signs of a broken heart, and left him alone. In Boston, so very different from his little Cheshire village, he found himself employment. Being young and strong, labouring jobs were easy to find. He threw himself into working, took his pay, ate whatever was available, and slept, not allowing himself to think. He drifted around this way for over three years, until employed by a wealthy merchant, with a home in Cape Cod.

At first taken on as a labourer, his employer, fascinated by Jonathan's accent, began to talk to him. He said very little about himself, but the merchant soon realised that what he had here was wasted as a labourer. This young man, was not only strong, quiet and hard working, but well educated. He could read, write, and had a very quick brain and was numerate. Jonathan was persuaded to leave Boston, to take up a position as a clerk in Cape Cod.

The merchant's daughter, a flighty girl of about eighteen, took an immediate liking to him. "Hannah," her father said, "this is Jonathan, my new clerk. He is from England." At first sight she knew she must have him. Over the following months she flirted and talked to him with no result. She became more and more fascinated. This handsome young man was so refined, he knew all about English poetry, and Shakespeare's plays, she had never met anyone like Jonathan. She baked little treats for him, blueberry muffins, cheese biscuits, gingerbread, and fudge. He was always charming, polite and considerate, but there was something missing, a spark of life was gone. She decided that he must have a broken heart, but was determined to win over his affection.

Eventually it was her mother's plan which succeeded, nearly twelve months later. Taking her mother's advice she packed a meal into a basket. Fresh lobster, newly baked biscuits, and sweet ricotta cheese pies, made with wafer thin phillo pastry. Along with the food she took a bottle of her father's best Tennessee whiskey and two glasses.

She skipped along to meet him from work. "It's my birthday today," she smiled, "I am nineteen, you will come and share this meal with me, won't you?." Seeing her eagerness, he could hardly say no, and taking the basket followed her to a secluded place in the sand dunes.

"Drink to my health?" she asked, pouring two glasses of whiskey. He almost choked, never having tasted anything so strong before, but it left a warm glow in his stomach, and made him feel relaxed. He enjoyed the meal, food unfamiliar to him, and laughed as she showed him how to tackle the lobster. As the level of the whiskey bottle dropped, she got him talking, and found out about Sarah.

She put her arms around his neck. "I can be Sarah. Close your eyes and let me make you happy." It was very easy, the whiskey dulled his senses, and he made love to her, but calling out, in his mind, Sarah's name over and over. He felt surprisingly good, comforted in some way, though with an underlying guilt at imagining that she was Sarah. They became a couple from then on, and he no longer mentioned his lost love, but he never stopped thinking about her. They drifted into marriage, she blissfully happy, and he content enough. The marriage was a hasty affair, as by now Hannah was pregnant, with the son Jonathan was never to see.

Chapter Twenty One

Sarah tried to put Joseph out of her mind. She knew that he had business in York, and he said that he would be back, but when? From what he had told them at dinner, he had spent the last nine years, wandering around the country. He might well return, but it could be next week or next year. She tried to carry on as normal, but silly things reminded her of him. She sat sewing in the garden with her mother, as the afternoon was mild, but the rich brown colour of the autumn leaves, were the same colour of his horse, and she could not concentrate. He was there in her mind, with his wickedly twinkling eyes, and she could not shut him out.

Ten days after he left, she was in the kitchen, surrounded by children, making barley sugar. They liked Aunty Sarah's barley sugar more than anyone else's, not just because it tasted better, but because she always let them help her to make it. They had to be on their best behaviour for safety reasons, as sugar was to be boiled in a decoction of barley, with Sarah's special ingredients of saffron and lemon oil added for extra flavour, but she kept them in order by telling them stories. The twisted brittle toffee, was just about set and the children began to get excited. She did not see him come through the door behind her. "Can I have a piece too, Aunty Sarah?" he asked, joining in with Joanne, who felt she couldn't wait any longer.

Totally surprised, and disarmed by his sudden appearance, she gave him a beautiful smile. "Oh, Joseph, it is good to see you, I am so glad you came back." He put his arm around her waist, "Couldn't keep away. Now, how about a piece of this toffee, before these little monsters eat it all." He pulled funny faces at the children, making them giggle. Mary came in with Jane, and welcomed Joseph. The barley sugar was distributed among the children, and Jane, being for once a tactful Grandma, bravely took them all back to the mill to play and to feed the pigs, suggesting that Sarah might take Joseph for a walk, to catch up on the news.

They walked towards the woods. The trees, with their changing colours were a beautiful sight. He stood behind her, arms around her waist,

"Season of mists and mellow fruitfulness!
Close bosom-friend of the maturing sun,
Conspiring with him how to load and bless
With fruit, the vines that round the thatch eves run".

The way he recited her favourite poetry excited her. He turned her round kissing her, igniting a new kind of love, beyond her imagination. Her desire for him was matched, she thought, as she felt him swell hard against her. This was not only love, but a rampant passion, making her heart beat twice as fast, and taking her breath away. "Sarah, I have spent the last ten days dreaming that you might feel the same for me. I could not keep my mind on my work, I had to come back to see if you wanted me." She ran her fingers through his hair. "I have never felt like this before, and I longed for you to return, but we know so little about each other."

He sat her down in the autumn sunshine, and told her all about his life. How, after completing his training in London, he left the uncle who raised him, and had been travelling ever since, learning so many wonderful things, in this age of revolution. She was intrigued as he told her of how he chose his horse. He had seen the Duke of Wellington's horse. It was pensioned off in the paddocks of Strathfieldsaye, the Duke's beautiful country home. The Duke had ridden the horse in the battle of Waterloo, from four in the morning until twelve at night. A fine animal, 15 hands high, rich chestnut, and called Copenhagen. Joseph had searched until he found himself a similar creature, not quite 15 hands, but of a beautiful colour and temperament, and naturally he also called it Copenhagen!

Sarah told him of her life. He was shocked at the wickedness of parson Richardson. "The devil can 'cite Scripture for his purpose," he commented, "but Shylock was an innocent compared to this Richardson. It is so typically Christian of Henry, not to have told me all about it." He did not think that it was shameful, as she did, that she could barely read or write. "You have so much knowledge, it can hardly matter." Her heart stood still for a moment as he carried on. "With a strong husband by your side, you need not worry your pretty head about such things." Jonathan had said much the same, a long time ago, perhaps Rebecca was right about destiny, perhaps Joseph had always been meant for her. She did not mention Jonathan by name, only saying that she had once loved someone who had gone away. "We have all had past loves," he smiled, "It is the future that we must think of. I was born on November 1st, All Hallows Eve. In Scotland, they say that gives me double sight, and I can see a future for us." "I was born on the winter solstice, December 21st. What does that make me?" she asked playfully, "A witch, I should think, with all your skills, and the power to steal a man's heart!" He took from his coat, a small gold box.

"With your love of Shakespeare, I suppose it should be a box of lead, but it is not Portia's box, and I would only have the best for you." The box was beautiful, and he laughed at her, "Dare you open it?"

"All that glisters is not gold,
Often have you heard that told,
Many a man his life has sold."

She opened the box. Inside was a tiny bag, made to look like a strawberry, and filled with emery. "Rebecca told me that you are quite a seamstress, and if you keep your needles in this, they will stay sharp."

Sarah had not thought she could be so happy, as she walked home with Joseph, hand in hand, and carrying his box. He stayed two days, but this time he told her exactly when he would be back. He had done some work for a man in York, who was a landowner, outside Chester. "He is yet to pay me, but he wants me to take a look at his corn mill for suggestions of improvement, so I shall return on Saturday." he promised.

After he had gone, James talked seriously to his daughter. "It delights your mother and I to see you so happy. We want you to know that you have our blessing whatever the outcome." He hugged his precious daughter. There would always be a special bond between them, and he felt that if she was to marry, there could be no better husband than Joseph.

To his word, he was back on Saturday. He arranged to stay with Henry and Rebecca, but insisted on paying for board and lodging. They welcomed him, and Rebecca was secretly relieved to have the money, as another adult mouth to feed was a great strain on their budget.

That very evening after dinner at the farm, he took Sarah outside. As he kissed her she felt that she could never have enough of him, and wanted him to hold her for ever. The air was chilly, so he put his jacket around her shoulders. They looked up at the stars in the clear sky, "Bassanio's candles of the night," she sighed. "Yes" he agreed, "but they could be diamonds. If you marry me, I will pluck one from the sky for you." Sarah had not expected this, so soon, but she could not stop herself from giving her answer, "Yes, oh Joseph, yes." He picked her up in his arms, off her feet and whirled her round. From his pocket he produced a ring, with a single diamond. "A star from the sky, always wear it to prove that you love me." She was swept along with his amazing plans. "John Clegg in Chester, has paid me by giving me his corn mill. I have great plans for improving it. He is a very wealthy man, with a huge impressive house. He also has a large farmhouse, no longer tenanted, and I have bought it for us! It needs some attention but we could soon put it right. It will be a wonderful place to live." He looked at her. "Doubts my love?" "No, please do not think that, but this is all so sudden. I had never thought of leaving my family." He cuddled her close to him. "All little birds leave the nest sometime, and Chester is not far away. Your father could even bring your mother on the coach service, the roads are so good now, there would be no problem. I could write a letter for you to send to them every week. Sarah, it will make a beautiful home, and we could fill it with our children."

What could she say, the wedding was arranged, first banns read that very Sunday. He whisked her off to Col d'Arbres, as the house was called, leaving Jenny to struggle with the wedding dress. It was, as its name suggested, a house on a hill, on the edge of a small wood. She was surprised to find it a hive of activity. Workers were busy limewashing the walls, and installing a new range in the kitchen. "He must have been so sure of me, to have gone ahead with all this," she thought, loving him all the more. To Sarah it was a very large house, but she loved it all as he showed her around. The kitchen was enormous, and the new range matched it. Leading off the kitchen was a wine cellar, a pantry, a spacious sitting room, and a laundry/ still room on the north side. Here workers were installing a large copper cauldron, with a fireplace beneath, especially to do the wash. Upstairs there were three spacious bedrooms. The largest, on the south side, was to be theirs, with the most beautiful view of the distant Welsh mountains. The carved staircase led up to another floor. The building narrowed at the top, and he showed her how it formed one spacious room, running the width of the house, with a large sunny window on each side. "This will be your soler, and we will have a chaise longue by the fireplace. Did you notice that each bedroom has a fireplace? We will be warm even in the coldest of winters. I will sit with you while you sew, and read out loud, our favourite literature, and new books which we will find on our travels." He swept her along to Chester and then to Liverpool in the three weeks before they returned for the wedding. Her head was spinning as he ordered expensive furnishings, including a huge bed with the thickest and lightest feather mattress that she had ever seen.

Sarah's main worry was the expense of it all, but when she voiced her concern, he reassured her. "Leave all that to me, I never even want you to think about such things." The last three weeks had been like a wonderful dream, but their lovemaking put everything else into shade. The passion and intensity of his experienced touch thrilled her so much, that she sometimes sobbed with pleasure, and even the way he looked into her eyes, made her ache for him. "The best is yet to come," he teased, "Wait until our wedding night."

Chapter Twenty Two

The night before the wedding, she sat on her father's knee, and wept. "I love him so much," she sobbed, "but how can I leave you all, and yet he has such great plans, I cannot spoil all that, and what about when I have a baby, I would want Grandma to be with me." James consoled her, "Sarah, Chester is on the coach connection, we can visit each other, it will be a big adventure, and I know you are both very much in love, you will be happy, I promise. You will be able to plan your own garden, taking cuttings and seeds from ours and Grandma's. You will be so busy, and we will have lots of news for each other each time we visit. As for having a baby without your grandmother. Do you think that she would let that happen? She would fly on a broomstick over to help you if necessary!" Sarah could not help but laugh, her father would never say such a thing to anyone else but her.

The wedding, held in the morning was a splendid occasion, with all her friends and family so happy. The wedding breakfast at the farm was spectacular, Emily, Jenny and Jane had worked for days, under Mary's instruction, on the preparations.

Before they set off on the coach for their new home, with Copenhagen unhappily trailing at the back, Jenny handed Sarah a parcel. "Something special," she whispered. Emily kissed her, "Goodbye mavournin, may the path be straight that's in front of you."

Tears sprang to her eyes as she hugged her parents and Grandma, but with all the excitement, the journey did not seem that long. A horse and cart was waiting outside the coach house to take them to Col d'Arbres. It was quite chilly, despite her new winter coat and gloves, and Sarah was glad to reach the house. Joseph introduced the driver, as Jack Johnson, who said that his wife was waiting for them at Col d'Arbres.

She greeted Sarah most respectfully, then saying, "Everything is done, Mr. Joseph, I hope it is to your satisfaction." She left with her husband, and Sarah looked around the house in amazement. Everything was in place. A kettle was singing on the range, the table laid, and a promising smell of something delicious in the oven. They went upstairs, Joseph carrying two of the bags. Carpets, curtains, furniture, were installed as if by magic, and their bedroom, was just as she had imagined, with a cosy fire lit in the fireplace, and a scuttle of coal for re-fueling.

He took her there, as they were on the big new bed, throwing off their heavy coats and pulling off their boots, not able to wait any longer. With an insatiable appetite they enjoyed each other, trying to make the moment last, but so greedy for that final fulfilment. They lay in each other's arms in a cocoon of happiness. "Welcome, mistress of Col d'Arbres, here is the beginning of our lives," he whispered.

It was very late by the time they got around to the meal, but there was no one to bother them, and it was not spoilt. The range was equipped with a warming oven, and they found it contained delicious chicken in white wine sauce, and an apple pie. Joseph suggested that they arrange staff for the house, but Sarah frowned at the idea. "I do not like the thought of servants, let's just ask Mrs. Johnson to come in to help me, and perhaps her husband could manage the stables, we only have Copenhagen, after all. I have great plans for the garden, and will need help with the heavy work. It would be good if Mr. Johnson would consider doing that too." Joseph reluctantly agreed, and as the Johnsons were returning next morning, promised to have a word to both them, and John Clegg, who employed Jack as a labourer.

Inflamed, by the excellent white wine from Joseph's own cellar, they went to bed. In the firelight, she slipped on Jenny's gift. An alluring nightdress, of blue-grey silk and lace, with tiny shoulder straps and a revealing low neckline. She stood by the flickering flames, filled with desire at the sight of his strong naked body, the nightdress tantalisingly showing off her breasts, and gold crucifix shining against her fair skin. He fell on his knees before her, and lifting the beautiful silk, kissed the hot wet place, the centre of her yearning. She gasped with pleasure at this new experience. He carried her to the bed, tasting her desire for the first time, and she moaned in ecstasy as he put his mouth to her.

"Open afresh your round of starry folds,
For great Apollo bids,
And when again your dewiness he kisses
Tell him, I have you in my world of blisses."

With the poetry, wine and new found pleasure, she wept as he skilfully brought her to climax. This was a different kind of pleasure, and after, as he held her, she found herself longing for the deep satisfaction of his full erection. He seemed to know all her feelings, leaving her wondering, if indeed he did have that All Hallows Eve, double sight, but again he did the unexpected. Kissing her breasts, he took the crucifix from her neck, and threaded the chain between her legs, before lowering himself gently inside her. She sighed with delight at his fullness. He did not move, but once again brought her to thrilling rapture, this time by rubbing the gold chain against her with his hand. Then with the ache for her almost unbearable, they began mutual love making. Relishing the joy of kissing her, gently nibbling her neck and breasts, feeling her writhe beneath him and hearing her strange little sighs as they reached the height of their passion together. Swathed in happiness, never would they have believed that anything could wreck their perfect love, as they slept in that delightful bedroom, without moving until morning.

He woke first, watching her as she slept, so beautiful, with her cheeks still flushed from their lovemaking. He woke her with a kiss. "I will go down to fill the pitcher with hot water, then we must dress,

Mrs. Johnson will be here soon." The range in the kitchen, was of the very latest design, with a hot water tank and tap built in, giving instant hot water. He refuelled the dying embers, and filled the jug. The washstand set, was Dutch, and a pretty blue design. They had found it at a tiny shop in Liverpool, and he had quelled Sarah's horror at the price, insisting on its purchase.

Mrs. Johnson, to her word arrived early, and Joseph left Sarah to make the domestic arrangements, while he rode across to see John Clegg. Mrs. Johnson was very willing to work for Sarah, and was sure that Jack would feel the same, but was worried, because she had no formal training. Sarah reassured her that it was just help in the house she wanted, as she had been used to at home. "I hope that we can become friends, with no formality," she smiled, "There will be times, when we may need a little extra help, though. Do you know anyone suitable?"

It turned out that Mrs. Johnson had a daughter, a hard working and sweet natured girl, but in a shameful position. Her eyes filled with tears, as she told Sarah the story. "She is unmarried, with a child of two years. As far as we knew, she never had a man, and she kept the pregnancy secret somehow until the seventh month. She would not tell us the name of the man concerned, and her father became seized with a kind of madness. He ranted and raved at her, making her cry, but she still would not tell, and then, oh it is so terrible, he beat her. Not just a lash of his belt, but he beat her senseless, if I hadn't laid into him, he would have killed her. He hit me too, blacking my eyes and making my nose bleed, before he came to his senses. He had never taken a hand to anyone before, and I was afraid that he would die of the shame and grief. Rachael, our daughter was delirious for days, sometimes unconscious, sometimes shouting and thrashing about. We all recovered slowly, but Jack is a broken man. Rachael would never tell us the name of the baby's father, and when he was born, his right foot was deformed. Jack and Rachael blame it on the beating, and although we all adore the child, he is a constant reminder of the pain. So perhaps now you will not consider us to be a suitable family for your employment."

Sarah thought nothing of the sort, and said so, going ahead with arrangements. Joseph became too preoccupied with business to make any objection, spending most of his time planning the renovation of his corn mill, and the building of a dam. Sarah had been shocked at the sight of it all. A real mess compared to her father's property, but she voiced no opinion, as her husband seemed so happy and confident about it. Every month he wrote letters for her to send to her father, and in them she told him of Joseph's enthusiasm. She also made sure that she included a snippet of news for everyone, her mother, Jenny, Rebecca, Emily and Grandma. The keeper at the coach house, always made a fuss of Sarah when she posted or collected her letters, and told her tactful versions of the district gossip.

They visited Sarah's family in time for her birthday. A most enjoyable visit, and although too short, made memorable by a gift from her father. A cameo portrait of Sarah, by his own hand, in a beautiful ebony frame.

On their return, Joseph proudly nailed it up in their bedroom. "My beautiful wife," he whispered as he held her close, admiring her father's handiwork, with the inscription at the bottom, in his fine handwriting, 'Sarah 1828'

Col d'Arbres had become a symbol of their love and happiness. On Christmas night she used the last of her dried pine cones, for the fireplace in the soler. She sat, sewing at Joseph's feet, as he read a new book out loud, another gift from her father, and most interesting. He had opened one of his special bottles of port, from the well stocked wine cellar. It was comet wine, he explained. A comet in the year, influenced the grape crop, and this was wine from 1811. He taught her how to open and pour it carefully, so as not to break the film which formed on the sides of the bottle, which he called beeswing.

"Never shake the bottle, or turn it the wrong way," he warned. "The film, when broken, looks like the wings of bees, and we do not want that in the wine." The fragrant allurement of the burning pine cones, and the strength of the fine wine soon stirred their desire, and the book was cast aside, as she touched his breeches, and felt him harden beneath her hand. They made love, as they had done many times before on the chaise longue, relaxing in each other's arms as their passion was spent. Sarah smiled to herself as she thought how they had enjoyed such sensual encounters, in every part of the house, even once in the wine cellar, her sitting on a cold low wooden table, with racks of expensive brandy above their heads.

The Johnson family proved to be excellent workers, anxious to please, and seemed relieved not to be working for John Clegg any more. Sarah could not understand why, she had only met him twice, a handsome man of about her father's age, not at all self conscious of a slight limp, which Joseph thought had been caused in a riding accident. She found him amicable enough, but asked no questions of the Johnsons. She encouraged Rachael to come to Col d'Arbres with her mother, and to bring the child. He was the prettiest little boy. "Like a lamb at foot, as George would say," she was later to write to Emily in one of her many letters. She was sure that the deformity of his foot was nothing to do with Rachael's terrible beating, but probably a general birth defect. How sorry she felt about Jack's guilt, etched on his face and carried on his stooped shoulders like the Ancient Mariner's albatross.

It delighted Sarah to have a child around, the only mar to her own joy, was that she had not conceived, but now as she organised her garden, she had hope. Her regular monthly courses were two weeks late, and she and Joseph were hugging each other in breathless anticipation.

Rachael's child limped happily around the garden with Sarah and his grandfather as they planted, in what Jack thought was a strange haphazard way. Sarah planted onions among her roses, knowing that this would make them more fragrant. Carrots together with marigolds and chives, which would not only look pretty, but keep away the wretched carrot fly. Basil was planted around the tomato plants, but Jack refused to believe that it would improve the flavour. Corriander was to be everywhere to attract the bees, and peppermint planted all around the house. "Ants hate peppermint, and so do mice," she told the astonished man. She set him to work planting a quickset hedge at the sides of the house for privacy. "Can't think why," he thought to himself, scratching his head, there is no other property around for at least two miles." The hedge, as its name suggested, would soon grow, being of living hawthorn stakes, set between the existing railings and pailings. "My little witch", Joseph called her, with all her knowledge of such things. She could imagine her fragrant and productive garden, which led down to the woods, and pictured herself showing her own child the flowers and the trees.

She was to be disappointed. Three days later, she woke with the familiar cramps, and blood stained the beautiful lace trimmed linen sheets. She wept bitterly, clinging to Joseph. He was to leave early that morning, and was loathe to leave her with swollen red eyes and sorrow written on her face. He wrenched himself away on Copenhagen, with a heavy heart, knowing that it would be late before he could return.

Mrs. Johnson arrived to find her rinsing the sheets, with tears in her eyes. "Poor lamb," she said, reminding Sarah of Emily, and making her weep even more. "Don't take on so, babies come only when ready to do so. This time next year you will have forgotten all about today, you will be so busy making pretty baby clothes!" She made Sarah cheer up. "What about Mr. Joseph, you must not make him sad. Let me help you prepare an extra special meal for him tonight. Jack caught a hare this morning. How about cooking that?" Sarah laughed, as she told her the story of Emily, and how she became pregnant after eating jugged hare, and drinking elderflower wine. "Poor Emily thought she was going to die, but she got a little bundle of mischief, Joanne, instead." She put the tinge of sadness of this story out of her mind, and said nothing about Jonathan, or of how Emily had at first rejected Joanne.

The day went quickly, as Sarah threw herself into the cooking and gardening, and by the time she heard Copenhagen's hooves, she looked herself again, with freshly washed hair and Joseph's favourite dress.

He hugged her as he came in, still dusty from the ride, but she did not care, and smiled as he teased her. "I have something for you, to make you feel better."

"Shed no tear! Oh shed no tear,
The flower will bloom another year.
Weep no more! Oh weep no more.
Young buds sleep in the root's white core.
Dry your eyes! Oh dry your eyes!
 For I was taught in Paradise,
To ease my breast of melodies,
Shed no tear."

"Oh, you lovely, wicked man, stop teasing me and using our favourite poet's work for your own ends," she said, knowing that she loved him to do just that. "Ah, I have here a box," he carried on, "What can be in it? You must guess, but I will help you, even if our friend Keats turns in his grave!" "Joseph, if John Keats knew how you inflame my passion with the way you recite some parts of his poems, he would probably do just that." He continued to tease, "A clue," he said, eyes sparkling in the wicked way that she loved so much.

"Gaze with those bright languid
Segments green, and prick
Those velvet ears, but prithee do
Not stick,
Thy latent talons in me."

"A cat, Joseph it must be a cat, please let me see." He handed her the box and inside was a tiny white kitten with green eyes. "I thought it had better not be a black one, my little witch," he laughed. She was thrilled with the tiny animal, and straight away called it Maurice. Maurice in turn decided that Sarah was his own personal possession, causing Joseph many a time to comment. "If he were a man, I would throw him out!"

They were not to know then, what a great part Maurice was to play in their destiny.

Chapter Twenty Three

In the twelve months since his arrival in that small box, Maurice had grown into a fine animal. A huge white cat, with green eyes and rounded ears, who thought he owned the world. He adored Sarah, following her about, tripping daintily alongside her as she gathered herbs, or installing himself on her knee in the kitchen. He was a cunning hunter. Although spoilt and well fed, he would stalk and kill anything which dared to cross his path. This resulted in many injuries, as he took on squirrels, rabbits, weasels and the like. He would patiently allow Sarah to bathe his wounds, and secretly, she felt that he thought he was some kind of brave knight, returning proudly wounded from the crusades! When her parents and Grandma visited, he had disgraced himself. As Sarah hugged her dear father, Maurice hissed and spat, getting himself banned from the house for the entire visit. Not to be outdone, he sat outside staring in a relentless and menacing way at the visitors. James found the cat's jealousy amusing, Jane decided to use her authority, by trying to make friends with the animal, getting scratched in the process, and Maurice remained quite shameless of his dishonourable behaviour, almost smiling to himself when the visitors left.

Sarah had still not conceived. A bitter disappointment to both herself and Joseph. He assured her that he did not care if she could not give him children, as he loved her so much, but that only made matters worse, leaving her filled with guilt. He was changing, little by little, sometimes sulky and distant, and it worried her. She made up her mind to talk to Jane about conception on her next visit. If anyone had a trick or two concerning such things, it would be Grandma. It did worry her though, that she had not conceived with Jonathan either.

Jonathan and Hannah, thousands of miles away, were happy. They had taken the horse and buggy to a neighbour's house. It was a good evening, though rather hot. Hannah proudly displayed the bulge in her dress. "Three months to go," she boasted, "we can't wait. You must come and see my bassinet, mother has re-covered it with the most beautiful lace." Jonathan put up with the baby talk, and drank too much whiskey to compensate. As they set off for home, the weather had become sultry and thundery, so he pushed the horse on a little faster than he should. Near home, the heavens opened with a sudden violent thunder storm. A crack of thunder made the already nervy horse rear in its harness, and the following lightning struck a tree with such ferocity that it was instantly felled. He saw it, as if time had slowed down, and managed to push Hannah clear with an almighty shove, that was to bruise her arm and side, but to save her life. He was trapped across his chest, and Hannah was unconscious. The terrified horse fought to free itself from the harness, trampling over Jonathan's legs, and fleeing for home. Hannah's father found them. They begged to take her home, but she would not leave her husband's side, as they worked for two hours in the rain to free him.

Sarah, asleep in Joseph's arms, saw it all. She saw them raise the tree, saw the blood seeping through his fine white shirt, and the angle of his broken leg. It was as if her own breath was fading, with his, as they lifted him. She saw a girl, heavily pregnant, holding his hand, but it was Sarah he looked at with his vivid blue eyes. He reached his free hand out to her and uttered hoarsely, "Sarah, Sarah, oh Sarah!" She sat up in bed, screaming his name and Joseph shook her roughly. "Who in God's name is this Jonathan?" She tried to explain about her insight, "The same thing happened with Elizabeth in the church, I told you about it." He was cold and angry, as this did not explain who Jonathan was, and with no care for Sarah's feelings, continued to interrogate her jealously. He eventually accepted the explanation, but there was a certain coldness about him from then on.

Jonathan died, as Sarah knew in her heart he would, within minutes, leaving Hannah, bitter and broken hearted. She swore to tell her child how its father had betrayed her as he died, how he had called out for that horrible English Sarah, with the mill owner of a father, who thought that Jonathan was not good enough! Yes, she would tell this child, and her grandchildren, and her great grandchildren, if she lived long enough, no one would ever be allowed to forget her heartache.

Joseph's mill project was not doing well. He had chosen a stout man with two sons to run it, but they were constantly in the ale house, and not a week went by without some problem or other. He was also quarrelling with John Clegg. Some of Clegg's cows had been rubbing against Joseph's dam wall, and he was incensed, galloping off on Copenhagen, shouting of revenge and compensation. He cancelled the regular order for his fine brandy and wines, and instead bought a large quantity of cheap wine, which made his sulky humour worse, and deepened Sarah's sadness. "After all," she thought "He would not allow me make my own wine, not even my favourite broom wine." She tried to cheer him, worried that it may be something more than just her lack of fertility, but he refused to discuss business at all, except to say that there was nothing for her to worry about.

One day, word came from a company in Kendal, Westmorland, asking for Joseph's services for repair to some complicated scientific machinery. His mood altered dramatically. "I shall not take you with me, my love. The journey is long and I will be fully occupied when I start work on their particular instruments. I will be away for two weeks, but when I return, we will celebrate. I will send the Johnsons home early, take a meal and some wine into our woods and make love to you, until we have made up for the time we have been apart. Is there anything that I can bring for you?"

Sarah told him about a very special cloth, imitations abounded, but the real thing came from Westmorland. "Kendal green cloth, I was always going to get some to make my father a jacket, but we never went to Westmorland, and I have that new glove pattern from Jenny, some fine kidskin or chamois, would make beautiful gloves for you." "How like you, Sarah, not to ask for anything for yourself, but you shall have something, never fear!"

She was very sad as she waved him goodbye, they had not been apart for such a long time, so she decided to keep herself busy. The day was fine, so she set off down the track leading from the house to the road. The house was quite isolated, the track being about a mile in length, and her nearest neighbours another mile after that. She walked along, happily thinking of Joseph's return, and looked forward to that special meal in the woods. As she reached the road, she turned towards the bend, where she knew was a pond. This was the only place in the area, that soapwort grew. She had tried to grow it up at Col d'Arbres, but there was no part of the garden or woods, damp or boggy enough. Maurice darted off, after a rabbit, making Sarah laugh. Such a fat and cuddly cat, at first sight, who would think he could be so ferocious and swift footed. "But then," she thought, "in that little body is the mind of a lion, king of all beasts." She had even seen him, in the past, sitting on the wall, tapping poor Copenhagen's nose with his paw, just to make sure that the horse knew his place.

The terrified rabbit, turned in its tracks towards the road, with Maurice in hot pursuit, into the path of a horse and rider, approaching the bend. The horse bolted in fright, brushing against Sarah and knocking her over. The rider, having gained control, ran to help her. "I am so sorry," he said, "Are you hurt?" He helped her to her feet. "You are Joseph's wife, from Col d'Arbres, what are you doing here?" It was John Clegg. Sarah explained about the soapwort, and of Maurice's relentless pursuit of rabbits. To her surprise, he lifted her up on his horse. "I will take you home, do not worry, I will lead the horse, he will not bolt again."

Sarah felt rather silly and embarrassed, but he chatted as they went along in a pleasant easy going way. Maurice trailed behind, ears slightly flattened, and in a bad humour. At home she explained to Rachael about the accident, and how John Clegg had brought her home, and asked her to make some tea for them in the garden. She did not dare offer a glass of wine, as she was only too aware of it's bad quality, and regretted not having made her own. He seemed enthralled with the garden, and very impressed to hear that it was Sarah's own doing. "Would you consider planning such a garden for me? Jones, my gardener has no imagination. Perhaps if you would do that for me, I could help with Joseph's problems." Sarah was surprised, "I thought that was all sorted out. There is a fence to keep the cows from the dam wall." She was shocked as he told her how Joseph owed him money. He spared her nothing at all. Joseph owned the mill, but he had borrowed money to renovate it. Joseph had agreed to buy Col d'Arbres, but had so far only made the first payment on it, leaving himself heavily in debt to Clegg. He smiled in a way that made Sarah shudder. "I will send Jones up for you to look at my garden. Don't worry, I feel sure that we can work something out.

He left her with a flourishing wave. Feeling sick, she went into the house, not noticing Rachael. "Please," Rachael whispered, Sarah looked at her, she was almost cowering by the pantry door. "Please have nothing to do with John Clegg, he is an evil man." This only added to Sarah's shock, and she nodded dumbly as she climbed the stairs to the bedroom. She pulled out the drawer, where she knew Joseph kept all his papers. What could she do, she could hardly read, and dared not ask anyone else to look at such things. She made herself study the pages. Isolating each word with her fingers, she began to understand a little. She found Col d'Arbres, and the words Pro Tando. This was one of Henry's phrases, little bits of Latin learned for fun, a long time ago. It meant an instalment, good as far as it goes, but not final. There seemed to be many mentions of large sums of money, and always that name, Clegg. She had seen enough, Clegg had told the truth, even the house was not theirs, and Joseph had kept it all from her.

She was filled with sickening anticipation as Jones, the elderly gardener approached with the horse and cart. John Clegg waiting at his home, displayed his utmost charm, as he helped her down, and took her to the secluded garden at the back of the house. He sat her at the wooden garden seat, and poured a glass of wine from a bottle chilling on a nearby table. She accepted the glass, but did not drink. "Your garden is beautiful," she said coldly, "I can see that you need no help from me." "Ah, that is where you are wrong. Did you look into Joseph's affairs, and see that I told the truth?" She nodded, and he carried on, "You are a beautiful woman Sarah. Did you know that my wife died in childbirth, years ago? A man has his needs, and I have no wife to satisfy mine. If you would let me make love to you, just once, here in my garden, my body would be sated. My desire for you is so great, and I am a man of experience, I could give you much pleasure." He stopped as she gave him a resounding slap across his face, leaving behind a great red mark. "Ha, you have spirit, pretty Sarah, but do this one thing for me and I shall cancel all your husband's debts." He snatched both her hands in his, "and an heir Sarah, perhaps the seed of another man may give Joseph the son he so wants, he would never know. I am a man of my word, I would leave you alone, and never say another word, if you would only just once let me enjoy your beautiful body."

Nausea and horror filled her, but there was no choice, everything he said made sense. If she did this one horrible thing, Joseph would be freed from all his worries, and life would return to their world of blisses again. She swallowed the wine and agreed, saying sorrowfully, "I will do this thing, as I believe that you are a man of your word, but I shall take no pleasure from it. Just do as you will."

He laid her down gently right there in the garden. She shut her eyes tightly as he grunted, thrusting inside her. Somehow she could see it all, as if looking down, but then she realised that it was not herself she was looking at beneath him, but Rachael. A younger

Rachael, with long flowing hair, fighting and screaming as he raped her. She saw him grab her roughly by the shoulders, "Not a word, you hear," he growled at her. "Or I will turn your parents out onto the road, and you can all beg for a living."

Back in reality his lust spent, he tried to revive her. Her eyes were open, but with a strange glazed look. He gently patted her cheek, and she blinked as if coming back into this world. He kissed her limp hand, "Come now, Jones will take you home, and we will never mention this again, I will keep my word, I will find a way of releasing Joseph from his debts, without arousing any suspicion. You will both be free.

At home she was violently sick. Mrs. Johnson made little comment, but tried to soothe her. "Too much heat, I shouldn't wonder," she said in a motherly way, "you must not go out in the sun without your bonnet." Later, slightly revived, she questioned Mrs. Johnson, "Rachael's hair is very pretty," she mentioned casually, as she brushed her own, has she always worn it so short?" The older woman's eyes clouded, "No, as a matter of fact she had beautiful long hair, but when the baby was born, she took the scissors and hacked it all off. It took a long time to get it back into any sort of shape, and now she says it will never be allowed to grow long again."

So, it had been the insight again, it was true what she had seen, and Rachael's baby's foot, his limp was just like his father's. Had there ever really been a riding accident? No, she was sure now, John Clegg had a deformity, and he had passed it on to his son. The son begotten by the rape of an innocent young girl!

She thought of parson Henry, long ago. He had told her that she could stop these flashes of insight. "I must stop them again, first dear Jonathan, and now this. I will put it all from my mind, that and John Clegg. He brought me home when a rabbit scared his horse, and I advised him about his garden. That is what I must believe, I will have no more of it. The power of the mind, Henry said, I will use the power of my mind."

Chapter Twenty Four

Sarah pushed the unpleasant events to the back of her mind, until it all remained as only something hovering in her subconsciousness.

She was so glad to see Joseph again. Running down the track to meet him, she was greeted by the friendly soft rumbling whinny, which Copenhagen seemed to keep for her alone. She was fond of the big animal, having won his affection by brushing his coat with lemongrass, to keep away the flies, and washing his eyes in the summer with witch hazel and water, to relieve them from the dust.

Joseph was all smiles, whisking her off her feet, and leading Copenhagen towards the house. Even Maurice welcomed him, fussing around his legs, and purring in his resoundingly noisy way. His work had gone well, and full of praises, the machinery owner made enthusiastic recommendations to colleagues, with the prospect of more such assignments for the talented Joseph. "Don't worry though," he assured her, "You will always accompany me in the future." There were tears in his eyes as he continued, "I will never leave you again, I love you too much." She was to remember this conversation in the future, in very different circumstances.

He was laden with gifts. First the Kendal green cloth, of beautiful quality, with matching silk lining and a dozen unusual horn buttons. She was thrilled, "There is enough here to make a coat, instead of a jacket. I will make it Newmarket style like yours, with a velvet collar, not the old Artois style with high neck and caped layers." He smiled at her enthusiasm. There was a quantity of first class kidskin, some fine muslin, and a length of pale blue cotton, of a quality she had never seen before. Not only was the colour unusual, but it was extremely strong as well as being soft.

"Now, a special gift for my Sarah," he teased, keeping it behind his back. "For once I cannot think of any poetry to describe it, so you must guess." As Maurice was sitting looking at all this with great interest, she laughed. "I do hope it's not another cat, my possessive Maurice would swallow it whole." In this frivolous mood, she casually mentioned how Maurice had almost killed John Clegg, and had only been forgiven, because she had given him some advice about his garden, making Joseph laugh. Assuring her that it was not an animal, he handed her the box. Inside was a beautiful mirror with matching comb. It had been worked from silver and ivory, and she was enchanted.

They planned their love tryst in the woods, for the next day, telling the Johnsons that they need only work in the morning. He had brought home some very fine wine, and a bottle of best brandy, telling her that there was more on the way. The meal was prepared with loving care. Tiny beef pies with apricot preserve topping beneath a lattice of pastry. Savoury prunes, one of his favourites. Prunes cooked until tender but firm, wrapped in tasty streaky bacon. Hard boiled eggs covered in sausage meat, breadcrumbs, and fried in bacon fat, and tiny fingers of rich gingerbread, made with treacle and cream. A bowl of firm, freshly picked raspberries completed the menu, as they headed for their special place in the woods. The food, wine and love making transported them into a time of their own, and it was not until the light began to fade, and the warm air cooled, that they realised how long they had been there. Their world of blisses had returned.

Sarah set to work on her father's coat with great enthusiasm. Joseph promised to take her to visit her parents at the end of the month and she was determined to have it finished. She was more than pleased with the result, then set upon making a canezou for herself and her mother. This was a short three tier cape of muslin, with long ends which tucked into a belt. She embroidered the capes with tiny flowers of grey blue silk, which would reflect the colour of her mother's and her own eyes. With time running short, she made the kidskin gloves for Joseph, and with the left over skin, managed also to piece together a pair for her grandmother.

They stayed this time, for ten days, making Sarah very happy, gossiping with Emily, Jenny and Rebecca. She was saddened at her mother's condition. Now totally blind, she relied on Jane for everything, but not only that, her life spirit seemed to have faded with her sight. She appeared content, with a lovely smile for James, but it was as if she was now resigned to sit and wait for the end of her days. She wore the pretty embroidered cape from Sarah, with great pleasure, listening carefully as James described it, but nothing would change her frame of mind.

James was moved almost to tears by the coat, remembering how they had always planned to go to Westmorland, for some such cloth. A fine green coat, with silk lining, a velvet collar, wide lapels and horn buttons. Joseph felt that he could have been jealous, if it hadn't been for Sarah's happiness.

Jane much appreciated the fine kid gloves, congratulating her on the tiny stitches. Sarah broached the subject of conception, telling her grandmother how disappointed they both were about not yet having a baby. Jane just laughed and hugged her granddaughter looking into her lovely eyes. "You need not ask me for such advice, my feelings are rarely wrong, you are with child." Sarah thought, yes her monthly courses were late, but that had happened before, and with all the sewing, love making and re-established happiness, she had not thought anything about it. "You be sure to get Joseph to write and let us know, but I will be surprised if I am wrong." Sarah firmly pushed John Clegg even further to the back of her mind, and hugged the secret of Joseph's baby to herself. This time she would not tell him until she was quite sure.

Although sorry to leave her parents, Sarah left happily with her secret. Her father gave her a box of pretty pearl buttons, and Grandma supplied her with packets of seed for her garden. She made up her mind what to make from the length of lovely blue cotton. She would make a gardening apron. It would have small pockets all down the front, for seeds. Each pocket would bear the embroidered representation of the flower produced by each seed, and would be fastened by one of her father's pearl buttons.

She could hardly wait to start the sewing when they returned to Col d'Arbres. James had given Joseph much advice about the running of his unprofitable corn mill, and he set about looking for more reliable tenants. The only cloud on the horizon was when he announced that he was going to see John Clegg. Again she swallowed her fear, but was sick with anxiety until he returned.

He was there much longer than she expected, and returned strangely subdued. She pretended not to notice, but the tension was making her head ache. Not knowing what else to do, she plied him with his new batch of brandy. It worked. Pleasantly drunk, he took her to bed early, and made love until he fell asleep in her arms, his face as relaxed as a child's.

He made no further mention of Clegg, and as far as she knew, did not go again to visit him. His mood improved and he threw himself into sorting out his mill, determined to find good workers this time.

Word came of more work for Joseph. The manufacturers in Kendal had indeed made many recommendations to associates about Joseph's abilities. This time he was to go to Shropshire, to a place called Much Wenlock. "We will go together," he told her, "The work is of the same type and will be demanding of my time, but Much Wenlock is a medieval market town, and I know of a very good inn, where we could stay. It is very central, and I am sure that you will enjoy the shops and markets. I have also heard that there is a ruined priory nearby, and at this time of year they hold Shakespearean plays there in the evenings. We will have a good time, and I shall earn lots of money!" He happily buzzed about making business arrangements, and Sarah had an idea of her own.

Although she had not seen Elizabeth since she was twelve, she occasionally wrote to her father, and James kept Sarah up to date with Elizabeth's news. She never married, but was content in acting as teacher to the children of her village. Elizabeth lived in Shropshire, and Sarah suggested that they might call to see her during the trip. Joseph of course had no interest in doing such a thing, but readily agreed to stay over one day, in order to keep Sarah happy.

With all the domestic arrangements made, they set off. Sarah felt guilty as Maurice and Copenhagen were left behind. The horse whinnied pitifully as they left for the coach house without him, and Maurice, shut in the house with Mrs Johnson, sulked in a corner of the kitchen, large green eyes wide, and rounded ears flat. The Johnsons would come to the house every day, see to the garden and the two animals, and open the windows as it was now August, and could be hot and stuffy.

It was strange to see Elizabeth again. Although only fourteen years older that Sarah, her once blonde hair was now white, and held back in an unflattering bun. Her dress, although spotlessly clean, and of good quality was grey, with not a ribbon or pretty button to be seen. Despite her sombre appearance, she made them very welcome, and took delight in hearing about Sarah's new life since her marriage. It was altogether a pleasant day's stop over, even Joseph was not bored, as Elizabeth was a good host. All was well until they were just about to leave. Elizabeth suddenly clutched Sarah's hand, and took her to one side. There was a terrible expression of fear in her eyes, "Sarah, write to tell your father about the baby, as soon as you can. Tell him the truth, tell him everything. Do you understand? I am afraid for you."

This was a complete shock. She had told no one about the baby, hardly admitting it to herself yet, but she felt caught up in Elizabeth's fear. She just nodded as she boarded the coach, realising that this friend from the past, did not know that she could not write a letter.

Yet more disquiet she pushed into the back of her mind. She tried to tell herself that perhaps Elizabeth had been left slightly insane after her experiences with parson Richardson. She said nothing to Joseph, just chatted happily about the coming two weeks at Much Wenlock.

Joseph established her at the inn, situated in the centre of the town. Their room was airy and comfortable. She missed Col d'Arbres, but to be in his arms at night was much better than being left at home. She watched him thrive as he worked on the problem of the defective instruments, knowing that he would be well paid. At the end of the two weeks his work finished and in receipt of generous payment, he announced that they would go to see the performance of Macbeth, that evening at the Wenlock Priory, but was startled by her reaction. "Oh, please don't, you must never call that play by its name. It is very unlucky, no actor would say it you know. You must always call it the Scottish play." He only laughed at her, "What's in a name," he teased, "and how could it hurt my own little witch!"

It was a lovely balmy evening, and the solitary soaring arches of the ruined priory made a most impressive setting for the play. Lady Macbeth's speech about the babe, made her shudder, and the atmosphere of the whole play, set in such a stage, made her catch her breath. This was really something to tell her father about.

They walked around the priory after the performance before taking the coach and pair back to the inn. They talked about the superb acting, but also how they both looked forward to going home to their own dear house. Then he produced something from his pocket, and dangled it in front of her. It was a pretty lace handkerchief tied with a bow of green ribbon. "A penny for your secrets, Sarah," he said seriously, "but perhaps your secrets are worth more!" Her heart almost stopped with guilt as he handed her the handkerchief. With shaking hands she opened it, finding a gold sovereign. "When are you going to tell me your secret Sarah? When are you going to tell me about our baby!" She covered her relief with laughter, "I could not bear to disappoint you, I wanted to be quite sure." "Ha, I miss nothing," he pretended to scold, "Do you really think that I had not noticed the missing monthly courses! Now we have made a start, we will fill Col d'Arbres with children. I don't mind how many daughters, and perhaps one son."

Their lives seemed complete as they headed back to the inn.

Chapter Twenty Five

Jack Johnson met them at the coach house just as he had when they first came to Col d'Arbres after their marriage. It was so good to be home, and there, just as before was a good meal standing in the warming oven for them. Copenhagen went wild with happiness as if he thought he had been abandoned for ever, but Maurice was nowhere to be seen. Jack reported that the cat had been most unfriendly, and that they had not seen him for the past two days. Sarah was worried, so she searched outside, calling his name, but there was no sign of the animal. Unhappily she unpacked their cases, and came across the box of pearl buttons which she had left on her dressing table. Her mind still on the missing cat, she climbed the stairs to the soler to put the buttons with her partly made gardening apron. As she walked through the door, she stopped. There was something wrong in here. Everything looked normal, but she stood quite still, sensing something. She heard it, a feeble miaow coming from the fireplace. It was a small ornate cast iron fireplace, with a narrow chimney, and Maurice was firmly wedged up it.

It had been no exaggeration that Maurice was not friendly while Sarah was away. At first he had held the Johnsons responsible for Sarah's departure, and refused to eat their food, seeking the company of the equally fretting Copenhagen. Each day he watched the movements of these people, and each day they did the same thing, left all the bedroom windows open. Nearing the end of the second week, he figured out his daring plan. Climbing the large walnut tree, he leapt from it to the roof of the porchway. With much breathless scrabbling he reached the top, and then it was simply a matter of a single leap through the window into Sarah's bedroom.

Sarah never allowed the cat upstairs, so this territory was alien to him, but he had to find her. Oh yes, she had been here. He hopped effortlessly onto the bed and rested, washing his paws and grooming his whiskers, bathing in her smell all around him. He contentedly dozed for a while, but then renewed his mission. All around the room was her smell, but that was all. He investigated the other rooms, but there was no trace of her there. Then, spying the stairs leading to the soler, made his way up. Yes her scent was here again, but were was she? He sniffed around the room, knocking over a bobbin of blue silk, and playing with it, kitten like, for a while, until he heard the noise. He padded up to the fireplace and peered up the chimney. He stiffened, fear bottle-brushing his tail, and spiking the fur on the back of his neck. Up that hole it was dark and black, and something was there alright, setting his feline mind reeling. A demon, one of those creatures all mothers warned their kittens about. He had seen them, in the dark in the woods, and sometimes in broad daylight on the road. He remembered well his mother's warning. Cats could see them, so could those stupid creatures who barked all the time, using their voices without necessity, and wagging their tails when the were not annoyed. These demons, his mother had said, must always be avoided. "They must never be approached, walk away respectfully, run if you have to, but do not annoy them". Now there was one in this black hole, he sniffed, smelling the soot. "I can smell him," he thought fearfully, "A bad smell, a death smell. He must have the Mistress up there, I must go. The man is not here, he should go, but there is only me to save her". He arched his back, and hissed and spat up the chimney. "I will get you, I will bite and scratch," he thought as he began to climb, stretching his paws onto the chimney's narrow sides, "I am coming, let her go. Bite, hold and scratch, rip and tear, that is what I will do. Let her go!" The space became much narrower, but he scrambled on. Suddenly the bird at the top of the chimney, the real cause of the noise, realised the danger from below, and in panic flew off. The echoing sound it caused around the cat's ears, made him lose his footing. Down he fell, claws raking the sooty surface. Reaching the bend awkwardly, with the force of his weight, he became stuck, jammed below the ribcage, unable to move back or forth. Soot fell into his ears, eyes and mouth, choking, eye stinging soot, adding to his terror, and then the silence, only his heartbeat and the horror of his imprisonment.

Two days had passed when she found him. Dehydrated and terrified, he heard her scream. "Joseph, Joseph, Maurice is stuck up the chimney!" Almost laughing, Joseph reached up the dark opening, and as gently as it was possible wrenched the distraught creature from the chimney. Luckily the cat had lost some weight, or the process would have been even more painful.

After he heard her scream, Maurice realised that the demon was no longer above, but below him. He yowled through the soot with his dry throat, and fought with all his might as it gripped him from below, pulling him into its fearful clutches. Suddenly he fell into the light, into Sarah's arms, and the demon was gone. He had won, he had saved her!

Joseph smiled as she cradled Maurice to her, not caring about the soot against her lilac dress. The poor animal was a mess. Fur caked with soot, his normally pink nose blocked and black, and his eyes sore and sticky. They carried him to the kitchen, and Joseph watched with proud contentment as his wife tended to the animal. She bathed his sore eyes with warm water and witch hazel, and dropped a little water into his parched mouth. Into some hot water she put two drops of camomile oil, and with the solution on a soft wrung out cloth, stroked his sooty fur. He relaxed on her knee, and allowed himself to fall into the blissful darkness of sleep, which he had fought for two days, knowing that it would then have meant certain death.

By the time they went to bed, he had revived enough to lick some chicken gravy from her fingers, and even had a small drink of warm milk. They left him on Sarah's chair for the night, feeling proud and satisfied at his victory.

Next morning Joseph woke to find no Sarah beside him. He was filled with a feeling of pleasure as he found her in the kitchen. She was sitting by the range, kettle singing on the hob, holding the blackened Maurice. "I thought so," he laughed with that wicked look in his eyes that she loved so much, "but I will have to get used to you doing this. You will be often sitting here so early, when the baby comes in March." "February," she corrected him, "I hope it won't be very cold, but we are always cosy and warm here in our house."

Like a cloud drifting over the sun, his happy countenance faded. "February? Sarah, when was this child conceived?" The sparkle had left his eyes and a frown creased his brow. Icy fingers of fear wound themselves around her throat. Desperately trying not to show her guilt, she answered sweetly. "I should think our baby started during our tryst in the woods, when you returned from Westmorland." He turned his back to her, looking through the window, but with eyes not seeing the lovely late summer morning. He spun around suddenly to face her again, making her jump, and sending Maurice fleeing into a corner. "You will tell no one, do you hear? I mean no one, not even your parents. We will keep your pregnancy a secret, until you can hide it no more!" He stamped out of the kitchen, saddled up Copenhagen and galloped off, not returning until late that evening.

She had lost him, she knew instinctively. His love had died, so suddenly, right before her eyes. A long dark shadow fell across Sarah's life. He made no accusations, but mostly ignored her. Staying away from the house as much as he could, and sleeping with his back turned to her. The only normality was the regular letter to her father. "I will write your usual nonsense, we do not wish to upset your mother in her state of health," he told her with a bitter edge to his voice.

Until the end of November she kept herself busy, trying to be sweet, loving and welcoming for him, but he remained set against her. She spent her time sewing baby clothes, roomy dresses for herself, and finished the gardening apron, filling its embroidered pockets with seeds for the spring, and fastening each one with its pretty pearl button. They had planned to spend this Christmas with her parents, fearing that it may be her mother's last, but Joseph changed his mind. "We will write to say that I am taking you to France and that we will not return until the spring."

She was sitting at her dressing table, combing her hair, and almost dropped the mirror at this announcement. He pointed to the growing child, now showing clearly through her nightdress. "You have made a cuckold of me! Do you think I am a fool? The only time you conceive is when I am away, after you have so kindly given John Clegg advice about his garden. Why was it on my return, that he told me how charming you were, and how helpful, and suddenly released all my debts, in the name of friendship! I did not live as a monk before we met. I have had many sexual encounters, but not left behind even one bastard, and all the times we made love, nothing, no baby. I don't believe that I can sire a child!" He snatched the beautiful ivory and silver mirror from her hand and pushed it in front of her face. "What if this were Alasnam's mirror? Would you dare to look into it then?" Sarah shuddered and looked away, she knew what he was saying. It was a story from Arabian Knights, about a mirror which clouded over, if a woman was unfaithful. He threw the mirror across the room, making her gasp as it smashed against the wall, representing their shattered lives.

"I am never going to tell him," she thought, "however much he suspects, after all the child may yet be his." He grabbed her hand, roughly pressing it to the baby. "It shows too much, you can no longer hide it, so now I must hide you. I will dismiss the Johnsons, you will stay in the soler during the day out of sight, and I will say that you have gone to nurse your sick mother. At the end of January, I will send for your grandmother to deliver the child. You will confess to her, and send the infant back to live with your family. Then with the cuckoo out of my nest, we will start again."

The room began to spin, colours blending into misty grey as she fainted. She came to, alone in the soler, feeling very cold as the fire was not lit. He appeared at the door, carrying a pillow and blankets, "We may as well start now," he said icily. "I no longer wish to share a bed with that mongrel's whelp inside you."

True to his word, he dismissed the Johnsons, and only allowed her downstairs to cook meals, or wash at night. He seemed to take delight in his cruelty, and there was little food. "How can I buy food, you are not supposed to be here," he snarled. For longer and longer periods he stayed away from the house, locking her in the soler. He ignored her pleas and tears. Distraught one day, she accused him of being as bad as parson Richardson. He slapped her across her face, leaving an almost instant bruise, shouting, "How dare you, it is you who are evil, compare yourself to that man." He could not bear to look at her. Her pale skin had taken on a greyness which did not flatter her, and despite the grotesque swelling of her belly, she was otherwise thin and gaunt from lack of food. She was no longer his precious Sarah.

In January he wrote the letter to Jane for Sarah to sign, stating simply that she was required for the birth of the baby next month. The letter was a relief, for it would be so good to see her grandmother. She would tell Jane everything, and go back with the baby to live with her parents. All this she clung to, saying nothing to Joseph, and not knowing that the letter was never posted.

Sarah watched the weather anxiously, praying that it would not snow, delaying her grandmother's arrival. From the beginning of February, she suggested that they write again, as Jane had neither arrived or replied. Joseph did as she asked, but she was filled with fear as she signed the letter, somehow knowing that her grandmother would not come.

Joseph now spent most of his time away from the house and was drinking excessively, leaving her locked upstairs. Maurice was her only companion, and Joseph sometimes even banned the cat from her company. Knowing that her time was near she became frightened, begging Joseph to go for her grandmother. She was horrified at his response, "I never wrote to your grandmother, no one knows of your condition. You have all the medical knowledge, my little witch, you can deliver it yourself. When it is born, I will take the brat, and leave it on the steps of the friary in Chester, the Monks will find a home for it." He turned and slammed the door in her face.

During the early hours of next morning her labour started. This was not as Sarah had expected, these were not just contractions, building powerfully towards their purpose, but throes of torturous cramps leaving her nauseous and weak as her waters broke. She banged on the door, screaming for Joseph. At last he came, looking at her in disgust as she bent over in agony. She held out her hand to him, "Please help me, Joseph, you are wrong, the baby is yours, when she is born, you will see, she will look just like you. Please get Mrs. Johnson or Rachael to help me." "Witch!" he spat at her, and slammed the door, locking it behind him. She heard him bringing out Copenhagen, and gallop off at greatest speed. "Oh please God don't let him be long," she prayed.

He did not return. Now late in the afternoon, she was soaked with perspiration despite the chill in the room. Surely such pain could not continue for much longer. She had assisted her grandmother with two births, but they had not been like this. The agony went on and on. Daylight was fading, and he still did not come. She fumbled to light the lamp between contractions, feeling the welcome warmth of the flame. The pain changed intensity. "It is coming," she thought fearfully, I must prepare and think only of the child now." She gave birth to a tiny baby girl, lying on the chaise longue, where they had once enjoyed such wonderful love making. She heard herself screaming, "Grandma, Grandma, help me," but no one came. Then she was not alone, as there was a tiny person with her, and oh so precious, her own child. She was filled with wonder and love as she cut and tied the cord and wrapped the child in a piece of sheet. The little girl was small, but seemed well. "Joseph's child," she said out loud, "Oh look at you, my mother's soft fair hair, but surely Joseph's child." She tried to put the baby to her breast, but there seemed no milk to give. She had become wasted through lack of food, and now dehydrated through the long labour. She drank the small amount of water left in the jug, and hoped that the milk would soon come. She was bleeding. Of course she knew that there would be a loss after the birth, but not like this. This was a steady pouring of blood, which she could not stop, and she felt so very cold. Joseph had left no coal for the fire and the chill reached through to her bones. She shouted with all her strength for him to come back, but the only reply was a pitiful miaow from Maurice, locked outside. Joseph had left her, she was sure of that. She remembered how he had sworn never to leave her again after he came back from Westmorland. She remembered the tears in his eyes as he told her how much he loved her, and despite everything, she still loved him.

Feeling weak, she padded a blanket between her legs trying to staunch the bleeding, and lay back on the chaise longue with the child. It was daylight when something woke her. Something brushing against her face. Light headed from the blood loss, it was an effort to even open her eyes. A spider! It was a spider, spinning a web across herself and the child. Horrified she flicked it away, feeling the child stir against her, but also aware of a fresh surge of blood between her legs. She looked down, so much blood, she was going to die. She touched the baby's head with the gold crucifix, which had hung around her neck for as long as she could remember, and kissed her.

"I name this child Mary, after my dear mother
 in the name of the Father,
Son and Holy Ghost
 Amen."

Now if they did not survive, the child would not be condemned to stay in limbus. She did not really believe that her God would do such a thing to an innocent child just because it was unbaptised, but her strong mother's love was going to take no chances. She held the baby close, and slipped into a comfortable velvet blackness, where there was no sorrow or pain.

Joseph at an inn miles away, awoke from his drunken stupor, and saw Sarah standing in the doorway. He shook himself as he stood up, "What are you doing here?" he snarled. She did not reply. She had a child with her, holding its hand. A girl child of about three years old, with pale blonde hair who wrinkled her nose in an insolent way. The child's shining hair, as fair as Sarah's was dark, was caught up at the top of her head in a strange way, hanging loosely down her back like a horse's tail. Sarah and the child were dressed alike, both with striped shirts, and of all things sailor's breeches! At the bottom of the breeches was attached something gold and shiny. He looked closely and saw it was a bell. "Have you lost your senses woman," he yelled, but she just smiled saying, "Goodbye, my love," and was gone.

The realisation hit him like an arrow in his chest. It was a wraith. He had heard about such things in Scotland. A highland superstition, a spectral appearance of someone who is about to die, which appears at a distance to warn of the event. Throwing money across the table, he yanked a surprised Copenhagen out of the inn stable and galloped home.

With his heartbeat thundering in his ears, he burst into the soler. She lay there, death still, with a perfect little baby in her arms. She could have been asleep, but for her colour, blue white and so cold. He saw the blood. All her life blood, soaked onto the chaise longue and pooled on the floor. He touched the child, not so cold, but also lifeless. His sorrow, remorse and love burst into a thunderous roar, followed by an avalanche of tears. He had killed her, as if by his own hand. Looking around the soler, he found her gardening apron, with its pretty pockets full of seeds and fastened with little pearl buttons. Lifting her and the child away from the blood stained blanket and chaise longue, he covered them with it. He ran to their bedroom, pulling off the counterpane of Welsh wool, a wedding gift from Henry and Rebecca, and wrapped them in it before carrying them downstairs. He laid them gently on the floor in the sitting room. Closing the door, he headed for the cellar and a bottle of brandy and began drinking it, sitting in her favourite chair in the kitchen, until the alcohol took away the pain and put him to sleep.

Jane awoke in a cold sweat hearing Sarah's screams in her sleep. Both she and James had been uneasy about Sarah, but this confirmed her fears. At first light she pulled on her coat and hurried up to the farm. James knew his mother too well to dismiss this premonition, and leaving Mary in her care, set off immediately on his horse for Chester. At a slow hand gallop he rode, for maximum speed without overtiring the horse. He was glad to have the warmth of Sarah's Kendal green coat, as the air was chilly, but was grateful that there was no snow.

It was almost dark when he arrived at Col d'Arbres, with both himself and the horse weary. There were no lights in the house, but Copenhagen was in the paddock and whinnied excitedly. James turned his tired bay mare in with Copenhagen, who happily trotted to her side, pleased to be reunited with his old acquaintance. Warily, James entered the kitchen, and in the gloom, saw Joseph slumped in a chair. He woke with James' touch, dropping the almost empty brandy bottle to the floor with a splintering crash. James lit the lamps, while his son-in-law stared at the flames with blank eyes.

"Where is Sarah?" Where is my daughter?" James demanded. "Gone," was the simple reply. James shook his shoulders, "Gone, you drunken lout, gone where? What have you done to her?" He said no words, just nodded towards the sitting room. James opened the door, to see the shape of a body wrapped in the wool counterpane. Lifting the cloth he saw his dear daughter's dark curls. Tears filled his eyes at the pitiful sight of her lips, once so rosy and red, now blue in death, and a child. A little baby, with fair hair like his own dear wife Mary's, but also cold and lifeless. He turned just in time to see the great iron poker coming towards his head. Joseph hit him again and again, but the first blow killed him. "No one must know my shame," he said over and over until he was sure there was no movement from his father-in-law.

Next morning he began to dig in the clearing of the woods. Maurice watched silently from up a tree, full of a strange fear that he did not understand. He dug for two days, a deep hole. "No interference from foxes," he thought. Through a numb alcoholic haze he dragged the bodies into the woods and buried them in the place where Sarah had once been so happy. With some dried bracken, he covered the disturbed earth, so that no one would know, but Maurice knew. Joseph returned to the cold kitchen, with its unlit range, and brought from his cellar a bottle of whisky and another bottle of brandy. Sitting on Sarah's rocking chair, he began to drink again. Despite the alcohol, reality began to return to his mind. Sadness crowded in as he remembered how he had missed her in Westmorland, and how he had sworn never to leave her again. "I am sorry, Sarah," he wept aloud to the empty kitchen, "I left you when you needed me, I left you to die." He continued to drink, now starting on the bottle of Scotch whisky, "I love you Sarah. I will never leave you again. Please come back to me. I will stay here to wait for you, and make you see how sorry I am. If only I had been there instead of John Clegg. If only Maurice had chased that rabbit under my horse. It should have been me, on Copenhagen coming around that bend in the road, then none of this would have happened". He rocked in her favourite chair, and drank the whisky until he could feel nothing anymore. The alcohol and the cold stopped his heart, allowing him to die a painless death, that he knew he did not deserve.

Maurice sat on Sarah's unmarked grave in the woods. All night he sat there, looking up at the full moon. At dawn he raised himself to his full height, and gave a heartrending yowl. Then, with his decision made, he walked purposefully off into the countryside.

Chapter Twenty Six

Part Three - The New Beginning

ANNIE - 1946

The year's shortest day, December 1946, seemed to Joyce to be the longest day of her life. She had been in labour now for four hours, but had been in a bad mood for a lot longer than that. Most of this hormone induced bad humour was directed at her husband Alex.

The weather was terrible, snowing heavily and oh so cold, but the day had gone like any other Saturday in their bakery and shop. Between them, with the help of Lottie, an older woman from next door, and her lodger Dennis, who was on the dole, but worked for Alex on the sly as he called it, they made bread and baked cakes. Saturday was always a busy day, and no-one, not even Joyce made any allowance for her pregnancy.

Joyce looked forward to Saturday evenings, and for the last two months they had settled into a pleasant routine. They spent the evening by themselves, in front of the fire, listening to the wireless, and Joyce made a special cold tea. Today she looked forward to cold roast beef, which they would eat with apricot jam, salad, some of that morning's Hovis bread, which she would cut thinly, but butter thickly, a jar of Lottie's pickled onions and a lovely trifle, made with jam swiss roll, soaked in Alex's expensive sherry, and topped with thick cream. This was real trifle, not like the insipid feeble things they sold in the shop, and Joyce much looked forward to it, thinking of how her mother would have scolded her for not having a hot meal on such a cold day.

Her mother lived in Yorkshire, and was a real Yorkshire lass, full of hospitality, yet they could never see eye to eye on anything. A great believer in good solid food, she could not bear Joyce's picky eating. "You are so thin," she would moan, "Look at your bones, our neighbours will think I don't feed you." Now, since Joyce lived in Chester, she escaped her mother's scolding, other than her letters telling her to eat for two. "If you carry on the way you usually do, you will end up with a weak and sickly baby," she warned.

Eat for two had become a joke between Joyce and Alex, as she had developed a passion for chocolate eclairs, and devoured them two by two. Indeed now she had a huge appetite, with Alex accusing her of eating the profits, as she consumed their pasties, pies and doughnuts.

An hour before closing time, Joyce noticed a slight discomfort, which as the baby was not due for another two weeks, she chose to dismiss as wind. She was taken aback just as they locked up, by a tremendous gush, as her waters broke. Then there was nothing. Alex turned as white as the snow falling outside, but Joyce wanted to ignore it, determined to enjoy the meal as planned. She felt so angry. Why was he panicking? It was her body this baby had to come out of, not his. She snapped at him, "Goodness knows what horrors I am going to have to face. I am staying for the meal!"

Alex couldn't eat a bite, but Joyce calmly munched through a vast amount of cold beef, pickles and trifle. The more panicky he became, the more irritable she felt. "I am not going before I have a bath," she announced, and banned him from the bathroom, while she sat soaking in the hot water. After what seemed to Alex like an eternity, he had never felt so relieved when eventually she was dressed and ready to go.

This was not to be any ordinary hospital birth. Alex, as always, insisted on the best, and had booked her into a private nursing home, where she was to be attended by her own dear old Dr. Hastings. Alex snatched up the car keys, as if he could not wait to get her out of the flat, so she dawdled about, fussing over the contents of her case, just to annoy him. Eventually he ushered her out with irritating haste into the car.

It was bitterly cold, but the heater of the car was beginning to take the chill away. For some reason, just as Alex sat in the driving seat, the engine stopped, and refused to start again. Unreasonably, and out of character, she teased him nastily. "Stupid car, your pride and joy. You think you are so big driving around in this thing, and now at the most important time, it's let you down."

She was right, he was proud of the car. He had bought it from an old retired colonel. It had spent the war, jacked up on bricks and covered with tarpaulins in a barn. A Riley Victor, made before 1938, when Riley sold out to Morris. One of the last real Rileys, lovely coachwork and delightful handling, with four doors, good leg room and stability, as the engine was mounted further forward. A wonderful vehicle, but now it just would not start again, and Alex, who for all his acquired talents, was no mechanic, and unable to do anything about it.

Dashing back up the steps to the flat, he found the keys of the old Morris bread van, and endured Joyce's sarcastic comments as she squeezed into the cold van with uncomfortable seats. "A fine start in life this baby is getting," she whined as the trusty old van made its way through the snow.

The matron at the nursing home greeted them with exasperating cheerfulness, firing Joyce's annoyance. She spoke to Alex as if Joyce was incapable of having any thoughts of her own. "You can stay here dear," she said to him, pointing to the waiting room. "Or if you wish you can go home, and we will telephone you with the news. Mother will be just fine with us." Joyce exploded, "Mother, I am not a mother yet. I have a name, and a brain, and we are paying you for this, so have a care!"

She saw with disgust, Alex shrink into his chair in the waiting room, so she turned as flightily as was possible for a woman in her condition, and followed the subdued matron. Being called Mother was to be the least of her problems. A starchy nurse took over from the fat matron, saying. "Now can we take a nice bath?" Joyce retorted, "You can if you like, but do I look like a person who would come here without taking a bath first?"

Worse was to come, they gave her a glass of castor oil and orange juice to drink. At first she refused, "It will hasten the labour and make it easier," the nurse insisted, so she drank the foul stuff. It was not long before it mixed with the pickled onions and trifle eaten earlier, and Joyce was violently sick, which was an unfortunate experience for someone in Joyce's frame of mind. "Satisfied now?" she snapped, "I should have stayed at home." Next came the razor and Joyce was totally unprepared for all this. "I must shave your pubic hair," the nurse said in a matter of fact way. Joyce was horrified, "What? Why? That's horrible, I won't let you, and that's that!" The nurse patiently explained the reasons of hygiene, and eventually Joyce felt for the sake of the child she had better give in. Although, how having such hair left in place could be so dangerous to a new born baby was a mystery. She felt it must be some sort of hospital propaganda. The last straw came with the enema. "No," she screamed when she realised what the nurse intended to do with the rubber hose and jug of soapy water. "If you even try, I will take that hose and wrap it round your neck!" She did not insist, but installed Joyce into a bed that was cold and too high, making her wear a stupid cotton gown, which was ridiculously short and fastened down the back, saying that her own pretty nighties were for later.

She sat stupidly in that bed for two hours before the pains began. A young man, he looked to Joyce younger than Alex, came to see her. "This is Dr. Jones," the matron smiled, "he will be attending you, as Dr. Hastings is at a wedding." It was all so very embarrassing, this handsome young man poking about her, so much so that her anger gave way to tears after he left. She looked up at the white ceiling, tears streaming. "What the hell is Alex doing, while all this torture is going on? Drinking tea and reading magazines, I shouldn't wonder."

Four hours into labour, the pains changed, and there was the young Dr. Jones again, but the pain was so bad, she was past caring. "Push now, my dear," he kept saying, but she did not know what he meant, her body was running away with her, with a will of its own. Then there was a horrible splitting sensation of pain, and a strange cry along with Joyce's screams.

Annie was born. She had lived on this earth before, but as it should be in such cases, she had no conscious past memories.

As if in a dream, pain, anger and hostility gone, Joyce looked at her beautiful daughter. Pale skin, chubby cheeks, little pink rosebud mouth, and dark curls stuck wet to her head. "Annie," she whispered, "I am going to call you Annie."

Dr. Jones smiled, "I can see that you are pleased with this young lady. A good size she is too, and such an easy labour and delivery, with no stitches. Wonderful! We will call your husband in now." Suddenly brought back to the real world she snapped. "No, I want to do my hair and put something decent on, he's not seeing me like this." The doctor seemingly used to such hormonal tantrums, shrugged, "Very well nurse will see to you, and I will tell your husband the good news."

Somehow she was washed, and dressed in her expensive pink nightdress and bedjacket. She brushed her hair and insisted on having her lipstick. The result was worth it, she looked as pretty as a picture, with Annie in her arms. Alex came in sheepishly, with a huge bunch of flowers, produced from heaven knows where. She had meant to tell him, all about the pain, the indignity, the fact that they said it had been an easy labour, and if that was easy, she was never going through it again, as to her it was sheer hell. She was going to try to make him suffer some of the pain, after all, he had got her pregnant, so why should he just sit back while she was going through such torture.

All these thoughts vanished as she looked at him. He looked so pale, young and vulnerable, just as he was when they first met, and she loved him more than ever. It had been through his brother Thomas that they met. Thomas was a year older than Alexander, and was the clever one of the family. He was attending Liverpool University just before the war, studying Archaeology, where he met Joyce, who had come from Yorkshire, with ambitions of becoming a teacher. They became friends, but when she was introduced to his younger brother, there had been some kind of instant magic between Alex and Joyce, as if they were made for each other.

That was in 1938. Alex could have not been more opposite to Thomas. Thomas was studious, but rebellious, always looking for an argument for the fun of the debate, whereas, Alex was shy, but easy going and full of fun. Joyce felt that his father treated Alex unfairly, always berating him for spending his wages, and wasting his life. Yet it was Alex, who along with the paid help, Sally and John, did most of the work in the bakery, always helped in the shop, and often did deliveries as well.

There had been a terrible row when he bought his motorbike. He saved without telling his parents, and took the train with Joyce to the Earls Court Show. It was unbelievable; there were hoards of people around the Velocette stand, but clutching the willing Joyce by the hand, he pushed his way through, and there it was.

A Velocette KTT Racer, Mark VIII. Wheel rims of high tensile steel, cone hubs in magnesium alloy. Mudguard pad, air filled, and rear springing oleopneumatic. He paid cash for the wonderful monster, £120. His father went crazy, calling him an irresponsible, good for nothing wastrel, which was most unfair, and his mother, who usually said very little, wept loudly, sobbing that her son had bought a death trap for himself, without a thought for his family.

The bike transformed their lives. He would visit Joyce after work in Liverpool, returning late to his parent's vexation, but he never once let them down. Always on time at the bakery when it was his turn on early shift, never did he say that he was too tired to do deliveries. Joyce and Alex loved to dance, and since the arrival of the bike, they had won several competitions. Joyce made herself beautiful dresses, copying the actresses on the cinema, and they would go to dance halls on the bike, with her outfit packed in a waterproof bag. They nurtured a secret dream of dancing together for a living, another Fred and Ginger they dreamt. Their hopes were all dashed. On the way back to Liverpool one night, the bike skidded on the wet road and crashed into an oncoming car. The cherished machine was wrecked, a complete write off. Joyce was kept in hospital overnight, with slight concussion, but Alex was in for a month with a horrifyingly smashed leg, which despite the valiant efforts of the surgeons, left him lame for life.

Joyce threw her wonderful dancing dream out of the window, realising then, just how much she loved Alex, and when he came out of hospital, they became engaged. His father promised that when they were married they could have the flat over the shop, so the future looked good after all. "How quickly things can change," she thought at the time.

Chapter Twenty Seven

Alex hadn't known what to expect as he entered Joyce's private room in the nursing home. What a relief it was to see her sitting up in bed all pretty and smiling. "You O.K.?" he asked, sounding just like Norris, their American friend from Burtonwoood Air Base. He laid the flowers on the bed and kissed her, relishing the taste of her lipstick, which she always wore when she felt good, and it made him smile. "Oh you clever girl, isn't she a beautiful baby? The doctor told me that you have called her Annie, are you sure that's what you want?" Ann had been his mother's name, which made Joyce's choice most poignant. "She has your mother's curls, what choice do we have?" she laughed, breaking his sad train of thought. "I am sorry I was so horrible to you about the car, I don't know what got into me." "Forget it love," he whispered as he kissed her again and brought a chair over to the bedside. Joyce saw the familiar flicker of pain, as he bent his lame leg to sit down. No one else would know, he never complained, but she understood how the old injury was affected by the cold weather, and had she been at home she would have rubbed it with wintergreen, and made him sit by the fire with his feet up.

He took Annie in his arms for the first time and looked lovingly at his wife. "She is so small and perfect. It was worth waiting for peace. Now we have a big, safe new world for her. We are so lucky." Joyce gently stroked the baby's hair. "She is not so small you know, 9 lbs, that is quite a size, it must have been all those vitamins and cod liver oil." "What about the chocolate eclairs, and doughnuts? if she eats as many as you have lately, we will make no profit in the shop at all," he joked. "You are right about my mother's curls, she would have been so proud, a grandchild named after her, and Dad, a little girl in the family, he would have been thrilled."

Alex's father had proved to be a tower of strength and a shrewd businessman, on the outbreak of the war. No one could believe it was happening. Neville Chamberlain had gone to visit Hitler in Munich during September 1938, when Alex was still in hospital with his broken leg. Chamberlain returned triumphantly, reassuring the country that there was no danger of war. "Peace in our time," he had said. How wrong he was!

By May 1939 Alex's father had quietly bought, from various sources, hoards of tea, coffee, sugar, condensed milk and what seemed to Alex to be a ridiculous amount of best Spanish sherry, and Scotch whisky. All this was stashed in hiding places at his house, under beds, under the stairs, in wardrobes, and in the box room of the flat over the shop. Conscription started, and they began to realise that even women were to be called up. His father advised them to get married. They took his advice, then Joyce left university, and although not fully trained, got herself a teaching job at the local school part time, she also began working in the bakery with Alex. Alex could not be called up because of his leg, and now Joyce had a reserved occupation they could stay together. Not only that, the cunning old man also gained an extra pair of hands for the business and he needed her as it turned out. His other staff, Sally and John, clung together in fright. The next thing anyone knew, they married without any fuss at the registry office, and signed up to work at a munitions factory in Birmingham. "We are not going to be parted," they explained, "If we work there we won't get called up, and if we get killed at least we will be together."

Their move proved to be very productive for Alex's father. They kept in touch and sometimes came to visit. It turned out that they made many black market connections, and if money was available they could provide almost anything. Alex's parents would regularly take their suitcase on the train, a sweet little old couple, going to visit their 'dear friends' in Birmingham. The case always came back packed with whatever was available, on one visit, straining the old man's back, as it contained almost half a jointed pig. With this source of goods and his precious hoard, he was making a fortune. They returned from Birmingham, always with tales of horror. Sally and John had almost been shot, just missed by a strafe of bullets from a low flying German plane. There were tales of broken glass, bodies, fires and awful destruction, but the work in the factory went on, and they always did their shifts together. Often their hands, and even their faces and hair were stained yellow with cordite, and sometimes they were desperately tired after spending the night in the Anderson shelter at the back of their tiny house. They had little faith in the thing, called after John Anderson, the Home Secretary. It was just an igloo of corrugated sheets, buried down a hole in the garden, with a concrete floor, and two feet of earth on top, but it was better than risking the house falling onto them in a raid. Unlike Chester, a city of shopkeepers, with no worthwhile interest to the enemy, and just somewhere on the way to Liverpool, suffering the odd stray bomb, Birmingham was a prime target. Night after night, John and Sally sat cuddling in their shelter, with Sally knitting socks for the troops. She became so good, that she could knit them in the dark, even the turn of the heel.

They used to say in those days, that if a bomb had your name on it, it would get you wherever you were. Alex's parents went to Birmingham, once too often. On the way home, with their heavy case, the train was bombed. There was nothing to find of them, no bodies left to identify, no formal funeral as a last farewell, Alex and Thomas were shattered. Joyce arranged a service at the church, but they all stood there in disbelief, as if in a waking nightmare, and it did not help at all.

Thomas was stationed in Scotland by then. He had been allowed to stay on at university until he took his interim examinations, provided that he attended a special military training school one day a week. After the examinations, he was to be sent into the infantry, but amazingly he refused to go. He argued himself into an interview in

London, where he told them in no uncertain terms, that with his education, he was not acting as cannon fodder for anyone. They found him a non-dangerous position in Scotland, doing land surveys, and he settled down there to sit out the war.

With the sudden death of their parents, Alex was now left with all the responsibility of the business and his father's financial affairs. Thomas wanted none of it, and shot back off to Scotland as soon as he could, telling his brother that he would have their parents' house, and that Alex was welcome to the business.

Alex needed to change overnight. He had to lose his innocent, happy go lucky ways, and become a sharp and wily businessman. Inexperienced as he was, he adapted well with Joyce at his side. They were shocked as they sorted out his father's money. There was far more than anyone could have imagined, so they quietly opened two building society accounts, and split the money equally between themselves and Thomas.

Alex went a step further with the black market activities, and became a bigger wheeler-dealer than his father. He was never short of eggs for the bakery, and somehow the authorities never knew, even though his shop sold the best cakes for miles around. Dried egg just did not have the same results, making Alex's products superior. Thanks to their American friends at the air base, Joyce was never short of silk underwear and nylon stockings. Never did she have to stoop so low as to paint her legs with gravy browning, and make false stocking seams with eyebrow pencil.

Alex ruled the bakery with an iron fist. He produced delicious Christmas cakes by using gravy browning and white sugar, instead of the traditional brown sugar. Once when there was a shortage of cooking fat, he went out, bought jars of petroleum jelly, and they used that for the pastry instead, producing wonderful vanilla slices! There was no nonsense about a baker's dozen with Alex. "That came from when bakers were flogged if a loaf was of short weight, so forget it, everything is weighed here. We might be in a war, but this is the twentieth century, not the sixteenth, a dozen is twelve from now on." "St Wilfred help us!" exclaimed Lottie, who was working in the bakery by then. "St who?" he barked at her. "St Wilfred, patron saint of bakers," she explained, crossing herself. Out of patience, he threw up his hands and left her to Joyce. He never knew whether that woman was serious or not.

With Alex's new found business sense, he and Joyce rode out the war successfully. Thomas was not so fortunate. Nicely settled in Scotland, he met Lucy, the girl of his dreams, and married her with what Joyce felt was indecent haste. Out of the blue came orders for his transfer, and this time his protests fell on deaf ears. He did not even know where he was going, but he and Lucy hugged each other full of fear. He had been inoculated against malaria and yellow fever, and you didn't need that if you were staying in good old Blighty.

He had never felt so sick as they took off in the Dacota. It was an oppressive flight, with all the windows blacked out, and not a safe route, they were going to Gibraltar. There they re-fueled and were given the news that they were headed for the Azores. "The Azores," he wailed. "There is nothing there, it's just a poxy string of three islands belonging to Portugal, in the middle of the Atlantic. What good will we be there?" This earned him a black look from his sergeant. "For Christ's sake man, shut up or I'll put you on a charge. If you want to worry about something, just think on, we have just enough fuel to get us to the airstrip. If we don't make it first time, we will all be shark bait." This statement had the desired affect, it was quiet for the remainder of the journey, except for the droning of the engine, mixing with the silent prayers of the men.

They unconsciously held their breath as they landed. A bumpy landing but as least they were safe. Not as safe as they thought. When the doors of the aircraft opened, they were greeted by a crowd of hostile natives, brandishing anything they could find as weapons, generally giving the impression to Thomas that they had no right to land there. Just as the situation was becoming critical, a dusty Jeep drove up, scattering the mob. Whoever the official was, he commanded some respect, and a way was cleared, albeit with some fractious mutterings.

It turned out that they had every right to be there. Winston Churchill had dug out an old treaty made with Portugal. It stated that if England was ever in dire need of help, that Portugal was obligated to give assistance. They could just see Winston's joy at finding that, and could imagine him saying. "Well we are in dire need now, so we will have the Azores!"

Thomas and company had been sent to oversee the building of runways on the islands, giving 'hop' distance to the allied planes. U-boats were devastating the shipping, as no planes could fly far enough to defend them. Now it was different, and from the Azores they almost wiped out the U-boat Atlantic patrol.

Conditions were bad, as the islands were not equipped for so many men. Their inoculations gave good protection against malaria and yellow fever, but polio was rife. Men dropped like flies from polio. There was no defence against it, and no cure. Everyone lived in fear, as they saw fit, strong colleagues taken by the merciless disease, and the best most of them could hope for was life in an iron lung. In an attempt to kill such germs, all personnel were ordered to immerse themselves in the salt water of the ocean, every morning, leaving it to dry onto their skin. Raw sewage from all the islands was pumped into that very water, carrying the polio virus, which no salt could kill, making the situation worse, but of course no one realised.

Because of the health hazard, the government made it a rule that no one must stay there longer than eighteen months. Unfortunately, a replacement for Thomas could not be found. He had proved to be too knowledgeable and efficient for his own good. Somehow he survived, thin and hair turned grey, but he, who as a child had always been the sickly one, came though it all without as much as a sore throat, although not getting back home to Lucy until the end of the war.

Now this was all behind them, there should never again be war, baby Annie, and Rory, Thomas's child of six months, had all the world to grow in.

Chapter Twenty Eight

Joyce spent ten restless days in the nursing home, being allowed out for New Year's eve. Her delight at being home was shattered by the surprise arrival of her mother. She had so looked forward to spending time alone with Alex and Annie, that the sight of her mother almost made her weep. It was not that Joyce did not love her, but she felt sure that she would interfere, and that is exactly what she did.

Mistaking her daughter's weepy greeting for depression, she set to work to remedy the situation. "Everyone feels depressed after giving birth," she announced cheerfully, refusing to believe Joyce when she told her how happy she was. By the time the week of her visit was over, Joyce really was depressed.

Her mother arrived with a case full of beautifully knitted baby clothes all in pink. Joyce was thrilled and amazed. "However did you manage to knit all these pretty little coats, dresses and bonnets so quickly?" The gift was tarnished by the explanation. Her mother was always brutally honest. "I call a spade a spade, and I always speak the truth," she often boasted. She had knitted the clothes a year before, for a wealthy woman in her district. The little garments were delightful, all trimmed with ribbons and lace. Sadly the woman's child had taken ill and died, so she no longer needed the clothes, and Joyce's mother was only too pleased to give them to Annie. Joyce whispered to Alex that night, "Thank goodness Annie is too small to fit any of that knitting. As soon as Mum has gone, I will give the lot to charity." Alex agreed, the story had made his skin crawl, but he failed to support Joyce on the subject of food.

His mother-in-law's ambition in life, seemed to be to feed everyone to bursting point. She cooked the most enormous dinners, and included delicious Yorkshire puddings, filled with gravy at each meal. To follow there was always something equally gluttonous. Apple pie, served with thick custard. Rice pudding, made extra rich by adding a large lump of butter during the cooking, bread and butter pudding made with cream, her menu went on and on. Alex betrayed Joyce by eating every morsel, proving to her mother that she did not feed him properly. Joyce would not each much as she was horrified by her weight and figure. All the chocolate eclairs, and other goodies, enjoyed during the 'eat for two' pregnancy, were still there, now as fat on her stomach and thighs. She swore to herself that as soon as her mother left, she would never eat another cake again. The last straw was when she started on Annie. "She should be breast fed," she scolded, "but as you seem incapable, at least put her onto condensed milk, that National Dried stuff you give her is no good!" If Alex had not been there at the time, Joyce felt she would have thrown her mother out of the door and locked it, but she saw Alex wink and pull a face behind the outspoken woman's back. "She is doing just fine," he said soothingly, firmly removing his daughter from his mother-in-law's arms. "Joyce simply did not want to breast feed, and my little Annie loves her bottle."

They both sighed with relief when she left at the end of the week. She cheerfully waved from the taxi, which would take her to the train, quite oblivious of all the distress she had caused. Joyce immediately went on a diet. She measured her body, and wrote down on a piece of paper, a record of the horrible fat. She put the tape measure and paper into the top drawer of her dressing table. "Next week it will not be as bad," she told herself. Sure enough, the measurements began to drop, but she could still not fit into her pre-Annie clothes. She could not get out either. Other than carrying Annie around the shop, it was too cold to go anywhere with her. Alex was now back at work, and Joyce missed the old togetherness of working side by side.

Norris, their American friend came to visit. He bounced in, bearing not gifts for Annie, but for Joyce. "It's O.K. I have Alex's permission, believe you've got cabin fever!" he told her, as he produced a beautiful cream satin slip, of a tactfully large size, with matching camiknickers and a small bottle of expensive perfume.

"These are for you, AND, Alex," he winked, "There I knew it, a smile, I'm magic you know." "You are a very naughty man," she laughed, "but thank you, these are so lovely, and I am feeling rather frumpy. By the way, what on earth is cabin fever?" "Ha, it's how the old settlers felt, when they were snowed into their cabins and could not get out for weeks, but I am sure it's not that bad, now that your mother has gone. Oh yes, Alex has told me all about the old moose, if you pardon the expression!"

Norris worked wonders. Despite Joyce's protests, he enlisted Lottie to look after Annie, and teased Joyce. "Come on, Lottie has had four children, she must know which end is which." Then he goaded Alex into locking up early, and whisked both his friends off to dinner. Joyce wore the new, large sized, but sexy undies, beneath an ex-maternity dress, belted into some kind of a shape. With a dab of the new perfume, she felt almost herself again. Norris laughed good naturedly at Annie's name. "Haven't you heard of Annie Oakley? Better watch out, you will need to keep the guns locked up. You will be buying a ranch next!" The evening was a great success, Joyce refused to eat dessert, but made up for it with an extra glass of wine. Norris had good news, but it was tinged with sadness, he was going back to America. He was only kept on after the war to organize the shipping back of equipment, and now his mission was complete. Alex could not imagine life without him, and it all came as rather a shock. Not as great a shock as the announcement that he was to be married to the girl he had left behind in Texas. They had known Norris for a long time, and he had many lady friends, with not a mention ever, of a fiancee at home. Nevertheless, here he was, planning his wedding and his future. "The way forward is antiques," he told them. "I am going to import antique British furniture to the States, and make a fortune." This idea was logical, as Norris was crazy about anything

English. He was supposed to have ancestors from Liverpool, and had been thrilled to find himself posted so near his roots. Alex and Joyce secretly thought that all Americans must have roots in Europe somewhere or other, and did not give his claim much credibility. "We could go into business, you find the goods, I'll find the buyers," he enthused, and a seed was sown for the future in Alex's astute mind.

There was a blank and empty space in their lives when he left, but he wrote with regular news. Photographs of his wedding arrived. Bethany, his wife seemed nothing like his former girlfriends. She was small and chubby, with short hair, but a sweet face. A far cry from his long legged, willowy English ladies. Soon news came of a baby on the way, a little girl like Annie, he hoped, but he hadn't told Bethany that, in case she was disappointed. He still talked of the antique business, although by now he was working for his father-in-law, who had something to do with the cotton industry. As time went by, they heard of the birth of baby Melissa, who for some reason they called Missy, and Norris was thrilled.

Annie was growing up in a different world. An England, struggling after the destruction and expense of war. She was a happy, placid baby, soon capturing the hearts of all the customers with her endearing smiles. By the time they got around to organizing the Christening, she was three months old, and already sitting up. Lottie was convinced that she was going to be clever, swearing that she had never seen a baby so forward, whatever that meant.

They invited everyone to the Christening. Thomas and Lucy came down from Scotland with baby Rory to be Godparents, and Lottie made up the third, as she had become something of a grandmother to Annie, much to the annoyance of Joyce's mother. Sally and John came from Birmingham. They had no family yet, and announced that they were thinking of going to live in Australia. Heat and wide open spaces, that is what they wanted. Thomas informed them that the heat in Australia would be terrible, and had they thought about the flies?

Hoards of flies, all the time, he carried on, in his usual over informed way, but Sally and John were used to him, and knowing that he meant well, listened patiently, but took no notice at all. Their minds were made up, they may not be going tomorrow, but Australia was were they were headed, after all what were a few flies and heat, compared to German bombs and cold air raid shelters.

Joyce looked radiant in her new outfit, bought for the occasion. A New Look suit, the latest fashion, with a full bosom and small waist. Despite the dieting, her waist had not returned to its normal size so she bought herself a tight, high waisted girdle and an uplift bra to achieve the fashionable shape. The garments were made from strong lastex and satin, and once inside them, the body was ruthlessly held. She squeezed into these while Alex was not looking, and suffered with a smile, for the whole day, not telling a soul the secret of her good figure. Lottie ironed Alex's shirt and trousers while Joyce dressed. "My, you look smart," she said admiring Joyce's new suit. "Your mother is watching Annie. You had better hurry and take these trousers to Alex or we are going to be late." Joyce took them, beautifully pressed, with neat turn ups. "I wonder why trousers have turn ups," she said absently, half to herself, as she turned to the door. "Because gentlemen turned up the bottom of their trousers on rainy days at the races, and then it became fashion," Lottie replied. "The things she comes out with," Joyce thought, "but I suppose it could be true. Alex thinks she is slightly mad, but we could not do without her. Oh how this girdle pinches!"

It was a long day, but Annie was on her very best behaviour, and charmed everyone. They held the meal at the hotel where they had their wedding, overlooking the river, but this was a much grander affair. Everyone seemed to enjoy themselves, even Joyce's mother, and other than Alex spending too much time 'talking shop', with a business colleague, all went well. Annie went to sleep like a lamb that night, and thanks to a surfeit of champagne, so did her Grandma!

Alex could not believe the sight of Joyce's foundation garments when she took off the suit. "Oh please, get them off, you must be in agony, and I love you as you are, you don't have to do that to yourself." He helped her out of the wretched things and made love to her with the tenderness of true lovers, but he made sure he used a Durex. She was still quite adamant that one baby was enough, she could never go through all that again.

Chapter Twenty Nine

Lottie became invaluable to them, looking after Annie now, while Joyce and Alex ran the business. Lottie's own children were all grown up, so she found great delight in caring for a little girl again. She had moved from Little Budworth in the countryside, to Chester, just before the war, and bought her tiny two bedroomed house, which she said represented her independence. Having Dennis, her lodger, helped with the expenses, and she was better off now than she had ever been in her life. Her daughter, and son-in-law who still lived in the village, could not understand why she insisted on the move to Chester. They did not see her as much as they would have liked, and in fact were rather hurt, but Lottie chose to ignore their feelings.

The truth was that she had decided to make a new life. A life where only she was the most important person in the world. She never tried to explain it, as she felt sure that to anyone else, it would seem silly and selfish, but as last, for the first time, she had no family responsibilities.

At eighteen, she had fallen in love with Roland. He was tall and handsome, but to her father he seemed a worthless lay-about. She was the only daughter. The middle child, amongst five boys. Her father made a living as a cheese maker, employing all the family, including her mother, unless she was about to give birth, which seemed almost every year. So many little babies she carried, without complaint, but so many little souls did not reach full-term, or were still-born. One of Lottie's worst memories was of a still birth. At only twelve years old, she had been with her mother during labour, the midwife saying that she was old enough to know what life was all about. Her periods started that year, and her mother told her that she was a woman now, but she felt like a very frightened little girl. That horrible thing was going to happen to her every month. She was to cut up two old towels, and use them to soak up the blood. They were to be washed and dried in secret, no way must her father or brothers know about it, and it was all her own responsibility. From then on she was given even more to do in the house as well as the cheese factory, and despite her protests was to leave school. When her mother went into labour Lottie felt apprehensively excited. Babies were lovely, she still remembered how her brother Freddy had been when he was little, but she would be expected to help care for this new little one, and it was really something to look forward to. It was a little girl, but blue and lifeless, Lottie was so shocked that she could not even cry. The midwife wrapped the child in a piece of sheet, and her mother said coldly. "There is a box under the bed, Lottie can do it." The little body, which should have been Lottie's sister, was handed to her. "Put it in the box," her mother instructed, "Tie it up and take it to the church warden." That was all she said, Lottie could hardly believe it. She had no idea then, how often this had happened before.

She did not just put the baby in the box. She made a little bed in it first with some old cloth, and picked a bunch of buttercups to put into her sister's tiny hand. Then she walked off to the church, with no one giving a thought to a twelve year old girl's feelings. She did not hand the box to the church warden, but sat on the step by the door of the church, with it on her knee for a long time. He found her, a kindly old man, well used to death and all it's trappings. "Oh, I see you have something for me." "No! It's not just something, it's my baby sister," she sobbed. He took her hand, "Come, bring her in. You see, she has not been baptised, so we cannot officially give her a Christian burial, but this is what we will do. Next time someone is buried, I will put this little box into the coffin. No one will know, but she will be buried then. I do not believe that God would not welcome a little baby into his churchyard, but you must promise not to tell. If you like, I will let you know when it is done, and then when no one is about, you can come and put a flower on the grave for your sister." She nodded, feeling a hundred years old. Over the years, before she left home at nineteen, she was regularly to put little flowers on three different graves, and no one knew, but the church warden and herself.

At nineteen the love between Roland and Lottie had almost reached bursting point. Being a good Catholic girl, she would not dream of having sex before she was married, but it was that intense longing for each other that led to their desperate solution, knowing that her father would never let them wed. Quite by chance, a friend of Roland's mother came to visit. She was in service with a doctor in Scotland, and had not been home for many years. Enchanted by the romance of the young couple, she offered to help. Her doctor was looking for a married couple to work for him, so she asked if Lottie and Roland would like to join her in service. She explained that near the doctor's home was a famous place, where you could be married, without either permission, banns, licence or priest, all you needed were witnesses, and she could easily provide them. So the plan was hatched. With all the money Lottie had saved, they set off on a number of train journeys, without a word to Lottie's parents, to the village of Springfield and the household of Dr. Henry C. Cairn.

The place for the marriage was Gretna Green. It was a legal marriage, but in her father's Catholic eyes, Lottie knew it would be sinful. The wedding was performed over an anvil, and was declared by the blacksmith. Lottie was uneasy about it all, but as Roland was happy, she made no complaint.

The doctor's house was impressive, but their quarters were very cold and sparse. The work was hard, with long hours from morning 'till night. Doctor Cairn's wife was pleased with Lottie, a willing girl, eager to please. Once she asked her to bake a bramble pie, the doctor's favourite. Lottie had never heard of brambles, but she said, "I can make a pie out of anything, you get the brambles, and I will surely make it." She could not believe her eyes when the brambles arrived, they were just blackberries. The doctor's wife had given them a fancy name, and it made Lottie feel very ignorant. Her pastry was excellent, and she baked many a pie from then on, earning praise, but never a penny more, or an extra hour to herself.

Roland on the other hand proved to be a disappointment to both his employer and Lottie. She felt that it was her duty to work even harder to make up for her husband's shortcomings. He was lazy and sulky, constantly complaining about his duties. "I have never heard of anyone wanting polish on the soles of their shoes," he moaned every day. The doctor's shoes were of the finest brown leather, and the polish was to extend to the space between the raised heel and the sole of the shoe. Roland's love making was equally selfish and lazy, leaving Lottie feeling confused and cheated as he rolled over afterwards and slept, without even holding her. This dismal performance in bed did achieve something, Lottie became pregnant. They concealed the fact for the first four months, but the eagle eyed doctor saw the signs. A baby was not part of their agreement the good doctor explained, as he terminated their employment. He turned them out without a thought for their welfare, and felt not a trace of remorse.

Roland got drunk, leaving Lottie on a tide of despair. There was no other way out, but to go home and face her father. They arrived, hungry, footsore and without a penny. Amazingly, he greeted them with joy, so relieved that his only daughter was safe. He frowned at her wedding certificate, and noticing her swollen midriff, insisted on a decent church wedding. No grandchild of his was to born into sin.

Although he did not approve of his son-in-law, the old man was good to him. He provided the young couple with a house, on the understanding that Roland would work in the cheese factory. Roland was as lazy as ever, finding so many ways to avoid any effort, that Lottie found herself working alongside him in the hope that her father would not notice his behaviour, and having to leave the baby with her mother. In no time at all she had become pregnant again, this time feeling tired and weak for the whole nine months, but just relieved to give birth to another healthy strapping son.

Three months later, in the year 1916, Roland went to war, called up to fight for king and country. He was away for two years, enduring the horrors of trench warfare. All the boys of the village went together, but few returned. He was one of the lucky ones.

Lottie could not bear the tension while he as away. With two babies, the worry of Roland's fate, and trying to help her father, she was exhausted, yet could not sleep. So she started to read, she borrowed a book, the only book her mother owned, other than the bible. It was a large volume, a dictionary of phrase and fable. She opened it to find an inscription on the flyleaf. It read 'To Elenor, in gratitude for your kindness'. Who could have given such a book to her mother? It was something which would not ever be remotely useful to her, and had obviously hardly ever been opened, but she knew better than to question anything of her parents, so it remained a mystery. Babies asleep, she began to read it. Set out from A to Z, just as any ordinary dictionary, it contained 1,145 pages, and during the long evenings, she read each one, forgetting any curiosity of the book's origins, and inspired by its contents. So many things she found in that book. Snippits of information filled her head. Another world was opening out to her, and she vowed that one day, when the children were grown and she had more time, she would study and find out even more about those people, places and literature. One day she would be more knowledgeable than Dr. Cairn's wife.

Roland arrived home unexpectedly, save for a few minor scars, physically unscathed, and took up life as before, but he drank every night to try to keep out the nightmares. Flashbacks of the mustard gas, the fumbling panic to pull on the gas masks in time, the sight of those who slipped in the mud and fell before they could put theirs on, and the horrible resulting death, all haunted his nights.

Before she knew it, she was pregnant again, but this time the baby, a girl did not live. "Get the priest," she screamed, "She is breathing, she must be baptised." By the time he had arrived, the child was dead in her arms. Desperately remembering the little boxes put into stranger's coffins, and the tales of unbaptised babies condemned for ever between heaven and hell, she clung to the priest. "I named her myself, I asked God to bless her, surely that is enough?" He thought for a while, and nodded, so baby Martha was given a decent Catholic burial.

Roland did not seem to share her grief, and was at her in bed again in no time. By this time she had begun to resent him, and was terrified to find herself pregnant again so soon. He was becoming more and more idle, but it was to Lottie her father complained. She continued trying to cover up, doing her husband's work as well as her own, hoping to pacify her father, but instead his anger only increased, as he was now becoming concerned about his daughter's health. This time she gave birth to a healthy girl, and was so relieved that at first nothing seemed able to mar her happiness, but she had decided that this child was to be the last.

When Roland came drunk to bed one night, she slapped him. "No, no more, I will have no more children, you will not touch me again!" She ignored his pleas, then his demands for his rights. Next morning he was gone, no note, nothing, but his clothes were missing, and he was never to be seen again, leaving Lottie alone to rear the children.

When she moved to Chester, she became free of all this. Her children now had their own lives, and this was her independence. Looking after Annie was a pleasure, as was working in the shop, but now Lottie could do as she pleased.

Chapter Thirty

Annie spent her first five years happily shared between her parents and Lottie. She had become a sociable little girl through spending many hours in the shop. Lottie marvelled at her intelligence, little as she was she could serve a customer and give change, under the proud guidance of her father. She was always very polite, as they taught her, knowing all the names of the regular customers, and always greeting them with a 'good morning' or 'good afternoon'. She went everywhere with Lottie, delighting in visits to the hairdresser for Lottie's weekly set. They always admired Annie's natural curls and made a big fuss, saving treats and sweets for her on the day of Lottie's appointment. She would sit, watching so carefully all the cutting and rollering, and loved the smells of the shampoos and lotions. Lottie would spend twenty minutes under a dryer, and in that time she would tell Annie a story, with her sitting on her knee, as the fragrant warm air blew around them. By now Annie knew every nursery rhyme by heart, even a couple of tongue twisters and almost every fairy story. Lottie was full of stories. Annie used to think she grew them inside her head, but sometimes they would find a book of one of the stories with wonderful pictures, so she decided that Lottie must have learned some of them, just as she was doing herself.

The library was another favourite visit with Lottie. It had a funny musty smell, not like the hairdresser's shop, and she was expected not to be noisy, but it was equally exciting. Lottie always chose four different books each week for herself. Once Joyce said that Lottie ate books, but Annie, overhearing corrected her, "No Mummy, she always takes them back each week!" Making her parents nearly choke with laughter. There was always a book for Annie, who knew that her Daddy would read to her before she went to sleep at night so she and Lottie chose one carefully every week.

Annie was always good for her father. He had a talent for getting her to sleep, and it was her Daddy she cried for when she recently caught the horrible measles, and needed to stay in bed with the curtains drawn, so that her eyes would not hurt. That week was the only time Alex had been known to neglect the business. He sat with his hot little daughter, and left everything to Joyce and Lottie as if he did not care. He told her stories of Uncle Norris, who she had never met, and who lived in America. He had a little girl too, called Missy, and they wondered together if she had ever caught measles. "She couldn't have more spots than you," he teased, "You are like a little pink leopard. I will take you to see her one day, America is a big exciting place, and just think of the clothes Mummy would have fun buying." He told her all about the motor bike he once had, and how he broke his leg. How he and Mummy had so much fun with Uncle Norris, and that the dressing gown he was wearing was made from Norris's American issue blanket. That made her laugh, but when she looked carefully at it, she thought how clever her mother was to have made it, with pockets and collar and braiding. "American issue blankets were much better than ours," he told her, "Ours were hard and scratchy, but don't tell anyone I said that!" She was almost sad to be better when he went back to work as normal, but because he stayed with her, the measles would always hold special memories for Annie.

Lottie had always said that Annie was a Daddy's girl. Even as a baby, she swore she could sense the pain in her father's leg. On days when it was bad Annie would cry as her mother rubbed the wintergreen liniment onto the old injury, and even now, she would get fractious and weepy at the smell of the stuff.

Being in her fifth year, she was to start school. Alex found a private establishment, run by two elderly ladies. It had an excellent reputation for good manners and education, taking a small number of children in each class, from the age of five to sixteen. Satisfied with their standards for his obviously intelligent daughter, he enrolled her, even though the school was on the other side of town. Lottie was to take and collect her on the bus, and this daily bus ride was the one thing which Annie was looking forward to.

Such journeys were always fun with Lottie. Sometimes in the summer, she would take Annie to the seaside, on the bus and then the train. All the way Lottie would point out interesting things and places. Once she was on the train, Annie knew all the names of the little stations, and would become excited as each one went by, bringing them nearer to the sea and the sand. All they needed for a perfect day, was a picnic, and a bucket and spade. Annie would be happy all day, but she needed to wear a sun bonnet and to be rubbed with nasty, sticky lotion, because her fair skin burned so easily. Alex would meet them in the car at the station on their return, and smile proudly at his tired little daughter, with her hair sticking in damp curls to her forehead.

Lottie assured her that school would be good, but Annie had doubts. Joyce took her to Densons, the school outfitters, and ruthlessly bought everything required on the list provided for new pupils. The stiff collars of the blouses were uncomfortable and the tie was not only restricting, but a complete mystery to Annie. The final insult was that she was expected to wear baggy navy blue knickers. Annie had always worn little sea island cotton underwear, and she made up her mind to lose those nasty blue things as soon as possible. Within a month, they had gone, stuffed down the back of Annie's dressing table, and Joyce could not be bothered to go back for more, in fact she did not find them until years later!

School at first was not too bad. Annie felt homesick, and was so glad to see Lottie at the end of the day, but she soon found out that her classmates felt just the same. They did drawing and painting, which Annie excelled at, and found herself praised by the teacher. They sang songs, and listened to stories, some of which Annie already knew, so that made her feel better, and every day they sang the alphabet and counted up to twenty. This was new to some of the children, but Annie had already done it all with Lottie, and to her it was fun.

The trouble started later on in the year, when they began reading lessons. Annie simply could not understand what the teacher was saying, so she was given the story book to take home. This immediately solved the problem for innocently Alex read the book to her every night, and she soon knew it word for word. The teacher stopped frowning and smiled at the results, as Annie read her page for the day, but she could not read, she only remembered which words went with each picture on the page. She got away with it, no one but Annie knew.

By the second year, when she was almost seven, she had it all off to a fine art. Writing was easy, she just copied whatever her friend wrote. She became so good at it that she could even copy from someone sitting opposite her, even though it was upside down, but all this had no meaning, she was just becoming an accomplished little cheat. At the end of the school year, during a hot July, Annie was faced with a problem. Her first exams were to be held that week. What could she do? She knew that at such times, children were seated separately. She would not be able to read the questions, or copy the answers from anyone else and her guilty secret would be revealed. She began to feel hot and sick at the thought of it all, but she could tell no one.

An unexpected event saved her. With no warning, her parents were surprised by a visitor. He walked into the shop as if he had never been away, it was Norris. To the scandalous delight of one of the regular customers, old Mrs. Holloway, he swooped around the counter and swept Joyce up into his arms. "My, what happened to all that weight you put on? You've got the figure of a teenager."

Alex was delighted to see their old friend again, and laughed as Joyce pointed out that the waistlines of both men had expanded over the years. Annie instinctively knew who he was as soon as she saw him, and made friends immediately. "Wow, Alex," he whistled as she came into the shop after school. "Can this be Annie? With that lovely pale skin, brown eyes, rosy lips and dark hair, she is a regular little Snow White." She was fascinated by his accent and boisterous friendly ways. "Where did she get those looks Joyce? You and Alex haven't got a curl on your heads." "She takes after Alex's mother," she explained, "There will be no need for any permanent waving for our Annie." "Funny how things turn out," he laughed, "Missy is the image of my Pop." "Love the uniform," he carried on, admiring the hated blazer and matching navy socks, so hot in the summer but yet so cold in the winter." What's this?" he asked, retrieving her straw boater from her hand behind her back. He popped it on top of her unruly curls. "What a picture, wish I could get my Missy into clothes like this. It's all jeans and tee shirts for her, most unladylike." Annie had never owned a pair of jeans, but the idea sounded most appealing, how she envied Missy.

Norris caused such excitement that Annie was allowed to stay home from school for the ten days of his visit. After reassuring her father that as it was the end of term, she would not be missing anything, he said that it would be a good idea to stay home, and of course she did not mention anything about the dreaded examinations.

Norris had returned to England on a mission. It was his first step on the road to his career in antiques, and if successful, his father promised to fund him for the future. His parents had sold their house and business on the East coast, and were going to move to Florida. His mother's arthritis was worse and they felt that the all year round Florida sunshine would be just what she needed in their retirement. Joyce and Alex could not imagine all year round sunshine, but it did sound wonderful. Norris was full of surprises. They had no idea that he had been born in that part of America. He had always referred to Texas as home, but it turned out that he just went to college there, met Bethany and stayed.

His parents were retiring in style. They had bought a large house, and inspired by his son's time spent in England, were determined to furnish it, according to their ancestry, with antique British furniture. Joyce thought to herself, "These Americans and their imaginary ancestors, they are obsessed," but she said nothing, not wishing to hurt their good friend's feelings.

The deed was done with amazing speed. Lottie took over from Alex while the two men sought out everything on Norris' father's list, including Lottie's mother's mirror backed sideboard, which put her a tidy sum in the bank. Now she could buy a car, if only she could pluck up the nerve to learn to drive. Norris' military shipping experience stood him in good stead, and the furniture was shipped off on its way, the day before he set off back to The States, leaving Alex and Joyce behind with great plans for the future.

Chapter Thirty One

During the next few years, Annie's educational problems went from bad to worse. Able only to read a limited number of words by recognition, she felt as if her web of deceit was catching up with her. What was that saying of Lottie's? "Oh what a tangled web, we weave, when we start to deceive." "No wonder I can't stand spiders," Annie thought.

At school they scolded her and gave her detention, which added to her misery, but did not do anything to help the situation. "Annie is constantly wool gathering," the headmistress pompously complained to her father. Neither father or daughter knew the meaning of this, but Lottie explained that it meant wasting time, and not keeping your mind on your work. Annie was lazy, Annie was naughty, Annie's general attitude was not good, her reports complained. Because she had always been bright, intelligent and quick to learn, her parents accepted the school's opinions of their daughter, and began to agree. Annie almost believed them herself. Yes, she would waste time, she would do anything to get away from the lessons. They said she was naughty, so that became a good shield to hide behind. They thought her unfinished work was due to laziness, but in fact she struggled desperately to achieve the little she did manage to produce. It never occurred to Annie that all this was not her fault, she was full of guilt and often felt as if she was drowning in despair. Neither did the school realise that she had a genuine problem, to them if you had the intelligence, you worked, and learned, and that was that. Her only relief was the art class. Here she did excel, painting and sketching came naturally to her, but it was often pointed out that she should put as much effort into her other subjects.

At the age of twelve she was caught out. Up until then she had always managed to avoid examinations by developing a succession of illnesses. She could cause herself a rash and temperature at the thought, with the very word exams, making her break out into a sweat, but her parents were too busy to pay much attention to it all, and usually treated these little ailments with an aspirin crushed up in jam, and a few days in bed. Annie, who could copy anything, had only needed one sick note from her mother, and from then on skilfully made counterfeit copies for any occasion.

It was the English teacher, Miss Roberts, who found her out. She sprung an unexpected test on the class, making them change seats, with the dire warning. "No copying, I want to see just how much of this you have learned." Annie unfortunately was moved to sit by an obnoxious boy, who kept his arm around his work, so that she could not see to cheat. Actually she knew the work quite well. The poetry by Lord Tennyson moved her, and William Blake's, The Tiger was her favourite. She had a talent for poetry, Lottie only needed to read it out a couple of times, and Annie would know it by heart. This was different, how could she read the question paper? The words danced about the page and she began to feel giddy and sick. Throwing her pen across the desk, she stood up and fled, leaving Miss Roberts and her fellow classmates behind in stunned amazement.

With the whole object of the test now ruined, the furious teacher left the class and found Annie sitting in the girl's cloakroom hugging her knees. She hoisted her to her feet, "How dare you disrupt my class. I have never had the misfortune to teach such a naughty and lazy girl as you. You will go to the headmistress and tell her what you have done, and at break you will report to me!"

Once, years ago her father had put a rat trap in the yard at the back of the bakery. The unhygienic creature was caught, but Annie got to it first. The poor animal trapped in the small cage was terrified and alone, so she let it out. The memory of it all staying vividly, as it was the only time in her life that Alex had really been angry with her.

Now Annie felt just like that rat, but for her there was no one to come to the rescue. The headmistress was particularly cruel, telling her how her behaviour was letting down her parents, that she was a disgrace to the school and a bad example to the junior pupils. All the time Annie tried not to listen, and kept saying silently to herself, "I will not cry, I will not cry."

She was to sit in solitary disgrace in the hall until break time, and as the rest of the pupils poured out of the classrooms, towards the playground, to laugh, talk, and eat their crisps and biscuits, Annie made her way back to the classroom to face Miss Roberts. "Sit down," she ordered. "If you have composed yourself, you can now do the test." Annie sat staring at the paper, picking out a few words, but it made no sense, and was for her, impossible. The dam wall holding back her tears cracked, and they silently fell, rolling down her hot cheeks, drip, drip onto the paper. Miss Roberts relented slightly, "What on earth is wrong? You recited both these poems for me the other day, and you put more feeling into it than anyone else in the class. Just answer the questions." The tears turned to sobs.

"I can't, I can't read it!"

"You can't read it? Good gracious child, what do you mean?"

"I just can't, look, the words jump about, and I don't know what the questions are."

"If you are having trouble with your eyesight, why did you not say so? Too vain to want to wear spectacles, I suppose, I shall send a letter to your parents. You must have your eyes tested at once."

She said all this in a reprimanding way, sighing with exasperation, but to Annie it was a miraculous explanation. Perhaps that was the problem. Perhaps with a pair of glasses, she would be able to read, just like anyone else. The thought was so comforting that she did not care how ugly the glasses might be, and she happily took the letter home to her mother.

Joyce was irritated by the letter, "How can there be anything wrong with your eyesight? Look at all the drawings you do, they are all over the flat, and what about that tablecloth you are embroidering with Lottie. That is beautiful work, how can you do all that if you can't see properly? That teacher is mad."

Nevertheless, off Annie went to visit the optician with her mother, but Joyce was not in a good mood. She and Alex were always so very busy. They were now running an antique export business, with Norris as transatlantic partner, as well as the bakery and shop. Although very successful, Joyce felt that these days, they scarcely had a minute to themselves, and she considered this latest episode with Annie to be a waste of precious time.

Annie obeyed all the optician's instructions, read the individual letters with both eyes and did not blink as he blew air into them and peered at her with a small light. Then she sat outside with her mother, confidently awaiting the results, and examining the racks of frames, of all different shapes and sizes. It came as a great shock and disappointment, when he appeared in the waiting room, and pronounced her eyesight to be perfect.

All the way home, and without sympathy, Joyce interrogated Annie about her problems at school. She sat her down in the kitchen with the newspaper, telling her to read it. She was horrified at the result. Her daughter could hardly read at all. As a mother she was upset, but as an ex-teacher she was incensed. "You are twelve years old, with a reading age of five," she shouted, "How can you have been at school for six years, and not learned to read?"

It caused a terrible rumpus at school, as to Annie's shame, her inability to read was proved. The headmistress and her elderly sister talked at length to Alex and Joyce, both attributing the problem to an unexplained laziness on Annie's part. So she was accorded no sympathy, instead in disgrace, she was to give up her beloved art lessons, and use the time instead for extra coaching. The headmistress knew of a retired gentleman, an English teacher, who would be willing to take Annie on at his home, every Wednesday afternoon, for the sum of ten shillings a week. Alex sighed at the extra expense and agreed.

Annie was proving to be an expensive child this year, not only in her education and the fact that she had grown out of all her clothes at an alarming rate. Her baby teeth, which had been like a set of perfect tiny pearls, had been replaced by large unruly crooked monsters, which seemed unable to fit into her mouth. Their family dentist, kind old Mr. Barber, confided to Alex that Annie's problems were beyond his skills, and recommended a visit to a private orthodontist in Liverpool.

Sorry that Annie seemed to be going through such an unhappy time of late, Alex decided to make a day of the trip to Liverpool. She was so pleased to be having a whole day with her father to herself, that she almost forgot the fear of the unknown orthodontist. They drove to Birkenhead, and left the car in the car park, as they took the ferry across the river Mersey. The water was not at all like the sea in Rhyl, where she had so often played with Lottie, it looked dirty and oily in comparison, but the ferry boat ride was just as exciting as somehow she knew it was going to be. Annie said how big the boat was, but Alex promised to take her to see some real ships on the Liverpool docks. The size of those ships was overpowering. He told her how his friends, Sally and John had sailed to Australia on a boat such as these, and how it had only cost them ten pounds each, to go all that way, because Australia needed people to work there. The ten pound passage, it was called then, too bad if you did not like it and wanted to come back, it was a one way ticket! Annie did not remember Sally or John, but they always sent a card at Christmas, with photographs of themselves and the children on their sheep farm, together with a long and happy letter for her parents.

They left the docks to visit the large department stores. Alex was enjoying all this and thought what a treat it was to see his daughter relaxed and happy. In Lewis' Junior Miss department, Annie noticed a lovely outfit. A simple straight skirted, black and white polka dot dress, and a pair of black patent shoes with tiny heels. To her surprise her father waved her towards an assistant. "Try it on," he said, and she, who had grown too tall and felt gawky, looked transformed. The dress flattered her childish figure, and the shoes made her feel so grown up. Oh what a happy day, the outfit was bought, and off they went to an elegant restaurant for lunch.

All too soon, it was four o'clock and they arrived at the orthodontist's surgery. Their own dentist, Mr. Barber, held his surgery in a room of his house. It was always warm and friendly, with his cheery wife acting as nurse. After every visit she would take the children to see her parrot, which lived, quite unchained on a perch in their sitting room. An obliging old bird, he was well used to generations of children, who would all feed him with a grape or a biscuit. He would allow them to stroke him and even sometimes talk, saying, "Mr. Barber wants his tea," over and over again.

This orthodontist's surgery could not have been more different, cold formal and clinical. Annie's mouth was x-rayed and examined in every detail. Impressions of her teeth were taken by pressing pink waxy stuff into her mouth, so horrible that she was nearly sick. After a while, Alex was called in, and Mr. Jarvis explained his plan of campaign. He spoke to her father as if Annie was not there, making her feel small and silly. He talked of two years treatment, with regular visits to him, of an appliance to be worn in her mouth, and of four extractions, all to cost a horrendous sum of money. Annie shrank further into the chair, thinking that surely he could not be thinking of taking out four of her teeth. They might be crooked, but Mr. Barber said how strong and healthy they were, she had never even needed a filling. As if in a nightmare, she heard her father agreeing to the treatment. "You are worth it my love," he smiled at her, "I can not have my pretty Annie growing up with crooked teeth."

All you will feel are a few tiny pin pricks," Mr. Jarvis assured her as he approached with what seemed to be a huge hypodermic needle. There were actually eight 'pin pricks', two for each tooth, and each was extremely painful. Annie, trying not to make a fuss, knowing the amount of money her father was spending on all this, clenched her fists and kept her screams silent in her head, as the horrible man wrestled four large double teeth from her mouth.

Almost fainting, she hardly remembered going home. Her mouth was so numb that she was almost choked, and the taste of the blood made her stomach churn. She could not speak, but clung to her father all the way, and still held onto his hand as she slept after he put her to bed like a baby. "If Daddy leaves me, I will die," she thought as she fell asleep, and he seemed to know, because he sat up with her all night.

Chapter Thirty Two

Annie's self confidence had reached almost zero. A month after the extraction of her teeth, she was fitted with the appliance. A brace it was called, and was a torturous device. A plate fitted onto the roof of her mouth, holding wires which went over her teeth. The wires put pressure onto the teeth, and each week her mother was instructed to tighten these wires with a tiny key. It was not just uncomfortable and embarrassing, but also very painful for each of the first few days after tightening, and she was severely warned that it must only be taken out to be cleaned. Such drastic orthodontic treatment was rare on this side of the Atlantic in those days, so Annie now felt herself labelled the girl who was taller than all the boys, who always got poor marks, who needed extra coaching, and who had something in her mouth, worse than false teeth.

This low self esteem was not helped by the tactless comments of relations. On one of her rare visits from Yorkshire, her Grandma looked critically at Annie and scolded her mother. "Goodness me, the girl must not be eating properly, I have seen better legs on a sparrow! Joyce, however did you let her get so tall and thin?" Annie hoped that her mother would come to her defence, and say as Lottie often did, that she was naturally slender, and that in later life would never have to worry about her figure, but she said nothing, just allowing the old woman to rant on, and leaving Annie with more emotional bruises.

A summer trip to Scotland with her mother for a week's holiday visiting Uncle Thomas, made Annie even more withdrawn. "Whatever happened to Annie?" he asked without thinking of her feelings. Uncle Thomas and his family lived such a different life, that Annie felt green with envy. He had four children, one boy and three girls, who bounded happily about, never seemingly reprimanded for anything. The children were allowed to slouch about in shorts and scruffy tee shirts, wore old leather sandals without any socks, and seemed to have no fear of anything. They climbed trees, drove their father's car when he was not looking, and swam every day in the loch, wearing just their underclothes. Annie had never done any of those things, and they felt that she was dull and boring.

Not only did Uncle Thomas have a house full of children, he also had pets. Joyce had never liked animals, so she kept well out of the way, but Annie was enchanted. There were two dogs, a cat with kittens, a tortoise and more white rabbits than Annie could imagine ever existed. When she asked her aunt how many there were exactly, she just laughed. "We can'a keep track of them. When there seem too many, we give a box full to the pet shop. You can take one home, and a kitten if you like." Annie's delight was soon quashed, as her mother would not hear of the offer, and they returned to Chester empty handed, except for her sketches of the little creatures on a plain pad of writing paper, which she showed to no one.

The extra coaching on Wednesday afternoons was only a moderate success. Mr. Mealing was very frail and elderly, but although he had once been a headmaster, he never raised his voice to Annie. Unfortunately, he did not appreciate her problems either, feeling that a remedial class was the best place for such pupils, where they would not slow down their more worthy colleagues. He did, however teach her to recite the alphabet phonetically, and showed her how to sound out words, which did help a little. He plodded on each week, doubting her intelligence, as she split words into two or joined two words together in illogical way, and sighed at her persistent carelessness as she spelt words with the letters in the wrong order. Every week he gave her a list of spellings to learn, not understanding, that a list of any sort was a recipe for disaster for Annie, and that she could not remember them from one week to the next. This lack of success went on week after week, until one day when she was fourteen, her life began to change.

She arrived for her lesson at Mr. Mealing's house, only to be told by the lady next door that he had gone away. She peered at Annie over the fence, recognising her as one of his pupils. "He has gone to live with his daughter in Cornwall, the house is to be sold."

Annie was free, now she could go back to the art lessons that she so badly missed, but then she thought about it more carefully. If she told the school or her parents about this, they would just send her to someone else. She would have to find somewhere to go on Wednesday afternoons. Her first thought was the river. She and Lottie had spent many happy hours there, walking over the wobbly suspension bridge and feeding the swans, but she might be seen. Often she and Lottie had met neighbours or customers there, also enjoying the idyllic setting. No, it would be have to be somewhere safe, where no one would find her, or this wonderful freedom would be lost.

A passing bus gave her the answer. The Zoo, it said on the front, so onto that bus she went. It was only two stops further than Mr. Mealing's house, and with the remaining money intended for his lesson, she paid the entrance fee and bought an ice cream. She felt rather conspicuous in her school uniform, but a visit to the ladies toilets, soon remedied that. Next week she would bring her jeans, but for now, she ruthlessly stuffed her blazer and hat into her bag, along with her tie, which constantly looked worse for wear. That tie had always been a bother to Annie. Repeatedly her mother lost patience trying to teach her how to tie the thing, but Annie had beaten it in the end. She just never untied it, slipping it over her head instead, and no one was any the wiser.

Visits to the Zoo became much looked forward to weekly events. It was a wonderful place to hide. Who would ever find her there, but not only that, it felt so peaceful and comforting. She took her sketch book and sat for hours, watching and drawing the animals. Gradually she became aware of the signs on the enclosures, and muddled and struggled to read them. Once when she could make no sense of the information above the tigers, she asked a passing keeper. "I have broken my glasses," she lied, "can't see a thing without them." She was fascinated, as he told her all about the animals, and about India. In this way she learned more than she ever had at school. Now she saw and remembered the countries on the maps of the world above the enclosures, and soon learned about their climate and vegetation as well as their animals. She found that often, parties of visitors toured the Zoo with a guide, so she would tag along with them, unnoticed, and gleefully listen to all the information. It was so good to be anonymous, uncriticised and free. To Annie, the Zoo was her refuge, the safest place in the world. Here it did not matter that she could hardly read, that she was too tall, her skin unfashionably pale and her hair unfashionably curly, instead of lank and straight. No one noticed that her mouth was full of metal, and that she could not use the lovely pale lipstick which everyone else wore, because her lips were so red, it ended up looking like clotted cream on a jam scone. There she could sit and smile at the animals, and they would just patiently look back at her. "I am looking at you, looking at me," she often whispered to them.

Changes were happening in her home life too. With the money left by his father and the success of his various business ventures, Alex decided that they were now in a position to devote all their time to the antique business. He kept the shop, but sold the goodwill of the breadround to an enthusiastic rival. The whole ground floor, shop and bakery, now became a showroom. Lottie of course was not left out, and soon adapted to selling antiques, just as she had to selling cakes. The sweet smell of the bakery was now replaced by the musty smell of old furniture and wax polish, and Alex and Joyce were in business. Norris sent regular lists of required pieces, and with that and the trade from the shop, they were soon doing well. He had moved from Texas to Florida, so that he could be near his parents. "Pop is getting on in years, but he is still nineteen in the head, so I am happier being able to keep an eye on him for Mom," he explained in his latest letter, and urged Alex to take a trip over to visit.

When he was sure that Lottie could manage the shop, with Dennis, who was still strong as an ox, to help with anything heavy, he arranged a family trip to America. Annie could not believe it. Spain was the furthest any of her schoolmates had ever been, and they were in the minority, but being Annie she did not want to boast, so when they finished school for the summer break, she did not even tell them. She hugged the secret to herself, a whole summer in Florida, with sunshine beaches and palm trees.

Before they left, there was another visit to the dreaded orthodontist. This time he filed her front teeth. "To make them more rounded and feminine," he explained. It was a horrible sensation, and Annie felt it right down to her toes. He seemed pleased with the progress and told Joyce that the treatment was almost over. Now he need not see Annie for another twelve months, but she must continue to wear the appliance during that time, to make sure that the roots of the teeth set in place. Joyce felt that this trip to Liverpool was a nuisance, in the middle of all the preparations, and was sure that they would never be ready, but eventually, Lottie shooed them out of the door, with promises to do absolutely everything, and they drove to Heathrow, to take the flight to New York.

With just two hours stop over, and no chance to see the famous 'Big Apple', they were off again, this time bound for Florida. Joyce was convinced she had been travelling for days, and felt grubby and crushed, in her pink linen suit, which had looked so immaculate at the start of the journey. Annie, on the other hand thrived. In the excitement, she forgot her self consciousness, and nosed about the plane to such an extent, that she was invited to meet the captain in the cockpit. She had fought against the skirt and blouse bought by her mother, and for once won, travelling in her beloved Levi's, and what she considered a sophisticated black tee shirt. Half way through the transatlantic flight, she fell asleep, with her head against the window, reminding her father of baby Annie, and making him wonder where the years had gone to. She also slept for most of the journey from New York, and on their arrival, by the time Norris met them at the airport, Annie was bouncing with life, and her mother was dead on her feet.

The moment they spotted Norris waving enthusiastically as he approached, Annie's self consciousness returned, and she cringed, waiting for his comments on her looks. He unashamedly hugged her parents, and gently held Annie at arm's length by her shoulders. "My, my, Snow White has grown up into a beautiful princess. Alex, how are we going to cope? With Annie and Missy, the boys will be lining up at the door!" He looked at Annie as if he really meant what he said. "Got a hug for uncle Norris then?" he asked, hugging her anyway, and did not seem to notice her amazement as he whisked the family out to the car.

This was another world, and Annie fell in love with Florida, as if a magic spell wrapped around her, an enchantment which would always pull her back there like a magnet. The very air was hot, humidity they called it, and Annie, who Lottie often called a little cold fish, because she felt the cold more than most, loved it and said so. Norris laughed at that, "Wait until I see Lottie, teasing you like that. She knows quite well fish don't feel the cold, they are cold blooded."

As they entered the car it was surprisingly cool. "Air conditioning," Norris explained, "warm outside, cool inside, over here." The car itself was large and comfortable, making the vehicles at home seem like toys, and of course everyone drove on the wrong side of the road. Annie settled down to absorb the scenery as her parents chatted. The whole place seemed to be coloured in varied pastel shades of pink, green and blue, even the tall shining buildings. Palm trees lined the wide roads, and these roads turned into causeways, running effortlessly over sparkling water, of yet more blue and green.

Annie gasped as they reached Norris' beach house. It was a huge sprawling place, with large windows and verandas, but incredibly it was just as its name suggested, right in front of the beach. This was a place of dreams. The beach was long and white, and the shimmering ocean stretched into the distance for ever.

As they stepped out of the car, a girl of about Annie's age ran down the steps to them. Annie recognised Missy at once, from years of photographs sent at Christmas by Norris and Bethany, but those had always been in black and white, she had no idea that Missy was a redhead. Not exactly red, her short hair, falling to the left in a part, and curling up at the nape of her neck in a most becoming way, was a light sandy colour, shining in the sun, and her eyes were the same vivid blue as the sky.

Chapter Thirty Three

Annie felt very dowdy in comparison, as Missy rushed to greet them in her little pink and green shorts and halter neck top. A picture of happiness and enviable self confidence, she swooped upon Annie. "Hi, you must be Annie. Gee, I love your hair, just got to grow mine too. Come on, we're bunking together, let's go and unpack." "Slow down Missy," her father laughed, "you two have got all summer to get to know each other, now where is Mom?" Missy took Annie's hand and continued to drag her and her case away up the steps of the house. "Still teaching, the kid was late. She will be another ten minutes yet, we will be down by then."

Bunking with Missy meant sleeping in her beautiful bedroom, decorated all in white and shades of green and blue, just like the ocean it overlooked. It was a huge room. "Like everything else in America," Annie thought. There were two pretty beds and a row of built-in wardrobes, which Missy called closets. Amazingly, Missy had her own bathroom, leading off from her bedroom, and her very own T.V. Despite her boisterous ways, Annie liked Missy straight away, just as she had taken to her father when he came to stay all those years ago when she was only seven. She was shocked when Missy smiled, revealing a mouth full of metal fittings, one covering every tooth and all connected by wires. She tried not to look, but Missy missed nothing. "Braces," she explained cheerfully, "to straighten my teeth." She was intrigued by Annie's appliance, and was envious that it could be removed. "That's just great, I wish I could have one of those. Daryl has braces too, and we clash when we kiss!" She went on to explain that Daryl was her boyfriend, and showed her the friendship ring he had bought for her. "He will be here tomorrow morning, so after his lesson with Mom, we can all spend the day together." "Is he handicapped?" Annie asked shyly, thinking it would be better to find out so that she would not make a fool of herself. Her mother had told her that Bethany was a teacher, and that she taught children with special needs from an office in their home. Missy was busy unpacking Annie's case, and admiring the strappy black patent shoes, which she had persuaded her mother to buy in a weak moment.

"Handicapped? Gee whiz no! Mom teaches dyslexics, and Daryl is really clever, wait until you hear him play the guitar. He's fantastic and he has never had a lesson." "What are dyslexics?" Annie asked, intrigued, but trying not to appear rude.

"Don't ask Mom that, she has been studying dyslexia for years, and will talk about it for hours if you give her the chance. Dyslexic people just think differently. They are usually very clever, and Mom says that lots of inventors have been dyslexic. Trouble is, most of them can't read. They can't understand conventional teaching when it comes to reading. They spell words in odd ways, and write things back to front. Daryl is sixteen and he had gone all through school until last year without being able to read, and no one knew. He just copied everyone else's work, he is good at that, a real young forger, Mom teases him. When he came up against anything he could not cope with, he would spill something, or cause a fight, anything to cover up the problem. By the time Mom met him last year, his parents were desperate, and half the time he was skipping school."

While she was telling Annie all this, she was still busy burrowing into the case. "We will have to get you some more swimsuits and shorts. Until then we can go through all my stuff, and you can borrow what you like." As she looked up, she stopped chattering, horrified to see her new friend with tears rolling down her face. "Annie, what's wrong?" "It's me," she sobbed, "What you said about Daryl, that is me too, I can hardly read, I am always in trouble, I cheat to get by, and in school they punish me for being naughty and lazy, but I am not, I just can't do the work. Are you sure there are really other people in the world like me?" In her typically unreserved way, Missy put her arms around Annie. "Hey, don't take on, you've come to the right place. Mom will sort you out, and you can compare school horror stories with Daryl tomorrow." She produced a tissue, for her tears. A Kleenex, she called it, making Annie smile at the many different words used in America. Everything seemed so easy with Missy, and her confidence was contagious. Perhaps her Mom could solve Annie's problems after all. She washed her face in Missy's bathroom, and took her hand with a shy smile as they went downstairs.

Bethany's photographs had not done her justice. She was small and fairly chubby, with hair as dark as Norris' worn in a short bob, but she was so sweet gentle and charming, that Alex and Joyce understood immediately why he loved her so much. She too, was dressed in pretty shorts, but with a baggy tee shirt on top in varying shades of pink. She patted her stomach, "I am not usually so fat. Alex wanted to wait until you came, before we told you. We are going to have another baby, after all this time. It must be the ocean breezes, we had given up hope years ago." Joyce smiled, but shuddered inside, thinking how awful it would be to go through all that again. Ocean breezes or not, she would make sure Alex used a Durex, as he always had, and did not get any silly ideas.

There was much celebrating over dinner, talk of the vacation, as they called it, of the new baby, and of course the business. It was late before Missy told Bethany about Annie's problems. When they were all in bed, she came to their room, and sat by Annie. "Missy tells me that you could do with some help. I will explain it to your parents and I am sure we can sort it out. I will see you both in the morning, don't let my Missy chat all night!"

At breakfast, Bethany explained about dyslexia to Annie's horrified parents, but with her charming reassurance, the idea that Annie may have a real learning disability seemed less threatening. Before Daryl arrived, Bethany and Annie did some tests. Annie who was almost fifteen turned out to have a reading age of a seven year old, but an

I.Q. of 145. "I can see your problems, love," Bethany sympathised, "but we can put it right. You have a high intelligence score and that has been your only help so far. Dyslexia is how you are, not a disease. You will be able to read, but sometimes some words will still puzzle you. The same with spelling, I will show you special ways to spell, but you will always spell the odd word in your own little way. There is nothing wrong with that, it will be just your way, and believe me no one will bother about it. Oh, here comes Daryl, shall we all meet up after his lesson for lunch?"

Daryl came up with Missy skipping at his side. He was just as easy to like, with a big happy smile. No one here seemed to notice braces on teeth, Missy said that most kids had them, so Annie no longer felt a freak. Daryl, being older, was taller than both girls, and was as good looking as Missy had claimed, with his short blonde hair. He had brought his guitar, which was slung over his shoulder, completing Missy's romantic image, but it was his shoes that Annie noticed most. He was dressed casually, in jeans, and a white shirt with no sleeves, but the laces of his sneakers, clumsily tied and half undone endeared him to Annie more than anything. "Just like me with the school tie, I bet he has struggled for years with those laces," she thought to herself.

After his lesson, Bethany served lunch on the shady veranda outside the kitchen. Hot dogs, large long buns with strange delicious sausages and fried onions inside. Annie had never tasted anything like them, but she declined the relish and mustard which Missy and Daryl piled onto theirs. "Stick around Annie," Daryl laughed as she pulled a face after having a lick of theirs. "We will soon turn you into an all American girl." The food was finished off with an amazing milk shake, full of ice cream and crushed strawberries, so thick that Annie could hardly suck it through the extra wide straw. She could not help thinking of Grandma in Yorkshire, and how she would approve of all the food she had eaten.

When both sets of parents had settled in the shade with a bottle of wine, Missy urged Annie to tell Daryl all about her school problems. Suddenly it did not matter any more, and Annie's years of guilt fell away, as all three laughed at the universal problems caused by dyslexia, and of the cunning methods the two of them had devised to survive in a world which did not understand.

"Missy's Mom says that we dyslexics often have extra talents you know," Daryl informed Annie without a trace of conceit. "I can play the guitar, what about you?" Annie frowned, she had never been any good at anything, but Missy and Daryl would not believe her. "Well the only thing I can do is draw," she admitted despondently. She was shocked at their enthusiasm, everyone at home had thought her sketching to be a waste of time, and that she should pay more attention to her other studies, so as the years went by, she had kept her work to herself. "Oooo, what do you draw?" they asked together, displaying an unconscious closeness which was in the future always going to keep them together, and making Annie realise for the first time, that she had a perception of some things in people as well as animals, which others missed.

"Animals mostly, I love to sketch animals," she told them, and then went on to confess about her secret stolen Wednesday afternoons at the Zoo. Daryl was full of admiration, "Wow, and you got away with that? I was always skipping school and getting caught, I could have done with you as an accomplice."

All this praise was given in a way which would not make Missy jealous. Annie could see how tactful he was, and how much he cared for her. Here were two people who did not think of her as odd, or even ugly, and Annie began to relax and blossom on that very first day.

With parents now dozing in the shade, happily lulled by the warmth, wine and the sound of the ocean, Daryl suggested that they should go over to his house so they could be noisy. "Danny should be back by now. He was going for a driving lesson after lunch," he told them and Missy explained to Annie that Danny and his Mom lived with Daryl's parents, and that Danny was his best friend. The boy's fathers had trained together, until they qualified as doctors. Michael, Danny's father had then returned to work in Jamaica, which was still a British colony then. They lost touch with each other over the years, until Michael turned up at the very hospital where his old friend was employed as a consultant. The reunion was marred by the fact that he was at the hospital as a patient, a patient with terminal cancer. Being a doctor himself Michael knew that his time was limited, so he sold his house and practice in Jamaica and came to Florida as a last ditch hope. He brought his wife and youngest son Danny with him, but left his two older sons with their grandmother as they were settled in good jobs. He had lasted for nine months as they battled to save him, with the most cruel of treatments. The hospital fees had gone well beyond the insurance and when he died, Danny and his mother Molly were almost left penniless after the funeral. By this time both families had become great friends and Daryl's parents insisted that Molly and her son moved in with them. Now they lived in a small apartment created on the top floor of the house to give them a feeling of security and privacy, but in fact they all lived together as one happy family, Molly and Daryl's mother Paula, feeling more like sisters.

    Determined not to dwell on the sad event of Danny's father's death, and the memories of the days of tears shed with their friend, Missy picked out two swimsuits, and with Annie wearing her shady hat, they set off for Daryl's house, which was just a block away. "Whatever a block is," Annie thought happily as she walked along in the delicious heat.

Chapter Thirty Four

Daryl's house seemed as impressive as Missy's, and also overlooked the ocean. As they reached the front door, it flew open, and a boy of about sixteen carrying a huge cardboard box, staggered out from it, almost colliding with Annie. Daryl took hold of the box to steady it, and introduced his friend. "Danny, this is Annie, she has come all the way from England, and you nearly squashed her!" No one had thought to tell her that Danny was black. She felt so ashamed and embarrassed. What must they think of her, surely the surprise must have shown on her face, but Danny defused the situation. He smiled his easy sincere smile, showing perfect teeth, no braces needed for Danny. "Hey Annie, you are as white as I am black! Come inside and we will find you some of Paula's special suncream, or you will be burnt as pink as a lobster in this sun. He put down the box, and ushered a very relieved Annie into the house with his friends.

Paula and Molly were sitting at the table in the kitchen. "Hi, Moms," the boys said together in a well practised chorus, which always made the two women laugh. They were cutting pole beans, ready for the evening meal, and listening to 'Elvis is Back' on the record player. "Ha, cocktail hour," Daryl said winking at his friends, "The Moms are drinking coke, but I bet there's some Barcardi in it."

Paula blushed, "Daryl, stop embarrassing us, and introduce this young lady. He introduced Annie, explaining in almost one breath, that she was Missy's friend from England and she was dyslexic too. Annie shook hands politely, feeling rather shy. Daryl rambled on with the introductions, "and this is Molly, Danny's Mom, the best cook in the world!"

Molly shook Annie's hand, but held on to it gently, looking into her eyes. "Well now Annie, sit down with us, I can feel something very special about you." "Oh, look out, Mom's got fortune telling coming on," Danny joked, but his mother took no notice, and kept Annie's hand in hers. "I don't tell fortunes, that rascal of mine knows that, but I can tell you about yourself, if you would like me to." Annie nodded, feeling a strange warmth towards this stunningly beautiful woman, who had lost the man she loved in such a cruel way.

"When were you born?"

"21st December. 1946."

"Do you know at what time? I feel it would have been late in the day."

"Yes, it was after dinner, Dad often tells the story of how Mum insisted on eating the evening meal, and how he could not wait to get her to hospital, because he would have fainted if she had given birth to me at home."

The conversation was drawing Annie and Molly together. Annie almost forgot where she was, as Molly carried on, still holding her hand.

"Capricorn, then, southern gate of the sun, the winter solstice. It is the most southern limit of the sun's course in the ecliptic. This is an important date to be born. You have talents which you must not waste, although they might be late developing, and this is nothing to do with your dyslexia. You have been given a special life, and you must use it to the full, but even more important, there is a choice you will have to make. Two men, you must choose the right one, or your special chance will be lost."

"How will I know who to choose?"

"You will know in your heart, but don't worry, you shall have help. Someone is waiting to help you, someone full of sadness, but who will be there for you."

She said no more, and the room was silent except for the whir and click of the Elvis L.P. which had long finished playing, and no one had thought to switch off. Molly broke the hypnotic magic, "Well then, enough of this, who wants a peanut butter and jelly sandwich?"

As if suddenly shaken back to the real world, Annie pulled a face. "You really eat peanuts, butter and jelly on a sandwich?" She could not think of a more revolting mixture, but they proved her wrong. It was not peanuts, but a spread called peanut butter, and it was not jelly either, it was a lovely tangy seedless jam, and the combination on a sandwich was delicious.

After much rummaging in the drawers of the kitchen, Daryl found a large tube of sun cream for Annie. "Scuba divers in The Keys use this, it won't even come off in the water. You can only buy it down there, so don't lose it. We want you tanned not burnt after swimming in the ocean."

Annie had not thought that they actually meant to swim in the ocean, and she felt rather silly. "I can't swim," she admitted, cringing at the anticipated reaction. "O.K. We will use the pool instead, and teach you," Danny said as if it was the most simple thing in the world. This house had the advantage of a pool at the back, just right for swimming lessons, as it was only four feet deep. Annie went along with the idea, but would rather have sat on the beach with her feet in the water. She feebly explained about her previous efforts to swim, first with the school, when one term, the headmistress hired the City Baths for an hour every week. Annie had been glad that the arrangements did not last, and that the school gave up on the idea. Her other attempts had been ridiculed by her Scottish cousins, who swam like Loch Ness Monsters, and called her a cissy for the whole time she stayed with them. This story delayed matters more, as none of her three new friends had ever heard of Loch Ness, or its monster and demanded to be told the legend, which fired the excitement of both boys, causing them to swear that one day they would go and capture it.

Eventually, they had Annie standing in the pool, with the water reaching to her armpits. Danny explained that his father had taught him to swim. "Everyone can swim, that's what dad told me. The trouble is that we think we can't. You know how frogs swim, well you just do the same, it will work, I promise." Annie felt sick, "The water will go up my nose," she whimpered, "it always does." A snorkel and mask was produced from somewhere, and fitted with that, Annie had no choice. By some miracle it worked, she did not sink, and by the end of the afternoon, she was swimming unaided.

Molly and Paula were full of praise for her when they came out with a tray of Coca-Cola and chocolate chip cookies, which were biscuits with yummy bits of chocolate baked into them, still warm from the oven. "She might stay to the side like Rikki-Tikki-Tavi's musk rat, but she can now swim," Danny boasted for her. Annie looked at her new friend with astonishment.

"Who on earth is Rikki-Tikki-Tavi?" They sat cross legged on the floor with the cookies and drinks, and Missy begged Danny to tell the story. "He is a great story teller. Go on Danny, please." "No, we will drag Daryl to the library tomorrow and get the book, and I will read it instead, there are some great pictures in that book. You will like it, Annie, if you like to draw animals. It is about a mongoose and how he went to live with a family in India. The story might sound childish, but it isn't. The musk rat was his friend, called Chuchandra, and he never went into the middle of the room, always kept to the walls, just like you in the pool Annie!"

Anne was almost too tired to speak as they ate dinner that night. Lovely food, fried chicken in some sort of savoury breadcrumbs, chips which they called fries, and a huge salad, followed by a chocolate cream pie, which her virtuous mother declined to eat, giving the two girls the opportunity to eat Joyce's portion as well as their own.

Alex was very proud that Annie had at last learned to swim, and secretly hoped that the lessons arranged for her to have each morning with Bethany, would be equally successful, but said nothing about it, not wishing to spoil his precious daughter's happiness.

She slept almost as her head touched the pillow, just about managing to say, goodnight, to Missy, but it was a restless troubled sleep. She had gone to bed with the thought of Bethany's 'dyslexic lessons' in the back of her mind, and as she slept, she felt the old familiar stomach turning fear of school, and her inability to understand. In her dreams, she saw herself at a large table, with a pen in her hand, trying to write something. The woman with her was angry. "Just do it," she scolded, I think you are being naughty." The frustration was too much to bear, and she saw herself throw the pen across the kitchen, as she fled through the door. Then she was crying and she was sitting by a stream, with her feet in the water. After a while, Missy was there too as she thought that Annie was hurt. "What on earth is wrong," she asked, trying to stop the tears from flowing. Annie told her about the horrible school work, but Missy did not understand. "Is that all, I thought something awful had happened to you," she said relieved. Anger rose through Annie's tears and she glared into her friend's vivid blue eyes. "Even you don't understand," she shouted, but then she saw that it was not Missy. Tears blurred her vision, and the air filled with the choking smell of wintergreen liniment, which her father used for his leg, as she sobbed as if her heart would break.

"Annie, Annie, wake up," Missy pleaded, shaking her friend. She opened her eyes, back to reality, in Missy's beautiful bedroom. "Oh boy, that was quite a nightmare you had. I was about to go to get Mom, I couldn't wake you up. You O.K. now? It was probably caused by all that chocolate cream pie we ate!" Annie smiled weakly, "Guess it was," she agreed, unconsciously picking up Missy's accent, and making her howl with laughter. "We are Americanising you already, let's go down and raid the refrigerator."

So began a lifetime habit, in times of distress. While the rest of the house slept, the two girls ate ice cream, left over chicken and cookies as they sat on the floor of the kitchen. Somehow their friendship had been sealed at the moment they met, and they sat easy in each other's company, giggling and gossiping until first light with the magical sound of the ocean in the background.

Chapter Thirty Five

Even with the meagre amount of sleep, Annie awoke strangely refreshed next morning after the cheerful overnight picnic, which had included orange juice with a generous helping of Norris' vodka in it, but it did not stop the overriding fear as she stepped into Bethany's office. Her chest tightened, as she felt like a fly, just about to enter a spider's web. She shivered, despite the warmth as she sat down. Bethany was sweet, kind and gentle, but now she was a teacher, and Annie felt the old, well known shutters of defence coming down. "I can't, so I won't," her subconscious whispered, "Run, hide, escape," said her mind as she sat in the chair, her pale skin looking ashen, wiping away the first traces of her suntan. Her hands became clammy, and without thinking, she rubbed them on her shorts.

Bethany saw it all. Bethany knew all these things. Feelings which until now, Annie had struggled with alone. First she produced a packet of chewing gum from one of the drawers in her desk, and offered Annie a piece. This was quite unexpected, and Bethany smiled as she could see the mental shutters lifting a little. Next came the sunglasses, "Do you like these?" she asked casually. Almost relieved, but feeling trapped in the web, and expecting to be pounced upon any minute, by something like a great spider from above, Annie nodded. Bethany remained relaxed in her chair, "Try them on." They were very trendy, with dark green lenses and although Annie liked them very much, the anticipation of unpleasant things to come was unbearable. Then she stiffened knowing that Missy's Mom was now turning into a teacher, as from a large folder she produced some sheets of printed pages.

Bethany explained that Annie need not try to read them. "Just look carefully at the lines of words, leave the sunglasses on, and don't worry if you can't understand it." Annie looked the best she could at three of the papers. Some words she could understand, but it made very little sense. "Good," said Bethany, it does not matter at all that you can not read it. Now take off the sunglasses and try again." She began and after a few lines down, the words began to move and the letters jumped about and blurred into each other. She gasped at the realisation. "So the glasses did help you then?" Bethany could not help but smile. "They are not prescription lenses, and we don't know how it works, but they do help a lot of people, and as they help you, they are now yours. Tomorrow we will play some games, so now back you go to Missy, you have plans for this morning don't you?"

Annie could not believe it, for here was someone who really understood. They had been in Bethany's office for an hour, and the time had gone so quickly. As for the magic sunglasses, there was a door opening, ever so slowly, but opening at last for Annie.

Missy, Daryl and Danny were waiting for her, and Daryl gave her a friendly slap on the back. "Bet you thought it would be hell. Did you get the chewing gum? Bethany is great isn't she?" They headed down to catch the bus to the library, which itself came as something of a shock to Annie. She had spent many happy hours browsing with Lottie, in the library at home, but this was so different. The library in Chester was a vast old building, with a huge flight of stone steps inside, and dark musty corners. This was a large flat building, all light and airy, with picture windows and white painted bookcases. "Do you like books Annie?" Daryl asked, with a strange look on his face. She told him how Lottie and her father read to her, and how she knew the stories by heart. Danny butted in, "We couldn't even get Daryl into the library until a few weeks ago. He used to feel that books were a threat, because he couldn't read." Daryl admitted to Annie that he had never read a book by himself, but with these two bookworm friends, he was beginning to try. Danny found The Jungle Book, by Rudyard Kipling, and there inside was the story of Rikki-Tikki-Tavi. Annie felt sorry to see Daryl, so fidgety, and was relieved to see him return to his normal happy disposition, as they left the library, and headed for 'Dunkin' Donuts'. Doughnuts were nothing new to Annie, she had grown up with them, but this shop sold nothing but doughnuts, of seemingly endless varieties. They sat munching the delicious fresh cakes, and Annie found it amusing that the other three thought it so very grown up to be drinking coffee!

The rest of the morning was spent back at Daryl's house, with Danny the storyteller. Missy was right for the book came alive in his hands. Danny did not just read it, he told it with such gestures and expression, that they sat enthralled, like little children. There in the book, were fine illustrations, not just pictures, of all the animals. Wonderful sketches of Rikki-TikkiTavi, Chuchundra, the musk rat, Darzee the taylor bird and Nag and Nagaina, the wicked cobras, with their hoods spread out. Danny told them that only Indian Cobras had the spectical marks on the back of the hood, he had asked at the snake centre when he had been disappointed to see that theirs had none.

Annie was filled with the urge to sketch again, and resolved to ask her father to buy her a plain pad and some pencils, but it would not be today. This evening they were off to visit Missy's grandparents.

"Hi, Pops," Norris shouted to the elderly man, sitting on the porchway of the sprawling wooden house. Missy, forgetting her grown up attitudes, ran like a five year old from the car, into his arms, giving Annie a pang of regret at her lack of such a kindly grandparent.

She almost stared when she was introduced as Missy was exactly like him. His hair was greying, but still had traces of her colour. It parted to the left, and curled up at the nape of his neck, just like hers, and wow, he had the same vivid blue eyes, and instant friendliness as his granddaughter.

Full of smiles, and with Missy still draped around his waist, he welcomed them into the house. "Ruby is in the kitchen, cooking up a storm for tonight. We're really excited to meet you folks from

England." The house was old, wood built, with ceiling fans and polished wooden floors, and the furnishings were just like the contents of Alex's shop. To Joyce, the whole place was a nightmare. "Fancy having to dust and polish all this lot," she thought to herself. She said nothing to Alex as he, after all, was responsible for locating and shipping all of it. Genuine antiques, and Norris' father Jake, obviously loved them all. Proudly he showed them round, until they came to the kitchen, Ruby's domain, white, sparkling and ultra modern.

Ruby made a big fuss, playfully scolding Jake for not telling her that the guests had arrived, and asked the girls to help her with the drinks, while her husband took the others into the garden. "I am a bit stiff these days, and my hands don't grip like they should. It's the arthritis, you see," she explained to Annie, but without making it sound as if she was complaining. "Jake has English ancestors, so he wanted to furnish our retirement home accordingly. He will tell you all about it later." "No doubt," Missy giggled, "it's the family history, passed down through generations, and coming from England, you are sure going to get it!" Annie told Ruby about the special stuff her father used for his leg. "It might help your hands, but it smells horrible. It always makes me want to cry."

The evening was passing quickly, with the girls helping 'Grandma' and admiring her glass collection. All the pieces came from her home town, a little place called Sandwich, and were made by the Boston and Sandwich Glass company. Annie as fascinated by the subtle colours, and Ruby proudly explained that they had been made using a Roman, three part moulding method. She told them how she missed the old town. Sandwich had grown slowly and kept it's original character. The town was built round Shawme Pond, an artificial lake, built to provided power for milling. Jake's folks had lived there for ever, but the climate was better for Ruby in Florida. They were here to stay, no more New England winters for Jake and Ruby. "Besides, now we live near this precious granddaughter of ours, and another little one on the way." "Yes I know, you and Gramps are hoping for a boy. Carry on the family name and all that!" Missy teased.

Over dinner, Jake told the tale, passed from father to son and daughter through his family, of his connections with England, how his great grandfather talked about the story, and how he in turn, had remembered his own great grandfather, the son of the man who had come from Liverpool, England. With all this enthusiasm, for her country, Annie wondered why Jake had never made a visit, but she thought it would not be polite to day so. Jake was enchanted by the royal family. "We watched the coronation on T.V. you know. I felt so sorry for Elizabeth, her father dying while she was on holiday." He spoke as if they were personal friends, "Poor King George."

Without thinking, Annie commented, "He was mad in the end, wasn't he? Poor Farmer George." Joyce looked at her daughter, horrified. "Annie, what are you talking about? Of course the king was not mad. In fact he was a very good and brave man. He wanted to lead the troops on D. Day, but his private secretary, Alan Lascelles stopped him at the last minute." Jake interrupted, "You have just got your history lessons mixed up Annie, you are thinking of George III, he died in 1820, you are 132 years out!" They laughed amicably, but Annie was embarrassed. She did not think she had ever remembered any history from school, and could not imagine why she should have come out with such a silly piece of information. The incident clouded the evening for Annie, although only Missy noticed. They talked it over in bed that night. Missy laughed, "Why worry? If you have got a mine of information in your head, it's got to be useful sometime, and English history is so much more interesting, ours is just boring. Let's sneak down and get a glass of that 'special' orange juice, a slug of vodka will help us sleep!"

The lessons with Bethany went on first thing every morning, no matter what other plans they had for the day. She made everything into games. Spelling tricks, word dominoes, snap, word jigsaws, rhymes and funny songs. It was as if someone had pulled back a great curtain, letting in the light, allowing Annie to understand. Danny was her other teacher. Within a week he had her swimming in the ocean, cheering her on, and at other times they would sit together reading a book, as Missy and Daryl played handball on the beach.

"You should be a teacher," she told him, with your positive attitude, you would be great. Some of the people who have tried to teach me were awful, we need more people like you." The others agreed, but Danny wanted to be a politician. "In the footsteps of our great new president," he said proudly, "He a man for the future, with his beautiful wife and young family. I have followed his progress from a senator, you should have seen his debate with vice president Richard Nixon on T.V. before his election. That is what I want to be into, his New Frontier. Health program and civil rights, I will be there. Annie was taken aback by the fact that here in wonderful, progressive, ultra modern America, people with black skin were prejudiced against, and it made her realise what a sheltered life she had led so far.

The four friends were growing closer each day, going everywhere together. Swimming in the sparkling ocean, adoring the dolphins at the Porpoise School in The Keys, where the animals were part of a family with the humans, and seemed to love each other, and watching in awe at The Snake Centre, as venom was milked from the fearsome creatures. Antidote was provided from here, for all over the world, and Annie felt privileged to be watching such a project.

During all this time she sketched, encouraged by Missy and the boys, until even her father started to take notice of her work. This pleased Annie more than anything, as she had never managed to interest him in it before. Of all the animals she sketched, the racoons were her favourite. Wickedly mischievous creatures, which lifted the roof tiles from people's homes, so that they could make nests inside, and illegally inhabited basements and laundry rooms. She had spotted one behind Bethany's washing machine, its tail poking out from the side, but laughed to herself and said nothing leaving the animal to its wayward devices. Their usual pastime concerned causing havoc with the garbage. Norris had invested in a Racoon-proof garbage pail, but unfortunately no one had informed the animals of its wonderful properties, and they found their way into it. Missy's Grandpa told her of how at their old home, racoons would steal the meat from the plate of their elderly dog, and that eventually they had to feed the poor hound inside the house. Beautiful creatures in Annie's eyes, they were bigger than a cat, with grey fur, a pointed muzzle and black bands across the tail and face. She drew them in roguish positions, adding devastated garbage bins and chewed washing baskets. She even drew a good likeness of Grandpa Jake, after a racoon with his big old gun, and Norris was so taken up with it, that he had it framed and hung in the kitchen.

Towards the end of the four weeks vacation, the real Annie had emerged, like a butterfly from a cocoon. Her hair had grown an inch, now reaching her shoulders, and was allowed to curl naturally in the humid atmosphere, with beautiful results, as she forgot the longing for long straight locks. Her skin was now coloured a light gold, thanks to the special Scuba cream from The Keys, and the sun barrier for lips, which was clear and shiny, added to the natural healthy look. All this was on the outside. The real Annie had begun to understand herself, and thanks to her new friends, even to like herself. The confusing world of education was untangling before her eyes, and now she knew that if there was something she could not understand, it was not her fault at all, for help could be found.

Chapter Thirty Six

There were only three days left before the end of the vacation, and Annie could not bear to think about it. How could she leave this beautiful place, with its sparkling ocean and sunshine, and her new friends, how could she leave them? Missy felt like the sister Annie always wanted. It was only four weeks, but both girls felt as if their friendship had been for ever. Danny bought her a friendship ring, becoming Annie's first boyfriend, and her return to England was about to leave a big aching gap in all their lives.

Alex took his daughter to one side that Monday morning and she was worried. He was wearing his 'business face' and she wondered what could be wrong, but he smiled at her and kissed the top of her forehead, where her hair curled tightest in the heat, as if she were still his baby Annie. "You have made really good progress with Bethany, and you are much happier now, aren't you?" Annie nodded, wondering where all this was leading. "Mum and I are so sorry we did not know how to help you with school before, and we ignored your sketching. We are very proud of your talents, we want you to know that. We have been talking to Norris and making enquiries. Would you like to stay here for the next year, attend school with Missy, and continue your lessons with Bethany? We must go home, but we would phone and write, and next summer we would come over again and all go home together."

Annie's eyes brimmed with tears, filling Alex with alarm as he feared that he had misjudged the situation. The last thing he wanted to do was to make her unhappy. She threw her arms around him, but to his relief there were smiles through the tears. "Oh Daddy, how wonderful of you. I would love to spend a year at school with Missy." Then she was solemn again, "I will miss you and Mom though." Alex smiled and hugged her, thinking how sweet it was that she had called him Daddy, when he had been Dad for years now, and that she had accidentally called her mother Mom!

Although exciting, it was a sad farewell at the airport as Joyce and Alex took off for home, leaving Annie behind. Annie, who in the next year was to become a happy confident young lady, as American as apple pie. She settled into Missy's school, so very different from the Victorian style establishment she had become used to at home. Although almost a year older than her friend, Annie was placed in the same class because of her difficulties, and with Bethany's help, coped with it all, even in those first few weeks.

Half way through the second week of September, just as she was feeling settled, the weather changed. It became dull and windy, with the threat of something called a tropical storm. Missy became subdued with the meteorological change, despite Annie's attempts to cheer her with tales of cold rainy old England.

A hurricane they said. Hurricane watch. Danny told Annie that it only meant that there was a risk of a hurricane, but it had often happened before and hadn't come to anything. All the same, Annie saw that every family in Pantry Pride bought bottles of water, batteries for their radios, tinned food and candles.

Hurricane warning they said. Annie looked at Missy and almost gasped with shock. A hurricane could possibly hit them, it could be heading for Florida, but it was Missy's fear that shocked her. Annie had felt fear, at school, and at the thought of doing exams, but as she looked into her friend's wide blue eyes, it was as if their minds linked for a moment. Terrible fear, as if some demon was coming from the darkened ocean, bringing some awful disaster, nowhere to run, nowhere to hide. Annie shook herself free, "Hey, come on, it can't be so bad. Let's go to see the boys."

Daryl and Danny did not seem bothered at all. Daryl informed them that in The Keys, at times of hurricane, they simply boarded themselves up in their houses and got drunk, but nothing cheered

Missy, not even the piece of Molly's Key Lime pie, which was the best anyone could make with its tangy filling and fluffy top.

Next morning Bethany woke them early, with a glass of juice. The weather was strangely calm, and the colours in the sky were beautiful. "We are going to Grandpa's, so get up now, and just take what is important to you." She gave both girls a bag, and asked them to hurry. They were going to Grandpa Jake's hurricane cellar. His home was inland and it was safer there. Annie felt numb, how could this be happening? Such things just did not happen to little girls from England. How could the ocean she loved, now have become such a threat? She stuffed into the bag, her pretty new undies, a toothbrush and her sketch pad, hardly noticing Missy as they rushed about. Soon they were in the car, collecting Daryl, Danny and family on the way.

It was like a party! The cellar which ran almost the length of the house, was simply furnished, and Jake and Ruby had set it out with books and games, together with a super array of food and drinks. Daryl's father settled Bethany onto a sofa in his doctorly way, telling her jokingly, that she was too pregnant to be taking part in such adventures as this, and frowned at Jake as he handed her a brandy, commenting that he supposed that just one would not do any harm. Jake smiled, and winked at Missy, "Orange juice for you youngsters, and lots of ice I think, it is too warm down here, even with the air conditioning." She helped him to hand out the glasses, trying not to show the fear, which Annie could see so clearly. They sat cross legged on the floor as Ruby switched on the T.V. Annie and the boys looked at each other, wide eyed as they sipped their drinks. They were well laced with vodka, but Missy did not even blink, looking a picture of innocence as she tasted hers. "So this is where she got the vodka idea from," Annie thought, "Secret boozing with Grandpa Jake!"

Good news, the weather map on T.V. was showing the spider like form of the hurricane, veering away from them. Daryl sat smugly, it had done as he said, and he grinned. "They never hit us, I told you that." They were actually only affected by a tropical storm, with lashing rain and howling winds, giving Annie a better understanding of her friend's fear. If a hurricane was worse than that, Annie did not want to know about sitting through one.

The biggest source of amusement was the revelation of the contents of the bags, brought along in such a hurry. Grandpa Jake, who was evidently well experienced in such times of panic, suggested that they take a look.

Annie's was first. "Well Annie would have walked around in her underwear for a week if we had been hit," the old man laughed, "but at least you would have been able to use your sketch pad to draw the looks on the boy's faces."

Danny's bag contained only two books, one about President Kennedy, and the other The Jungle Book, which they kept renewing from the library, but then to his embarrassment, something else fell out. It was the green ribbon, which Annie had lost from her hair the week before.

By this time they were all laughing at the strange and useless things brought along at a time of crisis. Daryl had refused to be parted from his 'six string', and squeezed the guitar into the car, despite protests from the others, but he, the harum-scarum one of the four, had also brought a complete set of fresh clothes, shorts, socks and underwear, plus a set of screwdrivers.

If there had been a prize, Missy would have won. All she brought was her Elvis Presley L.P. collection and a small shabby cloth, which turned out to be a piece of the blanket she had loved as a baby.

With spirits lifted, despite the raging storm, Norris got his father in the mood for reciting. Missy giggled, telling the others that this was another family tradition, special poetry. "Dad knows it too, but it has to be done by the senior man of the house." Jake who by now had consumed half a bottle of Jack Daniel's, was well in the mood, and began an amazing rendition of Samuel Taylor Coleridge's, The Rime of the Ancient Mariner, holding their attention, just like the old sailor in the poem. At first Annie wondered how he could remember such a long poem, but as he went on, the story progressed, and the ship was becalmed, she was not only enthralled, but recognised some of the verses. They sat listening in awe as the rain and wind lashed outside.

"Day after day, day after day,
We stuck, nor breath or motion;
As idle as a painted ship
Upon a painted ocean."

They must have done the poem at school in England, or perhaps it was one of Lottie's tales, because Annie began to realise that she knew the story quite well. They all cheered at the end, and Annie thought how true the third verse from the last was.

"He prayeth best, who lovest best
All things both great and small;
For the dear God who loveth us,
 He made and loveth all."

"Coleridge was so right," she thought to herself, "All living creatures should be loved, respected and cared for." Right there in Grandpa Jake's basement, she decided upon her career, she would become a veterinary nurse. She made up her mind that it did not matter how many horrible exams she may have to pass, she was going to do it.

During the frivolity, only Norris was aware of Bethany's concern, and her worst fears were realised. By the time they had all returned home, promising to see Jake and Ruby soon, the threatened hurricane had headed towards Lousianna, and had hit on the Texas border, around the area of her parent's farmhouse. She sat watching the devastation on the T.V. her face waxen pale with black shadows beneath her eyes, that Norris had never seen before. Frantically he tried to contact her family, first her parents, then her brother and sister, but all the lines were down. No one could help, they would have to sit tight and wait, but Bethany was worrying Norris.

The call came through at last, in the early hours of the morning. Bethany's brother and sister had lost their homes, but the good old Texan farmhouse of their parents, had only lost part of it's roof. No one in the family was hurt, but Missy's fear had not been unfounded. Just as she knew it would, the evil of Hurricane Carla had reached out to them in Florida, her mother was ill. Bethany's feet were swollen, her head ached and her vision was becoming blurred. In an uncharacteristic panic, Norris called Daryl's father, who dispatched her immediately to hospital, her blood pressure was sky high.

Missy and Annie, left behind, sat on the floorboards of the veranda facing the ocean, with arms around each other, and wept until the sun came up, when Molly arrived with Danny and Daryl. She shooed them into the house, scolding gently, "My, my, this will not do at all. I am going to make us all some pancakes, now off you go and put something on those eyes before the boys see you. I have sent them to put out the garbage."

Somehow Molly's presence lightened the situation and as they dressed, both girls laughed on hearing her shouting, her lovely accent more pronounced with frustration. A racoon had attacked the garbage pail again, and as Daryl and Danny were trying to pick up the mess, she was chasing the wretched creature with a broom.

Bethany was to spend the remainder of her pregnancy in hospital. Five weeks hooked up to monitors and lines, with Norris looking as pale and sick as his wife. Molly came in every day, the boys joining Missy and Annie for the evening meal after school. Molly's family had now grown temporarily to four teenagers, and she thrived, allowing herself to think wistfully how life might have been.

She resolved to teach the girls to cook. In Jamaica, no young woman of their age would be so incapable in the culinary department. After all the way to a man's heart had always been through his stomach, and besides, when Bethany returned with the baby, two girls with a selection of good recipes could be nothing but an asset.

There was no doubt in Molly's mind that Bethany and the baby would be just fine. She had a feeling for such things, life and unfortunately death. She had known about her husband's illness, long before he found out himself, but Bethany was different, and she told Norris so. She also told him that he would have a son.

Chapter Thirty Seven

In the following weeks, both Annie and Missy became enthusiastic cooks, under the watchful eye of Molly. She also taught them to be economical, as her own mother had done. "It is one thing to learn how to cook and bake," she told them most seriously, "but a woman should be able to produce a good meal from whatever sparse ingredients which happen to be at hand." She taught them the art of tasty soups, how to make twelve little cup cakes with just one egg, to add water to eggs for a super two egg omelette, never to add milk because it would separate, to make pizza without bothering to use yeast in the base, to make their own chilli powder, and how to make a pound of ground beef, go oh so far. The ideas were endless, and the girls absorbed them eagerly, remembering all Molly's secret hints with herbs and spices. By the time Michael was born, Molly felt that they had become fully fledged cooks, and was as proud as if they had been her own daughters.

Michael arrived a week before Thanksgiving. An induced birth, but an easy labour for Bethany, and mother and baby were allowed home in time for the celebrations. In the week after his birth, Bethany blossomed, and by the time they arrived home at last, she looked almost her old self again.

He was a beautiful baby, and although disappointed that he did not have her colouring, Missy could not have loved him more. She and Annie cooed over him and cuddled him at every opportunity, like a pair of clucky old hens, as Molly would often tease. Bethany took it all in her stride in her usual patient way, and Norris now back in the relaxed atmosphere with the new baby, which Bethany called organised chaos, lost the lines of worry from his face, and was able to appreciate his daughter's new found skills.

With secret help from Molly, the girls prepared the Thanksgiving dinner. The turkey was roasted to perfection, slightly spicy, thanks to Molly's secret basting ingredients, with delicious stuffing, made from apples, breadcrumbs, onion and salt pork, and all served with home made cranberry sauce. For dessert, knowing Bethany's passion for lemons, they made lemon meringue pie, and managed to get the meringue just right, something even Molly said that you could never guarantee.

The family settled back to normal very quickly, with Annie feeling that Michael was her little brother too. Seeing her fondness for the baby, Bethany asked her to be his Godmother. Although she enthusiastically agreed, it worried Annie, and eventually she confided in Molly.

"I am not sure that I can really be a Godparent," she tried to explain, as they sat with their feet in the ocean. "My thoughts of God are different. To me going to church means very little. My God is in the ocean, on the beach, in the trees in the garden, all around. My God loves all living things, not just people but animals too. I believe that we should be kind to each other, not hold grudges and fight. All the talk of sin and damnation seems wrong to me. My Godmother Lottie, she is more like an aunt, and a friend really, told me once that she will go to hell because she got her dead baby a Christian burial in church, when it had not been baptised before it died. What kind of a God would do that? I don't believe it, do you?" Molly had a strange far away look in her eyes as she took Annie's hand. "No of course that is not true, but Annie, in the future, your friend is going to need you to tell her your feelings . You will have to make her see that she is wrong." Annie saw her shiver, although the warm sun was beating down upon them. Then she was herself again, "You will make a perfect Godmother, so stop worrying."

Annie was relieved as they walked back along the beach. She told Molly of her plans to be a veterinary nurse and how she was determined to master the exams which she would need to pass. Molly assured her that she would succeed, but warned that life very rarely allowed such plans to be straight forward. "Do not forget your talents," she advised, "your sketching is a gift, you must use that too."

Annie took her advice, but not quite in the way Molly had meant. Always short of money, the four friends came up with a way of raising extra cash. Down the beach, away from the prying eyes of parents, Annie set up an easel, made ingeniously by Danny, and bought a large sketch pad. Daryl sat playing the guitar while Annie drew portraits of passers by, and displayed some of her racoon cartoons. Soon they had an extra income. Danny passed his driving test, and was allowed to drive his Mom's battered old Chevy. In his usual, all knowing way, he found a shop where they turned a blind eye to the fact that he was obviously not twenty one and sold him alcohol on a regular basis. They always bought vodka, as it was less conspicuous, they could hardly go home smelling of Jack Daniel's. They never bought cigarettes as Danny was convinced that they had caused his father's cancer, but they did smoke the odd joint of mary-jane, which was his name for marijuana. Danny was sure it was harmless, saying that the American tribes used it as medicine but Annie was not so sure. Yes it was a lovely relaxing experience, even better than the vodka, but sometimes their voices became so hoarse after, that she had doubts about its safety.

Happy months slipped by, with the strange feeling of having Christmas dinner as a barbecue by the ocean, not Annie's favourite meal, all that lighter fuel and smoke, but fun all the same. Then there was an emotional telephone call between Annie and her parents, which made her feel that they were too far away, until Bethany gave her a big hug. Michael grew at an amazing rate, a happy smiling child, looking so like his mother. His name was never shortened, which seemed strange to Annie, as Missy never received her full title, Melissa, even in school, but she made no comment about it. She was so fond of this family, especially her friend, and admired Missy's lack of jealousy over the baby. In fact the only trace of jealousy she had ever seen from Missy had been about Daryl, but he knew her too well to let it come to anything. As always he guarded her feelings, Annie could not imagine Missy with anyone but Daryl.

By the end of the school year, Annie had become as confident and easy going as Danny. With his, and Bethany's help, her reading was fairly competent, and with it came a greater understand of the world around her. She could now laugh off any silly mistakes, and would shrug apologetically at the odd weird spelling which would always creep in, especially if she was tired. Bethany sent a secret and glowing report of Annie's progress to Alex, and they all looked forward to spending another summer together.

But it was not to be, for a call came from Alex. Lottie had been taken into hospital, "Just women's problems," he said infuriatingly, "and she will be off her feet for a couple of weeks." He did not seem to think that her condition was serious, but now they had no one to look after the business, and the trip to Florida would be impossible, Annie would have to fly home by herself.

Thinking of her conversation with Danny's Mom, months ago, about the way even the best plans were often disrupted by unforeseen events, and with Lottie on her mind, she confronted Molly.

She became very serious.

"Annie, your friend Lottie is very ill. I have a feeling for such things. Your father says it is just a matter of an operation, and she will be fine, but that is not so. I am telling you this because you must help her. You must not let her die believing in all that sin, hell and vengeance. Do not be upset, death is part of the balance of our world, and you know in your heart, just as I do, that death is not the end. It is better to know, so that you can help. Now make sure that you do not waste the remainder of this summer, it will go too quickly. I know this will be on your mind, but it is no reason for you not to enjoy yourself."

"Will I be strong enough, Molly, and will I ever come back?"

"You have an inner strength that you have not even found a glimmer of yet. We will all miss you when you go home, but you will always come back to us, never fear."

Annie felt totally shaken, but she and Molly had some kind of unexplained understanding, so she nodded with a lump in her throat, knowing that it was all true, and she was right, time did go oh so quickly. All too soon she found herself in tears, packing her case. Missy cried too, promising to write, and not knowing how they could go back to life without each other. Annie would miss them all so much, little Michael, crawling everywhere now, and calling Annie in his baby voice, Daryl who was in a way her soul mate, through their similar problems, and Danny with their innocent shared hugs and kisses. Alex promised that they should all come back next year for another summer vacation, but it did not lessen the pain of parting.

However, once on the plane, she found herself looking forward to seeing her home again, and to being with Mom, Dad and Lottie once more. She was going to make Lottie happy, for Molly had advised her, and Annie did not for a moment doubt the wisdom of that advice. Neither did she realise that she was no longer thinking like a sixteen year old. There was much to do in her life, responsibilities, obligations and ambitions, and she was going to get on with it in the same calmly optimistic manner as that lovely lady from Jamaica.

Alex waited for her at Heathrow. He was tired, not just from the six hour journey to the airport, but from an exasperating week. Lottie was still not back at work and Dennis, without Lottie's supervision seemed to be neither use nor ornament. Since she had been taken ill, the man seemed to be more slow witted than ever. A tall well built man, his physical strength had always been an asset, and Lottie's instructions to him never seemed to go awry, but with Alex he was hopeless. He had been injured in the first war, a bullet through his arm, leaving two fingers on his right hand stiff and useless, but the mental scars had damaged him most.

Lying about his age, he was only sixteen, he joined up, never prepared for what was in store. The rain, the mud seeping into boots making feet rot, the terrible deaths, friends blown to pieces beside him, the blistering, lung destroying mustard gas and the sheer futility of it all had robbed him of his senses. His immature mind, in the body of a strapping young man, was reduced, in a form of self defence to almost that of a simpleton.

Alex had been putting a large order together, for an oil tycoon in Texas. It included a beautiful cheval glass, a full length mirror, mounted as to swivel within a frame, a fine mirror backed sideboard, with ornate carving and tiny brass handles, a chaise longue, which had been stored in an old country house, and was in remarkably good and original condition, an extra wide, six drawer chest of drawers in mahogany, and a long case clock. To his annoyance the chest of drawers turned out to be acajou, a type of mahogany used by French cabinet makers, and would not do for his transatlantic client. Not only that the top drawer was locked, so before resale in the shop, he would have to pay the locksmith to unlock it, making the whole thing an uneconomic buy. To make matters worse, the clock, an excellent piece, he had thought, engraved John Banks fecit, Chester, did not comply with the list in Baillie's Clocknames. It showed John Banks as from London, not Chester, bringing Alex's exasperation to boiling point. Now he would have to search again to complete the order.

All this tension disappeared as Annie came into sight. His little daughter, transformed into a beautiful young woman, with a tumble of dark curls down her back, and a relaxed and confident air as she waved, shouting, "Hi Dad," as she ran into his arms.

He looked tired, she thought as he took her case, but he was smiling as he walked to the car, with that all familiar limp which she had almost forgotten while she was away. "Another four months and I will be able to drive myself. Danny has been teaching me, and it can't be much different over here," she told him, making his stomach churn at the thought. He had taught her mother five years ago, and it nearly drove him crazy, now it would happen all over again with Annie. Trying to put it out of his mind, he listened to her pleasant chatter, enjoying the news of Bethany, Norris and her friends, and smiling to himself at her accent.

It was ten o'clock at night by the time they arrived. She had forgotten how charming her home town was, with its old buildings lit up for the night. Not the neon lights of Florida, but beautiful in a different way. She would miss the sunshine and the ocean, but this felt good too, although now everything seemed so small.

The flat and her bedroom seemed tiny now, but she was happy to be with her parents again, and she badly wanted to see Lottie. She asked her mother casually about Lottie's health, but the slight frown on her face told Annie all, as her mother tried to assure her that Lottie was doing well, and would soon be back at work. They talked until late that night, all three content at being together again. "We will have to buy you another school uniform," Joyce remarked. "Oh, please, no baggy navy blue knickers!" Annie squealed, making them laugh until their sides ached.

She could not sleep, the five hour time difference telling her body that it was only seven o'clock in the evening. The bedroom seemed so small and oppressive. She missed the sound of the ocean through the open window of Missy's room, and felt as if she would never settle. Eventually she got up and went to the kitchen. Instinctively she reached into the refrigerator for the orange juice. This was not the good old U.S.A. people here did not keep such products in the refrigerator as a matter of course, neither was there a supply of chocolate fudge ice cream, another one of the night time feasts so often shared with Missy. Norris always said that coffee kept you awake, so it would be no use drinking that. She tried one of the cupboards and found amongst bottles of wine brandy and whisky, a bottle of vodka. Taking a glass, she poured a large drink, and with it in her hand she made her way down into the shop below.

Her nose wrinkled as she smelled the old musty smell, so like Grandpa Jake's house. Did he miss her, she wondered? She put on the light and began to poke about. The mirror backed sideboard was lovely, with little drawers and glass fronted cupboards, all lined with faded green velvet. She pushed the pendulum of the clock and it started to tick, in a typical slow tick tock fashion. "Dad will be pleased," she said out loud, knowing that such clocks could be notoriously awkward when moved. People sometimes painted the walls around grandfather clocks, rather than upset the delicate balance by moving them. The chest of drawers was highly polished, and Annie admired the rich colour of the wood. She tried to open the top drawer, but of course it was locked. She looked in the other drawers for the key, then ran her fingers along the bottom between its rounded feet. No key. Remembering one of her own hiding places, she pulled out one of the heavy drawers, and there, sure enough, taped to the back was a key.

Feeling giggly with the vodka, she turned it in the lock and opened the top drawer. There was something in there, a thick green blanket, wrapped around a long heavy object. She pulled it out, swallowing the remaining contents of her glass before unwrapping it. It was a large gun with a sort of cartridge thing attached to it. Not an old gun like Grandpa Jake's, more like the sort of thing terrorists in the movies carried about. Childishly she held it, pointing it at her reflection in the cheval glass. "If I were a terrorist, this is what I would want for my birthday," she laughed at her reflection. Then she saw it. A spider, a huge, long legged thing, crawling across the chaise longue. For no logical reason, it made her cringe with horror, she never could stand the things. "Got you now," she whispered to it as it crept along. She aimed the gun at the beastly arachnid, but to her horror, it somehow went off.

Horrible explosions filled her ears as bullets flew from the barrel of the gun. The chaise longue, sideboard and the cheval mirror disappeared into pieces and a gaping hole appeared through the wall dividing the shop and her father's office. She stood wide eyed in dismay, still holding the gun, with what was by now an iron grip. The spider crawled away sulkily into a dark corner, quite unharmed, and the long case clock ticked solemnly away in the ensuing silence.

Chapter Thirty Eight

Alex dashed downstairs, fearing some kind of gas explosion, and could not believe his eyes at the sight of Annie with the gun. Something flashed into his mind, 'What had Norris said when she was born?' "Haven't you heard of Annie Oakley? Better keep the guns locked up." 'Good grief, where did she get it from,' he thought, his mind in a turmoil. She did not move, so he called her name softly, "Give it to me love, gently, that's the way." He had to prise it from her grip, her face a picture of horror. "Oh, what have I done?" she cried, "I didn't mean to, it just went off."

Joyce, having called the gas board, joined the scene of chaos, and began to shout and cry at the same time, reminding Alex of his mother-in-law, and leaving him feeling powerless to help the situation. The men from the gas board arrived, along with the police. The gas men were peevish as Alex explained the situation, but the police were positively hostile. Did Alex have a licence for such a weapon? They doubted it. Had he smuggled it in from America? Eventually satisfied with Annie's explanations and her father's apologies, they retreated with the offending gun, leaving the family to face the mess.

The chest of drawers originated from Ireland, the gun obviously smuggled in it and left by mistake. It was a Polish Kalasnikov A.K. 47, a lethal weapon invented in Russia, A.K. stood for Automatic Kalashnikov and 47 for the year of it's invention, 1947. The action of its bullets, which continued to tumble around after entry, had caused the devastation. The initial impact would make a small hole in a victim's body, but leave a huge gaping wound on exit, and seemingly it could do the same for a brick wall. Alex sighed, "Talk about Murphy's Law, the damned clock and chest of drawers are untouched." Then he put his arms around his 'girls' and took them upstairs, "No use crying over spilt milk," he said.

Joyce was decidedly icy with Annie next morning. Full of guilt, she escaped, to see Lottie. Prepared for the worst, she was relieved to see her looking quite well. Thinner, perhaps, that was all, but it was Dennis who gave the secret away. He did not actually say anything, but Annie could see by the way he fussed around Lottie, that he knew, and that Molly had been right.

She sat, with a cup of real tea, not the hot water with a bag on a piece of string that she had become used to. Lottie's tea was strong, sweet and laced with cream from the top of the lovely Jersey milk which she always bought. Annie had forgotten how delicious it was and wished Missy was with her to taste it. She explained the cause of the night's events, including a confession about the vodka. Lottie looked at her incredulously.

"Do you mean that it all happened because of a spider?" "I know you never liked them, but really, to point a gun at one. Have you been in The States too long? I have always told you that spiders are good, I can not imagine what you have got against them. Let me think, a spider saved a king's life once, Frederick the Great it was, Frederick II, king of Prussia, 1740 - 1780. He did not get on with his father. He loved art and literature, but it made his father angry, so to toughen him up, he locked poor Frederick away in the fortress of Kustrin and made him watch the execution of his best friend, Lieutenant Katte. The King's plan failed, Frederick only became more determined not to be like his father, and when the old man died, Frederick became a good king, banning all torture in his land. You are wondering what all this had got to do with spiders? Well, someone tried to poison Frederick, the cook put poison into his hot chocolate. A spider fell into the cup and died instantly, warning him, and saving his life."

Annie spluttered into her tea.

"Oh Lottie, what a fib, how do you make up such things?"

"Would I lie?" It is quite true, anyway if you don't believe me, now your reading has improved, you can go and look it up in the library for yourself. Meanwhile promise me that you will use this method for the disposal of spiders."

She pulled the plastic top from an aerosol can of polish, instructing Annie to pop it over the spider, then to push a piece of paper underneath, and put the offending creature outside. Dennis smiled as he poured more tea, it pleased him to see Lottie laugh, and it was good to see Annie again.

With her parents so busy in the shop, Annie was sent off to buy her own school uniform. She bought the blazer from the official outfitters, a size too big, so that she could push up the sleeves, Danny style, but she began to search around town for the rest. No more itchy stiff necked shirts for Annie, she found two soft silk blouses, plain white with a tiny edging of satin ribbon stitched around the collar and matching satin covered buttons. Luckily they were in the sale at the high quality shop, so they did not dent the budget too much. A plain navy skirt, with fashionable matching braces was found in a little boutique, together with a soft baggy V-neck sweater and some long over the knee socks. "Couldn't buy a hat," she told herself convincingly. "I am sure the outfitters would order one for me, but I won't mention the fact that I didn't ask them to!" When the purchases were complete she still had money over, so she bought three sets of pretty lace bras and panties from Marks and Spencer. 'If only the Misses Jones could see these,' she thought, picturing the horror on the faces of the headmistress and her elderly sister.

School started all too soon, and was almost as beastly as she had remembered. Alex had briefed the headmistress about Annie's dyslexia, but after he left, the two sisters agreed that if this dyslexia was her problem, they had never heard of such a thing, and that it was a fancy name for darn right idleness.

"That wretched girl," the headmistress wailed as she sent for Annie at break on the first morning. "Your uniform child, what is the meaning of the way you are dressed, and your hat, where is your hat?" The girl of a year ago would have cringed, but this was the new confident Annie. She stood straight, with her hands behind her back. "I do apologise Ma'am," she said sweetly, deliberately imitating Missy's southern drawl. She saw Miss Jones' colour rise as she carried on. "The blazer is on the large size, my parents are so horrified at my rate of growth that they thought it wise. The skirt, sweater and skirt were part of my uniform from my former school overseas. It would be a pity to waste what is almost exactly a match to regulation uniform, at least until I grow out of it. The socks are long because, with the change of climate, I do not want to risk catching a chill in this important year, and as for the hat, Densons have ordered one." She kept a perfectly serious face as she stood in front of the furious woman. She saw Miss Jones fight to regain her composure. "Well at least do up your tie properly," she snapped, glaring at the tie which had been tied with the same knot for years, and which hung loosely around Annie's neck as she had made no attempt to pull it up to the collar of the pretty silk blouse. "Thank you Ma'am," she said mischievously, as she left the room, imagining the explosion of temper after the door was closed.

That had been fun, but school was not going to be plain sailing. She had not really made any school friends before, and now she fitted in even less. They remembered her as the tall awkward girl with the appliance on her teeth. Now she was the girl with perfect teeth, beautiful complexion and the most amazing long hair, which bounced in curls down her back. She had some different kind of style too, but try as they might, it did not work for them as they attempted to copy it, probably because it was just confidence, Annie was only being herself. Annie was different, and now she liked it that way, but she missed Missy, how good it had been to have a friend close all the time. She was put to sit by a boy called Arnold Bears, what a name, but even worse, everyone called him Swot. A miserable boy with glasses, Swot was the super brain of the class, and sitting next to someone like that was the last thing Annie needed.

Her social life was abysmal, but surprisingly, the lessons were not too bad. This was the final year, the year of the G.C.E. examinations, five of which would have to be passed if she was going to get into veterinary college. Art of course was a joy, Maths had never been much of a problem, but all that algebra and geometry were so alien to her that she was allowed to study for a lower grade paper, simply covering general arithmetic, leaving her a whole afternoon free each week for private tuition, which the school presumed would continue, and would actually be secret trips to the zoo.

History was interesting and they were studying the period of the Industrial Revolution, the nineteenth century. "Yes, she thought, we must have done some of this before, because it seems familiar." There in the history book was King George, called Farmer George because of his great interest in the new farming methods, and he had been insane, just as Annie said on that first, embarrassing evening at Grandpa Jake's house. Also there was the King's rotten son, wanting to divorce Caroline his wife, after his father's death. "Beautiful, fashionable Caroline Spencer," Annie thought, "Why didn't he want her? She would have made a lovely queen." The staid history book had no answer, and neither did the history teacher, who considered Annie's questions to be off tangent. She was not actually qualified to teach history, and Annie was putting her into awkward situations, making her despair at the sight of the girl. What was wrong with the child? The year before she had hardly opened her mouth, but now she never stopped. Questions questions, wasn't Robert Owen, the man who looked after his workers, and whose factory was in Scotland, actually from Wales? Why did Edward Jenner use a poor little boy to try out the cowpox vaccine against smallpox, when people in the countryside must have known about it for years? What kind of a doctor would do that, and what kind of a mother did little James Phipps have to allow it to happen? Surely all landowners did not treat their labourers badly? Wasn't James Brindley, the engineer who built the canal to carry coal to Manchester, the one who could not read or write? On and on went Annie's questions disrupting the class, but forcing Miss Hallows to research the answers at the library in her spare time.

Miss Hallows was having a bad time with Annie, but it was Miss Roberts, the English teacher who she clashed with most. "Annie, take off those sunglasses in class," she barked on the first day, and why are you wearing make-up?" Annie explained about the tinted spectacles and that she wore no make-up, just a touch of Vaseline, on her lips and eyelashes to counter the change of climate on her recent return to the country. Her classmates secretly decided to try this trick themselves, but no one had the dark eyelashes or the naturally pink lips of Annie, so they abandoned the idea feeling jealous. She actually did very well in Miss Robert's class, but the woman never afforded any praise towards her. "Your spelling is appalling," she moaned "it is as bad as your accent. You are not with your Colonial cousins now, you must spell the English way." This made Annie so angry, so what, if Bethany had taught her to spell the American way, if it had been left to Miss Roberts, she would not have been able to spell anything at all, and as for Colonial cousins, what century was this woman in? Hadn't she ever heard of the 4th of July?

Unfortunately Miss Roberts also took the class for English Literature, and Shakespeare was a complete mystery to Annie. Her mother was too busy with the business, to be worried about such things, so Annie turned to Lottie for advice. Unfortunately, Lottie was self taught, and Shakespeare was not something she had mastered either, so Annie was left floundering and bemused. "The man could not speak English," she cried, throwing her copy of Twelfth Night across her bedroom. "How am I supposed to understand?" To make matters worse, there was to be a school trip to see the wretched play.

"Where did you say you are going tomorrow?" Lottie asked in disbelief. Annie explained it was a trip to Shropshire to visit the famous Iron Bridge, and then to see the play at some old priory. "That school," Lottie rasped, "Why don't they take you to Stratford to see a play. You could catch your death of cold sitting outside in some old ruin, it is September after all, and I am sure today's warm weather will not hold."

She was wrong, it was a beautiful day as they boarded the coach. Everyone was to sit next to their class partner, so Annie was stuck with Swot. He was late arriving and Annie sat, with her small transistor radio playing through the earpiece wishing she was somewhere else.

"If music be the food of love, play on," he said with a flourish as he sat down beside her. She just smiled and shrugged, not knowing what on earth he was on about. He chatted as they went along, which was odd as he had never spoken more than two words to her before. "Want a drink?" he asked, offering her a lemonade bottle. Not wishing to offend she took a drink, looking into his eyes with shock as she realised it was vodka. "Thought so," he carried on happily loosening his tie, "thought we might have the same tastes!"

By the time they reached Iron Bridge, half the bottle was gone, they knew more about each other than anyone else at school, and were experiencing an alcohol induced infatuation. The class ate a picnic lunch on the banks of the River Severn, and there were a few amused looks at Annie and Arnold's pre-occupation with each other.

They arrived at the priory, two hours before the performance, so were allowed the free time to look around the town. "Oh what a lovely little place," Annie said as she and Arnold walked around, now hand in hand feeling very tipsy. He showed her St. Milburgha's well and told her all about it. In Victorian times, maidens would throw crooked pins into the water, to wish for a sweetheart. "Well I don't have to do that, do I," she smiled as she squeezed his hand. 'I am going to like Much Wenlock,' he thought.

Chapter Thirty Nine

They entered the priory in an orderly crocodile and were allowed to wander around the grounds for a while, before the start of the performance. Annie was taken aback by the beauty of the place. The stage was set between the soaring solitary arches of the ruins, bathed in the gentle afternoon sunlight. As she and Arnold walked hand in hand, he told her the story of the play, to help, as she had experienced such problems with the book. It sounded so funny, the way he told it. Was this the same play she had flung uncomprehendingly across the bedroom? He also told her about Shakespeare's life, his perception of human nature, and of his everlasting influence upon other writers.

"John Keats, you know, the man who wrote the poem about the cat, which you like so much, was influenced by Shakespeare. The way you recited it in class last week was so good. Miss Roberts should have praised you. She is a pig. I wanted to say so, but I was too shy then!" She giggled and nuzzled his neck, "What has happened to us?" she laughed.

They took their seats and Annie was quiet as she looked at the beautiful surroundings. "A penny for your thoughts," he said playfully. She jolted, turning ashen pale and catching her breath. He put his arm out to prevent her falling from the seat, touching concern showing on his face. "Oh Arnold, it's you," she gasped. Too much vodka he guessed. "Of course it's me, just take it easy." The feeling was unexplainable, an absent, but shuddering fear. Perhaps that was what Lottie meant by the silly expression, "Someone has walked over my grave." Annie made up her mind to ask her, whatever it was, she did not like it. She shook herself back to normality and Arnold put his arm around her, not caring about the look of daggers from Miss Roberts on the other side of the stand.

The play was an education, as it was intended to be, but for Annie, it was an eye opener to the world of Shakespeare. The characters came to life with the actors in their rich period costumes. "If music be the food of love, play on," said Orsino, to begin the play. Annie smiled, glancing at Arnold, now knowing what he had meant on the coach when they started that morning. It was indeed a comedy, with Maria the maid so mischievous, and the drunken Sir Toby so funny. She clapped impetuously at the end, and Arnold promised to read other plays to her. "No vodka when we do the Scottish one though," he warned. "That would really spook you, it is bad luck even to speak the name of Macbeth."

From then on Annie's English Literature came on in leaps and bounds, but now with her interest raised, she asked many questions, driving Miss Roberts to almost the same nervous state as the history teacher. Annie looked up John Keats in the library for herself, and while she was there she also found Lottie's story about King Frederick and the spider. There it was, all true! Lottie was a mine of information, it was a pity about her strict and uncomforting religious beliefs, but Annie was working on that. Her gentle God was going to look after this woman she loved as much as a mother.

Annie held up the Literature class, by shocking Miss Roberts with her newly gained knowledge of Keats. "The child is like a ferret," the teacher thought. "I wish she had stayed in America, and why on earth doesn't she lose that accent!"

She mischievously watched Miss Roberts squirm as she carried on, class mates inspired not only by her obvious devilment but also by such interesting information. Keats ceased to be just the writer of part of their G.C.E. syllabus poetry, and became a real personality to them.

It turned out that he was a romantic poet, and according to the library, inspired a soft romantic style of dressing at the time, as well as a style of literature.

Born 1795 in London, he took Shakespeare as his model, just as Arnold had told Annie, but he had started his career as a licensed apothercary. He contracted T.B. from other members of his family. Consumption they called it in his time, when there were no inoculations for prevention, and of course no cure. He travelled to Italy when he was twenty five, in a poor state of health, hoping that the climate would suit him better, but his lungs were badly deteriorated. The blood spitting cough became worse and he died a year later. "I feel the flowers growing over me," he said as he died, Annie informed the intrigued class with a shudder, making Miss Roberts sigh. Now she would have to find out if all this was true.

Annie wrote regularly to Missy, quite blase about any irregular spelling. Missy would not hold such a thing against her, although she was much more careful with her notes to Bethany. She told her best friend all about school, the uniform, and most of all about Arnold. By now they had a special relationship, although nothing remotely like that of Missy and Daryl. Annie wondered if everyone found such love in their lives, as love it surely was. She doubted it somehow, "Missy is just one of the lucky ones," she sighed.

That October, the letter from Missy was most disturbing. Annie opened it after school, looking forward to the usual girlie chat, only to find it full of the fear of war! Annie had vaguely heard something on the news that very morning, something about Cuba, so very near to Florida. She and Missy had stood in Key West together looking out over the water towards that troubled country. It was only ninety miles away!

How could it be, this awful event which threatened to destroy the world? The letter had been written a week before, the situation must surely be worse by now. Missy said that U.S. aerial photographs showed rockets and launchers being built in Cuba. Soon Russia would have missiles to strike and take out all cities in U.S. People there talked about what to do in a nuclear explosion and many were buying fall out shelters! Danny was sure that the President would fix it, but Kennedy had only imposed a naval blockade. Determined restraint, Danny called it, after all what was the use of a U.S. air strike, there was no guarantee that they could destroy all the missiles. With tears in her eyes she read the last poignant part of the letter.

> *"I wish we were together. We might all be blown to nuclear dust, and I will never see you again. Daryl and I have decided to make love tonight, there may be no time to wait any more. We have talked about it, and neither Castro or Khrushchev are going to take that pleasure away from us. We are going to do it now, while we still have the chance, but we have to hope Danny is right about the skills of J.F.K.*
> *Love from your very special friend.*
> *Missy*

With shaking hands Annie switched on the six o'clock news. Her parents were closing up the shop and everyone was acting normally. There it was, 'Cuban Crisis' the radio reported. Russia and America on the brink of war, Kennedy and Khruschev locked eyeball to eyeball. Her parents were of little help. Exhausted at the end of a stressful day of business with a difficult shipping order, they felt there was enough crisis in their own lives to become suicidal about events beyond their control.

Arnold was more of a comfort the next day. Putting his arms around her, then pushing up his glasses in an authoritative way.

"Do you really think either side would fire nuclear missiles? Both would be annihilated in a puff of dust and they know it. It is just a political threat. If you want to worry, never mind about ban the bomb. What about the nuclear power stations. Zap a few of those and we would all die from the radiation, there is no escape from that. What good would it do to sit in a fall out shelter, if all the world is poisoned around you? It poisons everything, the dust would drift in the wind. Even a nuclear melt down as far away as Russia could send contamination here. Write back to your friend, and tell her I agree with Danny, it won't happen!"

While the world held its breath, Lottie prayed, instantly converted back to the vengeful version of God. Alex and Joyce battled with their consignment of furniture, including a grand piano, destined for Ohio, and Annie clung to Arnold, with his calm and gentle attitude. She relished his company but with a pang of envy for her friend. Had Missy and Daryl made love? She was almost a year younger than Annie. Now, that would put the cat among the pigeons, if her parents found out.

Two weeks later Khruschev backed down, the world sighed with relief, the missile launchers were dismantled and life returned to normal, or as normal for Annie as the cold November weather would permit. She missed the blissful Floridian climate more than ever now.

The deterioration in Lottie's health was scarcely noticeable, but as she always said, Annie missed nothing. Her movements were becoming more careful, and she was becoming thinner. As her strength failed, little by little, Dennis became stronger and more responsible, but his craggy face was etched with silent concern.

Annie spent hours in their company, careful not to let them suspect that she knew the truth of Lottie's situation. They talked on many subjects, Annie revelling in Lottie's general knowledge, and Lottie marvelling at the change in her Goddaughter after a year in the U.S.A. Annie's views on religion were even more surprising. What strong faith she had, although somehow she saw all the old teaching in an off tangent way, but how gentle, logical and comforting it all was.

Two weeks before Christmas, Lottie shocked Annie with an announcement.

"I am going to buy a car! I have money put aside. I was going to buy one years ago, when I sold my mother's sideboard to Norris."

"But Lottie, you can't drive."

"No, but Dennis can."

"Dennis!" I have never seen Dennis even ride a bike never mind drive a car. Have you been at the Cherry Brandy?"

They both dissolved into laughter. The drinking of Cherry Brandy was a hilarious but embarrassing incident from Lottie's past.

When Annie was just turned nine, Lottie offered to 'babysit' so that Joyce and Alex could go out on New Year's eve. Appreciating her kindness, they left a festive platter of delicate sandwiches, mince pies and a bottle of Cherry Brandy. Not being regular drinkers, neither Lottie or Dennis had ever seen this strong liquor before, and it was to be another nine years before Prince Charles would hit the headlines, being caught ordering it in a pub, whilst under age. The unfortunate prince accidentally causing the best piece of advertising the wretched drink ever could have received.

They presumed that it was to be shared with Annie, and was as innocent as its sticky, sweet shop taste implied. By ten o'clock the bottle was empty, and they were rolled across the sofa like a couple of rag dolls. Annie luckily did not like the taste and remained sober, but panic set in as she failed to rouse them, only managing to cause Dennis to fall to the floor, lying there motionless with his mouth open. Common sense prevailed, she knew that her parents always left a contact number on the pad by the phone if they were out. Shaking with fright, she carefully dialled it.

"Lottie and Dennis are ill," she wailed down the receiver, over the noise of the party. Alex and Joyce sped home, missing the letting in of the new year, expecting some terrible disaster, and finding their 'babysitters' in a drunken stupor. Lottie felt she would never live it down, but over the years it had all become a great source of amusement.

Lottie regained her composure, and shook her head.

"No I have not been at the Cherry Brandy. Dennis holds an up to date licence. He has been renewing it since the time before a test was required by law. When that law came in, anyone who had held a licence for a while, was automatically presumed to be able to drive, and given a full licence as a matter of course."

"Just how long is it since Dennis even sat behind a steering wheel?"

"Ha, miss clever, that does not matter. You told me your friend Danny gave you driving lessons last year. Dennis has the licence, you can teach each other, and I will sit in the back with my eyes closed! Don't look so shocked, come on, are you willing?"

How could she say no? This was going to be some adventure, really something to write to Missy about. Annie now caught up in the plot, suggested that they tell her father that she and Dennis were going to have driving lessons, but omit the fact that they were teaching each other. With this pact made, they filled in the forms for Annie's provisional licence.

They talked at length about the car. Annie felt that it should be small economical and easy to handle, so they decided upon a Mini. To her surprise and slight disappointment, Lottie went off by herself to order the vehicle, which was to be delivered on the day before Annie's seventeenth birthday.

What a shock, when it arrived that morning. This was not the economical Mini of Annie's expectations. A shining new Mini Cooper, stood there in all it's glory. Finished in British Racing Green, with a white roof and two white stripes down the bonnet. A chrome bar on the front sported two impressive driving lights, and matching chrome guards, protected the lights at the rear.

This was no vehicle for an elderly lady, whose time was running short, it was more like a boy racer's dream. Lottie kept a completely straight face as she showed it to her amazed God daughter. "Your provisional licence is valid from tomorrow, then we will be mobile." Annie could see a twinkle of laughter in Lottie's eyes as she carried on. "Of course you will be able to borrow it any time, once you have passed your test," she told Annie so seriously, but looking towards Dennis, who was still standing by the front door of the house, she could see a big contented grin on his face.

Chapter Forty

Lottie sat contentedly in the back, while the stoic little car endured all their efforts to learn to drive, with hopping of clutch and grinding of gears. Annie's previous driving in America, was in an automatic vehicle, therefore she had no experience at all with gears. Dennis' efforts were even worse, and after a week of frustration, decided to leave the driving to Annie, while he sheepishly sat in the passenger seat, seemingly oblivious to her mistakes and near misses. As time went by, Annie and the vehicle reached a mutual understanding and now they departed each evening for a smooth ride, as the powerful 1275cc engine took off with a growling purr from the exhaust. Within six weeks she had passed her test, "What a great start to the year," Annie thought as her father popped open a bottle of champagne to celebrate her achievement. "1963 is going to be a great year," she was to look back on that day of happy thoughts many times, knowing later how wrong she had been.

"Shall we go to visit my daughter tomorrow?" Lottie asked. "The young people will be Souling. You could join in the fun while Dennis and I put up with her scolding."

Annie had no idea what Souling was, but felt pleased that Lottie wanted to visit her daughter. Lottie and her daughter Margaret, just did not get on, and Lottie was not exaggerating about Margaret's nagging. "A bit like my Grandma," Annie thought, but was too polite to say so. Margaret could never understand why her mother insisted upon leaving the village, and was exasperated by her independence. Annie was not looking forward to her reaction to the car, and her feelings proved to be an accurate judgement of the situation, as Margaret looked positively explosive when she saw it. Her mother had telephoned the previous day, telling her about the car and the proposed visit. Margaret expected something like an old Morris Minor, and could scarcely contain her despair when she saw the rampant little Cooper, with Lottie sitting like the Queen Mother in the back.

There was a definite atmosphere as they sat down to the meal. Margaret, to be fair had made an effort, cooking one of her mother's old favourites, squab pie. It sounded horrible, and Annie dreaded to think what lurked beneath the crust of expertly made pastry. It was in fact a mixture of mutton, previously slow braised to perfection, with the juice thickened to a gravy, added to this were onions and apples, making the perfect filling. The pie was served with a bowl of steaming hot chopped cabbage, garnished with butter, and followed by baked egg custard for dessert.

At least at that point, Margaret was happy at being praised about the delicious meal, although she felt she needed to berate her mother's insistence on smaller than usual portions, complaining that it was no wonder she was losing weight. Annie felt sorry, thinking surely it would be better for Margaret to know about her mother's illness.

A knock at the door, produced a group of alarmingly odd looking teenagers. "Hello," called a tall boy with a blackened face and a ragged sweater, as he spotted Annie. "Won't you join us?" Margaret ushered them into the kitchen and handed out buttered scones. They were Souling and it was explained to Annie. An old custom when the poor would go begging for cakes on All Souls Day, but these days it was essential to dress for the occasion. The boy produced a piece of burnt cork to rub on Annie's face, making her look as grimy as himself, and Margaret's husband lent her his old gardening coat to complete the picture.

This was something like Halloween night in America, but Annie said nothing at first, not wishing to be boastful about last year's visit. They soon found out, the indelible accent picked up from Missy, gave her away, and they were enthralled by the details.

They passed from house to house, collecting all kinds of goodies. "Old Miss Potter is the best," they told her, "Just wait."

They rang the door bell, singing their Souling song.

"Soul, soul, an apple or two,
if you haven't got an apple,
a pear will do.
The roads are very dirty,
my shoes are very thin,
I've got a little pocket to put
a penny in.
If you haven't got a penny,
a half penny will do.
If you haven't got a half penny
God bless you."

A little old lady appeared at the door and asked them in. "I am sorry I have no cake, my dears. Would a drink to warm you, do instead?" All, save Annie, knew what was coming as they piled into Miss Potter's parlour. This was her best room, only used for visitors. It was crammed with furniture and bric-a-brac with dust sheets covering the sofa and chairs. She bade them sit down amongst the dust as she disappeared into the kitchen. The room was cold, as Miss Potter never entertained, and did not feel the need to light the fire in this part of the house. The seats were cold, as if icy damp was rising from them. She re-appeared with a tray of glasses and two dubious looking bottles. "A drop of Sloe gin," she beamed, "Made it three years ago, one of my best batches." The drop, turned out to be a whisky glass full, and the drink was so potent that it might just as well have been whisky. They finished their remaining visits in an alcoholic haze, and Annie felt sorry to leave her new friends after such a good evening, but guilty for leaving Lottie and Dennis to Margaret's wrath.

Lottie seemed exhausted after the visit, and alarmingly, three days later she was no better. She also developed a cough. Annie called to see her after school, to find Dennis administering a spoonful of strong cough mixture. As far a Annie knew, Lottie had never taken as much as an asprin before, always using country remedies passed on from her mother. Many a time she treated Annie's coughs and colds with a spoon of mixed butter and sugar, and a drink of nettle tea with fresh lemon juice. "Have you been to the doctor?" Annie asked. "Doctors," she replied resentfully, "I am not bothering with doctors, what do they know? They poke and prod, cut out bits here and there, and then what? They are no wiser than you or me, I am having no more to do with any of them!"

The cough persisted, but she seemed better in herself as Annie started her G.C.E. mock examinations, but they did not go well. The information was in her head, but the old fear of exams reared upwards from its secret place in her heart. She muddled the instructions on the history paper, ploughed through a wonderful essay in literature, on not quite the right subject, due to missreading the question, and by the time she reached English language, she was so stressed and tired that her spelling was appalling.

A frank and brutal report was sent to her parents, but her father only gave her a hug. "Let's phone Bethany, it looks as if we need some advice." Despite the cost of transatlantic calls, Alex stood by patiently as she talked to Bethany, and even allowed her to have a short chat to Missy, before speaking himself. "Fear," Bethany said, She realised how difficult it was, but Annie must relax. Something good did come out of it all, for Alex arranged another vacation in Florida that summer. "Something to look forward to," he smiled, kissing her forehead.

The month of May came only too soon, with the real exams now imminent and Arnold was a tower of strength, constantly calming her down. With one day to go, they abandoned all work and spent the day by the river, not telling anyone where they were going. It was a beautiful day, with buds blossoming and birds singing. They bought fish and chips, laughing as they shared it with the swans. Eating ice cream they took a boat trip, first on one of the large motor boats, which were for some reason all named after members of the Royal Family, and then in a rowing boat, with Arnold heroically doing all the work. They looked at all the huge riverside homes, making up amusing stories about the lives of imaginary people living there. A wonderfully relaxing day, ending at five o'clock as they kissed goodbye, wishing each other luck for next morning.

Strangely the shop was closed, yet her parents always stayed until six o'clock. A spidery web of foreboding began to spin itself around her, as she noticed a strange car outside Lottie's house. Annie did not need to be told, "No," she screamed to the silent street, "Not yet, oh please God, not yet." Lottie had died at four o'clock, passing away suddenly but peacefully in her favourite chair. The doctor was just about to leave, "I must see her," she insisted, ignoring the pleas of her tearful parents. Dennis took her by the hand to the bedroom, where Lottie now lay so peacefully, "I did not say goodbye," she wept. There was so much I needed to tell her, I was supposed to make her understand."

"But she did understand, my dear," said a voice with a strange lilting accent. She looked towards the door through her tears, it was the priest. Dennis had called Father O'Riley to give Lottie the Last Rites and he put his hand gently on her shoulder.

"She talked to me for many an hour, I know all about you Annie. You made her see how wrong she had been over all those years. Love is one of God's special gifts and she saw in the end that he would not punish her for doing her best for a dying child. After all, did not Jesus say for the little children to come to him? As for the love of this good man here, she would never be punished for that either."

Annie was taken aback, Father O'Riley was talking about Dennis. Lottie and Dennis had been lovers, why hadn't she ever thought about that? Annie went home with her mother, Alex staying with Dennis, armed with a bottle of good whisky. She was numb and sick, but she was not a little girl any more, she knew she must be strong.

Amazingly, she slept, a sound and undisturbed sleep, hardly able to believe it all when Joyce woke her. "How can I possibly sit an examination this morning," she thought, but knowing that she must. Her future depended on it, but how different the future would be without Lottie.

Annie sat at the desk, and began the maths paper. As if in a dream she plundered through the questions, and was unnervingly first to finish. "Look through your work carefully," Bethany had advised, but now Annie could see nothing but a blur of tears. Dabbing her eyes, she looked out of the window. How pretty the blossom of the old crab apple tree looked in the sunshine. "How old is it?" she wondered, "and how many different children have played around it?" She remembered how Lottie once told her that the bitter little crab apple was the ancestor of the Cox's Orange Pippin, the result of hundreds of years of selective breeding and improvement. Lottie's tiny garden was dominated by a Cox's tree, and for as long as she could remember, Annie had helped her pick the fruit. The pips rattled when the apples were ripe, and they always laughed as they gently shook each one.

"What about the apples, Lottie?" her mind cried out. "You have left me, you won't be there to pick them." Somewhere in the distance of reality she heard the voice of the invigilator, telling them to to leave the room in an orderly fashion. Without speaking to anyone, Annie headed for the car. There it stood, that sporty little Mini, which had given Lottie such pleasure. She sat in the driving seat realising Lottie would never ride in the back again. Resting her head against the padded steering wheel, she gave in to her grief and sobbed.

Chapter Forty One

In her will, Lottie left Annie the car, and also a letter. Not able to bring herself to open it at first, she drove to the coast, and sat on the beach at Rhyl, where they had spent such happy times when she was little. With shaking hands she opened the envelope. There was Lottie's, familiar handwriting, the beautifully formed, old fashioned script, so unlike Annie's, which although clearly legible, had not developed much further than printing. She began to read.

> *"Well Annie, if you are reading this letter, I am now with your gentle God, and as you have always known he was with me all the time. I have talked for a long time with the new priest at the church, and he agrees with most of your ideas. For years I have tortured myself, and now I find that my sins were small and forgivable, just as you told me. You are special Annie, not because I have loved you and helped to bring you up from a baby, there is something more. I first saw it when you came back from your stay with Norris. Something I can not quite explain, as if you are on this earth for a purpose, to do some good.*
>
> *I have left you the car, you probably suspected that I chose it for you right from the beginning. Dennis and I had some fun with that, he could not keep a straight face when you first saw it. I wonder if you are a veterinary nurse by now. Or perhaps the doctors were wrong, and I might have even lived to see you married to someone tall dark and handsome! Whatever is in store for you, enjoy it all, live life to the full, and be happy just for me."*

She folded the letter and stared out across the sea, which was now reaching high tide. This was no glittering ocean, but the cherished childhood memories gave it an important place in her heart.

At the very time she needed stability in her life, Annie's world was drastically changing. Her parents, deeply affected by the death of their friend, looked critically at their own existence. "Life is too short, we should be enjoying ourselves," Alex complained to Joyce, who needed no persuading. They would sell the shop and move to Florida. An income could still be made in a partnership with Norris, but someone else could have the hassle of exporting. The idea came as a bombshell to Annie, for they had not taken her plans into consideration at all.

How wonderfully tempting to give in, go to live in that idyllic place. To be with Missy, and to swim in the ocean every day, but what about her career? She was to go to college in September, and her practical assignment was arranged with Mr. Martin's veterinary practice. She badgered the poor man for six months to gain the position, working for nothing at weekends, and cleaning the surgery. Eventually she won him over, and he looked forward to the extra help, admiring her persistence, and rapport with animals. She could not let him down now.

For once even her father was brutally unsympathetic. The shop was to be sold, and that was that. He did soften after a while, seeing her point of view, deciding that he would sell the shop, but keep the flat above for Annie. The deeds would be registered in her name, and he would appoint his brother Thomas as guardian, while she stayed in England.

Uncle Thomas was not one of Annie's favourite people, and to her dismay, the wretched man decided to move back to Chester from Scotland, 'Back to his roots', as he wrote to his brother. "What about his family's roots," Annie thought, "Lucy comes from Scotland, and their obnoxious son Rory and his three sisters would surely detest such a move. Annie dearly wished that they would all stay put.

The much looked forward to vacation, was cancelled as the shop went on the market, and to make matters worse, Thomas moved his family with amazing speed, buying a house by the river and a partnership in an estate agency. He turned up on the morning of Annie's G.C.E. results and hovered about as she, so publicly rang the school for the news. She scraped a C pass in literature and history, failed dismally in English, probably due to stressed out spelling, attained an A in art, which was always a joy, and found herself with a B for maths, which was unbelievable, as she could not actually remember doing the paper, she had been so upset at the time. The English failure would prevent her admission to college and she was devastated.

What happened to the old critical and tactless Uncle Thomas, she could not imagine. He sat her down and patted her hand, ignoring the disappointment on her parents faces. "Don't worry, the same thing happened to Rory last year. Just do a re-sit in October, you will pass it then, and go on to college next year. I am sure Mr. Martin will take you on until then, and you will end up with more experience than anyone else on the course. Rory is having a great time now, studying engineering and you will see him at Christmas."

The all knowledgeable Uncle Thomas proved to be right. Early in November, news came of the re-sit, when she gained a C pass. Plans deferred to next year no longer seemed so far away. Mr. Martin took her on anyway, and although the pay was painfully meagre, Annie was at least happy in her work.

Despite his shock, indeed horror at some of Annie's spellings, Mr. Martin began to find her indispensable. She sorted out his files and organised his day, something his wife was embarrassingly grateful for, as she had never been able to do so herself. She also attended surgery, accompanied him on his rounds, and became involved with both patients and owners, with an obvious natural talent. She did however, on occasion give some strange advice about cats, but each time, Mr. Martin could hardly say that she was wrong, it just left him wondering where she got it all from.

One afternoon, a woman, who recently moved to the district, brought her cat in for a tranquilliser. The animal was bent on escaping, and had already gone AWOL for a week, making its way back to its old home in a village eight miles away. "Shut him in tonight, by the fire, and rub butter onto all his paws," she advised quite seriously, "you will not need to tranquillise him." Vet, client and cat looked at her in astonishment, "He will clean the sticky butter from his paws," she explained, "and as he does so, it will taste good. He will lick contentedly until he goes to sleep, and wake up feeling at home!" A note and a huge box of chocolates arrived at the surgery two days later, to thank her for the advice. "You are a strange girl," Mr Martin laughed as they munched the chocolates in the car whilst doing his rounds.

A buyer was found for the shop, and her parents planned the move to Florida after Christmas, having bought a house very near to Bethany and Norris. Annie steeled herself, fighting the temptation to give up everything and go with them, but she could wait. "Once I have my qualifications, I will be free," she told herself, and wrote explaining it all to Missy. It was not easy, she longed for the sunshine instead of this extra cold winter with early snow. It became so cold that the River Dee froze over, and people began to skate on it.

Annie borrowed some skates from one of the clients at the surgery, and met Arnold to join in the fun on her day off. They often skated at the Silver Blades in Liverpool, but this was such fun on the river, like being in a scene from an old fashioned Christmas card.

Her parents were visiting Grandma in Yorkshire, for a few days, so Annie took the opportunity to cook a meal for Arnold that evening. She planned to cook Spaghetti Bolognese, and although it was after six by the time they returned to the flat, the meal would not take long, as she had already prepared the meat sauce that morning. Arnold bought two bottles of red wine, and pouring a glass each she put the pasta on the stove and began to grate the cheese. The mantle clock struck six thirty, as they piled the food onto the plates. The rich sauce, savoury with onions tomatoes and garlic made them more hungry than ever.

Suddenly she cried out, "No, no, no," and clutching her stomach fell to her knees. A blur of sickening horror spread through her as she saw a group of people on a grassy bank. Just in front of her was young woman dressed in a fashionable pink suit. It was her pain she felt, and she like Annie was on her knees. Annie could see her through the mist, head bent, her hair was a light sandy colour, parting to the left and curling up at the nape of her neck. Annie's screams matched hers as if they were one. She put out her hand, knowing it was Missy, but then everything turned grey and there was nothing but Arnold's anxious voice.

He helped her to an arm chair, as she tried to explain the horrific vision. "It was Missy," she sobbed, "Something has happened to Missy!" The meal cooled and congealed as he tried to reassure her, but she had never been so frightened and clung tightly to him. All else failing, he plied her with the wine, and kissed and held her until she seemed to forget a little. They did not intend it to happen, but they made love for the first time, as much for comfort as anything else, and Arnold held her all night afterwards. He, thinking how wonderful, and she, wondering why everyone made a fuss about such an over rated experience, but Arnold was so happy, Annie kept such thoughts to herself.

It was not until next morning at work, that she heard the news. President Kennedy had died in Dallas, at seven o'clock the previous night, the victim of an assassin's bullet. Surely this terrible event could not be connected with Missy? Annie pushed the thought to the back of her mind, convincing herself that Arnold was probably right, her experience was a fainting fit, caused by the heat in the kitchen, after being so cold on the ice. "Anyway", she assured herself, "that was at six thirty and Kennedy was shot at seven o'clock. She was wrong, Kennedy was shot at six thirty British Standard Time, but pronounced dead at seven.

Two days before, Missy had been filled with excitement. She was to spend a long weekend with her maternal grandparents. An appointment was made in Dallas between Norris and a client that Friday, and knowing that this date coincided with the Kennedy campaign trail, his mother-in-law suggested that he bring Missy along. Grandma loved her life on the farm, but was always on the look out for excuses to visit the big cities to shop. Her husband had long backed away from such expeditions, but resignedly paid the credit card bills at the end of the month without complaint. She was also a great Kennedy fan, an ardent admirer of Jackie, and she and Missy looked forward to seeing her in person. Danny was most envious, Kennedy being his role model. A few months earlier he had spotted the Kennedy yacht, the Elegante, moored in Fort Lauderdale. He could hardly contain his excitement as he watched the beautiful wooden sailing vessel through his telescope, before being moved on by the police, but now Missy would have a much better view, standing alongside the motorcade.

Norris booked them into the hotel, and went off to meet his client as Missy and Grandma watched the Kennedy party arrive on T.V. They admired Jackie's elegant style, how beautiful she looked in her pink suit. Grandma told Missy how brave Jackie was, only just coming to terms with the death of their baby son, Patrick, and yet smiling and being so charming for the sake of her husband.

Missy and her grandmother went shopping that morning. Grandma bought her a look-a-like pink suit from Macy's, and a little pill box hat for herself. Missy loved the suit, although pink was not really her best colour, and stopped herself from laughing at Grandma in the hat, taking care not to hurt her feelings. They ate a hasty cream cheese bagel at mid morning and headed for the best position to watch the motorcade. Grandma being a wily old bird, knew just the place to wait. "Elm Street," she told the taxi driver, "We will stand by the railway bridge, on that grassy rise." She adjusted her new hat and fiddled with the jacket of Missy's pink suit, in the annoying way that all grandmothers seem to have, but Missy did not complain, they were having a great day.

The procession advanced at walking pace, the sunshine glinting on the open topped cars. Missy stood on tip toe as the motorcade turned from Houston Street, towards them. The Kennedys were in the second car, waving to the crowd, and Grandma pointed her trusty camera in their direction. "You must remember to send me some prints for Danny," Missy said excitedly. Just as she snapped the shutter, there was a bang. The president lifted his hands to his head, shot in the neck. Split seconds later another two shots, maybe three, rang out, exploding his head in front of Missy's eyes, as Jackie held him in vain, his life blood soaking into her pink suit.

Missy sank to her knees clutching her stomach, sickening horror spreading through her. "No, no, no," she screamed, not wanting to believe this was happening. Through the mist of tears and shock, she saw Annie kneeling in front of her, only as she put out her hand to reach her, she realised that it was impossible, her best friend was far away in England, then the world became grey, and there was only Grandma.

Chapter Forty Two

Missy wrote to Annie, re-living the horror of that morning, but did not mention the strange feeling that they were somehow together at the time. In fact she told no one, not even Daryl, as they might think she was crazy. If only she had confided in Molly, she would have been reassured, but she was frightened and felt she must keep it to herself. The assassination brought about a dramatic change in Danny, Missy wrote how devastated he was. He locked himself in his room for days, before he would speak even to Daryl. Now they were slowly coming to terms with the shock, and Danny's outlook on life was different. There were to be no more politics for him, he was going to be a teacher, teaching primary children. His idea was that all the kids who passed through his hands would learn right from wrong, to consider the feelings of others and to be tolerant and kind. "Get them young and perhaps they will learn, then the world will be a better place," he told his friends resolutely. Missy was sad, he seemed to have aged ten years, and now insisted on going back by himself to live in Jamaica, breaking Molly's heart.

Annie's tears mingled amongst the dried stains of Missy's on the letter, and she hugged it to her heart. So she was right, it had not been a fainting fit, but some kind of insight. She would not say anything more about it yet. When they were together, she would tell Missy, this was not something you could write about, and anyone else would think it absurd.

Annie missed her best friend so much, but loneliness was to play a great part in her existence for a while. Her parents took off for their new life after Christmas, and while it was a dream come true for any eighteen year old girl to have such independence, with her own flat and car, she now felt that they were too far away. Another blow followed in February, when Arnold left the country. His father was in the army, and was posted to Germany. She knew that Arnold had never lived in one place for long, but somehow she had never thought of him leaving. He was still studying, now at the local Tec, but as his father pointed out, he could do all that in Germany, and if he joined the Army later, he could look forward to a distinguished career. It was a tearful farewell, leaving Annie feeling rather let down by the fact that he chose career prospects above her.

Now there was just Uncle Thomas, Dennis and her job, but Dennis was to go from her life too. John and Sally, who had emigrated to Australia when Annie was just a baby, heard the news about Lottie, and whisked Dennis off to live with them. They never forgot his kindness to them before they set off to Australia, buying little treats for the journey, and since, always remembering the children's birthdays, and sending local newspaper cuttings to keep them in touch with life in their old home town. They genuinely loved him, Annie could see that. He was treated like their long lost father, and they looked forward to taking him home for the children to have a grandfather at last.

Uncle Thomas and family were not of much comfort. Most of the old animosity was no longer there, although his girls, all younger than Annie, were now jealous of her. That awkward cousin, from years back, was now a beautiful woman, with her own flat and a fantastic car. Life was unfair, they thought, and showed it.

Annie threw herself into her job, but the nights were lonely. Often she would take sick animals home to nurse, not just out of dedication, but for company. Mr. Martin could not imagine how he would cope when she started college, even though she would be assigned to him for a good deal of the time.

He was to rely on her even more. Three weeks before Annie was due to go to Florida, on the long awaited visit, Mr. Martin was involved in a car crash, his car was a write off and his leg badly broken. She could not leave him in such a mess, but sobbed herself to sleep that night after telling her parents that she would not be coming.

Annie took on all the responsibility, she drove the painfully injured vet in her car, and worked without a day off. The work killed the pain of disappointment, and the Martin family's gratitude was heartwarming. He was just about able to cope when she left for college, and by the time she settled down there, she realised what a strange existence she had been leading. Everyone seemed to have enjoyed a wonderful summer, talking of vacations in France, Spain and even good old Blackpool. Parties and fun after the slog of exams, Annie had missed all that.

The work was not easy, but the social life was good. She stayed in the college dorm when she was not on assignment with Mr. Martin, gaining many friends, and making up for her lost summer. She was the only one who could cook, and as money ran short, Annie's ideas were a Godsend. They would pool their money and watch in awe, as Annie turned the most meagre ingredients into tasty meals. Annie's scones became a legend, and sometimes she wondered if that had something to do with the hopeful procession of would-be boyfriends. She often laughed to herself, remembering Molly's saying about a man's heart and his stomach! The late nights and intensive study, took their toll and she was glad to be back with Mr. Martin for a while. Even the emptiness of her flat was appealing at first, "I am re-charging my batteries," she told herself.

There was no one special in her life, and after a few days she was lonely again. With a free afternoon, she picked up her sketch pad, and headed for her old place of solace, the Zoo. She sat in front of the tiger enclosure, just as she had done years ago. Times were changing, the beautiful tigress now was the proud mother of two cubs. Patiently she sketched, capturing the beauty of the large cat's face. Its eyes were like glowing amber, but Annie could see that behind that look of ferocity, there was now also contentment.

"Tiger tiger, burning bright
In the forests of the night
What immortal hand or eye
Could frame thy fearful symmetry?"

The voice behind her made her start, almost dropping her pencil. "The Tiger, by William Blake," he smiled. Annie nodded, recognising him at once, Jack Taylor was a client from the surgery. "What are you doing wasting your talents as a veterinary nurse, when you can draw like that?" he asked, "You should be at art college." Annoyed now, she crossly informed him that she was a trainee, veterinary nurse, and she enjoyed her work, which was more than most people could say, but she melted at his crestfallen look. "How is the cat?" she asked, changing the subject in a more friendly tone.

She could never have forgotten him or his cat. Tall, dark, handsome and eligible, as Lottie would have said, he rode everywhere on an old motorbike, which looked like a relic from the war. He even brought the cat into the surgery in a basket strapped to the back of the thing! The cat, a huge striped grey tom, was brought in to be neutered. Annie could still see in her mind, the look on that cat's face as Jack put it into the basket to go home. If cats could speak, it would have screamed. "What have you done to me?"

He settled himself on the bench beside her. "The cat, well his behaviour has not improved, if that's what you mean." The animal, it seemed was often aggressive. Jack pushed up his sleeves, showing scratches and bruises to prove it. He bought the cat after his wife left him, and it became a pampered kitten. Jack played with him constantly, but the play got out of hand, even the neutering did not help. Jack now lived with a big fat tom cat, bent on beating him up.

Annie fought the temptation to laugh, "This I have got to see, why don't you bring him back to see Mr. Martin?" Jack had a better idea, "Come over tonight, I will cook dinner and you can see for yourself."

She drove to his house that evening, feeling rather silly. She had talked herself into this, with a man of maybe ten years her senior, who she really did not know at all. He lived in a small semi, not far from the Zoo, and Annie could not help thinking that this was once a happy matrimonial home, and wondered why his wife had left him.

Tiggy, the cat sat on an armchair, looking completely innocent, allowing her to stroke its silky fur, and purring in a noisy but friendly manner. Jack was charming, and a delicious aroma drifted from the kitchen. He poured two glasses of wine and sat beside her on the sofa. Quick as a flash, a blur of grey fur pounced upon him, knocking the glass from his hand. He pushed the animal away but it was back for more at once. Embarrassed, he gave it a smack, knocking it off balance, but back it came again.

This time almost as quickly as the feline fiend, Annie gave it a shove with her foot, pulled Jake into the kitchen and shut the door. She explained her strategy to her embarrassed host.

"Cats can be like that, look at the tiger cubs in the Zoo, they fight all the time. One smacks the other, it yowls, then thinks what a good fight it was, and goes back for more. Tiggy thinks you are his fellow cub. When you smack or push him, in his mind it is a great play fight, that is why the situation is becoming worse. Each time he starts, walk away and shut the door on him, he will soon take the hint. It would be better to get him to play with a feather duster or a ball and string, and if he starts on you, stop playing, and shut the door again

Her theory worked, the big grey tom learned to respect his owner, and he and Jack, fell in love with Annie. Jack swept her off her feet, visiting her at college, taking her to expensive restaurants and trendy nightclubs, but the best times were when they went to bed early at his house. They would take a bottle of wine upstairs, or smoke a joint of marijuana, light candles and make love until dawn. He was an attentive skilful lover, unlike Arnold who had been so inexperienced, yet Annie felt there was something missing. Some spark, some intensity. She realised deep down she did not really love him, but decided that it was just her way. She would never experience the same kind of love shared between Missy and Daryl, so she settled down, happy with her lot.

The happiness was shattered, with such suddenness that it left her reeling. With Annie's final examinations looming, Jack's wife returned. Simply turned up out of the blue, and he welcomed her back with open arms, as if she had never been away, saying nothing more than sorry, to Annie as he returned to matrimonial bliss.

Her emotions veered from shock to hurt and anger, so she wrote to Missy.

> "How could he do this to me? We were friends as well as lovers. He said he loved me, while he still loved her all the time we were together. Making love in her bed, I was such a fool, he was always thinking about her. How could he do that? Now of all times to leave me, just before I take my finals, he has wrecked my life."

Chapter Forty Three

Jack did not wreck her life. A feeling of deadly calm arose from her heart, numbing her mind to the pain. She collected her belongings from the dorm and drove home to her flat. Climbing wearily into bed, she slept, not even hearing the anxious telephone calls from her fellow students. A deep and healing, dream filled sleep, where she was happy, she was in love. Real love, not like with Jack, there was no spark, no intensity missing with this man, who was neither Jack or Arnold. She felt a mental and physical closeness as they rode in a horse and cart through warm sunshine into a wooded glade with a sparkling stream. She set out a picnic, "No candles, Jack," she thought, "no ex wife's bed. This is the real thing, something you could never give me." The deep emotion she felt was intoxicating, as the man in her dreams stroked her hair, twisting it gently around his fingers, and telling her how he loved the way it curled in the heat. She put her arms around his neck, saying how she loved him. Their passion inflamed under the protection of the trees, and they made love slowly, gently, cherishing every precious moment. "I want to be with you for ever," she sighed. Waking refreshed, she still carried an echo of the happiness felt in the dream, but there was a shock to come, for she had slept for twenty four hours.

For the next few days, she ate, studied, and slept when she could stay awake no longer, but now dreamless sleep. Her whole being was concentrated upon the successful completion of her finals. It was a most important part of her plans, and nothing was going to stop her now. Calmness remained as she began the gruelling week of examinations. The old fear of such events was now dead, buried somewhere in the passage of time, as she ploughed through the papers with a strange new confident determination.

Annie did not join in the post exam celebrations, but telephoned her parents and arranged a flight to Florida, the very next day. The reunion with her family and Missy, was well overdue, and she could not think of anything more appealing. Despite the hastily arranged schedule, everything went according to plan on the morning of the flight. In her organised way, Annie tidied the flat, emptied the refrigerator, and fueled the car with just enough petrol to drive to Manchester airport, and back home on her return. With her father's promise of shopping trips, she was only taking a small bag. It stood on the floor of her bedroom, neatly packed, and she knelt down to put in her purse. At that moment she saw it. A spider, a huge long legged spider making its way across the floor towards her. Revulsion filled her, she hated the things. They seemed to follow her about, relishing her company. One had caused her to almost destroy her father's shop with that gun. Were they never satisfied? Could they not haunt someone else? "No," she thought, "spiders love spider haters, making a point of roosting in our rooms, when there are other establishments with much more suitable accommodation." As far back as she could remember, she felt an illogical loathing for the creatures. Even in nursery rhymes, she understood just how Miss Muffet felt, and the thought of Insy Binsy Spider, climbing up the spout, filled her with horror. Following Lottie's long respected advice, she coped with this spider, like all the others, popping over a plastic deodorant cap and intending to dispose of it in the usual way. Checking her passport, she picked up the car keys from the table, zipped up the bag, and set off for the airport, allowing herself plenty of time.

The car was to be left in the long stay car park, and she would have time to buy breakfast, before the flight to Heathrow. The food on the plane turned her stomach, and she did not intend to eat any of the ghastly looking stuff, all covered in plastic. This attitude was a mystery to her mother, who out of character, seemed to devour everything in sight during the journey, as if it was a nervous affliction to eat.

In good time Annie reached the airport, and found a place at the long stay car park. Bag slung over her shoulder, she turned the key in the lock, and was hit by the sudden memory of the spider. He was still there in the flat, fat body and wiggly legs trapped beneath the plastic cap. He would slowly die of hunger and thirst and Annie had done this. She, the caring one who worked for the good of all living creatures. She who had just battled to obtain qualifications for such a career. "It is just a wretched spider," she told herself out loud, but it made no difference. Conscience getting the better of her, and no longer able to stand the thought of the creature's torment, she threw the bag back into her car and slamming the door, headed straight for home.

At the car park exit the attendant demanded the daily fee. "What?" she shrieked," I only came in a minute ago." He shrugged, muttering something about kids of today in their flash cars, so she almost threw the money at him and drove home at a speed far greater than she knew she should. Snatching the keys from her purse, Annie flew up the steps to the flat and ran into the bedroom. To find what? The plastic cap was on its side and the spider was gone. Staring in disbelief, with anger rising to boiling point, she sped back to the car and drove like the wind, only by chance, noticing the petrol gauge, almost empty. With time relentlessly ticking by, she pulled up to the nearest filling station, using the last of the her U.K. currency. Now there were only dollars in her purse, and she would not be able to buy breakfast.

"Nearly there," she thought, all hot and sticky now, putting her foot down hard on the trusty Mini Cooper's accelerator. Out from nowhere, a police car appeared, and her heart sank as he pulled her over. Of course she was speeding, what could she say? The police officer took his time, reprimanding her and examining her driving licence before giving her the ticket. By now anxiety turned to panic, and Annie's hatred for spiders was unbelievable.

She missed the plane, which was supposed to make the journey to Heathrow so easy. Despair followed panic as the calm, unruffled, not a hair out of place, woman behind the desk, informed her that there was no other flight for three hours. Annie's cheeks were hot and her hair dampened around her forehead making her feel so very dishevelled, as she explained the situation to 'Miss Perfect', the checking assistant. A spark of humanity showed through the woman's movie star make up. She contacted Annie's connecting flight desk at Heathrow. There would be very little time to spare, but as she was carrying no cases for the baggage hold, the New York flight would wait for her.

She only just got to the plane on time, they were calling her name at the airport, and her fellow passengers looked at Annie as she boarded, as if holding her responsible for the delay. She sunk into her seat with a feeling of guilt as they took off at last. Feeling emotionally wrung out, she ordered a large Jack Daniel's, swallowed it, pushed her bag beneath her knees and slept, waking later, to feel terribly hungry.

Lunch arrived on its plastic tray, and there was no choice now, but to eat it. The food, under all that wrapping was surprisingly good, and for the remainder of the journey, Annie became another version of her mother, and ate everything on offer. After sleeping during the last leg of the journey from New York, she met her parents, looking as fresh as a daisy, as if there had never been any Jack, exams or spiders, and decided not to bother telling her family about any of it.

Oh, the ocean, to be back at the beach, she never thought she would have been away for so long. Now she felt she could never leave again, and the house, what a wonderful ocean front home. It was situated so near to Missy, and she could hardly wait to see her best friend. She would walk along the beach to visit, as soon as she was unpacked.

Her room was beautiful, reminiscent of the one she had shared with Missy, with an ocean view, but decorated in varying shades of yellow and cream, with wooden louvre blinds, and matching doors on the closets and bathroom.

"I will just unpack Mom," she shouted, "I would love a cup of tea." Dropping the bag onto her new bed, she unzipped it, and to her horror, there on top of the special Beatles tee shirt, bought for Daryl from the Cavern Club in Liverpool, was the spider! Annie had flown the Atlantic with him beneath her knees. Grabbing the shirt, she ran through the lounge room, outside onto the beach, flicking the little beast onto the sand. "There, go and terrorise someone else," she shouted at the creature, moments later embarrassingly aware that someone was watching.

"How cruel," he scolded, "What could a small spider ever have done to you?" She glared at him, her brown eyes flashing with anger, and unable to stop herself poured out the whole spider story. "So there," she finished, "No one could blame me if I squashed the thing, and despite what you think, I care very much for all living creatures. I am a veterinary nurse!" Without waiting for any further comment, she turned and stomped back into the house, dark curls bobbing down her back in a provocative way that set his pulse racing. "Hope you know you've broken the law, that spider is an illegal immigrant," he shouted to her as she slammed the door.

"I see you have met someone," Alex smiled at her, "and you have only been here two minutes. Who is he?" "I don't care who he is Dad," she retorted with an unexpected bitterness. "He is a man isn't he. They come and go like double decker busses." He sat her down on the soft white leather sofa, there as no trace of anything antique in this house.

"Oh Annie, what is wrong? Tell your old Dad." She told him everything, it all tumbled out amongst her tears, even about the candlelit love making as well as the pain of rejection. Swallowing his shock and embarrassment, and resolutely determined not to show it, he hugged his daughter. "Put it all behind you love. You are here now, and never have to go back it you don't want to." Tears dissolved into giggles, with the relief of talking to him. "I must go back sometime, my car is in the airport car park!"

Refreshed, she skipped along the fine sand and walked with her feet in the ocean to Missy's house, where her friend was standing on the top veranda looking out for her. They laughed and cried, dancing about like little children. "I am home," Annie thought, "this is where I belong." "You and your parents are coming over for dinner tonight," Missy told her. "Won't you stay? It will be like the old days, we can talk all night, and raid Dad's vodka.

The meal was wonderful, Bethany and Norris had not changed a bit, but baby Michael was now a chatty little boy, intent on not going to bed, and an absolute handful. The most miraculous change was in her own parents. Who were these relaxed and youthful people? Perhaps they should have made this move years ago.

"You look so pretty, Mom," Annie whispered as she hugged her mother to say goodnight, and smiled as she watched them walk home along the beach arm in arm. When all the house as quiet, the girls crept to the kitchen. Armed with two tall glasses of orange juice and a large bottle of vodka they went out to sit on the wooden floorboards of the veranda facing the ocean. The air was blissfully warm and they sat as always, easy in each other's company, remembering how they wept in this very place years ago when Bethany was taken to hospital, and marvelling at the way that fate had a way of putting things right after all.

Missy topped up the glasses with more of her father's alcohol.

"Just look at Michael now, little scamp. When he annoys me, I remind myself of that awful time. My world was falling around me. I thought I was going to lose Mom, but you were there Annie. There is something special about our friendship, don't you think?   As if we are as one in a crisis."

Annie knew exactly what she meant, and with no reservations told her about the strange incident of insight on the day of Kennedy' death, feeling hardly any surprise on hearing Missy's version. Somehow they had both been there, minds linked by a destiny that was always to keep them together.

They drank half the bottle of vodka, staying on the veranda until the first shades of dawn, their years of being apart vanished and their problems evaporated. All but one very major one, Missy was two months pregnant!

Chapter Forty Four

Why didn't Missy go on the pill?" Annie thought as she walked home along the beach next morning, in time to eat breakfast with her parents. At least that was one thing that Jack did for her. Actually went along to the family planning clinic with her, sitting holding her hand in the waiting room, and even paying for the prescriptions. She thought then how sweet, loving and considerate he was, but now she knew it was pure selfishness. "He did not want any little Jack babies," she said under her breath, "No, he made sure that there would be no ties in case SHE came back!"

Missy and Daryl were different, they really loved each other, and although their baby was not planned, it was just part of their love and there were no regrets. Annie smiled to herself as she approached her parent's new home, thinking how Missy joked that they timed the pregnancy to co-ordinate with her visit, especially so that they would have her to help them take the flak from their parents when they made their important announcement.

"You've got a lovely smile, it is good to see you happy," someone said. There sitting on the steps of the house, was the spider lover from yesterday. "Your folks said you would be back this morning so I waited, this is for you." He handed her a single, slightly wilted red rose, not taking his eyes from hers for a moment. His hair was as fair as hers was dark. He wore it as long as Annie's, but pulled it into a ponytail, looking what her father would call a 'real scruff' with his faded tee shirt, ripped jeans and no shoes, yet there was something irresistible about him, as he smiled hopefully.

"Can I come in for breakfast?"

"What! I don't even know your name. Imagine what my parents would say?"

"It's Luke, and I have already charmed your Mom."

"How long have you been here?"

"Since last night, I can't get you out of my head Annie,"

"How do you know my name?"

"I told you, I charmed your Mom. What I can't understand is your accent, it almost sounds as if you come from Texas!"

Annie gave no explanation, but the way he looked at her as he spoke, as if holding her with his eyes, stirred unexpected and hitherto unknown emotions within her. Beguiled, she took his hand as they made their way up the steps to find her parents in the kitchen. "You won then, Luke," Alex laughed, "Well done, faint heart never won fair lady!" Annie looked wide eyed at her father. This Luke might be an axe murderer for all they knew, and here she was holding his hand, her mother was feeding him blueberry pancakes, and her father was encouraging it all. He was weaving a spell around her, just as the beach and the ocean had done years ago, and she could not break free, she did not want to break free.

Appetite sharpened by the night of girlie chat, the pancakes were delicious, but Annie suspected that her Mom had received some recent instruction from Molly, as her cooking was never so good. She could hardly believe the easy going breakfast, as Luke chatted away, telling them all about himself.

At twenty four, Luke was a little old to be a beach bum, but it turned out not to be his profession, he was a vet. "Of all things, a vet, "Annie thought embarrassed now, to think how, just the previous day, she had proudly thrown the fact that she was a veterinary nurse, at him. He originated from the Damariscotta Region in Maine, but fell in love with Florida at the age of ten. "The Sunshine State," he beamed, "pulls me back like a magnet." Annie knew exactly what he meant.

Luke explained that he made the first trip there with his father in their boat. Right down the Atlantic Intracoastal Waterway, 1550 miles, from Cape Cod to Florida Bay, and onwards. It was more than a vacation, it was part of his father's research. "What does your father do then?" Alex asked between mouthfuls of pancake. "Oh, he is a professor," Luke replied casually. Annie's third pancake suddenly lost its appeal. What would this brilliant professor father think of her. A veterinary nurse with wacky spelling who until the last few years had spent her time trying to avoid any kind of education. "What kind of professor," she asked sadly, thinking how foolish all this was, he was only having breakfast and she would probably never see him again.

Laughing he took her hand.

"What kind of professors are there? Absent minded or crazy. Pop is both, but he is great. Really down to earth, no time for apple polishers."

Annie made a mental note to ask Missy what an apple polisher was, but said nothing as he carried on.

"Pop forgets where he puts everything, because he always has something to do with work on his mind. Mom took my sister and I away for the weekend once. He forgot we had gone, and did not even feed the dog, which is quite something, as boy does our dog bark if he does not get fed. That dog has some kind of body clock. At eight in the morning and five at night we have to feed him. He goes to his bowl and sits patiently for about five minutes, if he has to wait longer than that, he starts. Poor animal, Pop shut him out of the house that weekend, couldn't understand what all the noise was about! Anyway, talking about Pop, he loves his job, and he is real good at it, but he types everything because his hand writing is awful, and uses Mom as a dictionary because his spelling is even worse, which explains why his pet name for her is Webster! We are a crazy family. We hold clam bakes on the beach, stay up all night playing monopoly, get drunk on home brew beer, which explodes in the cellar and sometimes sleep out in the garden under the stars just for the fun of it"

"Well you still haven't told us what you were doing travelling the Intracoastal Waterway," Alex insisted, unintentionally breaking the spun glass enchantment between his daughter and this likeable young man.

"He studies Algology, the branch of botany concerned with the study of algae. That's what we were doing, collecting samples, but wow, what a good vacation it was too. It was the first time I ever had Pop all to myself, and we have been best buddies ever since. Now he is investigating the possibility that plants grow on other planets, Astrobotany, they call that. Perhaps the first man to walk on the moon, will have Pop trailing behind collecting plants."

Annie's plans to meet Missy at Daryl's house now seemed to include Luke. On the way she told him all about her friends, about the year long stay with Missy, congratulating him on identifying the Texan drawl resulting from living with her, and which was somehow as deep seated as their friendship. She also told him of Missy's pregnancy, wondering why on earth he was so easy to talk to, and whether she should be divulging her friend's personal secrets to a stranger, even if she knew in her heart that she was falling in love with him.

Molly came to the door, hugging Annie like a long lost daughter, which indeed was how she felt. Luke respectfully stood back, waiting to be introduced, chuckling as Annie explained how they met on the beach. Strangely, the spider story had become a funny escapade, and Annie even laughed herself as she told it. Molly shook Luke's hand and welcomed him, but Annie noticed a strange expression on her face as she held his hand for a few seconds more than necessary. Paula appeared from the kitchen, preceded by the delightful old familiar aroma of chocolate chip cookies and fresh ground coffee, and made a great fuss of Annie. "Daryl and Missy are in the pool," she said, "Introduce your friend and we will bring out the refreshments."

Paula took out a huge plate of freshly baked cookies, and Annie went to help Molly bring the coffee. Fragrant rich ground coffee laced with cream and sugar, coffee was never like this in England. Molly touched Annie's cheek.

"Stay a minute dear, do you remember when we first met? I told you then of two men. That you must choose the right one, or the meaning of your life would be lost. This is the one Annie, I am well aware that I am not the person destined to help you decide when the time comes, but I can see it so clearly. Please take my advice, don't let him go."

Luke had no intention of going anywhere, and soon endeared himself to everyone in Annie's life. The news of Missy's baby sent shockwaves through their families, but the situation was soon accepted and in no time Molly and both expectant grandmothers were knitting baby clothes. There was no insistence or pressure about marriage, but Missy and Daryl always intended to marry and had no qualms about bringing the date forward a few years. Norris created a position for his new son-in-law to be in the antique business, and converted part of the house into an apartment for the new family, until they could save for a place of their own.

Annie and Missy excitedly planned the wedding, to take place at the end of August, a week before Annie's return to England. She found Luke's reaction to all this surprising. "You are so lucky, it must be the best thing in the world to have a child with the woman you love," she overheard him say to Daryl.

Luke spent every day in Annie's company. He was not only taking a vacation, but writing a thesis on cetaceans, so Annie accompanied him to the Porpoise School in The Keys. Annie had visited there before, but this time with Luke, she was not just a visitor. The relationship between trainers and dolphins was touching. These animals were indeed part of a family here.

Some were second or third generation captives, never animals taken from the wild. That, they all agreed was unbearably cruel. Such dolphins often killed themselves, driven by the distress of captivity, never would that happen here. Others were rescue cases, nursed tenderly back to health but bearing scars from horrific injuries. To Annie's surprise the school was involved in a medical research programme. A few mentally handicapped children came twice a week, and together with the trainers, played in the water with the animals. The creatures showed amazing understanding and gentleness towards those little human beings with such problems. The smiles on the children's faces was a joy to see, but evidently, there was more to it than pleasure. The children were improving, taking tiny steps towards a more normal life, and the dolphins seemed to love it.

They rode about in Luke's battered old Eagle Jeep. "As battered as Jack's motorbike," she thought, "but that is where the comparison ends." With Luke it was different, there was nothing missing in her love for him, yet she felt Luke was holding back. She tried cooking a meal for him in his trailer. Not the most romantic place, but it was his home after all. Despite two bottles of wine, passionate kisses and a stunningly beautiful starlit night, they still did not make love.

The wedding was upon them in no time. and the girls spent the night before at Missy's house, while Daryl went off to get drunk at Luke's place. They missed Danny, he would be with them for the wedding tomorrow, but Daryl was disappointed that he refused to come from Jamaica sooner. Now he would come straight from the plane to the wedding, not giving them time for a reunion chat.

Bethany kissed her daughter goodnight and she deliberately left tempting tit bits in the refrigerator, knowing of the girls' habits, but this time there would be no vodka. "Not good for my grandchild," Norris teased, dangling a bottle in front of them, he had known all along what they got up to.

They talked for most of the night of Daryl, Luke, the baby, how they missed Danny and how their lives were intertwined and Missy patted her stomach.

"Do you think I will make a good mom? Things won't change, will they Annie? You will come back for Christmas, and maybe stay?

I need you with me more than ever now. I won't be different will I? This is my last night of being Missy Blake."

Annie hugged her, with assurance that all would be well, and reminded her to brush up on all Grandpa Jake's stories. "You might not be carrying the Blake family name from tomorrow, but you will soon have a little one to pass all the family history on to."

The wedding was most unusual. At Key Biscayne the guests assembled on the beach at nine in the morning. The ceremony was to take place on a boat, with just the captain, the celebrant, the happy couple and their parents. A calypso band played as they sailed out into the sparkling ocean, and the guests tucked into a barbecue breakfast of bacon, scrambled eggs and toasted bagels, accompanied by glasses of freshly squeezed orange juice mixed with champagne. "How selfish," Joyce remarked to Alex, "Not holding the ceremony in front of the guests." "How wonderful," whispered Luke, squeezing Annie's hand.

Molly looked anxiously at her watch, where could Danny be? The festivities were almost over before he arrived. Annie was aware of the devastating affect of Kennedy's death on their friend almost two years ago, but he was now a different person. There was nothing left of the old mischievous Danny who she had once known and loved. This was a cold and serious young man, accompanied by a beautiful girl. There was no hint of warmth as Annie hugged him, and he was decidedly formal as he introduced Kathleen. Her skin was as fair as Annie's, but sun kissed with tiny becoming freckles. Her flaming red hair cut into a Mary Quant style bob, added to her beauty. Kathleen was Irish, with looks and a beguiling accent which would melt any man's heart. Her captivating accent, stirred an infuriating spark of recognition in Annie's mind. The accent of someone she had met once, perhaps when she was little, someone sweet and kind, she couldn't quite remember, but that was where the charm ended. Kathleen displayed none of the congenial, easy going and friendly nature, so characteristic of her race, as she wrapped herself around Danny's arm with all the allure of a boa constrictor, making Annie think about Lottie's old story of St. Patrick, and how he drove all the snakes and toads from Ireland! As the boys went off to the bar table for more champagne, she stood alone with Annie and rounded upon her. With temper as flaming as her hair, and green eyes flashing, she hissed.

"Danny has told me all about you Annie, so just you listen to me. He is mine now, you keep off. I've got a place at college, teacher training in Dublin, and Danny is coming with me. Don't get any ideas about coming to Ireland to visit when you get home, I don't want you anywhere near us. I am going to have him all to myself, away from this place, and that suffocating mother of his. He will marry me, because he loves me. I will not have to trap him like your stupid pregnant friend over there."

Annie felt as if she had been slapped across the face. Unbelievably as he boys returned, Kathleen just smiled sweetly, until the end of the reception. Annie watched with aching heart as Danny said goodbye to his mother with just a peck on the cheek, wondering how he could now be so hard after coming from such a demonstrative and affectionate family. He shook Annie's hand formally, but she held it, saying something which surprised even herself.

"Goodbye mavournin, may the path be straight that's in front of you."

Danny looked bewildered, but Kathleen's eyes widened. "What does she know about Ireland," she thought fearfully, "This hateful English girl, with an American accent, now she is talking like my old granny. I haven't heard anyone say that for years." Then Annie shook her hand.

"Goodbye Kathleen, take care, I am sure St. Patrick will be at your side as soon as you set foot in Ireland."

Chapter Forty Five

Annie felt she could say nothing to anyone about Kathleen, but Molly knew. She sobbed as she confided in Annie, not understanding the girl's hatred and, the change in her son.

With no idea of the situation, the happy couple set off for their honeymoon, for three weeks on Bethany's parent's farm, and Annie was left with only one remaining week with Luke. She felt confused, as he said he loved her, but not once did he ask her to stay. He talked about Christmas, when she was due to return. He would be back in Maine by then with his parents, but promised to come down to visit. How could he want to be with her almost every minute of the day, and yet be so negative about their relationship for the future?

They said their goodbyes on the beach, where the spider had first brought them together. "Can't stand public farewells," he told her and Annie's tears at the airport were not just for the parting from her parents, but for what she felt was the end of the only real love she would ever feel.

The sturdy little green car waited patiently in the car park, just as if she had never been away, and she shed a few more tears, this time for Lottie as she sat behind its familiar sporty steering wheel. Although the British weather was kind, her flat felt cold and dingy. "Perhaps I will save and refurnish it," she thought, "and paint the walls in Florida colours. "No," she decided peering into the empty refrigerator, "I don't want to live alone any more. I will give notice to Mr. Martin, and stay in America with my parents after Christmas. With no available food supplies she opted for fish and chips, and sat in the lonely flat eating them with her fingers out of the paper.

She dragged her heavy suitcase into the bedroom. So many lovely things bought by her parents, had caused the purchase of something not much smaller than a trunk to bring them all home. There on the floor, was the overturned deodorant cap, she picked it up and fresh tears, turned to sobs for Luke. That spider had a lot to answer for. She lay on the bed and cried herself to sleep, waking cold and stiff in the morning. Mr. Martin would be expecting her at nine o'clock, so she dressed and hurried out, stomach turning at the sight of the smelly chip papers left in the kitchen. Gingerly she dropped them into the bin outside, thinking how there would never be any racoons in this garbage. The Beatles on the car radio, sang 'Can't Buy Me Love,' only adding to her depression as she drove to work.

A week with Mr. Martin was healing and theyhey were so busy that she was grateful to go home and sleep. The end of the week was chaotic, with two emergency operations, due to a car accident, resulting in late surgery, irritable patients, and unreasonably irate clients. "If it was a life and death fight for one of their animals, they would not complain," she whispered to her boss.

An extremely unlikable old man waiting with a cat of a similar disposition overheard. "You are a clever Dick, aren't you?" he sneered at Annie. Out of the blue one of Lottie's bits of information came into her head, and she smiled at the grumpy old man.

"Well thank you for that compliment Mr. Rogers. You must be aware that in the 1920's, a husband and wife scientific team, George and Gladys Dick, isolated the streptococcus that caused scarlet fever. They were the original clever Dicks, I am very flattered!"

The old grouch grunted, then silently stared down at his cat and behaved impeccably for the remaining waiting time. Mr. Martin took Annie out for a drink after work, "What a day," he gasped, "but it was worth it to see you shut Mr. Rogers up." Cheered by the glass of brandy, she drove home feeling relaxed for the first time in a week.

Balancing a pile of files, her purse and keys, she locked the car outside the shop, and walked around the back to the flat. Her mind still on Mr. Rogers, she did not at first see the figure sitting at the top of the stairs by her door. Startled, the files slipped from her grasp and tumbled down the stone steps, scattering around in the street below. The crouching person, sprang to Annie's aid, causing her to scream, before realising who it was. Luke! Luke standing sheepishly before her, dressed most respectably in a black polo neck sweater and grey trousers. The Luke she loved, hardly ever wore shoes, never mind dressed like this. There was an unfamiliar awkwardness between them as he took her hand. "Aren't you glad to see me?" His appearance was so unexpected, she did not know what to think. For a week she had been trying to numb her mind against his memory, and now he was here as large as life.

"I have to know if there is someone else. I could not bear to be a temporary romance, and I know that you were seeing someone before you came to Florida. I talked to Molly about it, and she told me in no uncertain terms, that if I wanted you, I had better get over here right now. So here I am, I even bought suitable clothes to compare favourably with any English rival."

He smiled his captivating smile, and held her with his eyes as no one else ever could, until she melted into his arms. Pushing the tattered files through the door, he swept her up in his arms and carried her into the flat, by some instinct knowing the location of the bedroom. This was more than love, it was unbridled lust. Their clothes were strewn around the bedroom as he kissed and teased her before giving into their deepest desires as their mutual doubts and fears faded away. Passion spent, they slept in each other's arms until first light crept through the still open curtains. Annie woke, five fifteen, she must leave for work in just over three hours. She lay watching Luke as he slept, Molly was right, he was the one, but she was sure that she would never have to make the choice that her Jamaican friend feared.

"No one else in this life could make me feel like this," she thought happily, and in a way she was right.

She loved everything about Luke, even the way his front teeth were slightly uneven. Gently she touched his fair hair, thinking sensually of how she had kissed his body hair of the same colour last night. He woke, bleary eyed, and taking her into his arms, made love again, slowly this time, delightfully savouring every moment, as if in a dream that she wanted never to end.

It came as quite a shock to find the time at eight o'clock, hardly giving her time to shower and dress for work, and with no time to cook that English breakfast promised to Luke. He refused to stay in bed, laughing at the shower attachment over the bath. "Few homes over here have purpose built showers," she explained, "and we don't have MacDonalds for early morning breakfast either." He joined her under the running water, splashing and getting her hair wet.

"I love the way your hair curls. Um, I am getting really horny again."

"I can see that but, stop tempting me and control yourself, or I will never get to work this morning. I will come to see you at lunch time."

"No way. I am not letting you out of my sight. I will come to work with you. I am a vet after all, surely your Mr. Martin could find me something to do."

There was no dissuading him, and they walked together round to the car, with Luke looking himself again, in old jeans a sparkling white tee shirt and an obviously well loved old leather jacket. "Glad you put your sneakers on," she teased, "You could hardly go barefoot here." He smiled a wicked smile, "Careful, or I will carry you back up there, and you will have more than bare feet!"

He could not believe the car. "Jesus, Annie, what a beast! Mini Cooper isn't it, listen to that engine." It was all she could do to stop him from examining under the 'hood' as he called it, but she was no way going to be late for work.

Luke's appearance with Annie, in the waiting room, offering his professional services, came as quite a surprise to Mr. Martin, but he smiled and shook the young man's hand. "Well I don't need to ask what is going on, I have never seen our Annie so happy. How long are you staying?" "Oh until she agrees to marry me," he said very casually, making Annie spill the tea she had just made. "You haven't even asked me," she spluttered.

To the amusement of Mr. Martin, two old ladies with sick cats, and a young man with some kind of rodent in a box, Luke took her hand and fell to his knees. "O.K. Miss spider hater, will you marry me?" Her reply was accompanied by claps and cheers from the small audience, making the cats nervous, and causing frantic scratchings from the creature in the box.

With Luke's help, surgery was dispatched in no time, but an emergency farm call came in at eleven o'clock. Leaving Annie to hold the fort, the two vets went to assist. The result was a beautiful calf, and Luke smelling of manure returned in time to go for lunch.

They bought pork pies from 'The Creamery'. "I have heard all about English pork pies, um very good," he munched. "Now to a jewellers, I want an engagement ring on your finger before this day is out. Can't believe this town, you are living in a history book, Annie." With her feet hardly touching the ground, they headed for the largest jewellers, mainly because he had already spotted that they accepted American Express. They were really not dressed to visit such an exclusive shop, but the assistant treated them with utmost civility, having learnt that Americans, however eccentric, always spent well, appreciating British workmanship.

She rejected fancy clusters of sapphires and emeralds, and fell for a single diamond. "A pure flawless diamond, symbol of our perfect love," he whispered as he slipped it onto her finger. "A star from the sky," she replied, wondering what had made her think of that, "I will love you for ever Luke."

They tried to telephone her parents, but there was no reply. "Well let's ring Molly," Luke insisted, full of enthusiasm, "If it wasn't for her I would still be breaking my heart across the Atlantic." There was no reply there either and a tiny seed of fear began to sprout in Annie's mind. "Where could they be? It's eight in the morning to them," she thought nervously. There was little time to ponder on the mystery, as the remainder of the afternoon was filled with yet another busy surgery, and Mr. Martin was very pleased to have Luke's willing assistance.

Thrilled with the romantic engagement, his wife insisted that the young couple join them for dinner that night, so instead of the omelette and salad, Annie had intended to prepare, they dined on prawn cocktail, steak and chips, and chocolate mousse, together with two bottles of champagne, not returning to the flat until after midnight. They tried again to reach Molly and her parents, with still no reply. Annie was feeling worried.

"What about your folks, shouldn't we call them too?"

"What! Risk leaving a message with Pop. That would be worse than Chinese Whispers. No, let's go back to The States as soon as we can, to tell them, and why wait to get married. What about hiring a boat like Missy in Key Biscayne, but just the two of us, no fuss just lots of champagne. We could have a party with respective parents later. Please say yes Annie, and stop worrying about your elusive family. We can get up at five in the morning to call them. If they are in bed, they will just have to get up."

She willingly agreed to it all, although feeling guilty about leaving Mr. Martin, but that faded away as he took her into a world of bliss with his lovemaking.

It was chilly at five in the morning and Annie sat wrapped in a blanket as Luke tried again to call her parents. He tried three times, each time now, with the operator telling him that line was unobtainable. He tried Molly again with the same result and Annie's pale skin took on a hue of grey as she listened to the ominous sound.

She could not go back to sleep, or eat the bacon and egg Luke cooked for her. They dressed for work and tried again, but this time the operator informed Anne in a matter of fact way, that all the lines were down in that particular area due to the hurricane." "What hurricane?"

she shrieked, "What do you mean?" "Hurricane Betsy," the calm voice replied with no emotion at all. "It hit the Florida coast last night and our communications are a real mess."

Memories of Missy's fear in that tropical storm years ago flooded back, but this was no tropical storm, this was the real thing. The big one that people warned might happen one day, the one that didn't turn last minute and veer off somewhere else. Why hadn't she known? What had happened to that strange communication of insight with Missy. "Of course," she thought, "Missy is in Texas, holed up in a log cabin on the border of her grandparent's farm, she would not have been there to feel the horror," Annie's strength failed, she sank into Luke's arms and sobbed.

The calm logic which Luke had inherited from his mother took over. "We could not reach them, they must have evacuated," he assured her. He rang Mr. Martin and explained the situation, then sent a telegram to his family. "Only way to be sure they get the right message," he said, winking at Annie. The telegram read,

> *"10th September, 1965 - quite safe - don't worry*
> *- in England with the girl of my dreams. - Luke"*

With a great deal of persistence he managed to get them onto a flight the next day, not to Miami, but to Jacksonville. There they would hire a car for the 400 mile journey from north to south, but neither of them cared about that.

The journey was gruelling, taking three days before they arrived at Grandpa Jake's home, which was where Annie hoped they would all be. Once in Jacksonville, they began to hear horror stories of Hurricane Betsy and Luke decided it would be wiser to buy an old camper instead of hiring a car. "Good old American Express," he joked, wondering how he was going to cope at the end of the month. Although old, the vehicle was clean inside, and fairly roadworthy. They stocked it with bottled water and tinned food until it almost groaned. Then after adding packs of candles, two large ice boxes filled with cans of soda, and two jerry cans of gas, they set off. On the way, Luke replenished the ice and bought a large supply of insect repellent. "You will soon find out," he replied to Annie's questioning look.

Nothing could have prepared Annie for the sight of the devastation. Trees, such a part of the area's beauty were snapped or uprooted. Chunks of buildings and roofs seemed to have been bitten off by some nightmarish monster, but worse was the beachside. Luke's trailer park was gone, nothing left at all. "Oh Luke, your thesis, all that work washed away overnight," she said sorrowfully. "Posted it," he grinned,"I did not know how long it would take me to get you to agree to marry me, and I was not intending to come back without you, so I posted it!" The fact that he had been so determined, made her love him all the more, and she smiled her first smile in three days. The beautiful homes of her parents, Norris and Bethany, were now a sickening sight, reduced to rubble, as the wind and the angry ocean had ripped them apart.

There were no traffic lights working and cops and military people were directing the traffic in the sweltering heat. Annie delved into one of the ice boxes and handed out cans of cola to each one of these people they passed. Their gratitude was touching, it seemed ice was like gold in this heat with still no power in most areas. Through the strewn rubble and trees, Annie found it difficult to pick out the way to Grandpa Jake's, but eventually she found it. Roof draped with tarps and bricks, windows broken, but still standing. They were greeted by the barking of three strange dogs which gave the place an eerie feel.

Annie's arrival came as a tremendous shock. She was right of course, they were all there with Grandpa Jake and Ruby, and to see Annie, who was supposed to be safe in England, tumbling out of an old camper loaded with supplies, like some kind of female Santa, was incredible, but even more unbelievable was the change in her mother.

Joyce was always smart, to the point of stuffiness, even her beachwear was less than casual, but now she was dressed in a little green top and shorts, which Annie suspected belonged to Bethany, and her hair was loosely clipped with bobby pins. She looked younger than ever, as she ran to her daughter, and she, the Mom who could not stand animals of any sort, was followed by the strange dogs, happily scampering about her feet!

Chapter Forty Six

Fear. Joyce knew now that most people lived uneventfully, complaining and bewailing their fate, not appreciating the good parts of their lives, not being thankful for the little things that may have gone unnoticed through familiarity. Fear changed all that for Joyce. The last few days taught her that if you are trapped with fear snapping at your heels, and manage to escape, the world is a different place if you survive.

Before the evacuation of the beaches, Bethany explained the plan. Having been brought up on the good old Texas/Lousiana border, she knew only too well what to expect. "Fill the car with gas," she ordered, in the efficient way of one painfully aware of the situation, she handed Joyce a box, "Take any tinned food and some clothes."

Still not really aware of the danger, Joyce dutifully filled Alex's briefcase with the documents, while he went off to fuel the car. There was nothing worthwhile in the way of tinned food, so she filled the box with a jumbo pack of bathroom tissue, bought on special offer, weeks ago, and all Alex's bottles of Scotch whisky, vodka and gin. "Take the most important clothes," she decided as she plucked her best evening gowns from the closet, together with Alex's tuxedo. His leg was stiff, but they still danced, if rather sedately, at many functions with Bethany and Norris. "These clothes certainly must not get damp in the storm," she said to herself. Innocently she closed the wooden window shutters, "Just in case we have a broken pane," she thought, "I would not like glass to fall onto the carpet."

They managed to set off just before the evacuation call. The car radio took on a sense of urgency as they followed Norris to collect Daryl's family. "Beaches evacuate now," the disembodied voice urged, "follow the signs to the shelters."

They were not going to a shelter, but to Norris' father's place, where there was a large cellar. Jake and Ruby lived inland, so they headed for the nearest causeway leading to their part of the mainland, and were shocked. Lines of cars blocked the huge roads, crawling at almost walking pace, vehicles piled with possessions and surprisingly, animals. No pets were allowed in the shelters, giving their owners no choice. Leave them to fend for themselves or get out now with your animal in the car. Dogs, cats, birds and even a monkey peered from the car windows, with their grim faced owners, some fleeing to friends and relations, but others with no destination. These people were just driving, as far away as they could get. There would not even be a hotel room for them, no establishment would consider taking in pets.

The journey seemed to take an eternity and by the time they arrived at the house of the kindly old couple, the sky began to darken. "Just wind and rain," Joyce told herself, as they bolted themselves into the cellar, but those elements turned themselves into an express railroad train, and roared around them, unstopping and relentless for hours. She clung to Alex, for the first time realising how much she loved him, more than her life itself. The cellar shook and trembled, shutters were torn from the house above them, glass splintered and ceiling fans crashed to the floor. What felt like an explosion above the heads of the terrified cellar inhabitants, was in fact part of the roof tearing away, leaving the chimney looking akin to one of the few trees left standing, stripped of its foliage. They crouched like rabbits in their darkened cellar. The power gone and afraid to use candles, they relied upon a small battery powered torch to comfort little Michael.

Eventually, as with all nature's fury, the violence passed and they emerged from their burrow of safety into bright daylight. The sun smiled down upon them as if nothing had happened, a beautiful day with bright blue sky. The rays of sunshine only highlighted the terrible damage, but at least the house was still standing. Jake explained that what on the outside appeared to be a sedate and vulnerable wooden house, was old indeed, but custom built and strongly reinforced.

Like busy ants, they set to work, the women sweeping and mopping while the men dragged tarps across the gaping hole in the roof, securing them with bricks and ropes in an effective but haphazard looking way. Joyce laughed about her feeble attempt to put together hurricane supplies. What use were party dresses in a situation like this? Bethany lent her some shorts and tops, and hugged her for the booze and bathroom tissue. "Look what Joyce brought," she said to Jake, "Absolute essentials," the old boy chuckled.

The next day she went with Alex to survey the damage to their home. They were prepared, from the news on the radio, but Alex dreaded her reaction. Instead of the expected tears, she smiled, kissed him and shrugged, "What do we pay insurance for? We will rebuild, perhaps with a small pool this time!"

On returning to the car, they heard a noise. A pitiful whining came from beneath some nearby rubble. Shining a torch between the broken cinder blocks, bricks and splintered wood, Alex saw the face of a dog. Before he knew what was happening, Joyce, who before all this was forever worrying about chips to her nail polish, began to burrow under the debris with her bare hands. As Alex tried to prise an opening clear with a broken plank, Joyce clutched the animal's collar and with an adrenaline powered pull, yanked him free.

Saurus, as his ostentatiously bejewelled collar identified him, was a fully grown Afgan Hound, with once silky fur and a pampered lifestyle. How could he tell his story? That of being a fashion accessory to a rich woman. Of being impeccably behaved, well fed, groomed and shown off, but never loved. Now his sleek body was thin, paws sore and coat matted, but this new mistress was kind. There was love in her touch as she stroked him, and she did not object as he kissed her face in gratitude, although he knew that it was really not good manners to do so. Surely this mistress would not turn him out, and drive away leaving him to face the fury of the monster from the sky. The new Joyce was not going to do any such thing. Alex fell in love with her all over again, as they bundled the smelly dog into the car and Joyce sat with her arms around its neck as if it was a large stuffed toy.

The appearance of Saurus was good for little Michael, taking his mind away from his recent fright. They cut off all the dog's matted fur in the best way they could, resulting in a deliriously happy, much cooler but scruffy looking mutt, but they all loved him just the same.

After that Joyce took to roaming around in the car, and by the fourth day she found another two dogs in need of help, to join the family. Jake and Ruby thrived on this new found usefulness in their lives, and suggested that they might set up a temporary centre for lost pets, as people would soon be frantically looking for them. Joyce took off Saurus' collar, some owners could claim their dogs by all means, but there was something about the Afgan, he loved her and she intended to keep him.

She never expected Annie to turn up amongst all the mess, but here she was, looking beautiful, with an engagement ring on her finger. Joyce felt so happy for her daughter as she described Luke's determined quest to win her hand, and Molly shook her head, laughing as he described her advice. "Get yourself over there fast, and for heavens sake smarten yourself up, is what Molly said. So that's just what I did. She even dragged me to Sears for some more suitable clothes, and then I was off on the next flight." "How precious Annie is," Joyce thought, andll those years of growing up seemed to have flashed by, but now she was going to be a better mother, never again would she be too busy to sit and talk.

Luke and Annie offered their professional services to the community, without payment at first, until the government stepped in, as so many animals were lost or hurt. The state buzzed with roofers, **builders and glaziers, some honest, some not so honest, but repairs** were on the way. As the telephone lines were restored, Luke called the Porpoise School in the Keys to see how they had fared. He and Annie wept at the news. The storm had washed everything into the ocean, including the twelve dolphin family, and no one knew the fate of the animals. They decided to go to help with the restoration for a while, so that Luke could be on hand to assist if any injured dolphin managed to return. The dolphins' love for their trainers and homes proved strong. Within a month they had all returned of their own accord, and were fairly unscathed by the experience. Basic instinct, still there, even in third generation captives, saved their lives, but this was their home. With what appeared to be sheer delight, they swam about fussing their trainers and watching the rebuilding with interest. They played, splashing the builders as they worked, enjoying their mock anger and laughter. The men were sorry when the work was complete, but clapped and threw fish to their new friends as they happily swam into the new tanks, their new homes.

It was to be a full five months before Annie and Luke found time for their marriage, slipping away in secret to Key Biscayne as planned. Just a private boat ceremony with lots of champagne, but made extra special by the ocean's wildlife. As they returned to the shore, a school of dolphin appeared, swimming in front of the boat, as if escorting them with their blessing.

Alex and Joyce, were secretly disappointed to have been excluded in such a way, but Annie's happiness and the party on the following day, made up for it. Missy, still in Texas with Daryl and her other grandparents, wept over the phone as Annie told her the news. The baby was due in a month so they were staying until the rebuilding was complete. Missy was excited as her parents were now building a smaller house for themselves and a separate two bedroomed one for Missy and Daryl on the same plot, with a shared pool. There was much to be said for thoroughly insuring your property, most of the expense was met by the insurance claim. Despite the wonderful future,

Missy needed her parents, and missed Annie more than ever at this stage of her pregnancy.

They were still all living at Grandpa Jake's, with a few unclaimed animals, thankfully including Saurus, who Joyce deliberately kept in his clipped and scruffy disguise. She was not to know that his former owner had moved to California, and now sported two poodles, dyed pink to match the colour of her car. These animals walked beside her daily, causing much admiration, with their green jewelled satin collars and leads. She gave not a thought to the abandoned Afgan, who, no thanks to her had never been so happy. Annie sketched her Mom and the happy animal, putting a smile on the face of everyone who saw it pinned up in the kitchen. Luke was enchanted with her sketching, and was sure that she could put her talents to good use somehow. He put up his hands in mock horror when she told him how they used to sell her racoon cartoons on the beach so that they could buy alcohol and the odd joint!

Whilst the rebuilding was in progress, everyone was thankful for those hefty insurance premiums, which before seemed such a nuisance. Luke was very organised in such matters, and had taken all the relevant papers with him on his trip to England, stuffed into his small bag, containing not much more than his old jeans, a selection of tee shirts, underwear, and his sneakers. "So casual, but so careful," Annie laughed. His trailer and all his possessions were fully insured, so the young couple had no financial worries. They decided to live in Florida, a small studio apartment on the beach would do them nicely for now, and by a stroke of luck they secured jobs at the same veterinary clinic, due to reopen in six weeks time. Annie sent instructions to Uncle Thomas in England to close up the flat and store her car until further notice. "Don't sell them yet," Luke urged, "there is no hurry. We can go over for a vacation sometime, and you can sort it all out then. Perhaps we could have the car shipped over here, I know how you love it."

With everything becoming settled they planned to enjoy the time on their hands before starting work. Hopefully they would be with Missy in time for the birth of the baby, "Don't go having him early," she teased over the phone, "Luke is a vet after all, and will deliver him for you!" Missy laughed, and was rewarded by a kick from her unborn child. "So it's going to be a boy is it? By the way it's kicking right now, you are probably right."

Now it was the matter of visiting Luke's parents. He had not even told them of the engagement yet, let alone the marriage, yet he called them regularly, telling them all about Annie.

"They will love you," he assured her, but Annie felt horrible doubts. What would they say when their son turned up suddenly married? His highly educated family of Puritan stock. They descended from early settlers, not the original Pilgrim Fathers, but not far from it. Annie's mind conjured up a picture of people dressed in dark clothes and strange hats. People who took great care not to enjoy themselves. This vision did not correspond with Luke's description of his folks, but Annie could not rid it from her mind.

Chapter Forty Seven

Alex watched with growing concern as Annie and Luke packed the old camper ready for the journey. They were to drive all the way up to Newcastle, Maine, visiting Luke's parents, sell the vehicle, then on by air to Texas to be with Missy, and finally fly back to Florida, in time to start work.

An arduous journey, in Alex's eyes, and a strange way to spend a honeymoon. They would be away for six weeks, a great deal of the time spent travelling. Luke assured his father-in-law, that the rusting camper was mechanically sound, and Alex, whose talents did not stretch to such matters, was hardly in a position to argue. They cheerfully turned down his offer to borrow the family car, so instead he enrolled them in Triple A, and insisted that they accept an envelope containing two hundred dollars, for any emergency.

Laden with gifts for Missy and the baby, with many hugs and much waving they left Grandpa Jake's big old house. It was fully restored now, and appeared to have taken on a glow, with what seemed like a small commune residing in it. Annie smiled at her mother, still waving in the distance. The new style Mom, wearing shorts and no shoes, with one arm around her Dad and the scruffy Afgan at her feet.

They would take the journey in easy stages, the camper allowing them to sleep, when and where they pleased, but the most important stop for Annie was Cape Cod. On the way she told Luke the story of Grandpa Jake's ancestor, originally from Liverpool, so near to her own home town, and how he came to settle in Sandwich, Cape Cod.

Luke listened with interest as they drove along.

"Evidently he worked his passage over here with a broken heart, leaving the girl he loved behind in Liverpool."

"If he loved her, why did he leave her? I would never have left you."

"I am not sure, I think her father disliked him or something. Anyway he came to Cape Cod and married a wealthy merchant's daughter. He died in a storm, crushed by a falling tree, and never got to see the son his wife was carrying. He broke her heart when he died, and she became bitter and depressed, because with his last breath he called out, not for his wife, but for the girl he left behind in England. She swore to tell her child, and her grandchildren, if she lived long enough to have any, of how he let her down. Never to let the pain and injustice be forgotten, as long as there was family to remember it. Her parents were beside themselves with worry, as she became more and more withdrawn for the remainder of her pregnancy, but when the baby was born, she changed. Apparently the child looked the image of his father and her heart melted. She realised that her husband had died saving her life, pushing her clear, putting her safety above his own, so he did love her in his own way. It was nobody's fault that his first love was not to be. She told the story to her son when he was old enough to understand, and also taught him the poetry her husband was so fond of. They made a pact to keep the story alive through the family, although I supposed it might have changed a little in the telling over the years. Grandpa Jake knows all the poetry, so does Norris, and I bet Little Michael will soon. It has to be told by the eldest man of the family but Missy knows it too, and will tell her son."

Luke pulled the camper over to brew some coffee, chuckling at the fact that Annie was so sure of the sex of her friend's baby. He handed her the steaming hot drink, laced with powdered milk, which was easiest to carry, and did not taste all that bad. "Hope you are not disappointed, Missy could have a daughter you know. It's a good story though. Do you want to know my family history?"

Annie certainly did want to know. She was desperate to make a good impression, so any family information would be a good idea. She made some sandwiches, while Luke told his tale.

"Mom's folks were from England too, don't know from which part, she could probably tell you. They were Puritans, I told you that before. Wherever they came from, people hated the Puritans. They were well educated, deep thinking people, who did not like the pompous church, with stained glass and statues. They wanted everything to be simple and pure. They were persecuted by their neighbours who considered them to be finicky and forever carping, so many of those Puritans left to make a new life in America. They needed to charter a ship for the journey, but as there were not enough of them do so, they solved the problem by taking other people with them. Just ordinary people wanting a new life, not of their religion, but citizens willing to work alongside them in the new settlements for a while. They called these people Strangers, and kept themselves as separate from them, as possible. The Strangers called the Puritans Saints, and wanted nothing to do with their weird ways. Anyway, Mom's folks got married a month before the voyage began, and the new wife was ill all the way. It turned out that the poor thing was pregnant, and it was only through determination that she survived. Many people died from T.B. the close quarters of the ship, spreading it like wild fire, but Mom's folks luckily, seemed to be immune. Some of the group would have died from scurvy through the poor diet on the voyage and lack of fresh supplies afterwards, but the natives advised them to eat cranberries, which saved their lives. The baby was unfortunately born five weeks early, to a still sickly mother and the date of birth was noted. The couple were accused of fornication, and despite the tiny child, were both put in the stocks for a whole day as punishment! Or at least that is how the story goes."

Annie shuddered, "How Puritan are your family now? What are they going to say about us?" "Stop worrying," he tried to reassure her, "I have told you they will love you, so just forget about religion. Over the years many church groups still have Puritan ideas. Mom belongs to the United Church of Christ, one of the most liberal and progressive in the country. She joined when she was at college in Boston, but she never goes on about it." Annie still looked apprehensive. "Hey come one," he said nuzzling the ticklish place on her neck, and making her squirm with laughter. "Pop is probably an atheist, and my sister and I think that God is all around, part of nature and the natural progression of life. We are not so frightening surely?"

From Cape Cod they telephoned Annie's parents, to the relief of her father, who was very glad that his doubts about the soundness of their transport seemed to be unfounded. They found the town of Sandwich at the western end of route 6A. Following Grandpa Jake's instructions, they visited the glass factory, where Luke bought Annie a pretty little vase of the typical subtle colours, which she would treasure for ever. Ruby's collection of glass was beautiful, but remained untouched except for occasional cleaning, and hurricane storage! Annie intended to use her treasured gift to fill it with flowers, wild flowers, whenever she could. Ruby was right about Sandwich's charm, most of its original character was still intact, built around Shawne Pond, an artificial lake providing power for milling. Annie felt sad to move on, and wondered what Grandpa Jake's man, who came here from Liverpool, all those generations ago looked like. Perhaps he even had light sandy hair and vivid blue eyes, just like Jake and Missy.

She began to feel apprehensive again about meeting Luke's parents and could hardly appreciate the beauty of the area as they neared their destination.

Newcastle covered about thirty miles, and consisted of three villages. Sheepscott village, where his Mom's folks had first settled, Damariscotta Mills, and Newcastle itself, Luke's home town, which was almost entirely residential. People living here earned their living mostly from farming or fishing, or commuted to larger towns.

They pulled up outside the house at about four o'clock, with Annie wishing that she had been able to take a shower and change into something more presentable than her Levi's and pink shirt with Cape

Cod, emblazened on the front. "You look beautiful," Luke whispered, as he dragged her from the camper, "Stop worrying."

The house was quite something, a sugar biscuit kind of house, old colonial, federal style. The porchway and the mailbox were festooned with balloons and ribbons, and a huge poster hung over the door, saying 'Welcome Annie and Luke'. A large dog of distinctly mongrel origin, lumbered down the steps, almost tripping over its feet, excitedly welcoming Luke and then Annie. The grey hair on his muzzle betrayed his age and although his eyes were slightly clouded, Annie recognised that look. The look of Good Dog, friendly dog, altogether nice dog! Blue, the dog was swiftly followed by Luke's family. Not stiff and starchy Puritans, but three people happy to see them. His father, the super educated professor, seemed to have the same gait as the dog, but also to Annie's relief, the same look of welcome in his eyes. His mother and sister Ruthie, were female versions of Luke, with their blonde hair, long legs and slim build.

Ruthie immediately looked at Annie's left hand, and practically bounced with excitement, forgetting the eighteen year old facade of elegance she was trying to master. "Mom, you were right, he has done it. They are married!" Annie's horror and shock at this statement was short lived as she and Luke were swooped upon with hugs, kisses and congratulations, and were swept into the house for a glass of champagne. Ruthie explained as they sipped their drinks.

"My dear brother has always maintained that when the right girl came along, he would take off and marry her with no fuss. Not tell a soul, just turn up at home and have a party later. For weeks now Mom has been saying, "Annie is the one, Annie is the one," and since you told us you were coming, we have been sick with anticipation."

How wrong Annie's feelings had been about these people, they accepted her with all their hearts and started to plan a barbecue party for the next day. Luke noticed a shadow of doubt on Annie's face and put his arm around her. "Annie thinks barbecues are all lighter fuel and chemical smoke, she doesn't know we are barbecue experts here. It's one of my talents you are yet to experience, I will show you my love." "You know me all too well," she laughed.

After dinner that night, full to the brim with superb, mouthwatering lobster and laughing at Luke's comment that Pilgrims considered lobster only fit for pigs, they sat with a brandy to relax. Annie admired the old gun on the wall, which seemed older even than Grandpa Jake's. "Don't let her touch it," Luke squealed, proceeding to tell his family Annie's story of the A.K.47 and the partial demolition of her father's shop! Ruthie was most impressed saying that her nearest brush with disaster was falling out of a tree when she was twelve, earning herself a stay in hospital with concussion, and adding a few more grey hairs to her father's head.

It felt strange to be sleeping in Luke's old bedroom, sharing the big old bed he had slept in as a teenager. "All my hopes and dreams were hatched in this room," he told her, "and now they have all come true." Annie found a small wicker basket on the dresser, containing foil wrapped sweets. "Fudge," Luke munched, "Home made, a sort of personal welcome from Mom." It was so good that Annie resolved to find out the recipe.

They slept, almost immediately, in the bliss of a real bed, instead of the cramped camper, too tired to make love, but in the comfort of each other's arms.

Annie woke early, it was only six o'clock, but she could not go back to sleep. By six thirty she was fidgety, so pulling on her jeans and shirt, she tiptoed downstairs, hoping to make a quiet cup of coffee.

A delicious aroma wafted from the kitchen, as Annie opened the door.

"Good morning Mrs. Miles, Luke is still asleep, so I thought I would make a cup of coffee, I hope you don't mind."

"Annie, of course I don't mind. After all you are my other daughter now aren't you? Besides, it is good to have company, no one else in this house is an early riser. Come we will have a coffee together, and why don't you call me Webster, I would like that. It's my pet name, Leonard never calls me Pauline."

"Luke told me all about that," Annie smiled, "Webster, as in dictionary, I can relate to that, my spelling is often a bit weird." Webster was making blueberry lemon bread, and preparing ricotta cheese pies for breakfast. Annie with a love of cooking, was fascinated as her new mother-in-law explained that only Maine blueberries were good for such recipes. Large ones, usually found in the shops would sink to the bottom of the loaf.

They worked happily together and by eight o'clock breakfast was ready and many recipes had been exchanged. Blue, who was until now, snoozing on the porchway, pushed open the door came into the kitchen, and lumbered up to his food bowl, Webster winked at Annie. "Wait a while, and see what happens." Just as Luke had described, after five minutes of patient waiting, Blue began to bark and howl. "That will move the rest of the family from their beds," she laughed, as she fed the funny big animal, "They know breakfast is ready now."

Sure enough they appeared, Luke staggering down wearing only his tattered jeans, swooping Annie into a big hug, before sitting down. "Ah, I see you and Mom got together. Two brilliant cooks, we should be in for a treat."

Breakfast consisted of,

>   Freshly squeezed orange juice.
>   Blueberry lemon bread.
>   Ricotta cheese pies, made extra special with a spoonful of Grand Marnier.
>   Sauteed ham, with pineapple slices.
>   Strawberries with heavy cream,
>   and freshly ground coffee.

"So different from bacon and eggs at home," Annie thought, "Dad would love this." "Wait until you taste my barbecued steak," Luke grinned, "Don't look so doubtful, I will show you how it's done." He was right, there was no taste of lighter fuel at a Miles' family barbecue. Luke took a large old can, with holes punched around the bottom and underside. Looking to Annie, like one of his settler ancestors, he placed the can onto some pebbles. Into the can went some crumpled paper and a few dry sticks, then a handful of charcoal pieces. The paper was lit through one of the holes in the tin, and left to burn. When the coals glowed hot, he pulled them out with tongs, to the barbecue stove, and built the fire around them. Soon the whole stove glowed, with no trace of the off-putting lighter fuel smell, and as the steak sizzled, he took some small wood chips, dampened them, and placed them on top of the coals. The result was a real smoked flavour, and Annie was converted.

They ate, danced to the Drifters and the Beachboys, and became thoroughly drunk on Leonard's infamous home brew. He was the most un-professor like person Annie could imagine. Yes, he was dedicated to his job, and indeed rather absent minded, just as Luke had said, but he was a real family man, taking an interest in the music of the day, and willing to try anything new. Obviously he adored his family, which now seemed, without reservation to include Annie. He was also a collector and many weird objects adorned the house. As she was so interested, he showed off his peace pipe. "The curling smoke from it is called pukwa'na," Leonard told Annie most seriously. Luke hovered in the background and teased, "Pop bought that when he was first in college, don't ask what he smoked in it!"

Leonard took it all in good part. It seemed he also fostered a great love of the sea. Not just gathering algae, but an interest in coasts, rocks, routes etc. His most prized possession was a quater waggoner, an old book of sea charts. He told Annie how Newcastle had once been famous for its ship building, full rigged ships, clippers and Downeast-ers, all came from its yards.

They spent two wonderful weeks with Luke's family, with Annie joyfully accepted as new daughter, and sister to Ruthie. They took delight in showing her the sights, and were captivated, watching her sketch as they went along. Most of her work included illustrations of Blue, who always managed to wheedle his way into the car as they went out. She looked in awe at the ancient shell heaps on the banks of the Damariscotta River, these large deposits of shells, left so long ago by Indian tribes. "We are wrong to call those people Indians," Leonard spoke up, on a matter close to his heart, he had always been a champion of any injustice. "We should call them Native Americans really, but old habits die hard. The problem started when Columbus landed on Cat Island. The silly man thought he was on one of the Indian islands, so unfortunately he called the natives Indians."

They took picnics to State Park on the River Road, enjoying days of wooded trails and the sandy beach, but most remarkable in Annie's eyes, was an eagle's nest, said to be at least eighty years old, which every year, produced one or two eaglets. It had to be viewed through field glasses, but Annie's artistic eyes picked out every detail, and it was sketched, a prized reminder of their vacation.

Annie was fascinated by the little family cabin cruiser. The very boat in which Luke travelled the Intracoastal Waterway with his father, as a child. It was lovingly maintained, and sported a fresh coat of paint. They took trips in the boat, watching the seals and puffins, and visiting Pemaquid Point, with its famous lighthouse, sitting astride unique rock formations.

Annie and Luke stood watching the pounding surf at the foot of the lighthouse rocks, so happy in their perfect love. "Let's have a baby," he whispered, for her answer she kissed him. "We will bring her here next year and show her the lighthouse," "Or him," Luke said as he hugged her, but somehow knowing in a delightful way that he would have a daughter!

"What plans were you two hatching up there?" Webster asked playfully. "Ah," Luke replied, winking at Annie, "You will find out soon enough."

Blue looked up at them, as if reading their thoughts, and smiled his strange doggy smile.

Chapter Forty Eight

Towards the end of their visit, they were lucky enough to see the beginning of one of nature's phenomena, the alewife run. The alewife turned out to be a fish, similar to a herring, Annie thought, and given its name because of its rotund shape. As fat as an alewife!

At Damariscotta Mills, only two miles from Luke's home, the valiant fish climbed the falls, every May, to spawn. A wonderful sight, attracting people from miles around. Annie couldn't wait to tell Missy about it, it would be only two days before they flew to Texas to be with her.

In pouring rain, sheltering beneath Leonard's old golf umbrella, they left Luke's family at the airport, having made plans to spend Christmas on the beach with Annie's parents, and New Year in the snow with Luke's.

They boarded the plane, after kisses all round and a big hug for Blue, waving goodbye, mercifully unaware of the sometimes cruel designs of destiny.

Luke nuzzled Annie's dark curls, as she sat beside him on the flight, head on his shoulder, fast asleep. He frowned, noticing her hair felt damp and forehead hot. "You O.K. Annie?" he asked anxiously. She winced as she woke, with abdominal cramps. It was the last day of her period, and she should not have been feeling like this, and anyway, she never experienced much pain, compared to that of some of her friends. Luke asked the attendant for some asprin, but the cramps came on and on in waves. There was more and Annie was frightened. A horrible sense of foreboding through the pains, a long dark shadow falling across her happiness. Hot, nauseous, and feeling embarrassed she tried not to make a fuss, so sorry to see the anxiety on her husband's face.

The flight seemed to take an eternity, but at last the plane began its descent, with Annie almost screaming. Then it stopped, no more pain, but now a spine chilling sense of loss. She said nothing of her feelings, for how could she explain such a thing? She was almost herself again as they reached arrivals, but Luke still held her hand anxiously.

Daryl was supposed to meet them, but there was no sign of him, and no message either. Annie began to panic, "Missy, there is something wrong with Missy. Daryl wouldn't let us down otherwise." Luke tutted sympathetically and patted her hand. "She is only having a baby, she will be fine. They are probably at the hospital, and have forgotten all about us."

"The pains, and the panic on the flight," Annie thought, "I might have known she was having the baby, and I was feeling her pain, but there is also something else terribly wrong."

Luke calmly called a taxi to the ranch, where the housekeeper confirmed their suspicions. Missy was having the baby. Taking yet another taxi, Annie felt light headed all the way to the hospital, where at last they found Missy's grandparents and Daryl, and were greeted with good news. Daryl was always happy-go-lucky, but Annie had never seen him so ecstatic. Missy was safely delivered of a son, the son Annie knew all along she would have. Daryl, known for his squeamishness, gallantly held her hand the whole time without passing out, and mother and baby were in the best of health. Visitors were restricted, but Annie was allowed in, secretly needing to re-assure herself that all was well.

"Come and meet Nathan," Missy whispered as Annie tiptoed into the room. She looked lovely, with a flush to her cheeks and blue eyes sparkling with happiness, no sign of the gloom that still lurked in her friend's heart. Giving Missy a hug, she peered into the crib by the bed. "Oh," she gasped, "he is just like you. His hair, and look how it parts and curls up at the back just like yours." Missy smiled proudly, "He has really blue eyes too, Daryl is so thrilled. He stayed with me all the time, and do you know it wasn't all that bad." She gently lifted Nathan from the crib and put him into Annie's arms. "You are Aunt Annie now, doesn't that sound funny." The weight of anxiety should have lifted with all this proof of happiness and health, but it still hovered around her, a ghost of apprehension, which Annie could not shake.

Perhaps fate allowed them to spend those happy weeks with Missy, without knowledge of the horror to come. Annie had partially experienced Missy's labour, and knowing their closeness, she felt it was hardly surprising, but the dreadful premonition that she pushed to the back of her subconsciousness, was real too.

Leonard, Webster and Ruthie, drove back from the airport, feeling rather lost without Luke and Annie, but talked about New Year as they went along to cheer themselves. The sun fought its way from behind the clouds, and shone, glittering on the wet road, as if joining in their better frame of mind. Blue scrabbled from his place on the floor of the car, and sat upright on the back seat, smiling his special doggie smile, feeling, if not understanding, his family's happy plans. Only Leonard saw the tyre blow out on the oncoming car, Webster and Ruthie were unaware as he swerved, to avoid it. In split seconds, a truck behind the disabled car tried to stop, skidding, jack-knifing into Leonard's path. They felt the impact only momentarily, then nothing. The lives of a happy family, gone in an instant, as the car exploded into flames. Somehow Blue was thrown clear, his long tail gone, and fur melted and singed to his skin. He dragged himself as near to the flames as he could. Hot smell, death smell. Dog was supposed to protect family. He had always been Good Dog, but he had left them. He could not reach them. It was his fault. He stood shakily on his feet, sure now that he had become Bad Dog. Lowering his head, he turned and slunk like a wolf away from the scene. "Bad Dog must die now, and never go on," he thought, and found a sheltered place to curl up. He felt no pain as he fell asleep, waiting to be taken to his fate, as is the way with all Bad Dogs.

He woke hot and thirsty, not understanding what had happened. Blood had congealed and matted to his fur where his tail once had been, and his skin seemed to crack as he moved. Stiffly he made his way up to the road. There were no broken cars, no fire, just lines of traffic. Hope rose through his pain and confusion.

"Perhaps I am not Bad Dog after all, I must go home. I will lie on the porch, push open the door and go to my bowl. They will be there, they will feed me. Nothing will be wrong if I can just do that."

With that thought sustaining him he plodded on.

The police identified the car by its licence plate, and subsequently, the family by dental records. Frantically they tried to contact next of kin, for inquest and burial. Luke and Annie were the only relatives, but no one knew where to contact them. A search of the house revealed no clues, but Luke's former university came up with an address. His thesis on cetaceans, had been written for the veterinary science department. He had posted it months ago, before the hurricane, when he went in search of Annie in England. They still had the address of the trailer park, but Dade County Sheriff's office could not help, the trailer park was destroyed and no one knew where Luke had gone afterwards.

Luke's friend and colleague, John Ingram, an Associate Professor, teaching at the university, took time off and set out on a mission of mercy to find him, this was not the kind of news to be broken by a stranger. Knowing that much of Luke's thesis had been written at the Porpoise School, he headed straight for the Florida Keys.

John also drew a blank there. Yes they knew Luke and Annie well, they were good friends. Did he know the couple were engaged? Unfortunately no one held an address, other than that of the trailer park, but then one of the young volunteers, sorting out fish for the dolphins overheard the conversation and interrupted. She knew no address, but remembered a conversation with Annie.

"They were living in a big old house, her grandfather's I think. Annie said it was inland, away from the beach, the hurricane did not do so much harm there. The point is, she also said that they were running a shelter for lost animals from there. Surely there must a register of that somewhere."

John set off armed with this clue. He was tired, feeling he had set himself an impossible task, and if he ever found Luke, how was he going to tell him such horrific news.

After three weeks with Missy, sharing in the delights of motherhood, Annie landed back in Florida, happy and refreshed. Jake and Ruby made a party for their return, and the world seemed to be a joyous place. Bethany, Norris and Michael were still with Missy, and the new houses on the beach were almost complete. Daryl's parents and Molly were already moved into theirs, busy decorating, and Annie and Luke would be going to their own beachside apartment at the end of the week, in time to start work, so the old couple wanted to make the most of their remaining guests. As they celebrated, toasting the health of great grandson Nathan, Annie promised to have them all over for dinner after they settled in. Her hosts had become almost as much her grandparents, as Missy's.

Joyce's heart sank as she took a telephone call the next morning. Were they running an animal rescue station? the voice enquired. Immediately fearful of losing her beloved Saurus, she was tempted to deny it, but there were still the beautiful Siamese cats, whose owners must surely be missing them, so she quickly lied. "Yes, but only for cats, we cannot take dogs." Surprisingly the caller was not looking for a lost animal, but for her son-in-law.

John arrived at Grandpa Jake's, early next morning. Luke's joy on seeing his university friend turned to trepidation, at the expression on his face. Somehow Annie knew it all immediately, John's words seeming like an echo of what was already in her head. The world swam before her eyes, and she fainted into Luke's arms.

How could this be? This unjust and terrible thing. Why did it have to be their car? Why them? With all the bad people in the world, why did it have to be that kind sweet family, who had taken Annie into their hearts?

Jake and the family rallied around them, giving support also to John, who felt almost guilty now for giving the bad news. Arrangements were made for him to fly back to Maine with them, and it wasn't until then that Luke appreciated the goodness of his friend, and apologised for his apparent ingratitude. That night, neither Annie or Luke could sleep and they stood outside in the balmy June air, looking up at the moon. What an icy unfeeling planet it seemed that night. If anything grew up there, Leonard would now never know.

Blue made his way home, a three week journey of hell. Which way? How could he tell? He was ten years old, a big age for a dog of his size, and although strong and fit, the twinge of arthritis he had begun to feel in the last year, reared into firey agony as he limped along. His paws were sore now, with broken claws and ragged pads, but he knew he must keep going. Other dogs he met on the way, shunned him, more than that they feared him, he smelled of death and they could take no chances with such a creature. He always managed to find water, but never much food. Desperate he raided a garbage pail, a strictly forbidden act for Good Dog to commit. This misdeed was suitably rewarded as a great fat woman flew shouting and screaming from the house and hit his back with a heavy broom. Filled with remorse he plodded on, with no tail to put between his legs, only a terrible sense of loss. From then on he was reduced to eating grubs and worms, and by the time he reached familiar territory, his once overweight form, sported prominent ribs and hip bones.

Oh, the all familiar rough road, where he had scampered as a puppy, and later walked sedately with his family in his old age. Home at last, he limped up to the house. Forcing his weary legs to mount the steps of the porchway, he pushed at the door with his sore dry nose. It did not move, so he tried again, it would not open. He listened then sniffed, ghastly realisation bristling the unburnt fur on the back of his neck. The house was dead. The smells, the sounds, the spirit, all gone, he had been right all along, he was Bad Dog.

He rested his weary head on his paws and waited for death, not for him the sweet release of going on, but the everlasting darkness of the undeserving.

Chapter Forty Nine

They arranged the funerals immediately, as the inquest was already complete, a harrowing time which only added to their anguish. A simple ceremony followed by cremation, as was Luke's way. It was all over by the third day, when they stood hand in hand on the rocks of Permaquid Point by the foot of the lighthouse, where not so long ago, they had visited together as a family. In tears they sprinkled the ashes of their loved ones into the surf below, both unashamedly sobbing as they walked back to the car.

Now they could no longer put off visiting the house. The painful task of sorting it out, was almost too much to think about. Reluctantly they drove along the rough road, where Luke had played with Blue as a puppy, past the tree Ruthie had fallen from when she was twelve, up to the house, where there was once so much happiness. At first they did not notice the strange heap on the porchway. Annie stopped, "Luke, what is that? It looks like a dead animal." Never in their wildest imagination could they have guessed, but something made Annie run on to the creature. "Oh, God help us, it's Blue!" She took the filthy, smelly body into her arms, not bothering about her expensive lilac silk dress, "He is alive, he is breathing."

Somewhere in the distance, Blue heard their voices, but more important, he smelled their smell. Luke smell, Annie smell, like Mother Dog smell, he forced his eyes open to look.

Blue was in a bad way, but almost selfishly they would not let him die. If such a case was presented in the surgery, Annie knew that Mr. Martin would have put the animal to sleep. They carried him into the house, and Luke took a chance, sedating the dog, knowing that the anaesthetic could kill him in his condition. As a medical team, they worked together quickly, cleaning wounds and removing burnt fur, not allowing themselves to be appalled by the terrible injuries. The house lost its sorrowful memories as they fought to save Blue. They dragged two sofas into the kitchen, and spent twenty four hours a day attending to him, Annie whispering into his ragged ears, by some strange sense understanding his thoughts, "Good Dog, Blue is Good Dog."

A week later he was standing, if shakily on his four healing paws. A shadow of his former self, and quite a hideous sight to see, with bald crusted skin, where fur once grew, and an ugly mess where there should have been a tail. One of his floppy ears was still ragged, the injury too long sustained to respond to suturing, but there was life now in his slightly clouded eyes, and best of all after seven days of nursing, he gazed at Annie and smiled his special doggie smile, knowing that he was Good Dog after all.

Luke, Annie and Blue stayed in the house through the summer and the fall, until a buyer was found. The nursing back to health of their canine friend easing the pain of sorting out the family's belongings. They lost their super jobs at the new ultra modern veterinary clinic in Florida, and two months rent in advance for their beachside apartment. They also missed Daryl and Missy's return to their new house, and the pleasure of baby Nathan's first few month's development, but all that was trivial, compared to losing a family. If it had not been for Blue they would have just packed up the house and fled, but as it was, they also experienced a healing process along with the dog, and began to come to terms with their grief.

By November when they packed the car to return to Florida, and handed over the house keys to the new owners, there was something to celebrate, Annie was two months pregnant. A new life, begun where Luke had spent his happy childhood and Annie talked about the baby as they set off.

"We will bring her to see where you grew up. We will show her the lighthouse and explore the tidal pools. We will tell her all about your happy family, and I will make fudge for her, from your Mom's recipe."

Luke smiled as they left the rough road for the last time, with Blue happily perched on the back seat of the car, and imagined how life would be with his wife and daughter.

Jake and Ruby suggested that they stay with them for a while, at least until they found a place of their own, and they were delighted to do so. Blue, now fully recovered, but badly scarred, loped around the grounds with great delight, coming across the still unclaimed Siamese cats. Amazingly they took to him straight away, it was as if those normally cantankerous felines could sense his past torment, they played and purred beside him, followed him around and slept on top of him in his basket. Even Grandpa Jake had to admit that the dog could smile.

Luke brought a strange gift for Jake and Ruby, from his parent's house. Annie agreed that it was the perfect choice, as some of Jake's collectables were as weird as Leonard's. A shark, mounted on a wooden frame, a credit to it's taxidermist, if rather a sad looking creature. An inscription on the brass plate screwed to the frame read, 'The shark flies the feather', Luke never could fathom that out, but wise old Jake was thrilled and came up with the explanation.

"A shark will swallow anything which drops from a ship, metal, cloth, pitch wood, but will never swallow a bird. They avoid any feathered thing."

On reflection Luke thought this may possibly be true, at least it would explain the inscription.

With every intention they set about looking for a home of their own. Having a large dog and a baby on the way made a small apartment out of the question. Luke was offered a position concerning conservation in the Everglades, and Annie accompanied him most of the time, both losing interest in house hunting. Somehow as Annie's pregnancy advanced, she and Luke did not want to leave Jake and

Ruby, feeling as content there as Blue and his cats. As their hosts felt the same, in the big old house they stayed, converting the small bedroom next to theirs into a nursery.

Missy thrilled at Annie's advancing girth, and when together they talked endlessly of babies, as Daryl and Luke, drank beer, watched the game on television, or carried little Nathan off to see the ocean or Grandpa Jake's chickens. He was almost a year old now, a beautiful child, so like his mother and great grandfather, with his light sandy hair and vivid blue eyes. His first tottering steps were taken from Joyce to Alex on a visit to their home. Alex was holding an ice cream, and the little boy let go of Joyce's hand, taking two steps towards it. Alex was enchanted, and the idea of soon having a grandchild of his own filled him with joy. Annie was booked into a fine new hospital for the birth. Luke would stay with her, just as Daryl had with Missy, and all they needed to do now was wait.

In the early hours of the morning, she woke from a nightmare, finding that her pains had started. She felt unreasonably frightened, not quite remembering the dream, but left with a feeling of desperation. Creeping from the bed she reached for her bathrobe, but cried out, bending over with the next pain. Luke woke with a start as she held out her hand to him, eyes strangely glazed. "Please help me," she fell to her knees as he scrambled out of bed to her aid. "Oh, please don't let him be long," she muttered. Luke was most alarmed, she seemed almost delirious. "I am here, don't worry, I am not going anywhere without you, we just need to get to the hospital."

Ruby tucked a blanket around her, promising to call her parents and Missy, as they carried her to the car. She also, felt concerned by the strange vacant look about Annie between the contractions. The hospital checked her over and assured Luke that all was well, but the labour was long and she hardly seemed to know him. Now, late in the afternoon she was soaked in perspiration. Luke worried, surely such pain could not continue for much longer. Then the pain changed intensity. "It is coming, I must prepare and think only of the child now," Annie whispered, as if to herself in a rasping voice. Her eyes seemed unseeing as she gave birth to a tiny baby girl, and she screamed out, "Grandma, Grandma, help me," as the baby came into the world.

Her eyes re-focused as she held the child, and almost unbelieving, smiled at Luke, quite herself again. "Oh look, isn't she beautiful, she is so like you, with her fine blonde hair. I love you so much Luke."

His happiness and relief was shortlived, as he saw the anxiety on the doctor's face. "Too much blood," he thought, watching a steady pouring of Annie's life blood, which with his medical knowledge filled him with fear. She was rushed to theatre as he tried to reassure her, "It's just the placenta, they will soon put you right," but she, as a veterinary nurse knew the consequences only too well. She felt so very cold, a chill that reached through to her bones.

As the anaesthetic took hold she tried with all her strength to shout for Luke to come back, but the only reply was the pitiful miaow of the white cat, locked outside the closed door of her mind, and she slipped into a soft velvety blackness, where there was no sorrow or pain.

Chapter Fifty

Annie walked, strangely light footed along the dark corridor towards where the sun shone through an open door in the distance. There was someone standing outside in the sunlight, and as she approached he held out his arms to her. Recognising him now, she ran to him, full of joy. Her long skirts rustled as he danced her round and round with happiness. She relished his kisses and enveloped by his love they walked, hand in hand, along the banks of the stream in this place she knew so well. They made love in the meadow, amongst the wild flowers and the sweet smelling grass, his eyes as blue as the cornflowers growing around them. Satisfied and content she lay in the safety of his arms, kissing him again, and running her fingers through his hair, delighting at the way it curled up at the nape of his neck. They stayed in the warm sunshine for a long time, Annie filled with a blissful, healing happiness.

He sat, after a while picking daisies to make a daisy chain for her hair, and smiling, placed it between her dark curls.

"You must go back now, remember you have a husband and child. Our children are our destiny, you will see that one day. You must go back and be a mother to your daughter." Memories of Luke and the baby came flooding back, but she hesitated, "How can I go back Jonathan? I don't know how. I am afraid. It is safe here, I think I should stay." He gently twined his fingers round one of her curls. "Do you remember little bits of Latin, learned long ago, just for fun? Remember De Novo, afresh, from the beginning?" Still confused, she nodded. "That is your answer. You were given a chance, afresh, from the beginning, to start again, you know you must go back."

The ominous buzz of the monitor signified death, as the doctors tried to save her. Pounding volts of electricity into her heart, and oxygen into her lungs as they fought desperately trying to defy the will of nature, until first, a flicker, then a steady beep, was their reward.

Annie's coma lasted for two weeks. She was never alone, Luke stayed at her bedside, unless he was in the maternity wing, changing and feeding his daughter. She did not yet know her Mommy, but Luke made sure she knew her Daddy. Jessie was not going to be a little lost soul in a hospital crib. The family took turns to visit continually, Alex and Joyce seeming to have aged ten years overnight. Missy sat for hours with her friend, but hardly able to speak, her blue eyes swollen and bloodshot. Molly came at four every afternoon, armed with a flask of sweet coffee, and a tasty morsel to eat. For half an hour every day, she would shoo Luke outside for some fresh air, while he ate her special offering. Alone with Annie she set to work scolding, "You have got to come back girl for you have a husband and child. You can not waste your special chance now, you must come back!"

Alex sat with Annie's limp hand in his, remembering the time she had four teeth out, at the beginning of her orthodontic treatment. She was so ill, he had almost carried her home, and he was so worried that he had sat beside her all night, holding her hand, afraid to let her go.

He could hold back the tears no longer. Days of forced optimism and bravery for Joyce's sake took their toll. The doctors had brought her back from the very jaws of death, but Alex could see his precious daughter slipping further away each day. Now there was another little girl, Baby Jessie. Luke was with her now, feeding her and telling her that Mommy loved her too, and that they soon would all be together, but his face was gaunt, with dark circles beneath his eyes, and in his heart he felt the same fear as Alex.

"We lived such a hectic life," Alex thought, "How stupid we were in those days. We never spent enough time with our own child, we did not even appreciate her artistic talents." His head bowed as the tears flowed, uncontrollably now, splashing onto his and Annie's intertwined hands.

He did not see her eyelids flutter, or see her frown, not knowing that the sound of the steadily beeping monitor, represented her own heartbeat. "What's wrong Daddy?" she whispered, her throat as dry as parchment, as she squeezed his hand.

Two days later, and a little stronger every day, she received a surprise visitor, Uncle Thomas. Alex of course, had let his brother in England know of the tragic situation, but not understanding the strength of brotherhood, even in those who never before seemed close.

Thomas and Lucy were anxious and alarmed at the news of their niece's condition, but there seemed little they could do, other than make sympathetic noises over the telephone. "I must do something," Thomas told his wife restlessly, "I can't just leave him over there with no family support." Entrusting the business to the less than capable hands of his son Rory, who so far managed to ditch his engineering course at university in the final year, and found it impossible to secure any gainful employment other than that of assistant to his long suffering father, Thomas set off to comfort his brother.

It came as a great relief to hear Alex's good news when he landed on United States soil for the first time, especially as he had almost expected to be attending a funeral. Alex was touched by Thomas's concern. As brothers they were never good companions, seeming to have nothing in common, but now in middle age, they were both fathers, and Thomas understood only too well how Alex must have felt, with the life of his child, hanging so precariously in the balance.

By the time Thomas visited Annie, she was weak, but smiling, propped up on her pillows. Missy called that morning, brushed her hair and left a supply of blusher and lip gloss, which lifted everyone's morale. "Well now Annie," he said with a big relieved smile. He was still rumpled from the flight, and his wiry grey hair, unruly with static from the plane. "You have given us all quite a fright you know, and here I find you as pretty as a picture. Your husband is coming up soon with the baby, Aunt Lucy would love to have been here to see you and the little lass."

He pulled a small bottle from his pocket, just as Luke came in with Jessie. "Gin, Uncle Thomas?" Luke asked mischievously. He had only met Annie's uncle once before, when he went to find her in England, but in that short time they had struck up a rapport, mainly based, to Annie's amusement, on fishing off the highlands of Scotland. "Not gin, lad," Thomas assured him seriously, "I was supposed to sprinkle this over your wife here." Annie's eyes widened. "Uncle Thomas, they have me on a drip, I don't need to be splashed!"

They were seeing another side to this man, as he scooped Jessie out of her father's arms and perched on Annie's bed, beaming in a most besotted way at the child. They had not seen him when his own children were born up in Scotland, and although knowing him to be a devoted father, had no idea how delightful he found young children. How could they know that he would have continued adding to his very own personal population explosion, if Lucy hadn't called a halt to it with the aid of the Family Planning, and the Dutch Cap!

He gently stroked the baby's pretty blonde hair, as he explained about the bottle, adding to Annie's understanding of how lucky she was to be alive.

"As you know, your Aunt Lucy is a great one for local history and legends. When I decided to come, she drove off on a sudden whim to Holywell, you know Annie, that little place up the coast. In Holywell, as its name suggests if you think about it, there is a well, which is supposed to contain water with healing properties, holy water. She went to see the Sisters of Charity, based there. Lucy doesn't care about different denominations of the church, Catholic, C. of E. it's all the same to her, and I suppose she is right, we all have the same God after all. She told the sisters about you Annie and they gave her this bottle of holy water and promised to pray for you, so I had better take a photograph of you and Jessie here, and send it to them in thanks."

"There is quite a story about the well," Thomas continued, "It is really St. Winifred's well. The poor girl was pursued by the Welsh Prince Caradoc, who desperately wanted to marry her. I don't know what was wrong with him, but Winifred flatly refused to be his bride. Perhaps she wanted to be a nun, or maybe he smelled or something, I don't know, but he finally snapped as she refused him once too often. He chopped her head off! The head rolled down the hill, and where it stopped a healing spring was formed. It's a pool more than a well, Lucy says, with crutches lying around, no longer needed by people healed in the water. Anyway Annie, we felt so helpless over in England, that we thought we would give it a go."

Annie felt very privileged as he handed her the bottle, still strangely cold although it had travelled in his pocket. "Why don't we use it for Jessie's Christening?" she beamed, although feeling tired now. "Couldn't you get Aunty Lucy out here for a family affair?"

So Thomas stayed, a month in all, on a joyous visit, so different from the tragedy expected. Lucy flew out the join them, as excited as a child herself, experiencing her first flight. Rory and the girls stayed behind for educational and financial reasons, and Rory, their irresponsible, never been able to commit to anything son, came into his own. With the responsibility of the business squarely left on his, to date, unreliable shoulders, he set forth with enthusiasm to prove himself, without the all knowing, but unintended criticism of his father.

After three weeks, Annie was allowed home, still too thin and a little weak, but so glad to be released from the four walls of the hospital room and the controlled environment of the air conditioning, into the blissful Florida sunshine and fresh air. Jessie was as rosy and bonny as her mother was pale and thin. A happy and much loved baby, who on the day of her Christening gave Annie her first real smile. A, "We have made it Mommy smile," she told Luke later on.

The Siamese cats took one look at Jessie and fled up the big monkey puzzle tree, just about the only large tree to survive the hurricane unscathed, but Blue was enchanted. The big old raggedy dog sniffed the newcomer. Baby smell, Luke smell, Annie smell, all joined together. This small person must be good, like little Nathan perhaps, but better, this one belonged to Blue. Eventually the cats overcame their irrational fear, and baby Jessie found herself growing up surrounded by family, friends, animals, the breezes of the ocean and the peace of the countryside, but how sad they felt it was that she would never know Luke's parents and his sister.

As well as her natural grandparents, Jessie was also considered granddaughter to Ruby and Jake. "How lucky she is to have such grandparents," Annie said to Luke one day, watching them all play on the beach with Jessie and Nathan. "My only grandparent, Mom's mother is a real old dragon, I don't remember her ever saying anything nice to me. She is still alive, living with Mom's brother in Yorkshire, Mom feels guilty about that, says the old girl must give him hell!"

"Ah, but it was your Grandma you called out for when you were having Jessie," Luke reminded her, but she did not remember that. In fact she remembered nothing about the labour until she held Jessie in her arms for the first time. It must have been the drugs. She thought they must have zapped her with a little too much, because she hadn't even known that Luke was there, all she felt was the pain and a desolate, deserted loneliness, and as for having Grandma at the birth, she could not think of anything worse.

If she was to have another baby, she would have refused any drugs, but there were never to be any more children for Annie. The operation to save her life had put an end to that. She, who had been so sad to be an only child, had through no fault of her own, condemned Jessie to the same fate.

Luke cheered her from those gloomy thoughts. They were happy, they were in love, they were healthy and with Jessie their family could be complete. From his parent's estate they were financially secure, and Jessie was growing up with Nathan. Sweet Nathan, with Missy's hair and blue eyes, who little as he was, loved the baby. He was as much as a big brother to her as any child could wish for.

Chapter Fifty One

Part Four

ANNIE - JOSEPH AND COL D'ARBRES

Jessie woke excited, full of happy plans for her third birthday. Nathan was coming over that morning and they were going to help Mommy make a cake for her party.

The children skipped about Ruby's feet as they went to collect special eggs from the hen's straw nests. Nathan carried a little basket and Jessie chose six big brown ones for the baking. There would be five other friends coming to the party, but Nathan was her best friend. Nathan would always be her best friend.

Jessie and Nathan sat watching Annie make the cake. Carefully taking turns to crack the eggs, and beat the mixture with a wooden spoon. They watched hopefully as Annie scooped it into a cake tin, ready for the oven. "Can we lick the dish?" they asked, both at the same time. "Really, you two are like a pair of pirate's parrots," Annie scolded playfully, and Nathan made Jessie howl with laughter, giving his impression of a parrot's face. "What happy children," she thought, "So lucky to be growing up together." She watched as they licked the mixture from their fingers, and turned a blind eye to the fact that Blue was getting some too. Nathan was as serious as Jessie was flighty, not alike in personality as either of his parents, he seemed to think deeply about everything, even at this tender age of four.

They bounced with excitement when both Daddies arrived at lunch time, equipped with Daryl's guitar and a box of balloons with streamers. "These two will be worn out by six o'clock," Luke said, but there was no way he could persuade them to go for a sleep after lunch. Somehow, they were scrubbed and ready in time for the party. Jessie's little jeans, were replaced by a feminine party dress with matching shoes, and Annie tied her hair up with a green ribbon.

"Why won't Blue wake up Mommy?" she asked with anxiety in her baby voice. Blue always barked for food at five o'clock, and Jessie was right, he was still in his basket.

Annie knew before she reached him. The dear old dog's life had ended, and he lay curled up in his basket. Jessie began to cry as Annie called Luke over. There was nothing anyone could do, he was gone.

How do you explain death to a three year old? "Daddy make him better," she pleaded, sobbing now. They tried to make her understand, but she blamed her parents, not being able to cope with the finality of death. She backed away from them, "You are horrible and mean. You are animal doctors, you could make him better." Running to his basket, she put her little arms around the old dog's neck and wept. The party table stood laden with cake and goodies in the kitchen, and the balloons and decorations seemed to make the situation worse.

Missy met the guests at the gate and turned them away, explaining the sad state of affairs. It was Nathan who made the breakthrough. Nathan, at four years old, and as innocent of the cruel realities of life as Jessie. Crying himself, he put his arms around her, "Look Jessie, Look at his doggie smile. Mommy says no other dogs do that, you know Saurus doesn't, he must be happy, but if you carry on crying you will make him sad." Daryl glowed with pride at his young son's diplomacy, as the sobs turned to sniffs and the family gathered round. "Where will he go now Daddy?" she asked, a question not easy to answer.

Luke sat on the floor by the basket, noticing that the cats were cowering in the corner, big blue Siamese eyes wide with the fear of death.

"Jessie, Blue did not look like other dogs did he?"

"No Daddy, he could smile."

"Not just that Jessie, what about his fur and ears and tail?"

"Silly Daddy, Blue hasn't got a tail."

"Ah, but once he did have a tail, and lots of fur like Saurus."

"Did he leave his tail somewhere?"

"No, he was in an accident, before you were born, he was living with my Mommy and Daddy and my sister. He was happy living with them and used to always travel in their car."

"Like he goes shopping with Mommy?"

"Yes just like that, but the car crashed and Blue lost his tail and was very ill."

"What happened to your Mommy and Daddy?"

"They died, sweetheart, and I cried just like you did for Blue, and there is nothing wrong with that, but you must stop crying now. Nathan is right, if you cry too much after someone dies, you make them sad. You don't want to stop Blue from being happy, do you?"

"Will he go to be with your Daddy now?"

"Yes, I think he will, we will try to smile, then they will all be happy at last."

She was so sweet and innocent. Luke had never thought of death this way, but now he felt that it was true. Too much grief would hold a loved one back, it was time to start telling his daughter all about his family and to keep the promise made before she was born. To take her to see the lighthouse, and all the places he loved so well as a child.

They buried Blue under the monkey puzzle tree, where the cats often perched, and every time they picked flowers for Annie's little glass vase, they would leave one under the tree for the dog.

She grew up fast that summer, full of questions and vitality. Annie was relieved to see she showed no signs of the dyslexia, she had found so disabling herself, and Daryl seemed to be having the same luck with Nathan, but Jessie's world was about to change. A change which, in her little way she hated, and one which would shape her life in the future with far reaching consequences that no one could ever have foreseen.

Luke was offered a job in England! A two year contract at Manchester University, lecturing on his speciality, conservation, and captive breeding of endangered species. An opportunity in his field, which both Luke and Annie felt should not be missed.

Jessie could not understand, surely they were not going to leave Nathan, and all the people she loved. How could she live anywhere but the big old house where the smell of Grandma Ruby's furniture polish, and the whir of the old ceiling fans represented love and security. It was a sullen child who boarded the plane for England that January, leaving the Florida sunshine, so much part of her life, in exchange for the dull grey cold of England.

As the university was in easy travelling distance from Chester, they decided to stay in Annie's flat for a while. Uncle Thomas opened it up, had the dust cleared away, and lit the fire in time for their arrival. The town, with its encircling sandstone walls, historic buildings and two level shops tugged at Annie's heart, making her wonder how she could not have missed this place, but the weather was cold, and the flat seemed dingy, depressing the spirits of the little family. The air was cold and damp and Jessie insisted upon sleeping in their bed, complaining of the chill, but they suspected that it was the comfort of her parents she really sought, as she now slept with her thumb in her mouth, a habit lost as a toddler. Everyone huddled about in coats and carried umbrellas, and Annie, who always felt the cold more than most, developed chilblains on her feet and ankles to the point of agony, until Aunt Lucy advised her to rub them with geranium oil, and urged her to buy a pair of warm high boots. Luke's job was wonderful, with him fulfilling a lifelong ambition, but the only joy in Annie's life was the car. She wept as it came out of storage, a foolish thing to do, as it filled Jessie with alarm, but the joy of seeing it again, and the memories of Lottie were too much to bear.

The car brought a new dimension to their lives as now she and Jessie explored Annie's childhood ground. Equipped with coats, gloves and boots, they walked all round the park, Jessie gazing in wonder at the small streams running between the rockery, frozen into icicles. They bounced across the wobbly suspension bridge spanning the river, feeling it sway beneath their feet and took bread to feed the swans. Jessie wanted to know who the big white birds belonged to, and was amazed when she was told they all belonged to the Queen. Annie did not tell her that swans were originally kept for killing. In days of old, a swan was a valuable bird, every part of it was useful. Its flesh was used for meat and its skin stitched together to make quilts, then stuffed with its soft down. The skin between its toes, sewn together made tobacco pouches, and in the middle ages, its bones were used as flutes. All the feathers were utilised. Primary wing feathers, used by bee keepers to 'comb' bees, small stiff feathers from each wing used by clock makers for oiling clocks and watches, and the quills used as calligraphy pens. Lottie told Annie once, that Lloyds of London, still used a swan quill pen to record shipping losses, but Annie felt it prudent not to tell her sensitive daughter any of this. Lottie had always been a mine of information and one day Annie would share it all with Jessie, but this was not the time.

Another joy unfolded, with the task of house hunting. Uncle Thomas and Rory supplied her with bundles of leaflets, trying to steer them towards a more suitable home. Annie turned it into a game for Jessie, making up funny stories about people who they imagined once lived in the homes. One grand, too modern, four bedroomed house, not all to Annie's taste, but worth a look for the fun of it, sported a ghastly mural on the wall of the lounge room. Great yachts sailed across the wall, interspersed by out of proportion birds, and fish leaping from the water. "Who on earth painted that?" she wondered, and they pretended that the house belonged to an old sailor. "With a patch over one eye, a hook for an arm, a wooden leg and a parrot on his shoulder," they chuckled together.

Luke, being so occupied with his work during the day, missed all this, but joined in the fun, as they told him their stories at night. Annie sketched their imaginary sailor, and poignantly, Jessie insisted upon sending it to Nathan. It was painful to see how she missed him, sometimes she would even call out for him in her sleep.

From all the unsuitable houses they visited, it was Rory who found the right one. He told them how it had stood empty for years, and then become neglected and almost derelict through unwise short term letting. The last occupants, not much better than squatters, had stayed for quite a while, and were at one stage threatening to claim the property through adverse possession, which as Rory explained, meant occupation of the house by a person not legally entitled to it, continually unopposed for a time specified by law, extinguishing the title of the rightful owner. Those people were all set to stay, but the owner must have found some way of threatening them, because they left overnight, taking all their junk with them in their old truck.

On Sunday they set off to see the property, following Rory in Annie's mini. Although not too many miles from town, it was in a secluded position, as Rory poetically put it. "Right off the beaten track, is what you mean," Luke teased Annie's cousin, who now relished his position in his father's company, proving himself worthy of parental praise at last. They reached the tiny village with a lovely old world pub, 'The Coach and Horses' where they called for a meal and a drink. Chicken in a basket they ordered, and to Luke's amusement that was exactly what they got, chicken and fries served in a wicker basket. Jessie, sitting on a cushion ate hers with her fingers, insisting on having ketchup, miraculously not spreading it all over herself. The beer wasn't too bad either, warm English beer had been a legend of amusement as Luke grew up in Maine, but this was fairly cold and the alcohol made up for Rory's chat.

"This place would have been the old coach station, and probably a posting house as well," Rory informed Luke. Annie could hardly keep a straight face, Rory was turning into his father, no wonder they had found harmony at last.

With the exception of Jessie's dislike of the 'bathroom', much needed after two glasses of lemonade, they were all in good spirits as they left to view the house. Through a broken old gateway they drove, Luke now with Rory leading the way. Jessie became excited, asking her Mommy if they could rig up a swing, or even a tree house in one of the great trees growing along the track. "For heavens sake, how much further," Luke asked, having heard of the mini's reputation for seizing up after splashing through puddles, which was just what Annie was doing in her car behind. He did not receive an answer, as now the house loomed in front of them looking like something from an Alfred Hitchcock movie. "Christ Rory, it's awful," he exclaimed, but Rory just went on in his super salesman way, about good investment and wonderful financial return after a couple of years.

Before he had chance to protest any more, Annie and Jessie tumbled out of the car behind. "Oh," Annie breathed enchanted, "Briar Rose's castle!" Luke could see no roses, but tangled brambles choked what once was a garden, reaching with other weeds, to the ground floor windows of the house, and what windows, most were boarded up, adding to the disagreeable look of the place.

Annie saw it all with different eyes as they pushed their way through the heavy front door, into the rooms darkened by window boards. Rory took Jessie for a walk outside, giving his prospective buyers a better chance to look around. Luke knew at once that he was defeated as his wife danced about on the dusty floorboards. He thought death watch beetle, she thought wonderful old house. The kitchen was huge, typical of such a property. "A family kitchen," she almost sang, not thinking for a moment that Luke did not feel the same. She tapped upon a badly boarded up wall, "I bet there is a fireplace behind here. Oh just think, a kitchen with an open fire." He trailed behind her, feelings now beginning to melt, not for the house, but for Annie's apparent love of the place. After all this was how he felt about his job, why shouldn't she have something to bring her joy too.

They met Rory and Jessie outside, her little boots and his highly polished shoes covered in mud. "We will take it Rory," Luke smiled, kissing his wife's forehead, and putting his arm around her. Jessie's eyes lit up, "Can we live here Daddy? Rory and me saw a lovely kitty in the woods, I picked him up and cuddled him, and he went, purry, purry, purr, much louder than the cats at home." Luke swallowed what he knew to be an irrational fear of rabies in stray cats. There was no rabies in England, and never would be with their quarantine laws, unless they ever built the threatened tunnel through to France, but they would never be stupid enough to go ahead with a thing like that.

While the two girls in his life sparkled with excitement, Luke shook hands with Rory, confirming the deal. "Couldn't we change the name though? it's such a mouthful."

Rory shook his head, "It would be unwise in country folklaw, and the name dates from Norman times. A hill with trees, a settlement in the vicinity of trees, which is exactly what the property is."

Annie lifted Jessie, whirling her round, making her giggle, "Anyway Luke, you will soon get used to it, I think the name Col d'Arbres is beautiful"

Chapter Fifty Two

The well proportioned white cat dozed amongst the glade of flowers in the woods. He woke, stretching and began to groom his fur meticulously, as his mother had advised long ago. She spent more time with him than his six litter mates, even after they were weaned, she carried on with her council. He looked up at the moon, round and bright as a cat's eye, throwing pale light around the woods.

"How many moons has passed since the Old One made his pact?" he thought. "How long since he traded his spirit self to the demons of the air." All cats knew such creatures must be avoided, his mother told him that they were not all bad, some were just lost and sad, but none should ever be trusted.

The Old One's brush with one such creature had been deliberate. He sacrificed his spirit self for the sake of the memories, now this cat had the memories. They had always been in his head, but his mother made sure that he understood the implications, if he should be the Chosen One. He was becoming old, and soon he would pass the memories on, as was the way, to the seventh kitten of his final litter.

His life, like those before him was lonely. Other cats feared him, his handsome white body and green eyes not fooling them. The memories, of fear, hate and love, all combined with a mission, from which any normal member of his species would flee, were sensed all too clearly by their sharp instincts. Despite this, females were overcome by his power, at their breeding time, they came growling and teasing, longing for the satisfaction of his strong body, and after, shaking with fear as he told them of the responsibility, which they must share, should they give birth to the seventh kitten in his image. The little white male kitten with green eyes, which would carry the memories, and signify its father's death.

He stood, stretching again, grooming complete, and sniffed the nearest flower, bristling with realisation. This one was powerful magic, not to sniffed at so lightly and prickles of fear ran along his spine as he looked inside one of its many bell shaped flowers. Foxes once, long ago, put these bells over their paws, enabling them to move unheard, unseen in the night. He could clearly see the footprints inside each flower, and backed respectfully away from the plant.

There were people in the house again, but this time they were not fearful. He had met a child, with something of the smell of the memories, but not quite right. He knew that he must not let himself be involved with these people, he must wait until the Mistress came, if he was to be the Chosen One, then he would know her smell, and he would protect her.

Annie found a place for Jessie in a private nursery school, where she played happily with new friends while her Mommy threw all her energy into renovating the house. No local tradesmen could be persuaded to take on the work, but eventually she found willing workers from the other side of town. They restored the windows, plastered and painted its walls, but the kitchen was Annie's masterpiece. Behind the boarded up wall, there was indeed a fireplace, but more than that, a huge old cast iron range. With resolute determination she had generations of crow's nests poked from its chimney, scoured out its ovens and hob, and black leaded it to arm aching perfection. "This will be a test of my culinary skills," she joyfully wrote to Molly, there is no thermostat, you have to drive the monster, but I love it. Chuckling as she posted the letter, knowing Molly's passion for any sort of new modern kitchen equipment, she knew her friend would he horrified at the thought of cooking on such a range. She deliberately forgot to mention that the kitchen was also equipped, on Luke's insistence, with a state of the art electric cooker, boasting an oven timer and a special ring which was supposed to prevent milk from boiling over.

In June they moved in, and even Luke admitted that their new home was perfect, but now Annie started on the garden. She managed to enlist the help of a strange old man from the village. Mrs. Annie, he called her, to her amusement, though she was never invited to refer to him as anything other than Mr. Selborne. He gladly accepted her tea and cake, and patiently talked to Jessie, but never would set foot in the house.

"Haunted," he confided after a while, "Take care Mrs. Annie, spirits take strength from the living, no one has ever lived here for long. Even the squatters eventually fled in the night, though it is said they could have claimed the place, "Best get the priest in for a blessing."

"Poor old dear," she thought, but he was a whiz in the garden, and said nothing to frighten Jessie, so she humoured him, needing his expertise. Together they cleared the weeds, soon coming across an old wooden trap door in the ground. "The well," he explained, "Best get it covered properly, lest Miss Jessie falls into it." By the next day it was securely clad with a metal drain cover, Annie was taking no chances. She was fascinated by the old man's description of water divining. Surely they did not dig wells on the strength of a branch of hazel tree. Not to be outdone Mr. Selborne took Annie and Jessie to search in the woods for a suitable twig to prove his point.

The clearing in the wood, as always was strewn with beautiful flowers. How such a wonderful variety came to be growing together here, Mr. Selborne could not imagine. Wild flowers and medicinal herbs, they seemed to go on and on blooming, providing posies for Annie's little glass vase from Cape Cod. Jessie bent to pick some more, "Not those sweetheart," she warned, "those with the bell shaped flowers are foxgloves, you must not pick them, they are poisonous." The funny old man found his branch of hazel, glowing with the excitement of showing these Yankee townies its power.

"Oh, there is the kitty," Jessie cried, running up to the animal and he did not run away, as most cats would, but just sat transfixed. Annie looked into his green eyes, and he opened his mouth in a silent miaow. Jessie picked him up and carried him over, "Can we keep him Mommy? He likes us, listen to him purr. You have a cuddle of him." Annie's unvoiced protests vanished as she held the animal. Jessie was right, he was gorgeous, reminding her of a poem she once learned at school, and she had never heard a cat purr so loudly. She pointed out that perhaps he might belong to someone, but if not they could keep him. "That is if he wants to live with us," she warned, but the cat and Jessie seemed to be of the same mind, and he trotted along beside them as they walked back to the house.

Mr. Selborne demonstrated his water divining skills, by holding the hazel twig over the well, but seeing the doubt on Annie's face, asked her to try it for herself. He suspended the two prongs between the balls of her thumbs and pointed her in the direction of the well. "Not everyone has the skill," he warned his sceptical employer, "but I can see it in you, and Miss Jessie here."

It was amazing, to the point of being spooky, as the stick twitched, then pulled towards the water. Jessie took a turn, and yes, the same thing happened. The old gardener smiled smugly, "There's many a mystery in the countryside so keep in mind my warning about this house!"

She dismissed his tales of ghouls and ghosts, but resolved to give 'Daddy' a treat, with a mother and daughter demonstration of the hazel twig as soon as he came home. Sadly he thought it was a trick, as it refused to work for him, and it rather spoilt their joy, but the cat was a different matter. "This is Mo," Jessie told him, pushing the great bundle of purring fur into her father's arms, and the cat was successfully established into the family. "Who said his name was Mo?" Annie asked, having hoped to call him Henry after a cat in one of Lottie's old stories. "He told me himself," she replied with almost convincing innocence.

Mo's ancestral memories did not include this, so much comfort and love. He loved the Mistress out of duty, but the child, he loved the child with all his heart. What delight, for bones now past their prime, to sleep on a soft bed next to Jessie, to hear her breathing and feel her warmth, but never did he forget his mission. At times, when the Master was out of the way, he felt the threat, but it was no more than that, just a raising tingle on the back of his neck.

He no longer needed to hunt for food, as they fed him generously. Now he chased mice, voles, rabbits and birds just for the fun of it, keeping his body supple and fit. Everywhere Jessie went, he followed, and to his great delight she began to take him for rides in the car.

At first Annie refused, trying to reason with her daughter, that cats, unlike dogs, would not want to be in a car. She was wrong, Mo loved the car, and as soon as the mini door opened, he would leap in, sitting on the back seat like any legitimate passenger. "Oh Lottie, I wish you could see this," she thought, smiling as she took Jessie to nursery school.

The watery summer passed, with the leaves in the wood turning beautiful brown and gold, and Mr. Selborne only came once a week now. The house and garden were finished, leaving Annie feeling restless and strangely tired. Luke suggested she take up some sort of hobby, horse riding perhaps. They lived in a perfect environment for it, and she was forever saying that from their bedroom window she could see a horse and rider in the distance. "There's the horse again," she pointed across the hedge trimmed fields, but Luke could see nothing. "You really must get your eyes checked," she told him exasperated, "You are spending too much time under artificial light."

With Jessie off at nursery school, Annie tried a session at the local riding school, but although she loved the horses, she found no joy in sitting on their backs, so the idea was scrapped that very morning. On the way home she stopped to buy a Mars Bar from a group of village shops. Perhaps the sticky sweet chocolate would give her a lift, she felt so tired these days. "Low blood sugar," she thought, undoing the wrapper, "this is just what I need." Still munching the bar, she looked into the window of the antique shop on the corner. No furniture stood in this shop, it was full of pretty plates, pot dogs and silverware. Peering through the glass she wondered how they could make a living, so far out of town. Something caught her eye in the window, so hoping that she was not still carrying the aroma of the riding stables, she stepped inside. A shelf of blue tableware at the back of the showroom distracted her, she thought it would look lovely on her Victorian dresser in the kitchen. She examined the large plates and tureens, but horrified at the price, thought it would be more judicious to consult Luke before making such a purchase. She returned to the original reason for her visit for amongst the silverware lay an ivory comb. The shop owner stretched his long effeminate arm into the window and handed the comb to Annie. She felt sorry for him, "As queer as a coot," her father would have said, but Annie thought what a sad life of shadows and secrecy this man must lead.

"Beautiful, isn't", he enthused, obviously at ease in the company of women. "Genuine ivory, inlaid with silver. It is only so reasonably priced, as it should have been part of a set. There must have been a matching mirror once, sadly lost in the depths of time." She needed no persuasion, and was not at all concerned about the lost mirror. Its beauty as she held it in her hand, seemed to warm her from inside, and she would keep it on the dressing table in her bedroom.

Outside in the car, Mo dozed contentedly on the back seat until a tail brushing fear jolted him into action. The memories, the reason for his existence, 'The man', he was there, he had reached the Mistress, and Mo was helplessly trapped.

Annie left the shop, smiling at the thought of her purchase, alarmingly coming face to face with a large chestnut horse. "Sorry, did we startle you?" its rider apologised, sliding from its back and taking the reins. By his dress, she took him for a member of the hunting fraternity, of whom she did not approve, but he was heart stoppingly charming, with a wicked sparkle in his eyes. "You bought the comb then," he carried on, without giving her chance to speak, "I knew you would."

Mo hissed and spat with all his might, scrabbling at the car window, with its infuriating tiny space left open at the top. He must reach her, he must stop this.

"I will see you again," the rider told Annie with a wink as he mounted his horse, and trotted down the road without looking back. She stood with her heart beating too fast, and the old feeling of vitality, which she had lacked for months flooding back. How could she be so attracted to this stranger? She loved Luke, a deep true love, this should not be happening.

Mo was in quite a state by the time Annie reached the car, and collapsed into her arms as she opened the door. She blamed herself, "Poor thing, I am sorry," she said, cuddling him, now feeling very tired again. "You have been in this car all morning, I should have taken you straight home."

The mystery rider stayed in her thoughts, however much she tried to push him away. She knew instinctively that it was he, she saw so often in the distance from the bedroom window. The ivory comb evoked exciting memories of his wickedly sparkling eyes and curling hair, so she put it into a drawer out of sight, desperately fighting a growing attraction for the stranger, and feeling weighed down by an oppressive sense of weariness.

Chapter Fifty Three

Annie no longer looked across the fields from her bedroom window, she did not want to see him or his horse again, even from a distance. Determined to pull herself together, she bought some iron tonic tablets from the chemist, the woman behind the counter assuring her that a course of those would put a spring in anyone's step.

The end of October remained fairly mild, producing mushrooms in all the fields. Confident, after instruction from Mr. Selborne of which species were edible, she set off to pick some, with Mo at her heels. Tonight's meal would be a real farmhouse treat, bacon sausage, tomato, mushrooms and fried bread. There were still a few late blackberries about, so on the way back to the house she started to pick them into a little dish. "Blackberry crumble for dessert," she thought happily.

A mouse scuttled from beneath the hedge. An unwise move, as Mo pounced immediately. The tiny rodent fled, at adrenaline fueled speed, with the great furry white monster close behind. Annie felt sorry for the mouse, but that was the way of cats, they could not help themselves. "Just don't bring it back for me," she called out to him, laughing at his antics in the distance.

Her happiness faded with the sound of hoofs and a gentle whinny. A soft nickering sound, which struck a chord somewhere in the very centre of her being. She hated herself for she was even growing fond of his horse! He dismounted, watching her mockingly with those wonderful eyes.

"Good afternoon, mistress of Col d'Arbres. Surely you are not picking those blackberries?"

"They are from my own property. No one can object."

"You of all people know not to eat the fruit after Michaelmas."

"Never mind what I am doing. What are you doing here?"

The conversation was interrupted by a long slow hiss. Mo crouched between them, ears flat, tail bushed, green eyes flashing, staring up at the man.

"Do call him off," he pleaded mockingly, but she noticed that he flinched at the cat's unrelenting stance. "Your manners have not improved with time," he said directly to the cat, then leapt onto his horse waving goodbye. "I will see you again," he called as he trotted away down the track.

Annie looked at her watch, how long had she been standing there with him? It was very late, nearly time to collect Jessie. She threw away the blackberries, and realised she was trembling. Picking Mo up, she hugged him, "Thanks, Mo, you did me a real favour, you are my very own personal guard cat!"

The next day Mr. Selborne came to tackle the fallen leaves in the garden. According to him, they must be gathered and made into compost for next year. Not wishing to challenge his knowledge, Annie, Jessie and Mo pitched in to help with the impossible task. Mo burrowed into the piles of leaves, looking for imaginary mice and Jessie encouraged him to such an extent that it was decided to complete the task when she was safely out of the way at nursery school.

They sat for refreshments on the bench under the walnut tree, which seemed to have given every one of its few nuts to the local squirrels. "Ah," the old man sighed, supping his tea. "We should beat this tree with a chain, it might produce more fruit next year." Annie could not believe her ears. "Beat the tree, what do you mean?" Looking a picture of sincerity he explained.

"A woman, a spaniel and a walnut tree.
The more you beat them.
The better they be."

Annie almost choked on her cake, "I hardly think that applies these days. It is almost 1967 after all, we are in the space age, and what about the women's libbers who burnt their bras for the sake of equality. They would lynch you if they heard you say that." Then she saw a wry smile creep across his weather beaten face, "It's just an old country saying," he said sheepishly. "Talking about old country sayings, when is Michaelmas?" she asked, "Is there something wrong with picking blackberries after then?"

The old man's humour faded and his face blanched to a shade of yellow. "That is old country law. Blackberries belong to the devil after Michaelmas, 29th September. Someone with the old knowledge must have told you that. Take care, Mrs Annie, there's ghosts about here that mean mischief, always have been."

Annie changed the subject, not wishing the conversation to reach Jessie's tender ears, but it did not ease it from her mind. That night with their daughter safely in bed, she broached the subject to Luke, causing their first real argument. "You are spending too much time with that silly old fool," he shouted, "Surely you have enough sense not to listen to his stories!" She pointed out to him that he had never been able to see the horse and rider in the fields, even though they were quite plain to her, and how the cat hissed at him when he came across her picking mushrooms. Luke hit the roof, "Sounds to me as if you are obsessed with this ghost! If he is one, deal with it, you can't see ghosts if you don't believe in them. Whoever he is, if I catch him around here, I will give him a thrashing!"

Annie had never seen her husband so angry and jealous. "Luke is right," she thought, "I must put a stop to this, it is threatening our marriage. They slept, with backs turned to each other, muscles tense with unhappiness, but he woke in the night and took her in his arms, making love gently, sweetly until all was well again.

Resolutely she set herself against that bewitching stranger, and indeed began to regain a little of her old energy. Her birthday was a cheerful event, with family fun at the Chinese restaurant by the old bridge. It was an unlikely wooden building perched over a shop, but with a feast of a meal and always much welcome for Jessie. The next day a gift arrived from her parents, only a day late. A beautiful cameo portrait of Annie in an antique ebony frame. A friend of Alex had sketched it from a photograph, and Annie was thrilled. Luke proudly nailed it up on their bedroom wall, holding her close as they admired the amazing likeness, with her name inscribed at the bottom. 'Annie 1966'.

A sudden shiver ran down her spine, with icy spider-like tentacles reaching around the back of her neck. Strange feelings were rising again, but she pushed them away before Luke could see anything wrong.

Christmas was a wonderful traditional affair, as they decorated the house with holly, ivy and mistletoe from their very own woods. Despite the joy of it all, Annie longed for the ocean, and looked forward to the time when they could have beachside Christmases again, with her parents and Missy, where there was no handsome horseman making his way into her heart, but she kept her thoughts to herself, lest she upset the festive spirit.

January came with terrible news from a friend of Luke. They heard it on the news of course, but this friend was based at Cape Kennedy, and his letter was an eye opener. Three astronauts, killed on the launching pad. Trapped inside the capsule, burned to death in a flash fire. The news told of tragic instant death, and the world mourned for the brave men.

The glamour of the new astronaut frontiersmen produced an adoration equal to that of the Beatles, but reality was a different story. The stress experienced by all those involved in the space programme was dreadful, with tranquillisers the order of the day before launch. Coco Beach was rife with sex, V.D. divorce, and children under therapy.

The death of the three astronauts almost pushed everyone over the edge. A fire started in the fated capsule, which was equipped with a safety lock, something like that on the door of Annie's new washing machine. The door worked on a time delay, and could not be opened for three vital minutes. In less than that time, an oxygen line broke, almost decapitating one of the men as it thrashed about. There were ninety seconds of screaming hell before they died.

Annie and Luke were sickened, how could they have been so careless about a time lock? Luke said bitterly that the whole space programme was a sham. Never did USA send up an experimental dog or cat in the early days, to meet its doom. Good old Uncle Sam, wouldn't do a thing like that. The public did not care about rats, mice and rabbits, so using them was just fine. They never even sent a monkey up, until they were sure they could get it back. "They are not going to the moon for the sake of science," he said bitterly, "It's just a ploy to beat the USSR, I am glad Pop is not around to know all this."

The next week brought icing sugar dustings of frost, and Annie made warming soups and stews, enjoying the facility of her range, with its slow oven and warming kitchen fire. She dressed Jessie in her soft warm coat, with fur lined hood, and pulled on her red mitts and boots. Mo was nowhere to be seen as they set off for school. Too late did he hear her start the car's powerful engine from his position up the walnut tree. Perched on a slender branch, he had gone to investigate a flimsy nest, clearly visible on the leafless branches, and crackling tantalisingly in the frost. The allure of what might be inside, momentarily overriding the need to seek Jessie as she called, he stealthily advanced along the branch, and peeped inside. He was to be disappointed, the nest was empty and the car was gone as he reached the ground.

Jessie sat with her teddy bear on her knee. "Naughty Mo," she told it, "he doesn't want to go to school today." She was full of excitement, for today, every child was to take a teddy, and lunch was to be a teddy bear's picnic. "We are going to draw a picture of our bears," she told her Mommy, "I will bring mine home tonight and we can send it to Nathan." Nathan would always be her best friend and the confident little girl skipped along to the nursery school door, so looking forward to her day. Annie switched on the car radio, feeling rather lonely without Mo as a passenger, and wondering where he had got to.

Still sulky, Mo padded around the garden, and sat by the front door for a while, but it was too cold. He had become a pampered house cat, gone were the days of curling up in bracken and leaves, to stave off the chill of winter. Bored, he set off down the rough driveway in search of sport, rabbit, mouse, hare, any would do with his mood set this way.

The wild life population, seemed to have gone to ground, huddled together no doubt, against the frosty morning air. Towards the end of the long track, almost at the road, his luck changed as he spotted the rabbit. Boredom turning to feral instinct, he gave chase into the field by the bend in the road. Ferocious and fleet footed he sped over the frozen boggy ground by the pond. The terrified rabbit turned in its tracks, across the road, with Mo in hot pursuit, into the path of an oncoming car, Annie's car. Swerving to avoid the rabbit, and seeing in slow motion horror that Mo was right behind it, the car skidded on the icy road, turning full circle and careering into a hedge. The seat belt, which Lottie had insisted enhanced the car's sporty image, locked with a wrench on her right shoulder, and she watched unbelieving as a spider's web of cracks formed across the laminated safety glass of the windscreen. To the music of the Beach Boys playing, Good Vibrations on the radio, a shower of broken toughened glass sprayed over her from the window on the passenger side, caused by collision with a stout fencing post as the car came to a halt amongst the shattered hedging. "Full tank of petrol," she thought, switching off the engine, "I must get out." She yanked at the door, but it would not open, the window mechanism refused to respond either and the passenger door was firmly blocked with hedging. Dark bare hawthorn and sloe branches poked through the broken window, like spider legs, trying to reach her.

Panicking now, although there was no sign of fire, she banged on the door with her fists, thinking fearfully of the terrible deaths of Luke's family, but someone opened it and helped her out. What comfort there was in his strong arms, such was her fright that she forgot to fight the attraction of this man with the wicked sparkling eyes.

"It is all over now," he soothed, dabbing the little cuts to her face, caused by the flying glass. "I am here to put everything right this time, come sit on Copenhagen, and we will go home."

Annie felt dazed and dizzy sitting on the large horse, but became aware of a secure warmth and joy at the sound of Copenhagen's hooves, clip clopping on the road as they went along, with Joseph chatting in an easy going way. Mo trailed behind, ears flattened, full of bad humour and guilt. 'How could he have let this happen?'

Chapter Fifty Four

The world swam into a watery haze as he carried her into the house. Up the stairs to the bedroom, she made no protest, enveloped in his love. He lay her gently on the bed, kissing her tenderly, arousing delightful long forgotten passions. "You sleep now my love, remember our precious love for each other, now sleep until you come to me."

Annie lay alone in the empty bed, where she and Luke had been so happy. Her pulse slowed down and blood pressure dropped dangerously, she felt nothing but his all encompassing love.

The man was gone. Mo slunk out from his hiding place in the kitchen, and cautiously made his way to Annie's room. He sniffed the air, "Full of the memories, what must I do?" he thought frantically, jumping on the bed where she lay death still. Confused and fearful, he patted her face with his paw, in the way that cats do out of love. She moved, almost imperceptibly, so he carried on, patting and making small pleading kitten-like miaowing noises.

She came back from the brink of death, head aching and nauseous. "Mo, where am I? Oh, I remember, I crashed the car." He snuggled to her, purring in his resounding way, and she put her arms around him, relieved that he was unhurt. She slept again, deep sleep, but this time in no danger. The spell was broken, Mo had won again, but he knew it was not over yet.

All the other children had been collected, and Jessie sat with her teddy bear, as the nursery school teacher telephoned her mother, but Annie heard nothing of the ringing by her bedside. Jessie did not want the special lolly, offered to cheer her up, she wanted her Mommy. In all her life she had never been alone like this, it was even worse than leaving Nathan. An hour later the teacher resorted to calling Jessie's father at work, not wishing to cause a panic, but not knowing what else to do.

By the time Luke reached Jessie, she was in floods of sobbing tears. "Mommy is lost," she wailed, with her arms tightly round his neck. "The car has just broken down," he told her, but she was unconvinced, and sat next to him in silence as they drove home. The horror was unbearable as they rounded the bend, almost home, coming across the mangled car in the ditch. "Mommy," Jessie squealed as they saw it, and it was no use telling her to stay in the car as he ran to look. "Thank God," he cried, sinking to his knees and holding Jessie as he saw the wreck was empty. "Let's go home love, and make a few phone calls, we will soon find Mommy now."

The front door stood open, adding to Luke's stomach churning fear as he headed for the phone. The police might know something, but he would ring the hospital first. Jessie heard Mo miaow loudly from upstairs, it was the kind of miaow he used the day she shut him in the cellar by mistake. A, help me Jessie, kind of miaow. She ran to find him. "Daddy," she yelled, "Mommy is here, asleep in bed."

He bounded up the stairs, scattering poor Mo as he reached the bed, "Annie, Annie, wake up." He patted her cheek and felt for her cartoid pulse. "Normal and steady," he said out loud, in response to his daughter's wide questioning eyes. Annie woke dizzy and sick, with a mild all over headache. "Mo was here," she told Luke, holding on to his hand, "What happened? All I can remember is that Mo was here, it was Mo who helped me."

"Definitely concussion," he thought, "She is showing classic signs." He explained about the car crash, and Jessie clung to the Mommy she thought was lost, as he dialled the ambulance.

Annie was hospitalised for a week, as they bombarded her with x'rays and tests. By the second day, she remembered everything, worrying the doctors by apparently putting a dent in her recovery. She said nothing about the horseman, not daring to. Was that part real? If it was, she must get away, right away, back across the Atlantic, because she remembered all too well their feelings for each other.

She was discharged from hospital with a clean bill of health, but the unexplained tiredness she had been fighting for months, seemed to have taken an unshakable hold upon her. The hospital prescribed 'happy pills', but she refused to take them. Did they really think that chemicals could cheer her? She wept about the car, refusing to believe it was a write off, insisting on repair, whatever the cost, and with her frame of mind Luke was not going to argue.

After two weeks of leave, he was obliged to return to work, which only added to Annie's melancholy. "Look," he said, feeling desperate, "I only have one lecture today, and that is not until two o'clock. Let's take Jessie into town. We could do some shopping and have a burger at Wimpy's for an early lunch."

Annie mustered as much enthusiasm as she could, with only determination, and her love for Luke keeping her going. They wandered round the shops at a relaxed pace, browsing through books at Smiths, and buying a giant pack of crayons for Jessie. She couldn't wait to use them as there were silver and gold crayons in the pack amongst a rainbow of other colours.

Annie and Jessie tried on jeans. "Ooo, these are lovely. Can we try them?" Jessie pleaded, pointing to the 'Jingler' range. Soon mother and daughter were modelling matching flared jeans and blue striped tee shirts. Jessie bounced about, showing her father with her shiny blonde hair in its pony tail bobbing, and the little gold bell stitched to the bottom of this special brand of denims tinkling as she moved. They bought the clothes, keeping them on and laughing as they walked along with the bells jingling. Luke felt happy to drop off both his girls in such a happy frame of mind as he set off for work, but as soon as Annie stepped into the house, the terrible fatigue returned.

"Come upstairs with Mo," she suggested. "You can play with your crayons while I lie down on the bed." Jessie trotted off to her room, followed by the faithful cat, and enthusiastically searched for her colouring books. Annie wearily dumped the shopping bags by the bed, and pulled off her clothes leaving them in a heap on the floor. Critically she looked at her reflection in the cheval glass. The long swivel mirror, bought as a housewarming gift by Uncle Thomas, who had joked that he remembered the story of Annie shooting such a mirror in her father's shop! "How thin and pale I look," she sighed. Suddenly the door banged behind her, making her jump and she swung round, eyes wide with fear.

He was there! Her horseman, right there in the bedroom. She realised that she had never let herself look at him properly, only really at his eyes, his wicked mischievous eyes. He was still clad in what she took to be his riding dress, with a fine muslin shirt and long silk tie. His dark hair curled over this ears, and she was tantalisingly aware of his strong muscular body. She stood still, wanting him, needing him, but yet trying to fight those feelings with what strength she had left.

"You did not come to me," he said with a heart wrenching sadness in his voice. "I have waited so long. Can you not forgive me? Do you not love me?" She did love him. He took her in his arms, and she found herself giving in to his kisses. Knowing everything now, remembering everything, and in doing so, willingly losing her special chance, just as Molly warned years before. Annie was fading away as Joseph made love to her, bringing her to climax again and again, with his fingers, his mouth and then finally his wonderful deep fulfilling manhood. "Now we will stay together," he whispered, holding her in the world of blisses, lost so long ago.

Missy, five thousand miles away, was cooking pancakes for breakfast. She had woken with a feeling of unease, a restlessness she could not quite understand, but she was a busy wife and Mom, so she carried on with the breakfast for her 'boys' knowing that Daryl was attending a special meeting with a client today. She was so proud of him. He had taken to the antique business with amazing ease, and was an asset to her father and Uncle Alex. He joked that he lived two lives, and in a way he did. In the morning he would be off in his business suit, but at night and at weekends, he was the same old Daryl, with his guitar and scruffy shorts.

Nathan pulled at her skirt.

"Mommy, why is Jessie crying?"

"What do you mean honey?"

"She is crying Mommy."

"How do you know? England is a long way away."

"I saw her in my room, I felt all funny, then I saw her with a man in a green coat. She was crying, but I couldn't reach her."

Missy felt a cold shiver, remembering the incident in Dallas with Annie. She also, had felt strange this morning, perhaps the children were connected by the same gift of insight. She told him not to worry, that it was just a dream, but was glad when Daryl took him to nursery school, giving her chance to think. By the time they were safely out of the way, the unease had turned to panic and she picked up the phone to call Annie in England.

Mo stiffened, and ran to the door, scratching and hissing. "Mo, what's wrong?" Jessie asked, letting him out and following him to her parent's room. She opened the door and he flew in like a demon from hell, stopping in his tracks when he saw Joseph with the Mistress in his arms.

"Too late," he laughed at the cat. "Mommy, Mommy," Jessie interrupted, running to the bed, but she was thrown against the wall by some invisible force, as Joseph glared at her with decades of hate in his eyes. "Other man's child," he spat at the little girl crying on the floor, "You will bother us no more!" He walked towards her, but Mo stood in his path. This was wrong, the cat knew, he held all the memories, he was supposed to guard the Mistress, but he could not forsake the child. He loved the child, and fighting the heavy responsibilities, he stood his ground, ears back, fangs and claws ready for action. Jessie crawled towards the door and fled to her room, with

Mo close behind, the Old One's sacrifice in vain, as he abandoned the Mistress for the sake of her child.

Jessie hunkered down by her bed, holding on to Mo, not daring to move. Then, squealing with fright she saw someone was in the room with her. A different man, an older man, with dark hair like Mommy's, wearing a funny green coat and some sort of cowboy boots

"Hush little one," he whispered, "I am here to help you." She and Mo sat looking at him, eyes wide with fright. The phone rang, but Jessie dared not move, letting it ring on and on. "Answer, Annie, answer," Missy pleaded, almost frantic on the other end of the line.

The old man helped Jessie to her feet and she thought he must have been out without his gloves, his hands were so cold. Mommy would never let her go out without gloves.

"The bell, talk to your mother's friend."

"You mean answer the phone?"

"Yes, please talk to your mother's friend."

Jessie backed away and ran downstairs to answer it, in the way she had been taught.

"Hello, this is the Miles house."

"Jessie, sweetheart, this is Missy. Can I speak to Mommy please?"

"Can't get Mommy. Something wrong with Mommy."

"Daddy then, get Daddy."

"Daddy is at work, can't get Daddy. Bye bye Missy, I have got to look after Mo."

Jessie put down the receiver, leaving Missy with fears confirmed. She called Joyce, "Don't make me try to explain. Call Luke and get him to go home now, just do it!" Missy sounded so upset, and the strange urgency in her voice, goaded Joyce into action. Not knowing Luke's number at work, she called Thomas instead. "Do you have Luke's number at the university?" she asked hopefully. Her methodical brother-in-law of course did have a record of it. Not understanding the gravity of the situation, he nevertheless promised to contact Luke.

"Is it important?" the telephonist demanded, "He is lecturing at the moment." "Surely a request to go home immediately, must be important," Thomas replied icily. Subdued, she passed on the message, and Thomas returned to work, without giving the matter too much thought.

Jessie clung to Mo, her tears dampening his fur, until the man in the green coat came again and he smiled at her. "Do not fear, your father will come, and I am here to help, but will you do something for me?" He seemed kind, and Mo obviously liked him, but she said nothing, just looked at him doubtfully. "I have a daughter, just like your mother, and a grandchild who would have been just like you. Would you help us?" Jessie nodded this time and listened carefully.

"You will forget what I have said now," he told her after, "but when you are with child yourself, you will remember. You will understand and come back here for us. Then we can all rest in peace, only you will be able to put an end to my eternity of loneliness." Jessie did not understand, but at that moment in time she was not meant to. The conversation was just a seed implanted in her mind, not something to be grasped by a child of not yet four years. He stroked the cat, "You are not Maurice after all, are you?" Jessie giggled, "No, silly, this is Mo, he is my cat." The old man tickled behind Mo's ears, "You have done well Mo."

Jessie heard the crunch of car wheels outside the house and ran to open the door. "Daddy, Daddy, please help Mommy, a bad man is hurting her."

So, he was back, her so called ghost. "Get into the car Jessie," he shouted angrily, throwing her coat at her and making her cry again. She looked around for the kind man in the green coat, but he was gone. As her father ran up the stairs, she picked up her mother's little glass vase from Cape Cod, and followed by Mo, quietly tiptoed out to the car.

"Jesus Christ," Luke yelled as he burst open the bedroom door, to find his wife in the arms of another man. He strode towards them, picking up Annie's clothes from the floor and throwing them at her. "Get dressed, and you take your hands off her you bastard," he snarled, making a grab at the man's shoulders, but his grip felt nothing, only icy coldness, as he felt himself hurled across the room. Annie watched, slowly pulling on her jeans, as if unseeing, her eyes were glazed a strange blue grey. Luke had seen it before, that was the way she looked as she was giving birth to Jessie.

He picked himself up, only to be thrown again, with a sickening crack as his hand hit the wall. "She is mine," the stranger rasped maliciously. "She has always been mine and he strode towards Luke with his face set in a mask of venomous hatred.

"No Joseph," an authoritative voice commanded. Both men turned to look, someone was with Annie. "Father," she whispered, tears falling from a her misty eyes. Luke cautiously stood up as the horseman faced the strange old man in the long green coat with black velvet collar. "Too late," Joseph scowled, "It is almost over, I have her mind and soul, there is nowhere you could take her. There is nowhere with more meaning to her than Col d'Arbres. Nowhere you could go where she could be free and safe."

The old man did not move. "This is not love Joseph, it is guilt. My daughter and granddaughter, are as long gone as we are ourselves. This young woman and her child have another life to lead, you have condemned yourself to this existence for nothing. Sarah forgave you, she would have died anyway, there was nothing anyone could have done, and the child, my granddaughter, was no other man's child, she was the child of your love, but what chance would a tiny baby like her stand without a mother. No Joseph, there was nothing you could have done to save them. As for me, you condemned me with your plans, my love for my daughter will never die, I could not let you make such a terrible mistake."

Joseph stood by the bed with drooped shoulders and bent head, staring at Annie. The old man lifted her into Luke's arms, light and cold.

"Take her where she feels safe and free."

"But where? He is in her mind, where can I take her?"

"You know in your heart. There is such a place for she has told you about it."

This was no situation in which to argue. Luke ran carrying Annie down the stairs, grabbing her coat and bundling her into the car, where Mo and his little daughter sat huddled in terror. He snapped the door locks shut, and filled with dismay at Annie's vacant eyes, sped away without looking back.

"Where?" What did he mean, I know in my heart? Where must I take her?"

Chapter Fifty Five

Luke drove on relentlessly, past the shop and flat where Annie grew up, and through the town. "I am by myself, it's up to me. No one can help us, for who would believe in a ghost? I must think. If I don't come up with the right answer, she is going to die, and Jessie and I are going to end up in an asylum." He was driving out of town now, past the school, where Annie spent so many unhappy years. She had told him all about it, how she secretly went to the Zoo, instead of going for remedial teaching.

"That's it," he yelled, making Jessie jump and start crying again. "The Zoo Jessie, Mommy told us when we visited, she said it was her refuge, she was free and safe there, a place where no one could find her.

They left Mo sulking in the car, and made their way to the entrance. The gate attendant was most apologetic as Luke asked for the tickets. "The Zoo closes at dusk," she explained, "It gives you barely an hour to look around, perhaps you should come back another day." He bought them anyway, not there to look at the livestock, but to save his wife. How could he explain that?

Jessie and Luke held Annie's cold hands as they walked towards the tigers. "The poem, the poem, she had a special poem for tigers. How did it go?" he racked his brains, "Jessie, the tiger poem, Mommy drew a tiger for you to colour. Do you remember the poem?

"Tiger tiger burning bright,
in the forests of the night."

That was all Jessie could remember, so they said it together, over and over, and a little of Annie, the wife and Mommy returned, as she smiled a weak smile. She seemed to want to stay at the tiger enclosure, but it was so cold Luke insisted on moving along, finding the bird house.

"Look there is an owl in that cage," Jessie pointed, "Baby owls snore. Don't they Mommy?" She tugged Annie's hand, but there was no response as she stared blankly at the bird. Desperately fighting for normality Luke butted in.

"Actually honey, they purr, not snore."

"You mean like Mo purrs?"

"Yes something like that. The babies purr under the comfort and warmth of the parent's wings."

They moved on, closing time drawing near, with hardly any improvement in Annie's frame of mind. "Reptile house, let's go and see some wiggly snakes," Luke suggested, with stage managed enthusiasm, as his heart was breaking.

It was gloomy and hot in the reptile house, so warm that they took off their coats. The snakes housed in illuminated tanks were in no mood for amusing these late visitors. "Look Jessie, there's a cobra, an Indian one like in Mommy's book. Watch out snake, here comes Ricki-tikki," he teased, wriggling his hand, pretending to be a mongoose. To Luke's relief, Annie took Jessie's hand, and they both stared at the snake, but what he did not know was that neither of them saw the reptile. At first there was only their reflection in the glass. Mother and daughter dressed alike, in striped tops and 'Jingler' jeans, but then they saw a country inn. Annie opened the door, Jessie tightly holding her hand as she saw the bad man from the house lying across the table. She wrinkled her nose, he smelled nasty as he stood up, shouting at them, "What are you doing here? Have you lost your senses woman?"

Annie just smiled, keeping tight hold of Jessie "Goodbye, my love," she said, and then they were back, looking at the disinterested snake, and Jessie whimpered, confused and frightened.

Annie picked her up and hugged her, "Don't be afraid, it's all over now," she whispered. Luke looked in amazement, even in the gloom, her colour was improved, and her eyes were no longer glazed but the clear deep brown, which had always made his heart melt. He put his arms around them both, "Annie, are you back with me?" She nodded, kissing him, squashing Jessie, who wriggled with pleasure. "Do you remember what happened?" he asked cautiously, "Everything and more," she replied, "I have memories of two people, no one would ever believe it." "I believe it, oh boy do I believe it," he sighed.

They never went back to the house, or even to Annie's flat, but lodged themselves with Uncle Thomas and Lucy, who secretly thought they had taken leave of their senses. Rory collected Luke's important documents, and a few personal possessions for them, and within a week they were safely back in USA with Annie's parents, leaving the house in Rory's enthusiastic, and now capable hands, to sell, rent, anything he liked, Annie and Luke no longer cared.

Their only worry was Mo, but sedated and packaged in a special box, he survived the trip. Annie buttered his paws on his first night as an American citizen, hoping it would help him settle in, and get over the shock of suddenly coming nose to nose with Saurus, who seemed a little too keen to welcome his groggy house guest. They need not have worried, Mo permitted the big kindly dog to help him lick off the butter, only too pleased to have found a friend with another story to tell. Nothing mattered now for Mo was with the Mistress, and more important with Jessie, allowed as always to sleep on her bed. The Old One's sacrifice had not been in vain after all, and the memories, no longer needed, faded, washed away by the sound of the ocean and the warmth of the perpetual sunshine.

Annie did not explain the true situation to her parents, instead putting the blame on the car crash. They knew there was more to it than that. Thomas for a start, seemed concerned about their odd behaviour and speedy departure, but as caring parents often do, they left well alone. Annie was back now, she, Luke and Jessie all seemed happy, so they counted their blessings, and settled down to enjoy their family.

Missy was the only person Annie confided in, finding her turn pale with horror at the story, but she did not tell her Sarah's memories. How could she tell anyone?

Chapter Fifty Six

Annie looked up from her typewriter. She was sitting at her desk, facing the sparkling ocean, its balmy breezes fanning her hair through the open window as she worked. They lived in their own beach house now, not too far away from Missy and her parents. Her work was almost finished, a great pile of paper in a file box, tied up with a green ribbon. It was her story, her own and Sarah's. She never intended it to be published, but one day Jessie would need explanations. Whenever that time came, Annie would give her the box, then she could read it and make her own judgements. Besides, Sarah deserved to be remembered, if only on paper.

Jessie was playing with Nathan and Missy on the beach. They were coming up to the house now, for cookies and milk, and to prise Mommy away from her work for a while. She watched the children walking hand in hand, "Yes, our children are our destiny," she said to herself.

Mo woke and came purring around her feet, "And what about you Mo? I don't actually know your story, do I? Could it be that you are really Maurice?" He gazed up at Annie with his large green eyes, and she scooped the purring bundle onto her lap.

"No, you are just my Mo. Just an ordinary white cat!"

EPILOGUE

ENGLAND - MAY 1987
Twenty Years Later

The new vicar and his wife stood beside the headstone in the graveyard of their ancient little church in the village.

"How on earth could she have known?" she asked her husband. "How could a young woman like that, come from America to immediately visit Col d'Arbres and dig up those bodies in the woods?"

"I believe she lived there for a while as a child," he replied vaguely.

"Harry," the wife cried in exasperation, "that's no explanation. Those people had been dead for over 150 years, she even knew their names, it makes no sense."

The vicar shrugged in his absent minded way. "Does it matter? They are laid to rest now, and the police are not bothered any more."

"I am just curious, that's all," apologised his wife, seeing how annoyed he was becoming with her prattle. "It is a beautiful headstone, but the inscription is so sad, Lord Tennyson, isn't it?"

James Brand
Daughter Sarah and baby Mary.

"A thousand suns will stream on thee,
A thousand moons will quiver;
But not by me thy steps shall be,
For ever and for ever."

"I suppose she could afford such an extravagance," the vicar said, thinking about the church's weather vane precariously about to fall in the next gale, unless he did something about it. "Did you notice that heavy gold crucifix she was wearing, it must be worth a fortune."

'Jessie'

sequel to

'The Reincarnate'

due for completion 1996

Raped and beaten to the point of near death, Jessie's world falls apart when she recovers and finds herself pregnant. She cannot bring herself to think about abortion, as the child may not be a result of the rape, but that of the man she had loved all her life. Feeling irrevocably defiled, she leaves her lover and sets off to Ireland, intending revenge upon her attacker, but strange dreams begin to invade her sanity. Memories surfacing from a seed planted in her brain as a child, compel her to go the England, where a horrific mission becomes clear.

But..

She is not to face it alone, someone is waiting, someone whose love was never to die.